# VITAL TARGETS

## MIKAEL CARLSON

Danbury, Connecticut

Vital Targets
Copyright © 2021 by Mikael Carlson
Warrington Publishing

Printed in the United States of America
First Edition
ISBN:    978-1-944972-10-3 (paperback)
         978-1-944972-07-3 (ebook)
         978-1-944972-11-0 (hardcover)

**Book cover designed by JD&J**

# Novels by Mikael Carlson:

– The Michael Bennit Series –
The iCandidate
The iCongressman
The iSpeaker
The iAmerican

– Tierra Campos Thrillers –
Justifiable Deceit
Devious Measures
Vital Targets
Revealed Secrets
Decisive Endgame

– Watchtower Thrillers –
The Eyes of Others
The Eyes of Innocents
The Eyes of Victims

– The America, Inc. Saga–
The Black Swan Event
Bounded Rationality
Boiling the Ocean

*For Betty & Lawrence Dallman*

# PROLOGUE

## VASSYL STRACHENKO

*Outer Harbor Hotel*
*Chicago, Illinois*

Vassyl flicks his cigarette in front of him and crushes it with his foot as he walks by. Time is of the essence, and this isn't a place he wants to loiter. There are far too many security cameras around. The disguise he is wearing will help defeat facial recognition technology, but he hasn't survived in this line of work by tempting fate.

The doorman performs his function while dressed in a 1920s era uniform as Vassyl enters the grand lobby. The Outer Harbor is not the fanciest hotel in Chicago, but it pretends to be. Located not far from the Navy Pier and only blocks from the Miracle Mile, it is a magnet for tourists and businessmen alike. It's also a strange location for his target to hole up, considering his father's political leanings.

Vassyl nods at the concierge, who is dutifully posted at his station. The assassin has dressed the part tonight. His business suit is stylish and well-tailored for something he purchased off the rack, and his shoes look like something he might have bought in Milan.

"Welcome to the Outer Harbor Hotel. How may I be of service?" the polite young woman behind the reception desk asks when Vassyl walks up to her.

"Good evening. My colleague and I are here on business and have a big meeting tomorrow, so he retired early."

"He needs to rest up?"

Vassyl smiles at the woman's attempt to be chummy. "More like he can't hold his liquor. He left some files down here for me to review when I got back so I wouldn't interrupt his slumber."

"Your name, sir?"

"Lars. Lars Ulrich," Vassyl says, trying to hide the remnants of his Eastern European accent. He's hoping that she's too young to recognize that the name he gave her is Metallica's drummer.

"Uh, I'm sorry, I don't see anything here for you," the receptionist says, scouring the shelves beneath the heavy oak counter.

"That's weird. My colleague texted me that he dropped it off," Vassyl says, pulling out his phone. "Yes, he says he left it with a guy named Josh."

"Oh, okay. Josh just ended his shift and left an hour ago. Let me see if he secured it in the back room. One moment please, sir."

The moment she disappears into the back office, Vassyl pulls out a plastic card and spins around the card encoder behind the counter. He inserts the key and punches in the target's room number. He hears the machine apply the information to the magnetic strip and turns the device back around.

The task complete, he leans against the counter and waits for the pleasant reception clerk to return. He spent weeks casing this hotel in preparation for this mission and practicing that maneuver. The whole exercise took less than five seconds. He considers himself fortunate that the hotel hasn't upgraded to the new RFID lock system yet. That would have taken far longer to pull off.

"I apologize, sir. There is nothing back there for you."

"Okay, well, maybe he meant to drop it off and got distracted. I will have to wake up sleeping beauty and find out. Thank you."

"You're welcome, sir. Are you a guest here, sir? Our elevators require a key card to access the upper floors."

Vassyl reaches into his pocket and holds up the card he just encoded. "Your beds are amazingly comfortable."

The woman beams. "I'm pleased to hear that. Have a great evening, and enjoy the rest of your stay. Good luck with your meeting tomorrow."

Vassyl thanks her and takes an elevator up to the fifth floor. He uses the ride to slide on a pair of black leather gloves. He makes a left down the corridor when the doors open, having already familiarized himself with the location, distance, number of guests on the floor, and security response times. The target's room is at the far end of the building, beside a stairwell that will serve as a perfect egress when the mission is accomplished.

He slides his hands into his pockets without breaking stride and retrieves his SIG Sauer P226 with one hand and suppressor with the other. He screws the device onto the barrel's threaded end as he walks, completing the task as he arrives at the room.

Without hesitation, Vassyl slides the key card into the slot, and the light changes green. He opens the door an inch, backs up, and gives it a swift kick to defeat the security bar. It flies open, taking a chunk of the jamb with it. The assassin charges down the short hall past the bathroom and closet and trains his weapon on the bed. He squeezes the trigger twice. The reports from the gun are muffled but not silent.

He expected his target to be sitting up and was surprised that he wasn't. Vassyl moves swiftly through the darkened room to confirm the kill. When his eyes adjust to the darkness, they grow wide at finding two holes in the pillow where a head should be resting.

Vassyl immediately crouches slightly and levels the weapon in front of him. He sweeps the room to the left, checking the small sitting area and its high-back chairs. The gun traverses the windows and continues over to the small writing desk in the corner. He knows that his target is here but trains his sight over to the hallway and its bathroom entrance a second too late.

A man dressed only in a pair of boxers barrels into him before he can shoot. They crash into the nightstand and the headboard, causing Vassyl to lose control of his weapon. He dodges an out-of-control right hook and slams his fist twice into one of the man's kidneys.

His target howls in pain as Vassyl hooks him under the shoulder and shoves him into the corner between the bed and the bathroom wall. Not wanting to waste time retrieving the gun on the bed, he opts for the messy way and goes for the U.K. Special Forces knife sheathed on his belt. He doesn't reach it in time.

The man punches him hard in the solar plexus and goes into full Berserker mode. He lets out a primal scream and swings twice, catching nothing but air before pushing off the wall and lunging at the assassin.

Instead of retreating, Vassyl steps toward him and plants his shoulder into the athletic man's chest. In the same motion, he grabs the man's torso with both hands. Momentum does the hard part. Vassyl channels the energy to throw him over his shoulder. He bounces off the bed and lands hard on the floor before jumping back to his feet.

Vassyl goes for the gun lying in the center of the bed. He recovers the weapon and is about to fire when the steel floor lamp from the sitting area crashes down onto his arms. The gun burps, but the bullet strikes the floor at the man's feet. The retaliation is quick, and Vassyl rolls away barely in time to miss getting a face full of steel.

Off-balance and in a compromised position, he tries to scamper off the bed and gets caught in the chest with the lamp's base after the man thrusts it at him. Vassyl regains his balance but has lost the initiative.

"C'mon! Come at me again!" the man shouts.

"Hello?" a voice says from the door as it opens and allows light from the corridor to pour into the room. "Hello? Is everything okay in here?"

"I need help! Call security!" the target bellows, still wielding the lamp as a weapon.

Vassyl's time here is up. He draws his knife as the guest enters the room to see what the commotion is. Not wanting to stab an innocent bystander, he crashes the butt of the blade down hard on the man's head, collapsing him to the ground. Vassyl bolts across the corridor to the stairwell as more guests poke their heads out of nearby rooms. It's a race against the clock, and he begins keeping the time in his head as he descends the flights to the ground floor.

He charges through the exit out into the street, thankful he didn't have to return through the lobby. After two blocks, he heads west away from the lake as the approaching sirens grow louder. Once he's far enough away to decrease the likelihood of being stopped and questioned, he removes the prosthetics and fake mustache from his face and tosses them in the trash.

Vassyl pulls out his brass Zippo and lights a cigarette, taking a long pull on it. That went horribly wrong. Capture isn't the most pressing concern now. He'll be out of the city and heading east in less than an hour. It'll take the police five times that long to comb through the hotel video, and even then, their facial recognition software will come up empty.

What worries Vassyl is what comes next. He isn't used to failure. Assignments that go sideways are not new, but he has never outright failed to eliminate a target before. It's not a trend he wanted to start now with this much at stake. When he answers for this debacle, Robespierre won't be happy either.

# FIVE DAYS LATER

# CHAPTER ONE

## SPECIAL AGENT VICTORIA LARSEN

*Grace Bay Sunset Resort*
*Providenciales, Turks & Caicos*

Victoria finishes applying her sunblock and sets the tube down on the sand beside her chair. She closes her eyes and feels the sun's warmth and the cool breeze from the water brush her face in a gentle caress. She squishes her toes in the powdery sand. This is the most relaxed she's felt in years.

Grace Bay has been perennially voted the best beach in the world for two reasons: its seven-and-a-half-mile stretch of soft white sand and the beautiful turquoise blue water that extends a mile out to a barrier reef. Add in world-class resorts and near-perfect Caribbean temperatures, and Victoria knows it will be hard to leave this slice of heaven.

"You're going to burn," a man with an unfamiliar voice says, silhouetted by the sun and casting a shadow as he hovers over her.

"Is this where you offer to help slather lotion on me in the hopes that I'll be eternally grateful and invite you to sit so you can strike up a conversation? Trust me, it isn't going to happen, buddy. Move on."

"They warned me that you were tough to get to know."

"I don't know who 'they' is, but I do know that you are still blocking the sun, and it's annoying me."

"Sorry," he says, taking a seat on the edge of the adjacent lounge chair.

She looks over her sunglasses at him. He's athletic, with a conservative haircut and an arrogance that marks him as an agent, likely from Washington. Nobody else dresses this dorky in civilian attire.

"Did you raid the airport gift shop on the way here?"

"Something like that. I didn't have time to pack. I'm Rigoberto Benitez, but my friends call me Rigo."

"What can I do for you, Rigoberto?"

He smiles at the diss. "I was hoping to talk with you, Agent Larsen."

"I'm not an agent anymore, or didn't you D.C. boys get the memo?"

"Your paperwork hasn't been processed yet. You may not be carrying your badge and gun, but you're still every bit of an agent as I am."

"You sure know how to spoil a girl's vacation," Victoria says, shaking her head as she slides off her lounge chair.

She begins to pack her things before pulling a mesh beach shirt over her bikini top and wrapping a white sarong around her waist. Rigo watches her but doesn't leer with the intensity that most men would. She finds it comforting that he's not a complete scumbag.

"My intention isn't to spoil your vacation. All I'm asking for is a few minutes of professional courtesy. Just listen to what I came here to say."

"There's one problem with that, Agent Benitez. I'm not remotely interested in anything you have to say."

"I'll bet you an overpriced lunch at that beach café that you're wrong."

Victoria looks over at the small eatery on the beach. It's close to lunchtime, and she is hungry. Despite her better judgment, a free meal might be worth hearing whatever crap Rigoberto came here to spiel.

"Fine, let's go, if for no other reason than you're the pastiest Latino I have ever seen and are about to burst into flames in this sun."

Rigo offers his arm, and Victoria brushes by him. He grins and follows her to the café, where they are seated. Victoria orders a Mai Tai when the waitress stops by for their order, and Rigo orders a Turk's Head produced at the local brewery.

"A beer? I expected you to get water."

"What the FBI doesn't know won't hurt *me*."

"Did they at least spring for you to stay the night?"

"Nope. I'm on the next flight off the island. There's no rest for the weary. How are you enjoying your vacation?"

The pair makes small talk about Grace Bay and other vacation destinations they have visited during the rare downtime between cases. Victoria prefers sun-soaked beaches and the warm waters of the Caribbean, while Rigo likes old European cities like Paris, Prague, and Budapest. She's thrilled to see that he can hold a conversation that isn't work-related while they enjoy lunch. This is going better than most of her first dates do. The check arrives when they finish, and Victoria holds it up between her fingers.

"Time to make your pitch."

"It's simple. I want you to come to work for me as a member of my team. I've spent months studying your record. The Boston Division never appreciated your talents."

"Yeah, well, they had a more conservative way of doing things. The whole FBI is like that," Victoria says.

"Not all of it. Lance Fuller is a stuffed suit more worried about his next promotion than actually running his division. Takara Nishimoto is a competent agent who would thrive under the right mentor. Unfortunately, he'll never get one there. Then there's Miranda from NERFC. She thinks you're a superhero. Or British royalty. I'm not sure which."

"Queen V," Victoria mumbles, uttering Miranda's nickname for her. "You talked to my colleagues?"

"I talked to almost everyone you have ever worked with, inside the Bureau and out. Seth Chambers said you were the most capable person he's ever worked with. That's high praise coming from a detective in the Massachusetts State Police. Diego Velez also sang your praises. He's recovering nicely from his wounds, but I understand you already know that. He appreciates you checking in on him as regularly as you do."

"Okay, I get your point. You did your homework. What are you investigating?"

Rigo takes a sip of his beer and sets it down on the table. "The SOF."

She should have known, but the admission hits her with the force of a hammer. She stares down at the unpaid check. She may lose this bet after all.

"Ian Drucker?"

"Half of the FBI is scouring the country looking for him, so no. We're searching for Machiavelli."

Victoria sits up a little straighter. The members of the Sword of Freedom are all dead except her traitorous colleague. She knows because she saw Sartre's body, killed Marx, and watched Trotsky blow his brains out. Drucker will eventually get caught, but convincing a jury that Isiah Burgess was the mastermind based on circumstantial evidence is the last missing piece to close the case.

"Machiavelli is already under indictment and awaiting trial."

"Is he?" Rigo asks, raising an eyebrow.

"Are you saying that you don't think Isiah Burgess is Machiavelli?"

"You were at the *Capitol Beat* broadcast at the university. You tell me."

"He confessed."

"You know better than that, Victoria. He might be Machiavelli, but 'might be' isn't good enough. I want to be sure in light of recent events."

"What events?" Victoria asks, sounding more like someone issuing a demand than asking a question.

Rigo rises from his chair and digs into the pocket of his shorts, which might as well still have a tag on them. He produces a money clip and drops the money for lunch on the table. With it is his business card that Victoria picks up and studies.

"Unfortunately, I have to get back to the airport. Your paperwork will finish processing at the end of next week. Come and see me at any point before then if you're interested in talking further. If you decide that you've had enough of the FBI, I wouldn't blame you and will wish you the best of luck."

"I would have paid," Victoria calls out as Rigo gets halfway to the café's entrance.

He turns back and smiles. "I'm hoping you'll get the next one."

She returns to staring at the card, knowing that this vacation won't continue to be as relaxing as she had hoped. Now Victoria knows that she has another variable to obsess over as she wonders what to do with the rest of her life.

# CHAPTER TWO

## OLIVER JAHN

*Times Square*
*New York, New York*

Times Square is a manmade canyon coined "the Crossroads of the World" where Seventh Avenue intersects Broadway as it creeps eastward while it snakes down Manhattan. Its trademark is flashing neon lights, giant digital billboards, and theater marquees. Times Square is a big, bright, and unforgettable tourist destination known worldwide as the spot where the ball drops on New Year's Eve.

The foot traffic congesting the sidewalks makes it a people-watcher's paradise, especially in the pedestrian-only zones established when the city closed off Broadway between 42nd and 47th Streets a few years back. That's why Oliver Jahn is here.

"I thought you hated this place," Mi Sun asks. He is keenly aware of her struggle to keep up as he deftly weaves through a crowd of tourists milling around at the crosswalk.

"I do. No self-respecting New Yorker likes this place."

"Why are we here, then?"

"Research."

Oliver veers off the side and notices that Mi Sun is thrilled to stop walking. She has been his executive producer since the days before his podcast went viral. When he was signed to a lucrative deal to bring that magic to a cable network, bringing her along with him was the one part of that agreement he wouldn't negotiate away.

"Research for what? The best overpriced cheap food that only a tourist would eat? The effect of mass advertising on the human psyche?"

"Neither, although good guesses. Look around you. What do you see?"

"People."

"Yes! What would we do without your uncanny sense of observation?"

"Oliver, I have a show to produce tonight. Can we dispense with the games and get to the real reason you dragged me uptown?"

"I see thousands of people who should be watching our show but aren't. Families from Kansas and college kids visiting from Georgia. Young and old, from all across this great nation, they're all potential viewers who choose to do something else at nine p.m."

Oliver watches Mi Sun look around, waiting for her to realize as she most certainly will that the fastest way to get back to work is to play his game. There is more to what brought him up here than complaints about their viewership.

"I'm sure some of them watch the show."

"It's the law of large numbers, yes. What are TNT's average ratings for the year?"

"We are first in our timeslot and second nightly with a 3.4 live plus same day. *Capitol Beat* is first with a 4.1."

"Why am I not surprised that you know that off the top of your head? I seriously don't pay you enough," Oliver says with a smile.

"No, you don't," Mi says, not returning it.

"What were the ratings last year?"

"About the same. A little higher, actually. We were at 3.5 million viewers."

"Exactly! Exactly my point," Oliver says, jittery and animated as if a triple espresso just kicked in. "Seven months into a presidential election year, and we have managed to lose a sliver of our audience."

"Everyone has, Oliver. Newspaper circulation is down, as are television ratings throughout the industry. The election will give us all a bump, but there are too many options for people to get their news. That's without considering the countless reasons many don't want to hear about the world at all."

"Lack of attention is an American character trait, but I refuse to blame our decline on ADHD or other entertainment options."

"It's hard getting noticed."

"Yet we did."

Oliver took a one-man show he produced solo in his basement and turned it into a media powerhouse. His viewership soared on social media, but only after Mi Sun came knocking on his door one day with a request to work with him. Her ideas are what catapulted his show to online streaming records. She's why he got noticed, and he needs to rely on her to do the same again.

"It's harder still to get people to tune in regularly once you are noticed," Mi Sun argues, ignoring Oliver's interjection.

"And that's why we're here," Oliver says, slapping his hands emphatically. "We need to get noticed."

"What are you going to do? Tear off your clothes and go streaking?"

"I want to attract viewers, not make them blind. No, I am immensely proud of our show because of what we are."

"Entertaining and partisan?"

"Honest. Nothing annoys me more than journalists who pretend to be disinterested bystanders to history. They wear masks of non-partisanship and hide behind shields of journalistic indifference. Everyone has an opinion, Mi Sun. We give people ours. I wish everyone had the same integrity instead of being pretenders who drag naïve people into their land of make-believe."

"You're talking about *Capitol Beat* and *Front Burner*?"

"For starters, yes. They hypnotize lemmings into believing that they're real news. That ends on Sunday night. We are going to take our show to the next level by convincing people that they aren't. That's how we'll get noticed."

"Uh, okay. How do you intend on convincing people of that?" Mi Sun asks.

"By finding a target to put in our crosshairs."

Cancel culture emerged as a means for people to exert control over a less-tolerant world by forcing the removal of problematic people from mainstream culture. While matriculating on social media, it has infused itself into all walks of life. It's now common for any individual to become an arbiter of right and wrong and appoint themselves judge and jury. Any individual offended by a comment or action is empowered to dole out punishment, thanks to the power they wield behind a keyboard. Oliver wonders how magnified that would be if he could leverage his platform for it.

"Oliver, we are in the middle of contract negotiations with the network. The lawyers are close to finalizing a deal. If you change the show's direction, it could give them a moment of pause. They aren't going to like that very much."

"A corporation owns the network, and they only care about one thing: money. The more our ratings grow, the more advertising dollars we rake in. They don't care how we do it, so long as it doesn't cost them revenue or prestige."

"That's depressing," Mi Sun moans.

"Reality usually is."

"Okay, so you've thought this through. Who do you want us to target? I'm assuming you have someone specific in mind."

"I do."

Oliver points over his shoulder. Mi Sun's eyes track to the building across the street and up its façade. She settles on an electronic billboard featuring journalism's newest and brightest star, Tierra Campos.

"Put on your helmet and sharpen your wit. We're going to take down *Capitol Beat's* shiny new hood ornament."

# CHAPTER THREE

## BRIAN COOPER

*Il Diplomatica Infuriata Ristorante*
*Washington, D.C.*

Brian checks his watch for the tenth time in the last five minutes. He's late, not that the political operative expected his guest to be punctual. It's an election year. Nobody working for a campaign can keep to a schedule.

"Brian. It's good to see you," Brevin Hawkins says when he reaches the table ten minutes later. "Could you have picked a more conspicuous place for dinner?"

"This is Washington. You are the campaign chairman for the Republican nominee, and I'm the disgraced chief of staff of your opponent. Someone will learn about this meeting regardless of where we have it. I figured that we might as well get a good meal out of it."

"The Diplomat," as it is colloquially known, is a popular destination for politicians, lobbyists, and tourists willing to cough up the cash for an eighty-dollar steak. It's known for its mouthwatering Bistecca Fiorentina that both men order along with their drinks.

"Do you want to make your pitch so I can say no now, or do you want to wait until after dinner?" Brevin asks, draping a napkin in his lap.

"What makes you think that you know what I want?"

"I'm not an idiot. You had a bad breakup with your ex, and you want a job with us to get back at her. It's hardly a unique story."

Brian isn't comfortable with the characterization of his relationship with Alicia Standish. But now isn't the time to argue the point, so he rolls with it.

"You're right. That's what I want. Since we're sharing, here's something you need to know about me: I don't like wasting time. I wouldn't be here if I thought your answer would be no. Hear me out. I think you'll agree."

"I doubt that, but go ahead," Brevin says, gesturing for him to continue.

"I've been watching your campaign. I've seen all the advertisements and studied Bradford's speeches. One thing became glaringly obvious: you don't have the first idea of how to beat Alicia Standish."

"I'm glad you're not sugarcoating things for me, Brian. We have good opposition research. I know exactly how to beat her."

"I know you think that. You could have pictures of her fangirling over Hitler at a Nazi rally and wouldn't be ready for what happens next. Alicia's superpower is her ability to turn weaknesses into strengths. She lost big on the Safe America act and was still in the top tier of candidates in the primary. She doesn't speak publicly about

Frederick Lamm's murder and blunts the backlash by sending a heartwarming note to the family that made her more endearing. Those are only two examples. Trust me, Alicia Standish will take anything you throw at her and turn it into a weapon."

"And you think that you can help us avoid that? How?"

"I spent years doing it for her. I know the game plan."

Brevin eyes Brian as he takes a sip of his drink. The former chief of staff is a political power player who has worked for the opposition for decades. He has every reason to be skeptical of the motives here.

"Why would someone who's spent a career working for Democrats suddenly want to work for an ardent conservative?"

"You already answered that question when you first sat down."

"We're not in the revenge business, Brian. Bradford is running because he wants to lead this nation and—"

"Bring back the American spirit, blah, blah, blah. I told you that I've watched all his speeches. This is about winning for me, not ideology. You can call it 'revenge' if you'd like, but nobody is more qualified than I to say that Alicia Standish is not fit to be the president of the United States."

"Says the man she fired."

"Twice."

Brevin smirks and offers a nod, appreciative of the admission. "We already have consultants on our campaign staff. Too many of them, if you ask me. Why would I want another?"

"Because none of them is me."

A waiter arrives with their dinners. The men talk about the race for president and some of the state races in general terms while they eat. When coffee arrives, Brevin comes to a decision.

"I'm sorry, Brian, the answer is no. I don't want you working for the Bradford campaign."

"Why not?"

"Frankly, you have too much baggage. You may have a genius mind for politics, but that comes with a price: the murder charges and conspiracy to interfere with an election against you."

"Both of which were dropped."

"What sounds more realistic? A son trying to rig an election to help his father because he wants to earn his approval? Or a political operative arranging it to look that way so he can put his candidate over the top in a race she was likely to lose? I ask because, for me, that's a coin flip."

Brian dabs his mouth with his napkin. He replaces it in his lap, taking the time to choose his words carefully. He certainly can't say what he wants to.

"Standish was going to win New Hampshire before any of that happened. It wouldn't have been worth the risk."

"You don't know that for sure."

"With all due respect, Brevin, I do. I'm not Machiavelli. I had nothing to do with the arsons, the intimidation, the hacking, or any of the nonsense that happened in New Hampshire. If I can't convince you of that, let me talk to the governor."

"Not a chance," Brevin says with a chuckle. "He doesn't make personnel decisions for the campaign; I do."

"That's my point. Do you really want to know what I bring to the table? The key to destroying Alicia Standish. If Bradford loses, you don't want to be standing there at his concession speech wondering if the decision you made here was the right one. I can guarantee you that everyone else will be wondering that. Let the governor make the call, and he shoulders the burden."

Brevin leans back in his chair. He understands that the outcome of this race will define his career. Like all denizens of the political world, self-preservation is foremost in his mind. The offer is more than a temptation; it's irresistible.

"Okay. I'll bring up the subject of your hiring to Colin and let him decide if it's something we should pursue further. If I were you, I wouldn't get my hopes up."

Brian offers a slight smile. That's all he needed out of this meeting. Anything that isn't a no is a maybe. A maybe can be turned into a yes with the proper application of skill and leverage. Fortunately, he has both.

# CHAPTER FOUR

## VASSYL STRACHENKO

*Theodore Roosevelt Island National Memorial*
*Washington, D.C.*

Vassyl sits on the concrete benches on the far side of the cross-shaped plaza. This island was transformed from swampy bottomlands to a manmade forest to honor the legendary conservationist Theodore Roosevelt. The wooded island features miles of walking trails and is a fitting memorial to the 26th President.

The assassin isn't here to enjoy the outdoors or admire the imposing statue of a somewhat angry Teddy Roosevelt staring at him from the other side of the brick plaza. He's here because this may be the quietest and least visited place in the entire D.C. metropolitan area, even on a Saturday morning. It's time to pay the piper for the failure in Chicago.

"How was your hike?" he asks Robespierre as the big man sits next to him dressed in appropriate walking garb.

"I didn't take one today. I had to meet with you instead. The last thing I expected to hear was news that Isiah Burgess is still breathing. I also didn't expect to wait a week to hear why."

"It wasn't an update that I expected to deliver," Vassyl says, scanning the treeline to ensure nobody is approaching via one of the four trails that leads to the monument. "And I couldn't exactly rush back here."

"Machiavelli is upset."

"I don't care," Vassyl snaps. "I don't work for him, and neither do you."

"That's true, but you do work for me. I don't expect you to understand how this works. We are equal partners. When he's upset, I get to hear about it. That annoys me. What do you think that means for you?"

"I get the point."

"Good. Do you want to tell me how that debacle in Chicago happened? You've been planning it for weeks."

"Burgess had to take a piss, and it saved his life. He caught a lucky break. That's the short story."

"It looks more like you let Isiah kick your ass," Robespierre says, pointing down at Vassyl's bruised forearms where he got smacked with the lamp.

"That's not how it happened."

Robespierre lets out a sigh. "You have bruises, and he emerged with no new holes and your gun."

"It's untraceable, and there are no prints or DNA on it."

"I would hope not, but that's hardly the point."

"Machiavelli should handle his own business if he thinks his people are so damn good."

"Machiavelli took four washed-up soldiers and crafted a plan that they nearly executed despite being set up to fail. You are a top-notch hitman who couldn't even take out a politician's kid. I would go easy on any comparisons until you prove yourself if I were you."

Robespierre's words cut deeply, and Vassyl would like nothing more than to tell him off and walk away. Unfortunately, he's not a man to be trifled with, and he's also right. Vassyl knows that he screwed up. It doesn't mean he appreciates the lecture.

"Fine, give me a mission."

Robespierre pulls out his cell and sends a file via Bluetooth. Vassyl grins and pulls out his device.

"You don't own a printer in that government office of yours?"

"This isn't something you carry around Washington, D.C. in a briefcase."

Vassyl opens the file and scans it. He has to reread parts of it to ensure his eyes aren't deceiving him as Robespierre patiently waits for him to finish.

"I hope you're kidding me with this."

"I'm not. And the whole thing got even harder with Isiah Burgess not dead."

"This is deep sea fishing without a rod," Vassyl says, gesturing at the open file on his phone.

"No, it's more like hunting Jaws in a rowboat. It starts by chumming the waters, and I have the perfect bait."

Robespierre transfers a second, smaller file.

"Make contact with him. If you follow the plan and improvise what you need to, the rest should take care of itself."

Robespierre rises and takes a deep breath of crisp morning air before staring back down at his hired gun.

"The next time we talk, it had better be because you are reporting success. Another failure will not be tolerated. Understood?"

Vassyl nods. Robespierre looks at him for a long moment before heading back towards the trail leading to a pedestrian bridge that crosses the river. Nothing more needed to be said. It falls on Vassyl to make things right.

He turns his attention to his phone and reads the dossier. He has no idea how Robespierre got this information when the FBI doesn't even have it. If they did, his newest target would already be in custody. He continues to scroll until he finds the information on the man's last known whereabouts. It looks like he's heading south this morning.

# CHAPTER FIVE

## TIERRA CAMPOS

*Cable News Studio Conference Room*
*Washington, D.C.*

Planning for the next show starts the moment after the previous one ends. Ideas for follow-ups and threads to pull are annotated and left for the morning crew. Their work begins early by sifting through overnight reports and reviewing developing stories. They create the first draft of the rundown and instruct bookers to start lining up possible guests.

Writers begin plying their trade around mid-morning. The executive producer reviews the scripts for the opening monologue and final thoughts segment and presents them at the one o'clock production meeting. That's when Wilson and I get our first chance to preview the program's direction and layout. We provide our input into guest selection, develop the questions, and begin work on the show's monologue and final thoughts.

All this is revised and finalized at six pm. Technicians load the approved scripts into teleprompters while other members of the team create appropriate graphics. It's a dance that plays over and over. Most of the time, it goes smoothly. Sometimes it doesn't. From the constipated looks on the staff's faces, it will be one of those days.

Brock Puttman enters with a handful of writers and production staff. He took over the reins of the show not long after my theatrics in New Hampshire. Hand-picked by the network, he has been at odds with Wilson and me from the moment he walked through the door. When we are handed the drafts for tonight's show, I realize that the dynamic isn't about to change today.

"What the hell is this?" Wilson asks after reading the first couple of paragraphs.

"What's the problem now?" Brock moans.

"Where do I start? Use of slanderous adjectives, unnecessary characterizations, inflammatory supposition…"

"Opinion masquerading as fact," I add, picking up the baton. "Overt leading questions, conclusions without analysis—"

"I get your point, thank you. We're taking the show in a new direction."

"Says who?"

"It comes from the top," Brock says, sticking his chin out as he smugly stares at me.

"Since when does DeAnna dictate the tone and tenor of *Capitol Beat?*"

"Since she runs the network and can do what she damn well pleases. Right now, it's a change in direction. She thinks we're out of step with the people."

Wilson leans forward. "How would she know? DeAnna lives in a two-million-dollar Vienna, Virginia estate and has a staff of ten people working for her. She hasn't been to a supermarket in her life, much less worked a day of it."

"It's her decision, and I fully support it. All of our competitors have moved in this direction."

"And their ratings have dropped," I argue.

"And so have ours."

"Not by nearly as much. I've been doing this since you were in grade school. People turn to us for news and analysis, not to make up their minds for them like our competitors are trying to do."

"Why shouldn't we, Wilson? Look around you. The people in this room are more informed than ninety-nine percent of the public."

"That's not what this show does," Wilson snaps, his face beginning to redden. We present verified facts and ask tough questions to create informed opinions that people use to hold their leaders and representatives accountable."

"How quaint. That's not how the world works now," Brock argues.

"Says who? Reliable, unbiased journalism isn't just what people want; it's what they need."

The corner of Brock's mouth curls up in amusement. Not only does he disagree, but he believes the exact opposite. It's why he should have been the last person on Earth selected to produce *Capitol Beat*.

"I will not argue this further. This is the script for tonight. End of discussion."

Puttman jabs a finger down on the papers in front of him for effect. The act was unnecessarily dramatic. He came in here expecting a fight. Why disappoint him? There is no way the great Wilson Newman would ever agree to read the nonsense on these pages.

"Then you'll be reading it yourself," Wilson says, leaning back and drawing his line in the sand.

"I'm okay with dead air," I say when Brock turns to me. "Do you think our audience is?"

He glances at one of his minions before studying our faces. "Fine. Have it your way. Have your revisions to the rundown and script to me by the end of the hour. I'll inform the network of your objections."

"You do that," Wilson sneers as he leaves the conference room.

A majority of the technicians and writers glare at us as they follow him out of the room. Wilson and I are on an island. There wasn't much support here. It's odd since Wilson has worked with many of them for years. Puttman must have used some leverage to get them to go along with this.

"That was tense."

"I'm afraid it's only going to get worse, Tierra," Wilson says, rubbing his temples.

"Why?"

"This was a test. I'm an old dinosaur set in his ways. Puttman knows that he isn't going to change that. You're a different story. They want to see how hard you'll push back against the changes they want."

"That sounds pleasant. Are you sure you want to retire?"

"I've never been more certain. This is going to be your battle. I hope that you're prepared to fight it."

Wilson pats me on the arm as he retreats out of the room with his stack of papers to make the revisions. I'm content to sit here. This is a disaster. I came to *Capitol Beat* because of the way they presented the news to America. If Puttman gets the changes he wants to see, I may have been better off staying at *Front Burner*. That thought sends a shiver down my spine.

# CHAPTER SIX

## OLIVER JAHN

*Tomorrow's News Today Studio*
*Hudson Yards, New York, New York*

Oliver follows the same routine he did when producing the show from his basement. He sits at his desk, eyes closed for about five minutes before cameras start rolling. He has never used a script. Those early shows posted to Internet streaming sites were done without one. He just made it up as he went along and didn't feel compelled to change that when he hit the big time.

The format is unchanged, and the studio was built to keep that small-time feel. The TNT studio is half the average living room size, and there is only one camera. When Ahn Mi Sun began working for him, she introduced the idea of displaying graphics over his shoulder during the broadcast, and they preserved that during the jump to cable news. Visual storytelling made a difference in connecting with the audience that other news programs only wish they can replicate.

The opening credits play, and Oliver slides his signature black glasses up higher on the bridge of his nose. It's an action he will repeat thirty times before the end of this broadcast, and is something that he's relentlessly mocked for. He doesn't care, so long as people are talking about him.

"Good evening, and welcome to the program where you, my loyal audience, learn about *Tomorrow's News Today*. As always, I am your guide through the great unknown, Oliver Jahn.

"Tonight, we're going to talk about pretenders. No, not the snotnose little kids playing cops and robbers, cowboys and Indians, or any of the other racist and politically incorrect games we engaged in as children. I mean adult pretenders. Trust me when I say they're worse.

"Take Wilson Newman, who single-handedly keeps Geritol, insert copyright and trademark here, so please don't sue us, big button cell phones, and denture cream manufacturers in business. I know, I know, you're saying that he has been a great reporter, and he has. Who could forget his coverage of Washington crossing the Delaware? And let's be honest, his interview with a defeated Robert E. Lee at Appomattox was a must-see…newspaper article because that's all that existed.

"His understanding of what journalism means is as old as he is. It's also as wrong as getting fired as a massage therapist for rubbing people the wrong way. No, I didn't mean it that way. Okay, yes, I did. He's the Great Pretender in the hierarchy of their realm, but a new coronation is underway in the cable news realm."

Oliver steals a quick glance at the monitor located off to the side of the camera that displays the image the viewers see over his shoulder. He has to suppress a smile when he sees a rat with a crown on its head.

"He's passing the torch on to Tierra Campos, the Summerville shooting survivor who capitalized on her victimhood and stumbled into a story that earned her a box full of prestigious awards. Yeah, I said it. That's what she did.

"Miss journalistic integrity was reporting on human interest stories in Washington. What was she even reporting on? Is anything of interest for humans down in the nation's cesspool once you strip the politics away? Probably not, but I digress.

"She is a worthy successor to the title of Great Pretender because she hides behind the same veil of non-partisanship. In case you forgot, Tierra Campos destroyed viable gun control legislation and almost derailed a presidential campaign. Then she doubled down on that in the New Hampshire Primary.

"And then there is *Front Burner*, the news for Millennials by Millennials. I mean that in the worst way possible. There is nothing wrong with the generation, only that the other generations think you're lazy, weak, and stupid. Don't believe me? Read their articles. Do it! I dare you. It should come with a terms of service agreement that every American should be forced to read, saying, 'this writing causes brain damage.'

"We should be thankful that Campos left *Front Burner*. Now we don't have to read her horrid writing. Of course, now she's spewing her nonsense on *Capitol Beat*. If you want to believe that she is an old-school journalist, go ahead. It's a free country, for now at least. But trust me when I tell you that she is gaslighting you.

"I could spend this entire episode telling you about the fraud that she is perpetrating on the American public. Oh, what the hell? We are going to spend the hour on it. I just decided. We'll start when our corporate overlords get done ringing the cash register during this commercial break."

"Back in two-thirty," one of the associate producers announces.

"*Congratulations. You killed it,*" Mi Sun says through the earpiece. He misses having her just off-camera, giving him visual cues. Sometimes, the old days weren't only simpler; they were better.

"Thanks, but don't congratulate me yet. This was Pearl Harbor. They didn't expect an attack or see it coming. Now things will get interesting."

"*Yeah. Remember how that war ended for the Japanese.*"

"You forget, Mi Sun. I'm a journalist. Rewriting history is what I do."

# CHAPTER SEVEN

## SPECIAL AGENT VICTORIA LARSEN

*Red & White Wine Bar*
*Navy Yard, Washington, D.C.*

There are hundreds of restaurants and bars within walking distance of Tierra's apartment in Washington's Navy Yard neighborhood. Her favorite is the Red and White Wine Bar, whose sign is a D.C. flag stylized with wine glasses instead of stars. Victoria made plans to meet her there the day after she returned from her vacation in the Caribbean.

The two women share a hug before ordering glasses of wine. Victoria talks about her vacation and how lovely Grace Bay is. Tierra outlines her ongoing struggle with the executive producer over the new direction of the show he's pushing. They are on their third glass by the time they are all caught up.

"You aren't working tonight?"

"No, Wilson is hosting tonight's show."

"You know, it's weird watching you on television instead of reading your articles on *Front Burner*. Have you talked to Austin?"

"Nope, not since I left. There's nothing left to be said between us."

"What if he apologized?"

Tierra forces a smile. "He won't. What's done is done, and I've moved on. The last chapters of the *Front Burner* book aren't worth rereading."

Victoria nods. "I heard Tyler and Olivia left."

"Yeah, not long after I did. I haven't talked to them either. It must be strange in that office now."

"I bet. Speaking of strange, I saw Oliver Jahn's attack on you last night."

"Oh, so you're watching my competitor now?" Tierra asks playfully.

"It's in a different time slot, and I only saw it in passing. Oliver didn't pull any punches, did he?"

"He's a hack. Oliver is the kid who played acted as the class clown to get more attention from the teacher. He's not worth taking seriously."

"Why did he suddenly decide to go after *Capitol Beat* and *Front Burner* while pounding on you in the process?"

"Who knows? His ratings are dropping. He's probably trying to boost them by tearing me down," Tierra says before taking a long sip of her wine. "You said you got a visitor down in Turks?"

"Nice change of subject," Victoria says with a smile.

"Moving on to a more interesting segment is what I do for a living."

Victoria explains her offer from Rigo. She has to explain the Critical Incident Response Group that he works for and what they do. Tierra listens intently. She was fully aware of Victoria's feelings about the FBI when she left.

"That sounds intriguing. Are you going to take the job?"

Victoria shifts uncomfortably. "I'm not sure. When I left the FBI, I swore I would never go back."

"I remember, but it's all you know."

"That's true, but not the big reason I'm considering it. I don't think the Bureau is convinced that Isiah is Machiavelli."

Tierra's face changes to a mix of surprise and anger. "He admitted it, Vic."

"He didn't, Tierra, and you know it. He acted guilty. It doesn't mean he is."

"His phone rang at that desk when I dialed the number you pulled off of Marx's phone. I was three feet from him and saw the look on his face. He knew he was busted."

"Or he was only surprised. You went into that interview believing that the governor was behind it. I'm only saying that you can't rule out the possibility that you made a mistake."

"I didn't make one in Brockhampton, and I didn't in New Hampshire. If Isiah can prove that he's not Machiavelli, more power to him. He's lawyered up, and they're sowing the seeds of doubt when they mount his defense. That's all. Isiah won't be able to clear his name because he knows he can't."

Victoria backs off. Tierra is angry and defensive, and that wasn't the intent of seeing her. She is the closest thing to a friend that Victoria has. Isiah Burgess isn't worth ruining that.

"I didn't mean to upset you."

"You didn't," Tierra says, forcing a smile. "I didn't mean to snap at you. I've just been fighting so many battles that I don't have the emotional bandwidth to take on that one. When do you have to decide to take the job?"

"I have until Friday."

"Well, let me give you some advice. You know how to be an agent. You should try feeling like a civilian before you make a choice."

Victoria cocks her head. "How do I do that?"

"You can start by finding something in your closet that makes you look less threatening."

"What's wrong with what I'm wearing?" she asks, staring down at her clothing.

"Nothing, if you work on Capitol Hill, are a lawyer, or are a federal agent looking to shoot someone."

"I don't look like that."

Tierra lets out a laugh. It's the first one to come out of her since she got here.

"Seriously? Vic, if I had your legs, I would never wear pants."

Victoria is not the type that gets self-conscious, especially about her looks. This is a rare exception. She takes Tierra's opinions seriously. Only a fool wouldn't.

"This is all I own."

"I'll tell you what," Tierra says, getting the waiter's attention and signaling for the check. "Why don't we go shopping? We'll make it a girls' night. You should try dressing like a civilian before you decide whether you should become one."

# CHAPTER EIGHT

## VASSYL STRACHENKO

*Stono River Motel*
*Charleston, South Carolina*

This is the type of place in which he would expect his target to hole up. It's rundown, filled with shady characters, and most of all, cheap. There are no cameras or any other kind of on-premise surveillance. The only downside is that it's only a few blocks away from a police station. Based on what he has seen so far, the police visit often enough that the squad cars can drive themselves here.

None of that seems to bother this guy. He has kept himself secluded during the daylight hours. Darkness is a blanket that helps maintain anonymity. He will buy the necessities of life at night. It's an appropriate but predictable play.

When he emerges from the cesspool that he calls a room, his head is on a swivel as he moves quickly to his car. It's too fast. He doesn't notice Vassyl lurking in the shadows of the hallway with the burnt-out bulb. It makes it easy for the assassin to come up from behind and stick the suppressor of his new gun in the small of the man's back.

"Get in."

Ian Drucker complies. Vassyl reaches around to unlock the back door and climbs in. He places his gun against the former FBI agent's head.

"Fasten your seat belt. Go for your gun, and I blow your brains out."

"It took you long enough."

"Really? I didn't realize you were in a rush to die."

"Have you ever been hunted by the FBI? No, I imagine not. It's not as romantic as it seems on television. I figured that no matter how long and hard I ran, Machiavelli would get to me before they did."

"I don't work for Machiavelli. I work for Robespierre."

"I'm a little insulted that they sent the JV team after me," Ian says with a sneer.

"You should be more insulted that one of them has a gun to your head. What does that say about you?"

"Fair point. Go ahead, do what you came here for."

Vassyl presses the gun into his temple and moves his finger to the trigger. The man looks like he has been put through hell. Unshaven and disheveled, with bags under his eyes, he's at the end of his rope. The merciful thing to do would be to end his suffering. Unfortunately for Ian, Vassyl is not the compassionate type.

"You didn't strike me as a quitter. I figured you would have more fight in you."

Ian stares out the driver's side window. "It's used up. Enough of the chatter. Do it already."

"Not yet," Vassyl says, easing the pressure from his index finger on the trigger. "What happened up in New Hampshire?"

"You mean, why did we fail? Marx got paranoid, and that made him sloppy. Had he not gone after Wilson Newman in a damn shopping mall, we wouldn't have gotten caught. Sometimes it comes down to something that stupid."

It was an honest answer, and Vassyl agrees with the conclusion. Marx got cocky and took risks he shouldn't have. There was no reason to try to take out the old man in that mall. Trotsky didn't have to run Tierra's colleague Olivia off the road on a highway. There are far easier ways to do both. It was Marx's arrogance born from a winning streak that led to a feeling of invincibility. He was very wrong.

"You know what happened to your friends in the SOF, right?"

"Yeah. The FBI killed all of them."

Not technically accurate since Trotsky committed suicide, but Vassyl doesn't bother correcting the man.

"And now you've given up."

"I don't know who you are, but you don't strike me as the kind of guy that struggling would make a difference with."

The assassin smiles at the compliment. "You know, Engels is a stupid name."

Ian laughs. "Well, I picked it while I was stationed in Germany. I thought it was cool at the time."

"You know, I almost admire you. You were the most dedicated of the SOF members. You joined the FBI to be in a position to pull off your mission. That couldn't have been easy."

"It wasn't bad."

"How did you get your background suppressed? The FBI doesn't hire people dishonorably discharged from the military."

"Your boss helped, but I'm sure you already know that. Why the twenty questions?"

Vassyl removes the pistol from the man's head but keeps it trained on him. Ian sits motionless in the driver's seat and doesn't try anything.

"I want to give you a second chance at life, but you may be too far gone. I can't afford to have a quitter on the team."

"Second chance to do what?"

"Exact some revenge."

Ian exhales and returns his attention to the view outside the driver's window.

"Not that I'm disinterested, but I'm a liability. I can't exactly move around the country freely and will attract too much attention if I do. I won't be of any use to you."

"I can get you where you need to be."

"Where is that?"

"Back into the belly of the beast. Our operation is something I think you'll have a keen interest in being a part of."

Ian perks up. It's the spark that Vassyl was looking for. *There is hope for this guy yet.*

"What's the mission?" Ian asks, his voice an octave higher and dripping with enthusiasm. Vassyl leans forward and whispers into his ear.

"We're going to kill Victoria Larsen."

# CHAPTER NINE

## BRIAN COOPER

*ZQJ Research*
*Reston, Virginia*

Tucked away in the Virginia suburbs is a political powerhouse with no equal. ZQJ Research has an innocuous name that Brian once thought was the initials of the group's founders. He was wrong. The assembly of odd letters was the odd brainchild of the equally bizarre man he is visiting. Z, Q, and J are the three least used tiles in the game Scrabble.

The pollster and his company are unknown entities to most Americans. To the political elite and their inner circles, they are rock stars. They have called the last five presidential races correctly, and three of them with a perfect score in the electoral college. The company has earned high marks even in less-predictable state races. That makes them the go-to source for campaigns to understand where they stand with the electorate.

At the heart of its operation is their eccentric leader with the name only a jeweler would appreciate. Brian doubts that Cubic Zirconia is his real name, despite not being able to prove otherwise. A recluse who refuses to do television and is rarely seen in public, for him, polling is a religion. While recent election cycles have destroyed the industry's credibility, their failures only burnished his image as the oracle of elections.

"Your punctuality is borderline annoying, Brian," the bespeckled man says without looking up. "I wasn't ready for you yet."

"I thought you were ready for any eventuality, Cubic."

The pollster leans back in his chair. "Nice flattery. Why are you here?"

"You know why," Brian says, looking around the spacious office. Cubic is a busy man and a workaholic, but everything in here has its place. It's impressively tidy.

"I have clients that pay me millions of dollars a year for the insights I spend months developing. There is no way that I'm giving that information to you. That's the end of the discussion."

Brian reaches into his jacket pocket and produces a tri-folded piece of paper. He holds it up before tossing it on the glass desk.

"You deal with statistics and probabilities. I am one hundred percent sure that this will change your mind."

Cubic stares at him intently before picking it up and reading it. "What is this?"

"There is nobody on Earth that understands the value of information better than you do. That wasn't easy to find. Your attorneys did a good job burying it."

"Nothing in here is true."

"Yes, it's inconceivable. I'm sure that one of your board members with a long history of womanizing didn't fly on a plane to an island that didn't have underage girls owned by a disgraced billionaire that didn't kill himself. Of course, I saw the unaltered manifest, not what was made publicly available. His name was on it, so maybe it's not inconceivable after all. Any public disclosure of that…well, you spend your days gazing into a crystal ball. What will be worse for your business? The revelation or the cover-up?"

"What do you want?" Cubic says through clenched teeth.

"You already know."

"And if I give it to you?"

"If you give me what you have and any updated information and trends up to Election Day, that information will never see the light of day," Brian says, making a promise that he probably can't keep.

"You play dirty, Cooper."

"Welcome to politics."

Cubic makes a few mouse clicks and shares an interactive election map to the television hung on the wall. All the data is blank, showing the five hundred and thirty-eight electoral votes up for grabs.

"Let's start from the beginning—electoral politics one-oh-one. Only a handful of states really matter, so let's dispense with the obvious. Colin Bradford is from North Carolina and will own the Deep South. Add West Virginia and Utah, despite his lack of appeal to Mormons. He will also get the Midwest, including Missouri and Iowa.

"Standish gets the entire Northeast, including the Maine Second District, and the West Coast. The margins are tighter, but she gets Wisconsin, Minnesota, and Michigan. We'll also give her Virginia and Indiana to Bradford. She's leading two-fifteen to one-oh-nine.

"It looks like previous cycles so far, except for Georgia," Brian observes.

"He'll flip that red again. The Democratic outreach machine has fallen apart there. Bradford will win Ohio, and Standish takes Illinois. They split Alaska and Hawaii. So, Standish needs thirty-one and Bradford sixty at this point. They have almost equal paths to victory.

The Southwest is interesting because it's critical to the race. If it shakes out like we think it will, Standish wins Colorado, and Bradford holds on to Texas by a couple of points because of her Safe America Act."

"Yeah, Texans like their guns," Brian mutters.

"That should cancel out his flagging support with Latinos, which is also why Florida will be close."

"Isn't it Latinx now?"

"Whatever," Cubic moans. "Our research shows seventy percent of Hispanics hate the term. Do you want to hear this or play pronoun games?"

"It's a gender-neutral neologism, not a pronoun." The pollster glares at him. "Sorry. Continue."

"Standish wins Nevada, Colorado, and New Mexico. For whatever reason, Arizonans don't like her, especially in Maricopa County. We have Bradford winning, but it will be a race to watch."

Brian leans forward in his chair and stares at the map. "You've got to be kidding me."

"I wish I were. There you have it, in red and blue: two-fifty-nine to two-fifty-nine with one state left in play."

"Pennsylvania."

"At least the race won't be a tie, but it will be a coin flip. Standish owns the cities and Bradford everything else. The Keystone State will be determined by turnout. The team with the best ground game wins the state and the election. Registered voters give a slight edge to the Democrats. Likely voters favor the Republicans."

"This is the first map I've seen like this," Brian says.

"That's because my colleagues in the industry are clowns. They skew their data to align with their thinking, not vice versa."

"How sure are you about this?"

"That's a dumb question for a man like you to ask," Cubic says. "If the election were held tomorrow, one hundred percent. You've been in politics for more than five minutes, so you know the drill. This map assumes the status quo. We both know it can and likely will change. They're called swing states for a reason."

"Will the conventions tip the scales?"

"In the short term, sure. For the election? It's doubtful without a seismic misstep. Scandals and surprises cause the needle to quiver, but most people have already made up their minds. Even the ones who claim they haven't lean in one direction or another. The only thing that will make a difference is something earth-shattering. A two-point swing in either direction will color this map differently."

"You said that Bradford's vulnerable with Latinos. What about other minorities?"

"White, working-class voters are his base. He does decent with women and college-educated voters. Minorities are a problem."

"What about Brockhampton and the failure of her gun control bill? Is that going to impact Standish?"

"The Safe America Act's failure cost her in the early primaries and about a quarter-point nationally in a head's up race. Those are pre-convention numbers. The people who hold Brockhampton against her wouldn't vote for her anyway, so it's baked in the cake. America has moved past it."

"People and their short attention spans," Cooper grumbles.

"Anything else? Or can I get back to work?"

"Thank you for your time, Cubic," Brian says, rising from his chair and showing himself to the door.

"Remember our arrangement. Don't even think about screwing me over."

"I wouldn't dream of it."

Brian leaves with a lot to think about. Cubic is successful because he studies the trends that the data shows more than the data itself. His polls are also extensive and thorough. He's willing to bet that, barring something monumental happening or dismal campaign performance, the map looks like that in November. That means both camps are betting on some report or scandal to cause a seismic shift in the race. Poor Pennsylvania. They are about to be at the epicenter of controversy in yet another national election.

# CHAPTER TEN

## TIERRA CAMPOS

*Cable News Studio*
*Washington, D.C.*

Even with my eyes closed, I know when the lights come back up. Wilson introduced the practice on the *Capitol Beat* set years ago. He doesn't like the hot lights beating on him when cameras aren't rolling. The production crew turns them down during commercial breaks, and I use the time to close my eyes and focus on the next segment.

When the end of the final segment comes, so does crunch time. I've been practicing this all day. Now is the time to set my nerves aside and get this done.

"Now for tonight's final thought," I say, turning to a different camera. "There are some high-profile personalities recently taking to the airwaves to proclaim a new era of how the news is presented and consumed. It is infused with humor, opinion, and outright attacks. Their goal is not to inform you; it's to do the thinking for you."

Words stopped scrolling in the teleprompter after the first sentence. It doesn't matter since I'm not reading them anyway. The control room technician turns it off, allowing me to concentrate on recalling this from memory without distraction.

"*What the hell are you doing, Tierra?*" Brock Puttman barks into my earpiece. In a departure from the past, I don't remove it.

"Modern media has always relied on sensationalism to increase circulation or gain television ratings. This is different. It's the manufacture of the news at your expense."

"The point of journalism is to hold people in positions of power accountable. It's critically important for any nation whose representatives and leaders are democratically elected. The current news cycle is dominated by misinformation, disinformation, and the unabashed injection of opinion as fact. The quote-unquote journalists you see on television lack curiosity and a drive to do real reporting. In some cases, they hold contempt for truth."

"*Jesus,*" Puttman moans.

"The news business needs a rebirth by reverting to its past. Our job is not to advance the agenda of others. It is not to cheerlead for ideological gains or punish those who don't think like us. Those practices that some characterize as modern journalism have another word associated with them: propaganda.

"We all have our likes and our dislikes, but opinions belong in op-eds. It is the duty and responsibility of any journalist to ensure that we don't permit our prejudices to show. That is not only good journalism — it's one of our basic tenets. *Capitol Beat* will always be here to bring you a balanced approach to the news. That is my final thought, and it is for the record.

"We will be back tomorrow with the latest from Washington and around the country. For *Capitol Beat*, I am Tierra Campos. Good night."

"We're out," a floor producer announces.

I didn't expect applause. I didn't expect complete silence, either. Unfortunately, that's the reaction in the studio.

"I think that you do this job better than I do," Wilson says, coming from behind the cameras to the front of the anchor desk.

"You're going senile if you believe that. Is it me, or is the crew a touch unenthusiastic about our stunt?"

"Probably. They know as well as we do what's coming next."

"Tierra!"

"And here it comes," I mutter.

"What the hell was that?" Puttman shouts as he storms up to the desk beside Wilson.

"It was my final thought. I'm pretty sure you watch the show enough to know that we end with that segment."

"That's not what was on the teleprompter!"

"I'm aware. I was the one staring at the camera. We changed it at the last minute."

"And you're not the one who's going to be fielding angry calls from DeAnna Van Herten when she hears about this."

"That's why they pay you the big bucks, Brock," Wilson says, slapping him jovially on the shoulder.

"You think this is funny?"

"We don't do comedy here, unlike our competitors. We do the news. As it turns out, also unlike our competitors."

"Oh, and you're the arbiter of what constitutes news now?"

The slight smile Wilson was wearing disappears from his face. "I've been reporting since you were in diapers. So yeah, I'm more of an authority on it than you are."

To Brock's credit, he knows that he can't argue that point. Wilson is a multigenerational icon in the news business. Nobody would dispute his prominence among the elite journalists in American history.

"That was a garbage ending. You don't get to say what you want," Brock says, pointing his finger at me.

"I think you forget the arrangement," Wilson interjects as I am about to yell back at the arrogant asshat we work for. "You produce the show, but we get control over the monologue and the final thought."

"Yeah, that's right. You do. We'll see if that's still the case tomorrow."

Puttman storms off, still fuming. A bashful technician sees the opening to approach and remove my microphone. I'm eager to give it to her, get to make-up to wash my face, and get out of here.

"That went well," I say as we watch him disappear from the studio.

"He's determined to get his way. Unfortunately, if this is coming from DeAnna, he just might. They are out to murder what's left of journalistic integrity."

"Any advice?"

"Yeah, sleep with one eye open."

"Maybe you should have gone into comedy, Wilson."

We both smile and let out a laugh. It feels good. There haven't been enough of either around here for months now. The way things are trending, there might not be any for a while longer.

# CHAPTER ELEVEN

## OLIVER JAHN

*Tomorrow's News Today Studio*
*Hudson Yards, New York, New York*

Oliver enjoys his job more than anything else he has ever done in his life. It does get dull and somewhat routine at times. Then there are days like today. As the opening credits roll and Mi Sun gives him the count, he can't wait to dive into this.

"Welcome to *Tomorrow's News Today*, I'm Oliver Jahn, and yes, that is a bottle of tequila on my desk. Yes, I am probably going to drink it before the end of this show. Why? Because the Queen of the Pretenders is at it again.

"Tierra Campos just got done with one of her childish final thoughts…who came up with that? Was it Wilson? He was a great anchor, you know, before I was born. But how arrogant is he to believe he has the final thought on anything? Well, whatever.

"Campos just got done with hers, and it's priceless. It's the crown jewels, Hope Diamond, and Mona Lisa found in a storage unit at auction kind of priceless. I'm going to put it up on our website because you have to see it. She tried to defend old journalism like it was the Magna Carta and made a joke out of herself in the process.

"What makes it so funny? She's fooling you, people. Tierra Campos doesn't believe in fair-minded journalism. Make no mistake — everything that she does and says is about her. It's why she left a good gig at that ridiculous *Front Burner*…wait, are they even still around? They are? Go figure."

Oliver glances off to the side and sees an associate producer nod. "I have proof of just how duplicitous America's favorite churro is. Okay, you're right. That's mean. She isn't that sweet. Now, someone will say that this is photoshopped. You need to know something personal: I'm not that good at that. Unless altering a photo involves drawing in penises, I'm no good. Seriously. No, this photo is real."

He glances at the monitor off-camera to see the photo replacing him on screen. He stays silent for a moment to let the audience's minds run with what they are seeing. It's not every day you see Senator Alicia Standish standing on the street with Tierra Campos.

"Does somebody want to tell me what this is about?" Oliver asks when Mi Sun cues him. "I mean, the only thing missing from this picture is the suitcase full of cash and a couple of kilos of blow.

"Tierra Campos manipulates you into thinking everyone is against you. During the whole Brockhampton fiasco, she led you to believe that Alicia Standish was public enemy number one. Now Campos is making deals or dinner arrangements with her like they're BFFs. She's the one with an agenda and the crazy conspiracy to control your lives. It's dangerous, and the Queen of the Pretenders knows it. Or she doesn't, which makes her even more terrifying. It'd be like Pennywise not knowing that luring kids to a sewer to eat them is creepy and wrong.

"We need to demand better. You can make a difference by using your remotes and pointing your clicks elsewhere. Don't reward Tierra Campos's bad behavior by giving her the attention she craves. It'd be like giving a sumo wrestler another Twinkie. He doesn't need it. He doesn't need it! We're back after this."

# CHAPTER TWELVE

## SPECIAL AGENT VICTORIA LARSEN

*Front Burner Washington Office*
*Washington, D.C.*

The place is a ghost town. The only thing needed to complete the image is tumbleweeds drifting across the office floor. Victoria takes the elevator up and is greeted by an identical desolate floor. After two failed attempts at negotiating the maze of corridors, she finds the office she is looking for.

"Knock, knock."

"I'm busy," Austin snaps before looking up from his monitor. When he sees her standing there, he jumps out of his chair, almost falling over in the process.

"Even for me?"

"Victoria? I, uh… I'm never too busy for you. Come in."

"I'm sorry to drop by unannounced, but there was nobody downstairs to do the announcing."

"Yeah, we have had to cut back staff. The front desk was the first to go. Things are…you look amazing!"

"Thanks," she says, running her hands down the sides of her sundress and staring at the white strappy heels that she's wearing. "You look like a train wreck. Are you having a falling out with your razor?"

Austin smiles weakly. "I'm doing three jobs here and don't leave this office much anymore. Please, take a seat. What are you doing in Washington?"

"Considering a job opportunity."

"With the FBI?" Victoria nods as she moves a pile of folders off the chair and gingerly sits, conscious that she's wearing a dress. "I don't think I would have expected that."

"It's partly why I'm here. Have you been looking into Machiavelli by any chance?"

Austin waves a dismissive hand. "That story is done. Burgess is Machiavelli."

"Have you confirmed that?"

He shakes his head. "Outfits with more resources than we have aren't even wasting their energy on that. It's a law enforcement matter now. Why are you asking? Are you saying that the FBI thinks it might not be him?"

"I—"

"Hey, boss, I…whoa," Logan says, walking into the office and seeing Victoria.

"Logan, you remember Agent Larsen?" Austin asks, breaking the awkward silence after Logan's mouth hangs open wide enough for Victoria to count his teeth.

"It's just Victoria now. How are you, Logan?"

"I…uh…I mean, wow. You look different."

"Thanks. I was advised that I needed a wardrobe change and was taken shopping," Victoria says, opting to leave Tierra's involvement out of the story.

"It works for you."

"Can I help you with something, Logan? Drool bucket, perhaps?"

"Uh, no, it can wait. I'll come back," the young researcher says, almost walking into the door jamb on the way out.

"I apologize for that, Victoria. He doesn't get out much either. We're an army of two just fighting like hell to keep the lights on."

"I noticed. What happened?"

Austin leans back in his chair. "Economic reality set in, I guess. Our advertisers bailed on us, and our top talent got poached, Tierra included. Leadership saw the writing on the wall and moved on to greener pastures. At least most of them did."

"How are you going to make it work?"

He grimaces and shakes his head. "We're not. We have enough cash on hand to survive a couple more months. I don't think it will even last that long. The dream is dead."

"Austin," Victoria says, looking down at the floor. "Have you ever thought that you helped kill it?"

"What is that supposed to mean?"

"You're a bright guy. You know. You forced Tierra out."

"Management made her an offer to stay. I'm sure she told you that. She declined."

"Because it meant that you would have to leave. You made it impossible to work together, and this team is your baby."

"*Was* my baby," Austin snaps. "Tierra was hosting *Capitol Beat* in her off-time. She was going to leave anyway."

Victoria understands Austin's tone for what it is: resentment. She waltzed into his office and ripped the bandage off that wound. Now she's going to pour salt into it. Too bad. He needs some tough love right now.

"You don't know that. What I do know is that you made Tierra's decision easier. You may have been the brains here, but she was the beating heart of this team, and this team was the foundation of *Front Burner*."

"You don't think I know that?" he says, now getting angry. "I sit at this desk every day regretting what happened between us, thinking about how I could have done things differently. It doesn't matter now. Tierra is gone, and *Front Burner* will be too."

"Don't you think you should tell her that?" Victoria asks in a soft voice.

"It doesn't matter. Tierra doesn't want to hear from me. Is that why you're here? To guilt me into apologizing when we both know it won't make a difference?"

"No, it was just a suggestion. I watched *Tomorrow's News Today*. Oliver Jahn's attacks struck a nerve. I think she would appreciate hearing from you."

"I'll consider it," Austin says, forcing a smile.

"Okay, I'll let you get back to work. It was good seeing you, Austin."

"Victoria? If you're going to be in the city for a few days, can you…I mean, would you want to have dinner some night?"

"Are you asking me out on a date?"

"No…well, yeah, I guess…"

Victoria smiles warmly and places her hands on his desk. She leans forward, tapping the toe of her shoe on the floor beneath her.

"I'll tell you what. Clean yourself up, get some rest, and give me a call. You know my number."

She smiles and heads out of his office into the vacant room that was once the investigative arm of *Front Burner*. She's accustomed to men flirting with her. The act of flirting back like that is a new experience.

"Have a good day, Logan," she calls out after feeling his eyes track her to the door.

"You too, Victoria."

She didn't get what she expected out of this meeting. Victoria came into the office to press him for information about Machiavelli and ended up with loose plans for a date. She can figure out later how that happened. For now, she's going to blame the sundress and wearing her hair down.

# CHAPTER THIRTEEN

## VASSYL STRACHENKO

*Back Bay Safehouse*
*Boston, Massachusetts*

Their rental in the Back Bay section of Boston is a far cry from the places where Vassyl is used to staying. Homes on this part of Beacon Street sell for over seven figures. Why anyone would turn a high-end apartment into temporary lodging is beyond him. It's amazing what you can find online in those rental marketplaces. If he owned this place, he would probably never leave.

"This is sweet," Ian says, entering the well-furnished safehouse after climbing the back stairs from the public alley.

"Don't get too used to it. You won't be spending much time here."

Three men are standing in the living area to greet Vassyl and Ian. There isn't much camaraderie among this group. They are here as hired guns, and this is all business.

"Take that damn hat off," Vassyl says, ripping the baseball cap off Sven's head.

"You have something against the Yankees?" the big Swede moans.

"No, but everyone else in this city does. I need you guys to blend in, not get into bar fights by flashing the emblem of their sworn enemy. Learn the customs here. Don't confuse real football with American football, and don't talk trash about the Patriots."

"American football is real football," Ian mutters.

"Who are the Patriots?" the slick man who looks like he's an underwear model asks after an awkward silence. He's dead serious.

"Where did you dig up these guys?"

"You have a problem?"

"Yeah, I'm out of steroids, Tiny. Can I borrow yours, or did you use them all?"

"Oh, you're a funny guy," the Swede says, taking a menacing step closer.

"Knock it off, all of you."

"Who is Gilligan here, and why did you bring him?"

"Gilligan is Ian Drucker. Maybe you've seen him on the news once or twice. He's only managed to evade capture for six months during an intensive national manhunt. That alone makes him more competent and better than any of you, so treat him accordingly."

"Yeah, right," the Euro-trash grumbles.

"Ian, this is the team. The flashy, GQ type is Dimitri. He likes tripping old ladies and kicking puppies in his free time. The big one is Sven. The little guy is Jackrabbit. Nobody knows what his real name is."

"And nobody ever will."

"Ian is critical to the mission I'm about to hand you. That's all you need to know about why he's here. This is why you are here."

Vassyl opens a safe and hands out folders to the three men. They waste no time sifting through their contents.

"Are you serious?"

"Is there a problem, Jackrabbit?"

"No, it just wasn't what I thought we are here for. I thought we were going after Campos, too."

"She is being handled by Machiavelli and Rasputin," Vassyl informs them. "This is our mission. Focus on it."

"Who the hell is Bertram Jackson?" Sven asks.

"The biggest heroin dealer in Boston and somebody you are about to get to know much better."

"Lucky us. Are we starting a drug war?" Dimitri asks, getting a scowl from Vassyl in return.

"Something like that."

"What's the hotel room for?" Jackrabbit says, holding up his key card.

"Since nobody would ever confuse you three as businessmen or residents, you're tourists. If you get stopped by the police or suspect you're blown, report there and call me. Do not return here. I'll investigate and let you know when it's safe to return."

"How will you know?"

Vassyl narrows his eyes. "Does anybody have any intelligent questions?"

"Yeah, what does this have to do with the goal?" Sven asks.

"Theirs not to reason why," Ian leans in and whispers to Vassyl before closing the short distance to a small modern bookcase and checking it out.

"What did you say, Gilligan?"

"Theirs not to make reply, theirs not to reason why, theirs but to do and die. Into the valley of Death rode the six hundred," Ian says without looking at him.

"Let's hope not," Vassyl mutters.

"Alfred, Lord Tennyson? The Charge of the Light Brigade? Anyone?" Ian only gets blank stares. "Okay, I expected Tiny here not to know that, but c'mon, guys."

"You talk tough. You don't have no FBI badge to hide behind. I think you're a coward. I would crush you."

Ian smirks and gives a slight nod. "Says the guy that can't tie his shoes."

Sven falls for a trick most kids learn in first grade. He looks down, and Ian swings his arm around, swiping the steel lamp off the bookcase. The Swede looks up just in time to catch it square in the face. He lunges at Ian, stopped only by Vassyl, who jumps in his way and sticks the muzzle of his gun into the man's chin.

"I don't care if you can't stand each other, but you will learn to work together. If not, let me know. I need Ian to complete this mission. I can replace your ass in thirty seconds. You're the expendable one. Understood?"

Sven gets the message. He takes two steps backward, continuing to glare at the former FBI agent.

"Good. Back to business. This mission is divided into two phases. The three of you have your two targets for the first one. Once that is executed, we'll complete the final phase together. Read through that file and start your reconnaissance. There is a lot of groundwork we need to lay to pull this off, and time is not on our side."

"What are you going to be doing?"

"Ian and I will scout locations for the big finale. From this point on, this team is operational. No mistakes will be tolerated. If anybody steps out of line, I'll kill you myself. Get moving."

The three men sit on the couch and chairs to review their files. Ian walks over and stares face-to-face with Vassyl.

"Big finale? I thought I was here to help you kill Agent Larsen?"

"You are."

"Then what's this other crap?"

"Marx was reckless, but that was a symptom, not the disease. His sin was lacking patience. It's what happens to most people when they deviate from a plan. Victoria Larsen is a worthy adversary. If we take her head-on, we might win, but the odds aren't in our favor."

Ian nods at the assassin. He knows all that, maybe too well since he lived it firsthand. Vassyl didn't answer his question, though. There are a thousand less complicated ways to permanently plant her in the ground.

"And your plan is better? How?"

"Because we're going to make Victoria Larsen come to us."

# CHAPTER FOURTEEN

## BRIAN COOPER

*WMATA Shaw-Howard University Station*
*Washington, D.C.*

Brian is used to waiting on a spacious Washington metro station platform from when he worked on the Hill. It rarely has been on the green or yellow line. His travels often necessitated using the blue, silver, and orange lines that traverse the city and into Virginia from east to west.

He is about to check his watch when the diminutive and eccentric Adika Patel comes up alongside him, wearing clothing that only makes her a shade more conservative than a prostitute. Brian gives her a quick once-over and shakes his head.

"They let you dress like this at work?"

"For what I bring to the table, the bosses let me wear what I want. They're lucky that I bother wearing clothes at all."

"That's a mental picture."

"It doesn't have to be left to your imagination, big boy. You just say the word."

Adika isn't wrong. She is one of the best opposition researchers in the country, and any firm would put up with her rebellious nature to have her working for them. There is no tidbit of information she can't uncover, given enough billable hours to pay for it. Alicia Standish had plenty of cash, and Adika was assigned as the project lead.

"What do you have?" Brian asks, ignoring her sexual overtures. Her status as the city's biggest flirt is almost as well-known as her professional reputation.

"You're no fun. Here," Adika says, slapping a thick folder into Brian's chest. "This is complete opposition research into one Governor Colin Bradshaw. Paid in full by Standish for America."

"She has this?"

"Do you think I work for some Mickey Mouse outfit that doesn't make good on its obligations? We delivered it to Angela Mays and Andrew Li three days ago."

"Andrew Li?"

"Yeah, he's working for them now."

"Interesting."

"There is some damning stuff in there, especially about race relations. The firm allocated a shitload of resources to work with me. That gave me what I needed to find all the skeletons in the closet."

If ZQJ Research is the premier polling firm in the country, then Olsen Research Associates is the industry leader in opposition research. While many firms specialize in working for one political party or another, Olsen has no such predilections. They will work for whoever can pay their exorbitant fees. It's capitalism at its finest. They don't let political inclinations get in the way of making a buck, or a few hundred million of them.

Opposition research is one of the most critical inputs for developing a campaign strategy. It can range from identifying an opponent's ideological missteps or inconsistencies to uncovering salacious personal indiscretions. The one commonality with all oppo is that it's wielded to strike at the heart of another candidate's weaknesses.

"How bad?" Brian asks, straining to look down the tunnel as most commuters do while waiting for a train.

"He's not the Grand Dragon of the Ku Klux Klan if that's what you're asking."

"Wizard. Grand Wizard of the Klan."

"Whatever."

"Enough to put a damper on the GOP outreach to minorities?"

"Are you kidding? What I found is enough to kill it entirely if Standish plays her cards right. He'll be lucky to end up with two percent of the black vote."

Brian frowns. There go Pennsylvania and Georgia, and this could even put Ohio in play. Republicans struggle enough in large urban areas. The GOP gains to help close the gap over the past decade would be wiped out.

"What about Latinos?"

"Standish doesn't need to drive a wedge between them and Bradford. They already don't like him."

"I know. Is there anything damaging in the folder?"

"No, other than he didn't lift a finger for any minority group as governor."

The air in the platform changes, and the growing noise announces that their train is coming. Moments later, the lead car screams past them and starts slowing. Commuters begin to crowd the edge of the platforms where they expect the doors to open.

"What do you need this for?"

"I'm weighing my options. I owe you one, Adika."

"You owe me more than one," she says, staring up at him. "Someday, I'm going to cash in. You had better live up to the price when I do."

She gives him an air kiss and pats him on the behind as the train doors open. Adika follows him and saunters into the middle of the car, keeping her back to them. She begins batting her eyelashes at a man in a suit taking up two seats with his excessive manspreading. The flirtation has an immediate effect. He eagerly makes room for her. Brian wonders if the poor sap knows that he doesn't have a chance. He almost feels sorry for whoever is given one by that firecracker.

# CHAPTER FIFTEEN

## SPECIAL AGENT VICTORIA LARSEN

*Meridian Hill Park*
*Washington, D.C.*

Meridian Hill derived its name from being on the exact longitude of the original District of Columbia milestone marker. The park has a long history, from serving as a former president's residence to an encampment site for Union soldiers during the Civil War. In the early 20th century, architects planned and constructed an Italian-style garden there, complete with the longest cascading water fountain in North America. It's one of the prettiest parks in all of Washington.

A couple walks toward Victoria hand in hand, and she smiles. This is a lovely spot for a quiet, romantic stroll with a partner. Her illusion is shattered when the guy's eyes linger on her for a few moments too long, earning him a disapproving smack in the chest from his girlfriend. She doesn't fancy herself a homewrecker, but at least she knows she's still got it.

"You're late," Victoria says, not bothering to shift her eyes away from the man and woman now arguing as they walk.

"It's good to see that your skills haven't atrophied," Agent Benitez says, coming up alongside her. He ditched his tie, rolled up his sleeves, and is carrying his jacket over his shoulder. She figures that's about as casual as he gets on duty.

"I haven't been out that long."

"Long enough for you to change your look. I almost didn't recognize you with your hair down and dressed like that," Rigo says. "Without meaning any offense, you look stunning."

"There isn't a woman in the world that would take offense to that compliment. Do you like it?"

She twists at the waist, allowing the material of her other sundress to flow around her thighs. It's an unusual feeling for her.

"Does a fat kid like Twinkies? The real question is, do *you* like it?"

"I don't know."

She does know but won't admit it to him. Wonder Woman had her Lasso of Truth and invisible jet. Victoria had her suit, heeled boots, and gun. She feels naked without them. They weren't the source of her power so much as tools that accentuated it.

"Why are we here?" she asks as Rigo admires the water as it flows down the thirteen basins of the fountain.

"We can reschedule if you want to meet in a stuffy office instead. I love this place. It reminds me of the one universal truth in life."

"What's that?"

"Shit rolls downhill."

"Clever."

"Mmm…not really. Come take a walk with me."

Victoria and Rigo begin climbing the slope alongside the cascade towards the upper fountains and the terrace.

"Have you thought about my offer?"

"Yeah, more than I should have."

"And?"

"I still don't know," Victoria says, stealing a glance at Rigo in time to catch his reaction. "What? Not the answer that you were looking for?"

"Honestly, I was beginning to think you weren't going to call at all. You waited until the last minute."

"Why did you tell me about Burgess down in Turks and Caicos?"

"You needed to know."

Victoria shakes her head. "Is it that, or were you hoping I would find the allure of your offer more irresistible?"

"Oh, I knew you would, but if I was really trying to manipulate you, I wouldn't have buried the lead."

"If you say so. I'm tired of being made promises that are never kept. It happened before Brockhampton, and it happened after it. Nothing changed even after New Hampshire. How do I know this will be any different?"

"You don't. There's nothing I can say to you that will prove my team is any different than your experiences in Boston. Only actions will. If you don't like what you see, resign. This isn't a trap, Victoria. You have nothing to lose."

He's right; she doesn't. Victoria has spent enough time teetering on the fence. It's time to fall off of it and see what happens.

"Okay. Let's do it."

Rigo pulls out his phone and hits redial. "Yeah, it's me. Call the Hoover Building and stop Agent Larsen's paperwork…yup, let me know when it's done."

"Just like that?" Victoria asks when he ends the call.

"Just like that."

"Impressive. You must have more clout than I thought you did."

"I don't. The CIRG does. My bosses are as impressed with you as I am. They can move mountains when they put their minds to it."

"Do I need to sign something?"

"Just this," Rigo says, handing her a pen and producing a filled-out application for the position.

Victoria scans the document. It specifies a promotion and a bump in salary. The end of the application contains a detailed resume highlighting some of her greatest hits, including the Devil Rancher and Ethan Harrington. Rigo was very thorough.

"I felt like a true-crime writer drafting that. It was amazing."

"I'm glad you were entertained," Victoria says, signing it. "Now, tell me about Burgess."

"It's better to start with the Sword of Freedom. We know that they were well-funded. So far as we can tell, they were in New Hampshire for more than two months before the primary. The safehouse they rented was paid in cash—"

"By a shell company. I know."

"Then you also know about their off-shore account. Unfortunately, we can't get access to it. Even if we did, I'm sure the money was routed through other banks in countries that don't willingly hand records to the authorities."

"Did you check Burgess campaign records?" Victoria asks.

"It was the first thing we did. Every transaction is accounted for."

"What about PAC money or funding the effort directly?"

"The finances for their political action committee check out," Rigo admits. "Burgess and his father are not independently wealthy. At least not enough to fund something like this. If the money came from outside the family, that means it's a conspiracy. Nothing we have found indicates that."

"It doesn't mean there isn't one."

"True. Here's the other problem. We can't place Isiah Burgess with any SOF member, much less establish the time and place they were brought on board. These guys didn't walk into a campaign office with an offer to create mayhem. They were recruited. The question is, by whom?"

Victoria frowns. So far, this is disappointing. "The primary was almost six months ago. It doesn't sound like you've gotten far."

"I would have been content to blame Burgess, but then someone took a run at him at a Chicago hotel."

Victoria raises her eyebrows. That's an interesting development.

"Who?"

"Nobody knows. We couldn't get facial identification or prints in a busy hotel bristling with cameras. The guy was a pro. Machiavelli wouldn't have tried to off himself. Maybe he's working with somebody else we don't know about."

"Or he is trying to make us believe that by arranging a fake assassination. I'm sure that will now be the foundation of his defense."

"That's why I need you on the team, Victoria," Rigo says, stopping when they reach the terrace level above the fountain. You see things that other people don't. Maybe your sudden appearance will change our fortunes in battle."

"What are you—"

Rigo nods, and their eyes move to the Joan of Arc statue. "Did you know that this is the only statue of a woman on a horse in all of Washington? There are plenty of dudes riding them, but no women."

Victoria closes her eyes, shakes her head, and sighs. "You walked me here on purpose, didn't you?"

"I may have spoken to your tenth-grade English teacher. Mrs. Wodtke remembers reading an essay you wrote about Joan of Arc back when you were a shy little wallflower. I can't imagine that, but she insisted that it was written with a passion she had never seen from you."

"People change, Agent Benitez. Joan of Arc was one of my favorite historical figures then and now."

"That explains why you were willing to martyr yourself to get justice in that Chelsea office conference room."

The memory rushes back. Victoria walked into the FBI's Boston Division and presented Lizzie Schwarzer's letters implicating Ethan Harrington in the massacre. The problem was, the room was filled with Massachusetts State Police officers eager to execute an arrest warrant against her on a trumped-up murder charge. Prosecutors eventually dismissed them, but it took weeks. The selfless act is still talked about in the office with awe and reverence.

"Yeah, we were both burned at the stake for heresy."

"Then she was canonized as a Catholic saint and is a heroine of France."

"I'm sure that meant a lot to her charred ashes."

Rigo laughs. "You're impossible to argue with, aren't you?"

"You'll get used to it. What do you need me to do?"

"Start by meeting Isiah Burgess. His lawyer keeps us from seeing him. You may have more luck."

"He isn't going to want to speak to me either."

"Maybe not. Spend a couple of days there trying to prove yourself wrong. You were in the *Capitol Beat* studio that night. He knows that you're friends with Campos. I'm hoping you can get through to him."

"Okay," Victoria says, not at all convinced that it isn't a waste of time.

"It's time to strap on your armor again, Supervisory Special Agent Larsen. You leave for Chicago tomorrow and then will meet us up in Boston."

Victoria glances back up at the statue. She's getting back in the saddle and hoping that she doesn't meet the same fate as her favorite heroine.

# CHAPTER SIXTEEN

## TIERRA CAMPOS

*Cable News Studio*
*Washington, D.C.*

I shake hands with my newest guest as soon as he emerges from the green room and is shown his spot at the anchor desk. Wilson has done this a thousand times, but it's still a new experience for me. Until I joined *Capitol Beat*, the only other in-studio interview I had done was with Ethan Harrington. It didn't end well.

The two-and-a-half-minute commercial break flies by in the blink of an eye. Many critical tasks need accomplishing before the next segment can start. Makeup reapplication, sound checks, guest orientation, video package confirmation, and lighting adjustments all contribute to a semi-orchestrated on-set dance that teeters on the brink of chaos. We get seated and down to business only seconds before the red light above the camera clicks on.

"We welcome into the studio our first guest this evening. Senator Johnathan Veach of Pennsylvania has spent two terms in Washington and is a shortlist favorite to become Senator Alicia Standish's running mate on the Democratic ticket this November. Thank you for joining us tonight, Senator."

"Thank you for having me, Tierra."

"It has been argued by pundits on both sides of the political spectrum that the possible choice of you as a potential VP pick has more to do with electoral politics than qualifications. While it's undeniable that Pennsylvania is one of the toss-up states up for grabs in the next election, you've also had a close relationship with Senator Standish during your time in the Senate."

"We have worked together on numerous bills and initiatives during our time in the Senate. I was a co-sponsor of the Safe America Act and was proud to vote for it on the floor. It was a good bill and would have been a great law. It's too bad that it was interfered with."

His comment was meant to get under my skin. I'm not sure why he is goading me, other than to curry favor with Senator Standish. It's no secret that there is bad blood between her and me, despite our recent attempt to bury the hatchet. Veach's brazen attempt at a slight on my own show does succeed in getting me a little riled up.

"*Don't respond to that,*" Brock orders through my earpiece.

"Your detractors argue that you have not had enough experience to hold such an important office should she go on to win the White House," I say with a sharper edge to my voice. "Your resume before the Senate includes mostly legislating at the state level. What would you say to critics about your lack of experience?"

"Experience comes in many forms. I have worked in leadership positions in both the public and private sectors, and I have extensive knowledge of the legislative process. I believe I am the best choice to be her running mate as I know what it takes to get her agenda through Congress. I think you know how it feels to step into a position like that."

I don't lose my temper like I would have six months ago. I only smile. The senator is playing games because that's what people do in Washington. I can play them, too.

"Do you think that the allegations of election crimes, including the hiding of contributors and failure to disclose millions in donations, could hamper your chances of joining her on the ticket?"

"*Aw, hell,*" I hear Brock mutter.

"The allegations against me and my campaign are unfounded smear campaigns. I'm surprised that a distinguished program like *Capitol Beat* would be willing to bring up Republican propaganda."

"*He's right about that.*"

"With all due respect, sir, three investigations have been launched into—"

"They are political hit jobs."

"Even when they are launched by a Democratic administration?"

Senator Veach glares at me from across the desk. He starts to say something and stops abruptly.

"Senator, a whistleblower who worked for your campaign has come forward—"

"Miss Campos, I'm here to talk about policy and Alicia Standish, not unfounded rumors and innuendo that no other media outlet is bothering to report."

"I understand your position, sir, but I am here to present factual information, allow you to respond, and hopefully finish my sentences without interruption. A whistleblower has brought forth allegations claiming that campaign donations were diverted for your personal use on at least two dozen occasions."

"Disgruntled campaign workers will say anything to claim the limelight."

"I believe that there could be some truth to that. Can you explain why this person would be angry enough to fabricate a lie under penalty of perjury?"

"I really can't say."

"Can't or won't, Senator?"

"This entire line of questioning is not in the public interest," Veach decrees, playing to the cameras.

"The public makes that decision, not you, Senator."

"Which is why every other news organization hasn't covered these ridiculous assertions."

"I can't speak to why that's the case, although I'm sure our audience is perfectly capable of drawing their own opinions. Speaking of opinions, in a Senate floor speech five months ago, you said that whistleblowers coming forward deserve to be heard.

That they are, and I quote, 'courageous individuals presenting information and should not only be offered our protection but our full attention.' Do you recant that statement?"

"In this case, yes," the senator says, forcing the words out.

"Because instead of an opponent, it's you who are subject to a whistleblower's accusations?"

"That one had credibility. Mine does not."

"*Move on, Tierra.*"

"I understand. Do you agree that there were accounting inconsistencies during your last campaign?"

"Any irregularity is being worked out with the FEC."

"Yes, that is the common practice, and mistakes do happen. Is it true that the Federal Elections Commission has served notice of the intent to fine your campaign over those infractions?"

Veach glares at me again as I wait for an answer. My internal clock begins counting. The silence goes from long to awkwardly long.

"It's a yes or no answer, Senator," I say, prodding him when it hits zero.

"I'm not at liberty to say. I would rather discuss policies important to the American people than whatever this interview is supposed to be."

"You don't believe that character is important?"

"None of this speaks to my character."

"In an interview that you gave last fall, you said the following. Roll the clip."

The package comes up, and a video of him fills the screen. I watch as he flushes with anger, knowing that the camera is off.

"*The character of any elected official is extremely important. How they conduct their private lives is indicative of how they conduct the people's business. Actions, not words, matter most. The people have a right to any information that shows the truth about their elected leaders' character.*"

"Do you still subscribe to those beliefs, Senator?" I ask when the clip ends.

"You took that interview out of context."

"No, sir, you may have been talking about your opponent, but you applied the comment generally. The whistleblower from your campaign swore in an affidavit that part of the money earmarked for campaign advertising use went to personal expenses. He, or she, alleges that it was spent on hotel rooms and lavish gifts for a staffer you were having an affair with. Is that true?"

"No. He's lying."

"We don't know for sure if the whistleblower is male or female, even if you do. Did you have a sexual relationship with any member of your campaign staff, past or present?"

"Of course not."

"Did you ever use funds for personal use?"

"No, and I resent being asked these questions and your accusations behind them."

"I'm accusing you of nothing, Senator. I have no idea if these allegations are true, and I'm giving you the chance to clarify your position for the record. The burden of any investigation is to show wrongdoing if it exists."

"Your bringing this up is the problem. You are giving these false accusations an audience. This is gossip and an attempt to smear me, nothing more."

"We'll leave it at that. Senator Veach, Democrat from Pennsylvania, thank you for joining us tonight. We'll return after these messages."

"You're a bitch. You will never interview me again," the senator says before he rips off his mic and storms off the set. I wish they had gotten that on video.

"*Nice job, Tierra. You just dug your own grave,*" Puttman says from the control room through my earpiece.

"I asked hard questions. That's all."

I hear him laugh. "*Okay, yeah. You did more than that. You just torpedoed his chance to become vice-president, and I won't be the only person who thinks so.*"

Brock's words are ominous and disturbing. I asked direct questions and pressed for honest answers. Since when is asking about something uncomfortable or inconvenient a crime in this country?

*

# CHAPTER SEVENTEEN

## OLIVER JAHN

*Tomorrow's News Today Studio*
*Hudson Yards, New York, New York*

Mi Sun commences her countdown. The nice thing about not using a script is that it provides ample opportunity for flexibility. Events unfolding around the world can be described in real-time. Topics that require exposition and discussion can be added and deleted. That's what he needs to do tonight.

He only hopes Mi Sun can keep up with the graphics, or the show will fall flat. Most of the time, she has only a vague idea about what direction Oliver will go and is forced to adapt to it. She has a gift for doing that. It's one of her many unique attributes that make TNT the success that it is.

"Good evening, and welcome to the only place in the world where you get a glimpse at *Tomorrow's News Today*. I am your swami, Oliver Jahn, and I have a different program for you than I planned on having a couple of hours ago.

"You see, I wasn't going to talk about Tierra Campos. Not at all. Then she appeared on her show tonight and went all Spanish Inquisition on a potential VP pick. I mean, she raked Senator Veach over the coals. And why? Because he's a bad guy that you shouldn't like? He's a politician. They're all bad guys that you shouldn't like.

"So, I lied…yes, like a politician. We're going to talk about Campos. Hey, hey, it's a dirty business, but someone has to do it. If any good comes out of this segment, it's that I'm going to take a shower when I'm through.

"You need to understand what happened on *Capitol Beating*. Yes, I know the name of the show. I renamed it. Tierra Campos didn't defame a sitting United States senator because she was interested in the public good. Nope, she wanted to make waves. It's the same thing that drove her to report on Brockhampton, and then again in New Hampshire. This is about her, people. She wants Peabodys and Pulitzers because she's selfish and arrogant.

"Campos pretends to be non-partisan, and that makes her a wolf in sheep's clothing. A dangerous one because she's in a position to influence a lot of people. The easy thing to do is ignore her like a zit or a boil. It's annoying, looks terrible, but it will eventually go away. She won't, so ignoring her isn't going to get the job done.

"People are claiming that this is a partisan attack on a poor, helpless school shooting victim who's only trying to bring America the news. There are two – and only two – true parts of that statement," Oliver says, holding up two fingers. "She was in the library at Summerville High School when a gunman opened up. Second, my attacks are partisan because I'm a partisan. I freely admit it. I don't try to trick you or make you believe that I don't have strong opinions. I absolutely do.

"My point is, Tierra Campos should, too. Instead, she's afraid to offend anyone and tarnish her carefully manufactured reputation, so she wears the mask of an objective journalist. It's a load of crap. Do not fall for it. Don't. Just don't," Oliver says, slashing his arms and flailing about. "You're all smarter than that, which is why you watch this show.

"I'm telling you this because I want you to know the truth about her. She is a pretender; the 'Queen of the Pretenders' as you all know that I like to call her, and she needs to be stopped. That's where you come in because you can make it happen."

Oliver glances at the monitor set up next to the camera and smiles. Mi Sun works with their graphics technician to pick the best ones to put on the show. As host, he's more than willing to pass off the responsibility for what makes for the most humorous parts of the broadcast. Mi Sun has never let him down and isn't now.

"There is power in numbers. It drives real change when channeled and appropriately focused. We're concentrating this power on one group of targets: those companies who advertise on *Capitol Beat*. I will provide a list of the offenders on my website and social media pages. Boycott every last one of them. Don't patronize their stores or use their products. Send every last one of them an email telling them why. Post to social media and like and share everyone else's posts about them.

"Then stop watching *Capitol Beat* and any show on that network. The loss in ratings and advertisers will get their attention. Trust me, these companies care about money — it's all they care about. I have some firsthand experience in this.

"Fake news became part of the modern vernacular because it exists. Reporters were making things up when they shouldn't have been. We called it out on this program countless times. It's wrong for reporters to blatantly portray opinions as facts in their stories, but it's far worse to blatantly trick people into believing that you're something you're not. That has to end, and you have the power to stop it."

Oliver stops and rubs his chin. It may be television news, but he likes to bring in an element of performance art to the broadcast. He understands the power of visuals, and it makes his reporting more authentic because it's relatable.

"Imagine that! You have the power to make real change in a world that seeks to strip it from you. Governments take your rights daily. Massive multinational corporations sell you crap products and then make it almost impossible to return them. Critical service providers like utilities make obscene profits and can't even find a way for you to talk to a live customer service representative. It's infuriating! I'm not sure how I still have hair."

Oliver runs his hand through his thinning black hair. Despite having access to hairdressers and makeup artists when he joined the network, he decided to keep the unkempt look that became a trademark during his podcast days. It worked for him then and still does.

"It is time for the people to stand up, not by protesting, rioting, or storming the Capitol Building. That takes too much effort. You can do it from the comfort of your home. All it takes is for you to spend your money elsewhere. Tune into different entertainment and news options, but keep watching this show. Please. I need to eat.

"If you hit Tierra Campos, and Wilson Newman, and organizations like *Front Burner* where it hurts, they will change. They have to. Media is the law of the jungle, and it's about survival. Do your part, then go on social media and tell the world about it. Hashtag "silence *Capitol Beat*" or "silence Campos" is a good place to start. I will be with you every step of the way. I'll explain how right after some messages from advertisers you need to support."

# CHAPTER EIGHTEEN

## VASSYL STRACHENKO

*Back Bay Safehouse*
*Boston, Massachusetts*

The men gather in the living area of their safehouse for a quick morning meeting to trade information and coordinate their activities. Jackrabbit's day is just starting. His target keeps to a somewhat regular work schedule. For Dimitri and Sven, the workday has ended. The man they were tasked to follow is a night owl, and they're looking forward to getting some sleep.

Vassyl is pleased with the early progress, but that's where his contentment ends. This is only the second full day that Ian has been with them, and he can already see the former FBI agent's attitude is changing. He has spent this entire conversation sitting at the dining table, stewing.

"All right. We need to establish patterns if we expect that to work. Jackrabbit, your target is more predictable. Sven, Dimitri, yours is going to require a lot more effort. Continue your surveillance."

"Yes, continue wasting time," Ian mutters from his seat at the table as he draws imaginary circles on it with his finger.

"What's your problem, Ian?" Vassyl asks, earning a scowl.

"You said we're here to take out Victoria Larsen. Why are we messing around with this?"

"These targets are essential to that end."

"It's a pointless and unneeded distraction. All you need to lure Victoria into a trap is let me show my face to a camera. FBI facial recognition will take care of the rest, and she will come running to wherever we want her to go."

"We were handed a plan and are going to execute it," Vassyl says, leaving no uncertainty about this not being up for debate.

"If you say so," Ian sings out, the disrespect in his voice causing Sven and his associates to watch Vassyl for his reaction.

"I do."

"You're not only inviting failure in; you're offering it a seat on the couch and a cup of tea. This plan, assuming there is one, is complicated and has too many things that could go wrong."

"You would know," Vassyl says.

"I would," Ian says, standing. "All too well. That's my point."

"These targets are essential."

"Says who? Machiavelli?"

"Robespierre."

"Yeah, whoever the hell that is. Do you even know? Machiavelli was a mystery, even to me."

"It was Burgess," Sven says, confused.

"Was it?" Dimitri asks the big man, not so sure.

"Who cares?" Ian snaps. "I want Larsen dead. That's all that matters. If you guys aren't going to do that, I'll do it myself."

"You don't make the rules. You don't even need to be here," Dimitri says, causing Jackrabbit and Sven to join him at his side.

"That's why I'm leaving."

Vassyl has seen enough. There is a time for patience and a time for action, and that transition has been made. He grabs the back of Ian's jacket when he turns for the door.

Ian was expecting that. He pivots on the balls of his feet and throws a punch. The quick assault doesn't have the intended result as the assassin deftly blocks it. Before Ian can reload for a second try, Vassyl pops him in the solar plexus and slides under his shoulder, creating an armbar from behind and bending his assailant over at the waist. There are dozens of moves available from this position, but Vassyl just opts to kick him on his backside and send him careening into the wall.

"You don't want to do this."

Ian doesn't heed the warning. He recovers and comes at him, throwing jabs that are blocked as Vassyl retreats. The assassin lowers his center of gravity and steps forward with his left foot before powering a roundhouse kick into Ian's upper thigh. The agent grunts and his guard comes down long enough for Vassyl to strike him twice in the face. Stunned, he too late to see the heel kick coming. It knocks him off balance backward. He crashes to the floor and slides into the wall again.

"All right, playtime is over," Ian says, jumping to his feet. Ian charges in a bull rush. Vassyl has more room to work with than he did in Burgess' hotel room. He curls and drops to the ground, pressing his boots to Ian's chest when the out-of-control agent reaches him. He rolls on his back, supporting the body weight on his legs, and then kicks out, driving him through the air upside down.

The hard landing disorients Ian. Vassyl pops up and moves like lightning as Ian climbs unsteadily to his feet. The former FBI agent turns to find Vassyl staring him in the face. The assassin grabs his throat and squeezes as he presses the suppressor of his SIG Sauer under the man's chin with his other hand.

"You're right. Playtime is over."

"Pull the trigger, please," Dimitri says, cheering Vassyl on.

"I'll even clean up the mess," Jackrabbit offers.

Vassyl gives Ian a condescending look. "Is there a reason why I shouldn't?"

"You said you need me."

"For this plan to work, I do." Vassyl leans in even closer. "Plans change."

"C'mon, boss. Kill the asshole," Sven says, still itching for revenge after being humiliated at their first meeting.

"I gave you a choice at that shitty little motel you were rotting in. I held a gun to your head and offered you death or realization of your strongest desire. You chose the latter and agreed to do it my way. That means you play by my rules. Did you forget that agreement?"

"No."

"Really? I think you did. You should have listened to yourself when you quoted Tennyson. You don't need to understand why we're doing this any more than they do. Follow my plan to the letter, or I will kill you right now. Choose."

"All right. We'll do it your way."

Vassyl removes his weapon slowly.

"Aw, man," Dimitri whines as the other two men scoff.

"You may think that you're hot shit, Agent Drucker, but you don't know me. What I've done. What I'm capable of doing. I don't want to hear so much as a complaint about the weather from you. The next time we find ourselves in this situation, I won't hesitate to pull the trigger."

Vassyl releases Ian, who stands there and rubs his throat. The beauty of humbling somebody is that it makes them compliant. At least temporarily.

"Get your stuff together," the assassin orders. "We have work to do today."

Ian skulks off to the bedroom without a word. The four men watch him intently.

"He can't be trusted," Sven says.

"No, he can't. Fortunately, we don't need him for long."

"What about until then?" Dimitri asks. "I don't want my throat cut while I sleep."

Vassyl turns to look at his other three mercenaries. "Keep an eye on him. If he steps out of line even once for the remainder of his time here, shoot him."

A broad smile grows on Dimitri's face as the other two men nod.

"Gladly."

# CHAPTER NINETEEN

## TIERRA CAMPOS

*Capitol Beat Network Offices*
*Washington, D.C.*

The conference room was already tense before DeAnna Van Herten entered the room. Her arrival was a pleasant distraction from the side-eye glances and nervous energy. The people present are all under Puttman's thumb. I can't count one member of the production staff or a single writer I can trust to be on my side. That leaves Wilson, who is stoic and undaunted as we await the start of this newest inquisition.

DeAnna Van Herten is the daughter of a high-powered media mogul. She attended all the right schools, knew all the right people, and helped her daddy build his empire until his death five years ago. Diminutive in size but not stature, she doesn't usually involve herself in VH Media's operations. Today is an exception. I should feel special, even though I know the opposite is true.

"We all know who everyone is and why we're here. Let's get going with this. What's the damage?"

"We've heard from seventeen advertisers who are receiving an avalanche of complaints about the segment," one of the men in glasses says from the other side of the table. "Three of them have canceled their buys. Three more are waiting to see what action we take. The remaining eleven said they reserve the right to cancel their contracts if things worsen."

"Are they worsening?"

"Yes, ma'am," the woman next to her chimes in. "Social media response to the segment is mostly negative. The hashtag 'Cancel Campos' has been trending since the interview. Posters are organizing boycotts against the show, the network, and our advertisers. They are pushing others to join them. The movement has gone viral, and it's growing."

"DeAnna, this is nothing new," Wilson argues, cutting off the prosecution's case before they really get rolling. "We've been through similar episodes when people didn't like one of my interviews."

"I remember. I also think it's important to highlight what impact your behavior can have on this network and our advertisers. There is enormous pressure on me to fire Tierra right now. I have personally talked to a dozen politicians livid over that interview. Dozens more have publicly called for your firing over it."

"Politicians will seize any chance to politicize things. It's what they do," Wilson argues.

"Everything in that interview was factual," I say. "There was no conjecture or speculation. There is an upcoming investigation, there is a fine coming from the FEC, and the whistleblower did swear those things under oath. I did nothing wrong."

"You accused a man likely to be the next vice president of illegal activity and marital infidelity!"

"I asked him questions based on available public information. I never accused him of anything."

"You can't be this naïve. The questions were the accusation. That's why other media outlets remained silent about it. The allegations are all that the audience will remember."

"You underestimate our viewers."

"And you are trying my patience. You embarrassed Senator Veach in front of millions of people. It was selfish and unbecoming of an employee at this network. What would you have done if you were in his shoes?"

"Not used campaign funds to cheat on my wife."

I regret the words the moment they come out. I'm angry, and it's playing right into DeAnna's hands. She is trying to provoke me, and it's working.

"I expect an apology for that disastrous interview and for demeaning Senator Veach on tomorrow night's show."

"What?" I ask, dumbfounded.

"That's not a reasonable request, DeAnna," Wilson says, rushing to my defense.

"From where I'm sitting, it's generous. Tierra should be packing her things. Maybe then she would know what to ask and what not to during her interviews, and this network's reputation wouldn't be getting attacked."

"Is that what you want to see journalism turn into? Ask only the questions that angry people behind a keyboard want you to? If you don't, they dox you and try to destroy you professionally? That's not America. That's a mob mentality."

"Whether you like it or not, Tierra, social media is where people gather to share opinions. It's the new public square," DeAnna says, quoting something she read somewhere.

"And you're attending a stoning in it."

"I don't think you appreciate my position, much less your own. Your actions started this train wreck, and it's costing this network dearly."

"No, our competitors did. Oliver Jahn started this because he sees me as a threat, not just his competition. I'm an enemy to be defeated. He weaponized the cancel culture for his own gain and to advance his own twisted style of pseudo-journalism."

"He has a point. The interview with Senator Veach aside, your arrogance brought this on."

I can't believe what I am hearing. For decades, *Capitol Beat* has been the gold standard for hard-hitting interviews and unbiased reporting. Wilson cultivated that reputation over decades of hard work before this show existed in its current form. VH Media and its irrational owner are willing to kill the goose that lays golden eggs.

"You used to vigorously defend the people who work for you, DeAnna," Wilson says. "Why did that change?"

"I am defending them. People have the means to speak up and voice their opinions. My job is to protect the health and financial viability of this network so that people have jobs they can come to."

"The way to do that is not to cater to the mob," I argue. "Cancel culture is nothing more than digital genocide. It's enforced censorship that stifles debate and penalizes people for opinions that a select few don't agree with. It was unleashed on me because I'm guilty of a crime: good journalism. And you're rewarding them."

DeAnna doesn't immediately respond. I scored points, but this isn't that kind of game. She's not here to weigh the case against me. Her mind was made up before she walked into this conference room. The meeting was only called to dole out the punishment.

"This conversation is over. You work for me, not the other way around. You will apologize to Senator Veach, or you will be permanently removed from *Capitol Beat*. I'll give you a few days to think about it. You could use some time away to gain some perspective. Wilson can cover your shows this weekend."

"If she goes, I go," he says, playing a card he's been holding back for a while now.

"Let me remind you that you are under contract, Wilson. The provisions in it are clear about you leaving without fulfilling it. I'm allowing you to retire early in recognition of your decades of service to journalism. That won't apply in this situation. If you leave, it's a breach."

She stands, and the rest of the room rises with her like she is the Queen of England. Wilson and I remain seated.

"I will let you know what night it airs," Brock says.

"See to it."

DeAnna waltzes out of the room, followed by her cronies. Brock lingers for a moment, a devilish smirk on his face that I would love to smack off of it.

"Sun Tzu once said, 'Victorious warriors win first and then go to war, while defeated warriors go to war first and then seek to win.' I warned that it would come to this."

Brock grins after delivering the line he probably worked on all night, then he walks out, leaving Wilson and me alone at the conference table.

"I hope he choked on whatever fortune cookie he got that from. Thoughts?"

Wilson stares down at his hands. He told me once that his arguments with the head of the network were always professional and reasonable. This was neither.

"Yeah, one. We're in trouble."

# CHAPTER TWENTY

## VICTORIA LARSEN

*Tierra's Apartment*
*Navy Yard, Washington, D.C.*

Victoria looks up at the ten-story building as she makes her way to the entrance. This place is amazing. Then again, a shoebox would be nice for her right now. She has been essentially homeless since she took this job. All her things are in storage up in Boston, and she's living in a hotel until the FBI makes arrangements for a place in Washington. It won't be here.

She isn't surprised that Tierra ended up settling in this part of the city. Navy Yard is a prime spot along the Anacostia River near Nationals Park and is filled with young professionals. Her building also features a rooftop lounge for residents, a fitness center, and a concierge. So, there's that.

It takes a couple of knocks on the doors to get Tierra to answer. It's odd since Victoria was announced ahead of time by the man in the lobby. When the door swings open, her friend looks terrible. She barely makes eye contact before retreating inside the apartment.

"Hey. Come in."

Victoria looks around. Her place isn't spacious, but it doesn't need to be. She has high ceilings, wide-plank hardwood floors, a private balcony, and floor-to-ceiling windows. Victoria would never want to leave this place if she lived here.

"What's wrong, Tierra? You don't seem like yourself."

"Nothing. It's just been a long day. Do you want a glass of wine?"

Victoria checks her watch. It's only a quarter to two. It's early for wine, and she is technically on duty, but Tierra isn't the type to be drinking this early. Whatever happened must be bad.

"Sure. It's Friday. I thought you were working tonight."

"So did I," Tierra says, taking in her guest's manner of dress. "I guess the sundresses didn't work out for you."

"They did. I liked them more than I thought I would," Victoria says, in a half-truth. "I decided to take the FBI job."

"I thought you might. Congratulations. So, what's up?" Tierra asks, handing Victoria a glass. "This sounded important."

"It is. I just got back from Illinois."

"What were you doing there?"

Victoria stares at her friend as she takes a sip, deciding how to say this. It will be a sensitive subject for Tierra, so there is no point in sugarcoating it.

"I was trying to convince Isiah Burgess to talk."

The statement is met with the anticipated amount of consternation. "How'd that work for you?"

"He was adamant that he had nothing to say to me."

"What did you expect? It's a ruse, Victoria. You, of all people, should be able to see that. This is nothing more than Machiavelli setting up his defense."

"I said that he wouldn't talk to me. He told me that he has plenty to say to *you*."

"I'll bet he does," Tierra mumbles.

"No, you still don't get it. Isiah says that he can prove he isn't Machiavelli. The problem is, he won't talk to anyone in law enforcement. He was adamant that he would only give the details to you."

Tierra stares down at her wine glass. The seconds feel like minutes as they pass and Victoria fights the urge to push for an answer.

"I've said all that I need to say to him."

"That's it?" Victoria asks, surprised by Tierra's indifference.

"You expected more?"

"Tierra, you're a friend, and I need your help. If that's not enough, you're also a journalist. One who has earned everything she has by being curious and jumping on opportunities when they present themselves. This is another one, and you're taking a pass?"

"Yes."

Tierra walks into the living area and stares out the floor-to-ceiling window. It's like Victoria isn't even here.

"What's wrong with you?"

"I have other things to worry about."

"Like what?"

"Seriously, Victoria, you need to start paying attention to the world," she snaps, catching the agent off-guard. "Oliver Jahn unleashed the mob against me. I ask a popular politician a couple of hard questions, and all of a sudden, I'm being canceled. The worst part is that it's working. DeAnna Van Herten summoned me to the network offices to dress me down and give me an ultimatum. I have to publicly apologize to Senator Veach by the end of the weekend or find another job."

"What? That's ridiculous. She isn't backing you?"

"Backing me? No, she's more of a cheerleader for the cyber mob than a supportive boss. She wants me canceled, and my own executive producer is falling in line behind her."

Victoria walks over to the sofa and takes a seat. That explains her attitude. Tierra's reaction to the drama at her network is still mystifying. It's not like she hasn't been in this position before. Work drama seems to follow her wherever she goes. It's one of the things the two women have in common.

"What does Wilson say?"

"He obviously disagrees with it, but what can he do?" Tierra says, also taking a seat. "He's under contract. We both are, but he has a lot more to lose by not playing ball."

"I'm sorry, Tierra, I am," Victoria says, her voice absent the sympathy she actually feels.

"Yeah, you sound it."

"Well, I am, but I'm handing you a golden opportunity to get closure on what happened in New Hampshire, and you're up here moping about your career."

Tierra straightens in her seat. "I don't need closure about what happened up there. I already have it. And as for my career, maybe I'm not as willing to jeopardize it as you are."

Now it's Victoria's turn to be angry. "What is that supposed to mean?"

"You know. You think the rules are meant to be broken. It's why you were always in trouble up in Boston. I'm not like that. I did it once out of anger with Ethan Harrington and was lucky that it worked out. I'm not doing it again. I'm not willing to throw away my life like you are."

The words sting. Victoria sets her wine down before she gets the urge to throw it at Tierra.

"Wow. They give you a couple of awards that nobody cares about, and it becomes the most important thing in the world to you."

"I earned my Peabody and Pulitzer! I plan on earning more, and I can't do that by being reckless!"

"No, you earned them by taking risks. And, for the record, I'm not throwing my life away. I fight for what I believe in. That's what you used to do before you started considering yourself more important than anyone else."

"Well, okay then. I thought you were a friend."

"I'm arguing with you because I am one."

"Another argument is the last thing I need. I think you should go."

Tierra leaves Victoria sitting in the living area and moves to the kitchen counter to pour another glass of wine. There is nothing more to be gained by pressing the subject. Tierra isn't going to help her. She isn't interested in anything but helping herself.

"Have it your way."

Victoria leaves without saying goodbye. She has never had many female friends. Colleagues, yes, but never anyone she could confide in on a personal level. Tierra was the closest thing, and Victoria feels like she lost that today. Washington can be a cutthroat town, brimming with unscrupulous people filled with ambition. She never thought Tierra would fall victim to that. She was wrong.

# CHAPTER TWENTY-ONE

## OLIVER JAHN

*Tomorrow's News Today Network Office*
*New York, New York*

Oliver had no problem waking up early. There is nothing like Manhattan in the early morning before the city that never sleeps roars to life, and its streets swell with commuters and tourists. He often sleeps late and misses this part of the day. Oliver's afternoons and nights into the early morning hours are dedicated to bringing his show to the world. Today, it's being spent preserving its future.

The two sides of the negotiation assemble in the conference room and shake hands. It's not the first time they have gathered here to discuss the network's renewal of *Tomorrow's News Today*. The circumstances are different this time, and Oliver plans on using that to his advantage.

"You've been busy," one of the network executives says. "There have been some noticeable changes to your show since the last time we met."

"No, the format is the same. We opted to narrow our focus."

"In an election year?"

Oliver smiles. "The two go hand in hand."

"You didn't just narrow your focus, Oliver," another executive says. "You seem to have a singular objective. TNT dedicated the last several nights to tearing down your competitors and talking about nothing else."

"That's true. I decided to declare war on journalistic malpractice."

"Did you clear that with anyone in this room?"

"With all due respect, sir, I don't need to. Our agreement with this network is that I maintain full control over topics on my show."

The executive stares at him with cold eyes. "A courtesy call would have been appreciated. We've received complaints from advertisers who aren't pleased with you smearing a school shooting victim."

"Tierra Campos is a public figure. Using that as a shield to criticism is childish and unprofessional."

"She's not using it. I'm saying—"

"Ethan Harrington. He was a victim before he wasn't. Campos went after him and got a Peabody and Pulitzer out of it."

"Let's get back to the business at hand," a lawyer from the legal department insists. "In front of you are all the agreed-upon points. I think we are close to making this renewal official."

Oliver wonders if the other suits in the room feel that way. They are clearly unhappy with him, as he thought they might be. Oliver opens the leather portfolio and checks the numbers. It's not as bad as he thought it would be. It's worse. He glances over at his lawyers, who are staring at him as they await guidance. He shakes his head and closes the portfolio without further review.

"What's wrong?" the first executive asks.

"These numbers don't work."

"I don't understand. We have already agreed to your price."

"No, we agreed to a price that was compromised on. That was last week. Our ratings have improved, and I don't believe that compromise is in our best interests."

"You had a small uptick, and we are pleased with that, but you're still the number two show."

Oliver nods his head slightly several times. "For how long?"

"Let's take a step back," the dweeb from legal says. "The network has made it clear that we want to keep you and TNT here."

"Then prove it."

"We are. This is a fair offer and commensurate with the value of your show."

"And I think it's an insult, especially for a long-term deal that should be considering TNT's future value. Until we close the gap, we are too far apart to continue this conversation today. If you'll excuse me, I have a show to prepare for tonight."

Oliver stands and exits the room, leaving the bewildered executives and the legal department wondering what just happened. His own lawyers hurry to pack up their things and follow him. They are equally baffled as they corner him near the elevator.

"What was that? You never told us that you wanted more money."

"Surprise!"

"This isn't funny. You hired us to help you obtain the best possible deal. We looked like idiots in there."

"You don't get paid to look like geniuses. I write checks to your firm to ensure my interests are represented. So do it. Get with their lawyers and iron out the deal I want—twenty percent more than our current contract, and not a penny less. Let me know when they agree."

"How do you know they will?"

"Because we're going to be the best show on cable news by the time I'm done. If those idiots don't pay up because of an extraordinary lack of vision, I'm sure some other network will."

Oliver takes the elevator down to the lobby, leaving his lawyers looking nauseated as they head back to engage the legal team. He's going to make them earn every penny of the obscene amount he pays them.

Mi Sun is waiting in the lobby and stands to greet Oliver. For reasons surpassing any semblance of common sense, they would not allow her to be present for the negotiations. She missed a hell of a show.

"Well?"

"I sent them back to the drawing board."

Mi Sun frowns. "You're taking a huge risk. If this goes wrong, we're going to be back in your basement wondering what could have been by the end of the year."

"I know, but I'm tired of being runner up. Those stiffs in the conference room seem to be content with it, but I believe that second place is for chumps. It's time for us to make our move, Mi Sun. For better or worse, I'm all in. Are you with me?"

"I've always had your back. There's no reason to believe that will change now."

"Good. Let's go. We need to take things to the next level. Beating *Capitol Beat* in the ratings isn't going to get this done. We need to destroy Tierra Campos."

# CHAPTER TWENTY-TWO

## BRIAN COOPER

*Republican National Committee Headquarters*
*Washington, D.C.*

Brian rides the escalator up from the Capitol South Metro Station and emerges onto First Street just in time. His contact's info was spot on—the Suburban waits for Monica Stengel to exit with a pair of roided-up bodyguards pulling security.

He draws their attention as he approaches, arriving at the vehicle just as their charge emerges from the white, nondescript building. One of the physically imposing and clearly armed men moves in front of Brian, his hand out to stop him.

"You're nothing if not predictable, Monica. I thought I was the only person able to keep to a schedule left in this town."

"It's okay, Jacques," Monica says, calling off her security detail. "Brian Cooper is a pain in the ass, but he's not a physical threat."

The man looks at his counterpart and gets a nod before stepping aside. Despite the assurance, Brian can feel the two men keeping a leery eye on him.

"What do you feed that guy?"

"Whiny Democrats," Monica says. "What brings you here?"

"You do. I'd like to have a chat with you."

"Make an appointment like everyone else. I'm the chair of the Republican Party, not a doctor at a medical clinic. I don't do walk-ins."

Monica wasn't elected to lead the Republican National Committee because she looks good on camera. She's political, intelligent, and tough as nails. As the end of her second two-year term nears, November's election will determine whether she earns a third.

"I would, but I can't, in good conscience, give you the chance to keep rescheduling until I give up. I'd like to have it this year when it will do some good."

Monica checks her Patek Philippe watch. She rubs it and looks at the car, searching for an excuse to avoid this. She knows she can't. Brian may have a toxic reputation, but he also possesses a wealth of information. Only a fool wouldn't hear him out, and the chair of the RNC isn't one.

"You have time. Dinner isn't until six. Let's go for a walk, and I promise not to bother you again."

"I'm not sure I want to be seen walking with you."

"My former boss is about to become the Democratic nominee for president. Your colleagues would expect you to talk to me and might even wonder why you didn't."

Monica directs her detail to give them ten minutes. She and Brian head toward Spirit of Justice Park with one of her security guards trailing them. Located just south of the House office buildings, the park is nothing spectacular and hardly an attraction in a city full of them. It was just a way for the Capitol Architect to hide an unsightly parking garage when it was constructed.

"It's hot today. I hear it may last all week."

"You didn't come here to give me a weather report. I agreed to listen, so I am. Make this quick, Brian."

"I want to work for Colin Bradford's campaign."

"I understand you pitched Brevin Hawkins that at dinner. I thought he may have been drunk and not heard you right."

"He did."

"I don't make staffing decisions for our campaigns. If you want to work on Bradford's, you need to convince Brevin."

"I'm working on that."

"Good luck. What do you need me for?"

"To put in a good word for me."

Monica closes her eyes and throws her head back slightly as she lets out a short series of laughs. "Not a chance. First of all, I know you. You may be the most well-connected man in this city, but you're also a snake."

"Ouch. That hurts. What's your second point?"

"You're a carpetbagger who spent a career working for the other side of the aisle. There is no way I'm going to welcome you with open arms under our tent. I don't even know why you'd want to work with us. You despise everything we stand for."

"Because this election isn't about policy points. It's about the future of America."

"Which is why we are fielding a candidate that strongly represents our values," Monica says, shifting into sales mode.

"Ideology doesn't matter if you lose."

"We're not going to lose."

"How can you be so sure? Is your plan for Pennsylvania that good? Because it hasn't been in the past."

Monica stops in front of the fountain. This walk is at its end.

"What makes you think…never mind. That's our business, not yours. We're done here. Have a good evening, Brian."

"I know how to beat Standish," he calls out, causing her to stop and turn.

"Even if you do, I own any recommendation I make to Colin Bradford. If it turns out to be a mistake, I'm on the hook. There's too much on the line in this election. I like to take chances, but you're a bridge too far. I'm sorry. It's a campaign decision, and I'm staying out of it."

"I understand."

"Why do I doubt that?"

Brian slowly walks toward her under the watchful eye of her beefy bodyguard standing fifteen feet away.

"No, I do. Look, Monica, I'm not oblivious to how this must sound. If our roles were reversed, I would have told you to pound sand and climbed into the car. You have big responsibilities and millions of party faithful to answer to."

"I feel a 'but' coming," she says, crossing her arms.

Brian forces a smile. "There isn't one. I do have one small request, though. Colin Bradford is going to ask you whether he should hire me."

"I doubt that."

"I don't."

Monica looks down at the ground. "And you want me to give my blessing when he asks?"

"I know you won't. All I'm asking is that you not say 'no.'"

Monica purses her lips together and nods. "I'll think about it. Have a good evening, Brian."

She walks off, moving at about half the speed Alicia Standish used to in her high heels when he worked for her. The meeting went better than expected. The odds were long that she would even speak to him, much less indulge in his request. With that barrier hopefully removed, he has one hurdle left to clear.

# CHAPTER TWENTY-THREE

## TIERRA CAMPOS

*Red & White Wine Bar*
*Navy Yard, Washington, D.C.*

I can no longer say any day is the worst of my life. That privilege was lost one beautiful morning in Summerville, Arizona, when a fellow student walked into my school library with a rifle and opened fire. Nothing can compare to the terror I felt at that moment. Students hit the ground and hid behind overturned tables, but it did little to quell the massacre.

I was in shock and paralyzed by fear when Josh pulled me off the ground. I managed to run with him and hide in a supply closet with some other kids. They barricaded the door, forcing the gunman to fight to get it open. He had cracked it enough to stick the barrel of the weapon in when the police showed up and killed him. There is no doubt that Josh saved my life that day. The same can't be said about the twenty kids who didn't live to see their graduation.

It was a horrible and traumatic experience that I will never escape. Years of therapy have allowed me to function, but it will never erase the pain and guilt of surviving when so many didn't. By comparison, today was nothing, but that doesn't help me feel any better.

I finished the last of the wine at my apartment an hour ago. When the temptation became irresistible to turn on the television and tune in to whatever drivel Brock was forcing Wilson to say, I left and came here. I'm not in a social mood and figured I wouldn't see anyone I know. That conclusion is shattered when Tyler and Olivia walk past my table.

"Hi guys," I say, getting their attention.

"Hi, Tierra."

"Hey."

Neither of them sounds or looks happy to see me. "What are you guys doing here?"

"We needed to get out for a while. You?"

"I've had a rough day. You want to have a seat?"

Tyler sneaks a glance at Olivia, who continues to stare at me blankly. "Maybe another time."

"Is this a date?" I ask, half-jokingly. Neither of them so much as cracks a smile.

"Hardly. We were comparing notes on job opportunities but we got frustrated," Tyler says, trying to keep things light.

"I heard that you guys left *Front Burner*."

"Yeah, thanks for checking up on us," Olivia says with an acidic tone.

"I'm sorry," I say, adjusting my napkin as the conversation turns awkward. "I've been meaning to. Things have been a little crazy for me."

"I'm sure."

"No, really. I've been thinking about you guys a lot."

"Aren't we special? So much that you couldn't take five minutes to pick up your cell phone."

"Olivia—"

"No, Tyler. Don't defend her."

"That's not fair, Olivia."

"Life's not fair, is it? *Front Burner* was a dream come true. Now it's as good as dead. Everybody we worked with and cared about has left."

"Except Austin and Logan, and they will soon," Tyler adds.

"The media organizations have all turned on us. Anyone who sees *Front Burner* on our resume doesn't even call us back. Do you know what that feels like? Of course not. You have a cushy job at *Capitol Beat*."

"It's hardly cushy," I argue.

"Yeah, I'm sure it's so rough for you," Olivia says, folding her arms.

"At least you're employed," Tyler adds. "We're wearing scarlet letters. I'm going to be working at Home Depot if I can't find anything soon."

I turn my attention back to Olivia and see the hurt and pain on her face. "I'm actually thinking about moving back home. I don't see much of a future here," she says.

"Is there anything I can do?"

Tyler frowns. Olivia has a much different reaction. I realize it was a stupid question, but what more can I say?

"Nah. Just go on doing what you're doing. Don't worry about us. Not that you ever started."

She walks off in the direction of the bar. Tyler lingers for a moment, watching her go.

"Tyler, I—"

"We left *Front Burner* because of you, Tierra. We thought the way Austin treated you was wrong, but that's not the whole story. We were also friends. As soon as you got to *Capitol Beat*, you forgot who we were."

"That's not true!"

"It feels that way. I know you're going through some stuff. I wish you well," Tyler says before following her to the bar.

I sigh. This day just climbed a few spots on the horrible list.

# CHAPTER TWENTY-FOUR

## VASSYL STRACHENKO

*Abandoned Mill*
*Loughborough, Massachusetts*

Vassyl pulls off of Interstate 495 and heads into the heart of the old mill town. The small city on the Merrimack River has fallen a long way from its glory days. Once hosting a thriving manufacturing industry, nothing is left aside from the dilapidated buildings the factories once occupied.

"Hey," Vassyl says, connecting the call to his cell that's paired to his rental car.

"We have a preliminary meeting set up with Snowman," Dimitri says, using one of the agreed-upon codenames. "We are ready to go for Monday or Tuesday night."

"Okay. I'll get the seed planted to ensure Yamamoto is there."

"Sounds good. Jackrabbit is also ready. His child keeps to a fairly set schedule."

"Okay. We'll walk through the plan tonight. Tell him to keep babysitting."

"Will do," Dimitri says before hanging up.

"You guys and your codenames," Ian mutters from the passenger seat.

"You're one to talk, *Engels.*"

Ian smiles. "Where the hell are we going? I feel like I need a tetanus shot just driving through here."

"Relax. We're almost there."

"There are plenty of places closer to Boston to kill me and hide my body, in case you were wondering."

Now it's Vassyl's turn to smile. "Oh, I know."

"What are we doing?"

"You're about to find out."

Vassyl pulls the rental truck into the parking lot of a residential complex, and then down a short gravel driveway between buildings to a small dirt construction lot. The apartment buildings are close, and the rehabilitated mill structure's westernmost point almost touches the dilapidated structure. The convergence makes for a nice chokepoint.

"Are you apartment hunting or something?" Ian asks, unimpressed after the two men climb out of the pickup truck.

"We're not here for that. We're here for those."

A pair of long brick buildings bordering the river look like they could fall any minute. The roof on the easternmost structure has collapsed, and vegetation is growing on the old factory floor. The closer building that houses steam boilers that power the mill isn't in much better shape.

"We've been checking out places like this for a couple of days now. This is for Victoria Larsen, isn't it?"

"Yes."

"Just kill her, Vassyl," Ian pleads. "I know you agree that this plan is too complicated. I can see it in your eyes. We're wasting time. Let's just get her to Boston and take her out."

"Any fool can do that," Vassyl explains as he surveys what's left of the structures. "The key is doing it how and when it has the most impact."

Ian shakes his head. "You're falling into the same trap that the SOF did. I hope your guys are as dedicated as you are because she won't be alone if you lure her here. She'll bring an army like she did at our New Hampshire safehouse. Ask Marx and Sartre how well that worked out for them."

"They're dead."

"Exactly."

"What do you think of this area? You were in the FBI. If you were going to conduct a raid on this place, how would you do it?"

Ian walks to the west side of the building and sees that there is no gap. He then walks over to the convergence and peers into the triangle-shaped area. It is full of debris and has propane and gasoline storage tanks near the tall chimney. Beyond that is a smaller canal that feeds into the Merrimack River. He moves back to Vassyl and surveys the apartment buildings to the south.

"There aren't many options. It abuts the river, making any approach or escape that way difficult. They will seal the bridge and leave a small force off to the southeast near the canal. Then they'll use those residential buildings as cover to come right through that gap there," Ian says, pointing the way he and Vassyl came.

"How many personnel would they bring?"

"It could be six; it could be six hundred. It depends on how much support Agent Larsen manages to get from the CIRG. It will be a tactical team out of Boston, at a minimum. Probably more if they expect massive resistance."

"Then we won't give them a reason to think there will be any," Vassyl says, looking up at the second-floor windows.

Much of the building has caved in, but not all of it. The residential buildings behind them serve as a natural funnel. There are plenty of other abandoned military bases and facilities that they have seen. All of them had glaring problems except this one.

"It's perfect."

"Are you kidding me?" Ian asks. "For starters, those housing units are too close. We'll never see them coming until it's too late."

"Let me worry about that."

"Okay, then let's assume this works. Where are we going to go? There are no escape routes."

"Yeah, there is."

Vassyl punches a speed dial number on his burner phone. It gets picked up on the first ring.

"Yeah?"

"Hey, Jackrabbit, I need to put your services to work. I need you to find us a boat."

"A boat? Are you serious?"

"I am. We need a small one, like a dinghy. I don't need you acquiring a damn yacht; just something easily transportable that has a good engine."

"Okay. It will take a couple of days."

"That's about all you have. Find it, and do it quietly."

Vassyl is hanging up when a secure message from Robespierre pops up on his prepaid burner phone. He opens it.

*Archangel Logan Mon 1130 Terminal C Confirmed*

Vassyl commits the information to memory and deletes the encrypted message. The time has almost come.

"Anything else?" the assassin asks.

"My God, you're serious about this."

He grins. "Look around you, Ian. This is going to be fun. We have some time. Let's take a closer look at what we have to work with."

# CHAPTER TWENTY-FIVE

## OLIVER JAHN

*Greater New York Student Journalism Association Forum*
*Brooklyn, New York*

The audience rises to its feet when Oliver is introduced. He spends a moment taking it all in. This is entrepreneurship at its best. What better use for an old movie theater than transforming it into an affordable event venue? They host all manner of social and corporate functions, from expos and competitions to conferences and retreats. The catering is top-notch, and they even repurposed the old concession stand to hand out snacks if patrons get hungry during the day.

It was the perfect place for the Greater New York Student Journalism Association to hold its annual conference. Present in this room are the best and brightest future additions to an industry in desperate need of new blood. The Wilson Newmans of the world are dinosaurs that need to go extinct. The young men and women here are the future.

"Thank you to the SJA for inviting me to be your keynote speaker," Oliver says from the podium. "When I first walked out on stage, I took a moment to appreciate this venue. It took foresight and financial risks to take an old, tired theater and repurpose it into something fresh and new. I doubt that many of you appreciate that, but you need to. It's how I started.

"Seven years ago, I began a podcast and posted it to streaming video services. You see, I was between jobs and watched the evening news one night after spending a day emailing resumes to job search sites. The more I watched, the less I liked the way that it was being delivered. Information that the reporters conveyed was utterly void of context. That allowed the people in power to spread lies without any challenge.

"So I pulled out a camera, rigged up a makeshift studio in my basement, and did my own news show. I injected humor because people need to be entertained to stay focused. Before long, my views grew to the point where I was picked up by a cable news network, and the rest was history."

Oliver waits for the applause to die down. He scans the faces in the audience. They are engaged and eager. He's thankful that the last bit didn't put them to sleep, but he needed to provide a little context of his own before he continues this speech.

"Why was I successful? It may be because of the snazzy graphics my producer creates or in my delivery, but that's just the presentation. It's that I hold people accountable when nobody else does. That's the key to your success as you venture out into the world.

"This forum has students from all over the tri-state area. Many schools with diverse but equally vibrant student bodies are represented. You all have one thing in common: the desire to become journalists. Each of you has wild ideas about taking the media world by storm. You'll face countless challenges in that journey. Some of you will make it. Others will not. Let me give you the most valuable piece of advice you could hear as you look forward to graduation and the start of your careers.

"Journalism isn't about the news. It's about recognizing trends. We are the first draft of history, and the most successful among us understand that it means adapting those words to fit the times. Right now, there is an ideological battle in this country, and everyone must choose sides. There is no fence-sitting with this much at stake.

"That's what makes people like Tierra Campos and media outlets like *Front Burner* so dangerous. If you've watched my show, and I pray to God that you have," Oliver says to chuckles from the audience, "you've watched me implore you not to fall for their deception. They chose sides, so let's not pretend they haven't. But instead of being honest about their agendas, they spend their nights poisoning your thoughts under the guise of objective reporting.

"Tierra Campos has attacked men of character and destroyed them because she doesn't like their politics. She covers for the racists and misogynists who want to destroy America and turns her back on the people who have already suffered long enough. Don't believe me? Look at her latest interview with Senator Veach. She wasn't pushing to get the truth out. She was trying to destroy him."

Oliver stops talking to let that set in with his audience. He sees many of the young adults turn their heads and get the reaction from their friends. Some are bobbing up and down. Others shake theirs, unconvinced. He doesn't need to do that here. This is about planting the seeds. His viewpoint will take root and grow over time.

"So, what happened? Well, they claim that the 'cancel culture' came after them. What is that? Is it a group of trolls on social media looking to destroy people because they have nothing better to do? Maybe. Or is it people who are using a platform to raise their voices after spending centuries in silence?

"The cancel culture is not a mob, at least in the derogatory sense of the word; it's accountability in action. People who don't do wrong won't find themselves the subject of their ire. The racists and misogynists, the haters, and the xenophobes who use their platforms to spread vile beliefs are the ones they target. The cancel culture does not stifle honest opinion – it discourages those from spreading the hateful ones that should be purged from our society.

"Why is this necessary? It's because journalists don't do their jobs. We're at fault for letting these people come to power or gain positions of influence. My peers and I did not use our microphones and cameras to take a stand, as was our responsibility. Someday it will be yours.

"We cannot live in a world that allows the wolves who deliver the news to hide in sheep's clothing. Tierra Campos, Wilson Newman, *Capitol Beat*, and *Front Burner* are only the largest of the cancerous tumors that plague journalism in this nation. It's why they must be torn out through boycotts and public pressure before we can purge the rest.

"I am happy to wield my scalpel because nobody else will. I will use my voice and my platform to ensure theirs gets taken away. Because, while I might be called a partisan hack, at least I'm honest about it. You deserve that truth. Now go and demand it from others. Thank you for listening tonight. I look forward to the Q&A where I get to interact with all of you instead of lecturing."

Oliver steps back from the podium to thunderous applause. The emcee steps out on the stage, clapping before she shakes his hand. The woman gestures to him again, and the deafening ovation grows even louder. He never fancied himself a giant among journalists. He now knows that he's heading in that direction.

# CHAPTER TWENTY-SIX

## TIERRA CAMPOS

*Cable News Studio*
*Washington, D.C.*

This place has all the energy of a morgue. I thought that there would be excitement over my anticipated mea culpa to our viewers, most of whom don't believe I should offer one according to the latest polls on the subject. I was surprised that pollsters would bother asking a question on the matter, but they did.

The production staff is another story. They are almost unanimously on team Puttman, either willingly or due to threats to their jobs. Most don't acknowledge me as I head to Wilson's office. It is beginning to have the feel that *Front Burner* did in my final days there.

"Knock, knock," I say, rapping on the door jamb as I enter and close the door behind me. No matter how early I arrive, he always seems to beat me.

Wilson takes off his reading glasses and leans back in his chair. "I was watching a clip of Oliver Jahn's speech yesterday to the Student Journalism Association. Did you see it?"

"I did. He hit a new low."

"That's an understatement. Are you ready for tonight?"

I look down at my hands as I clench them together. "I'm not doing it, Wilson."

"What?"

"You heard me. I'm not apologizing for doing nothing wrong."

Wilson closes his eyes. He knows what this means. So do I.

"Tierra, DeAnna isn't bluffing. Even if you made the most convincing case in human history for her to keep you, she'd still fire you out of spite."

"Do you want me to apologize, Wilson? Run out there on air and say I made a mistake? Be contrite for asking real questions on stories that nobody else wants to cover because it doesn't advance whatever agenda they are pushing?"

"Of course not."

"Then what do you want me to do? Because if I apologize to placate DeAnna Van Herten, she will wield that as a weapon against me forever. You know that's what she'll do. She'll own me."

"I know, I know. But an apology gives us time to fight this."

"Us? What us? You're retiring. You won't care what happens here in a few months."

"I will always care," Wilson argues, his voice changing as he takes offense to the accusation.

"Then why are you fighting me? You know that I'm right. I am losing everything I care about. *Front Burner* is in trouble, my friends think I have turned my back on them, and the online trolls are after me with their virtual pitchforks. This battle may be unwinnable, but I'll be damned if I'm not going to stand my ground to the bitter end."

"What are you going to do?"

"I don't know. Victoria Larsen stopped by the other day and told me that Isiah Burgess wants to talk to me. I'm thinking about agreeing to a sit-down."

"That's not a good idea. Not right now."

"Wilson, it's a story."

"A dead one," he says, leaning forward. "You have been adamant that Isiah is trying to lay the foundation for his defense. I agree with you. If you meet with him and Oliver Jahn finds out, it gives him a week's worth of material for his show."

He's right. I will get crucified, but I'm also tired of hiding. Oliver is going to criticize me, no matter what. When you're damned if you do and damned if you don't, then you might as well do.

"He already got what he wanted. He's about to be the top-ranked news show on television."

"It won't be enough. This may have started as a ratings ploy, but Oliver Jahn made this personal. He hates you, for whatever reason, and never wants you to work in the industry again. If you do this, he may get his wish."

"He might already have gotten it. Are you okay doing the show tonight?"

"Tierra—"

"Yes or no?"

Wilson nods, and I get up to leave. There is nothing more to be said. I make my way out of the building, mercifully being ignored by the few people I saw in the corridor. I have no idea if this is the right thing to do. I don't know what the right thing is anymore. All I can do is stay true to my beliefs and hope for the best. Time will tell if that's enough.

# CHAPTER TWENTY-SEVEN

## BRIAN COOPER

*U.S. Navy Memorial Plaza*
*Washington, D.C.*

When Pierre L'Enfant laid down the plans for a grand capital for the fledgling United States, he envisioned a memorial that would celebrate the Navy's rich heritage. It didn't materialize until Admiral Arleigh Burke decided that two hundred years was enough time to talk about it. This memorial is the triumphant homage to a navy that started in 1775 when eight small wooden ships won its first battle at sea.

Memorial Plaza is located on Pennsylvania Avenue, across from the National Archives, midway between the U.S. Capitol and the White House. Millions of people visit each year to pay tribute to the men and women of the sea services and admire the largest map in the world set in granite at their feet. It's a great place to arrange to bump into an old friend. He only needs to get here.

Brian admires the statues that ring the plaza, but his thoughts are elsewhere. All the pieces are nearly in place. All that remains is for the Bradford campaign to call. There are no guarantees, but he's done all he can. The wait gives him the chance to tie up one more loose end.

"How are you, Brian?" Nathan asks after he pretends to notice him from across the plaza and walks over.

"I'm doing well. You?"

The two men share a hug like they haven't seen each other in ages. It has been a while, but not that long.

"I can't complain. I'm putting in long hours, and it's making the wife cranky, but we're managing."

"How are the kids doing?"

"Good. It's summer break, and they're driving us crazy, so I'm counting the days until school starts. Are you ever going to have any kids?"

"Nah. I'd need to find a woman that will put up with me first. Alicia Standish is made of rebar and concrete, and even she couldn't."

"I'm pretty sure work wives don't count. I don't think she was your type anyway. What do you need?"

"Any information you can give me on the FBI investigation into the SOF."

Nathan and Brian go way back. They met at a bar when they were both new to the city. His friend went on to find a wife and have a nice career in the FBI. Brian dedicated himself to becoming a Washington power broker. Despite the separate paths, they remain in contact and have an arrangement to share information with each other.

"I don't usually question your inquiries, but I have to ask this time. Why are you so interested?"

"They almost cost me my freedom, remember? Besides that, Machiavelli and the SOF were a threat to the primary election. I can't afford to get blindsided like that again. I'll spend the rest of my work years asking if you want fries with that if I am."

"Who are you working for now?" Nathan asks.

"Myself for the moment. I'm trying to get a consulting gig with the Bradford campaign."

"I didn't expect you to go over to the dark side of the force."

"You have that reversed. Alicia Standish is Darth Vader. She can't be allowed to be president."

Nathan shakes his head. "Be careful saying that to an FBI agent. We have some bad experiences with those words."

"I know. This is important. Machiavelli and the SOF framed me. I need to make sure there aren't remnants of it still in the wind."

"You know I work for SIOC, right? We aren't directly involved."

The FBI's Strategic Information and Operations Center is its enterprise-wide global command and communications center. It was created as a platform to maintain situational awareness and synthesize information for Bureau leadership. They also support field commanders in significant investigations and tactical operations. That's what Brian needs Nathan for.

"You can't tell me that SIOC isn't in the know. Machiavelli used the SOF to disrupt a presidential primary. If you aren't paying attention to that, I'm going to start wondering where my tax dollars are going."

Nathan smiles. "We have a team in D.C. checking them out. So far, they haven't been able to connect the SOF to any outside supporters. It appears that all the members of the group were killed."

"Not all of them."

"Yes, Ian Drucker. The Bureau missed some big red flags with that guy. Nobody has been able to figure out how he made it into our training program. The background check should have disqualified him immediately."

"Have you found him?"

"No, he's still at large."

"That's disappointing. I'm going to be looking over my shoulder until Drucker is caught. What about the money trail? Someone paid for the SOF to do what they did. Was it Machiavelli?"

"It came from an off-shore account. It's going to be a dead end. It could be Machiavelli. It could have been a foreign power. It could have been Santa Claus."

"That would be out of character for St. Nick. You said, 'team.' Only one is looking into this?"

"We have significant manpower issues right now. The group looking into this is one of the CIRG's best. Trust me, if there is something to find, they'll find it. They even managed to get Victoria Larsen to help. I know you're familiar with that name."

"Yeah, her exploits in Brockhampton have become a thing of legend in political circles. And she stuck it to Alicia, so I'm a fan right now."

"We all are. I don't have anything more to give you. I can let you know if anything develops with the investigation."

"I appreciate it, Nathan, thanks. Give my best to your wife, and don't let the kids drive you nuts."

"No promises," Nathan says, shaking Brian's hand before the men part ways.

Brian heads back to the Metro station. One team is not going to get this done. If Nathan made anything clear, it's that the FBI isn't taking seriously the threat the SOF posed. If you can mess with a primary election in one state, you can mess with a national one. Especially if the race comes down to Pennsylvania.

# CHAPTER TWENTY-EIGHT

## VASSYL STRACHENKO

*Boston Common*
*Boston, Massachusetts*

Vassyl picks up a map from a quaint building that marks the beginning of the Freedom Trail. His target is sitting on one of the short concrete walls that separate grassy islands from the heavily used pedestrian walkway. She is either expecting to meet someone or in no rush to be anywhere. With time to burn while she waits, Vassyl purchases a map to help him look like a typical tourist.

He followed his target from Logan airport to see what her destination would be. This wasn't what he expected. Boston Common is a green oasis in an otherwise bustling city, differing from Central Park only in size if not beauty. Most Bostonians would probably resent the comparison with their archrival city.

Vassyl didn't want Ian around for this, and sent him back to the safehouse when they arrived in the city's center. Sven and the boys are more than capable of babysitting his volatile and untrustworthy problem child. The whole mission could be blown if he decided to do something irrational.

A man walks over to her, causing her to smile. The two hug as Vassyl pretends to stare down at his brochure. He doesn't recognize the black man who looks like he can handle himself. When he catches a glint of gold on the man's belt, it explains a lot. He's law enforcement of some sort.

The two begin ambling up the concrete path. Vassyl keeps his distance, trying to admire his surroundings rather than focus on the pair up ahead. He begins to close the distance as Ian's words rattle around his head. This mission is complicated, and it would be too easy to ensure the job got done right now. Unfortunately, he doesn't make plans. He executes them.

He moves in even closer, remembering that his silenced SIG Sauer is at the safehouse. It wasn't wise to have it on him at an international airport. Vassyl wouldn't need it for this. He doesn't go anywhere without his knife.

Only meters away, he could do them both right now. There are enough exit routes out of the common to ensure the chances of escape are in his favor. By the time anyone reacts, he would be on his way to the safehouse. With the city surrounding him, the police wouldn't know where to look. After lying low for a couple of days, he could get out of Boston with his mission accomplished. It's worth the risk.

The only problem would be the cameras. Vassyl can't see them but is sure they're around. He walks up to the pair when they stop in the middle of the path. It's now or never.

"Excuse me. I seem to be lost. Can you tell me where the Boston Massacre site is?" Vassyl asks, going heavy on his accent.

"You're heading in the wrong direction. It's about a half a mile back that way," Victoria Larsen explains, pointing.

"You need to follow the brick path laid into the sidewalk. It will take you where you need to go," the man with her says.

"Like the Wizard of Oz?" Vassyl asks.

"Yeah, only this one isn't yellow."

Vassyl fusses with his map. "Thank you. It's my first time in Boston. I'm afraid I keep getting lost."

"It takes a little while to get used to the city," Victoria says. "It's pretty old."

The assassin smiles. It's not even close to old compared to what he's used to. Most big European cities were around for centuries before anyone even knew this continent existed.

"Yes. I see that," Vassyl says, noting the positions of their hands and determining where their weapons are. He will have to be fast. The man is cautious and alert. He already knows that Victoria Larsen is the same. He could still pull it off, but the odds of success have gone down some.

"Good luck. Enjoy the city," the policeman says with a nod.

The two turn their backs to him and start making their way up toward the pond. They may be good, but they are also trusting and prone to mistakes. This one could cost their lives.

Vassyl reaches into his pocket and pulls out his Zippo. He lights a cigarette and heads back in the direction of the Freedom Trail. Now that he's met his target, he doesn't understand why Ian speaks so highly of her. She may be a great federal agent, but she isn't as invincible as her former colleague thinks she is. Vassyl knows that he'll get the chance to prove that soon enough. Victoria Larsen's day is coming.

# CHAPTER TWENTY-NINE

## SSA VICTORIA LARSEN

*Boston FBI Field Office*
*Chelsea, Massachusetts*

Victoria walks into a building she never thought she would return to. The Boston FBI's headquarters in Chelsea was her first assignment after graduating from Quantico, and was her professional home for years. She almost left it once following her reinstatement after the Brockhampton debacle and then left it again a few weeks ago. Now she's back wandering its halls again.

The team is waiting for her arrival on one of the upper floors. She makes small talk with some former colleagues along the way. Fortunately, she has been able to avoid the one person she has no desire to see.

"Victoria? Is that really you?" Takara asks, walking over to her.

"Hi, Takara. It's good seeing you."

She extends her hand, but he moves in and gives her a hug instead. It's a show of emotion that she's unaccustomed to from him. Out of the cases they worked on together, the most she ever got was a high-five or pat on the shoulder.

"I can't believe you're here."

"Don't get used to it. I'm based out of Washington."

"I knew you would never leave the Bureau."

"Oh, I had every intention of leaving. I was pulled back in kicking and screaming."

"You're a terrible liar. I met Agent Benitez and the rest of your team when they got here."

"Then you're ahead of me. I haven't even met them yet."

"Takara! Did you get a chance to—?"

Special Agent in Charge Lance Fuller stops talking when he sees Victoria standing with Takara in the corridor. The awkwardness of the moment ratchets up a few levels. Victoria's relationship with him has been hot and cold during her career. He has gone from sworn enemy to ally and back countless times. He was the former of those two when she left this place for what she thought was for good.

"Special Agent Larsen."

"Supervisory Special Agent Larsen now."

"Congratulations. I would have figured that you were out of the Bureau by now."

Victoria crosses her arms. Lance tried to force her out a couple of times and must be incensed about her standing in his building still carrying a badge. The agent-in-charge of the Boston Division had this penchant for passive-aggressive behavior that drove her insane. It's good to see that he hasn't lost his touch.

"You're not that lucky. Or that successful at getting me removed."

Lance scowls before catching himself. "What brings you to Boston? I'm sure you aren't here for nostalgic reasons."

"No, she isn't. Victoria is a member of my team," Rigo says, striding up to them.

"Is that so?"

"It is. Is there a problem, Special Agent-In-Charge Fuller?"

"No, no problem," Lance says, suddenly on the defensive. Fuller may technically outrank Rigo, but he has a swagger that the Boston Division head only wishes he had.

"Excellent. The CIRG continues to appreciate your support of our investigation. We will let you know when we need any additional use of your facilities or personnel, and we look forward to you accommodating them."

Victoria stares at Lance. She has seen that face before. He would love to tell Rigo to shove it, but he can't. This investigation has the attention of the FBI director himself. One thing Fuller won't do is jeopardize career prospects.

"Of course," Fuller says, moving back down the corridor.

"Apologies, Agent Benitez," Takara says, shortening his official title to something more colloquial. "Agent Fuller has a lot on his plate. He's up for a promotion and doesn't know if he'll get it."

"Because he's an egocentric bureaucrat who's too stupid to understand that he doesn't deserve it," Rigo says, causing the corner of Takara's mouth to curl. "Anytime you want out of here, Agent Nishimoto, you say the word."

"It was great seeing you again, Vic," Takara says, nodding at Rigo before heading back down the corridor.

"You lasted longer in this place than I would have. Come on. Let's go meet the team. Well, half of it, anyway."

Rigo and Victoria make their way into a conference room, and the déjà vu sets in. She stops outside the door and stands there.

"What's wrong?"

"Nothing. The last time I stepped foot in here, I was arrested for murder and led out in cuffs."

"Trust me. The audience is much friendlier this time."

They walk in, and the three men and one woman seated at the table stop what they're doing. She is greeted with smiles, which is a nice change of pace.

Victoria, these are Special Agents Amanda Wheatley, Shawn Tucker, Dennis Dugas, and Steve Mueller. Shawn is the veteran on the team. He's been with me for a couple of years now. Steve is the rookie. He only came on about a month ago."

"Yeah, and now that I'm not the lowest rung on the ladder, we have someone else to get the coffee," he says playfully.

"Maybe she'll at least get the orders right," Shawn interjects.

"Whatever you say, mister triple shot, half caramel, half vanilla latte, with nonfat milk and extra drizzle on top."

"At least *you* got it right this time."

Rigo smiles. "Amanda, why don't you catch Victoria up before this gets out of hand?"

Amanda spends the next twenty minutes walking Victoria through the various aspects of their investigation. It is a more in-depth version than what Rigo gave her, but the conclusion is the same. No matter which direction they take, it comes to a dead end. Rats have better luck with their mazes.

"When Rigo offered me this job, my first thought was that you guys hadn't gotten very far, despite your best efforts. Now I see why."

"The money trail is the most promising to yield results," Shawn says.

"And the most frustrating to get them," Dennis adds. "Anybody willing to get caught up in this would have covered their tracks. Even if the banks decided to hand over the information, it would take years to unravel the transactions."

"That's why we're hoping that you can help."

"We're out of ideas. We tracked down everything we could from Sartre's hard drive. Most of it didn't lead anywhere."

"And nothing brings us any closer to confirming the identity of Machiavelli."

"Any thoughts, Vic?" Rigo asks.

"Yeah. We need to go on a field trip tomorrow. Let me make a couple of calls."

"Please tell me it's a Sox game at Fenway," Amanda says.

"Over my dead body," Dennis objects. "They play in my division. It's the baseball equivalent of supporting ISIL."

"The Orioles suck anyway. You'll survive."

"A field trip to where?" Rigo asks.

Victoria smiles and pulls out her phone. She has both men saved as favorites. One of them will be up for this. She isn't sure about the other.

"You'll see."

# CHAPTER THIRTY

## BRIAN COOPER

*The National Mall*
*Washington, D.C.*

This is Brian's favorite time of day in Washington. The National Mall is beautiful at sunrise. The air is still fresh, and the area is mostly devoid of the tourists who will invade it like the Bay of Pigs in a couple of hours. It's also the best time to catch up with busy people, especially ones who don't like you. That sums up Marvin Leer.

"Why would I want you as a source?" the reporter asks, seated next to Brian on the bench.

"Why wouldn't you?"

"Because I don't operate that way. My job is to uncover and publish facts, not spread propaganda."

Brian shakes his head. That's the seventh lie he's told, and they've only been sitting here for five minutes. Marvin will spin any story for an additional hundred clicks.

"Really? Would Andrew Li agree with that?"

Surprise flashes on Marvin's face before he recovers. "I don't know what you're talking about."

"Sure you do. Andrew Li leaked information to you in New Hampshire that Angela Mays and several high-level staffers reached out to Burgess for jobs when the Standish campaign was on the verge of collapse."

"How do you know that?" Marvin asks.

"It doesn't matter. By the way, none of that was true, mister I uncover and publish facts."

"It sounded credible," Marvin says with a shrug.

"Most lies do."

"Andrew Li got a gig with the Standish campaign when Burgess called it quits, and you're unemployed. How's that for irony? Unless you aren't unemployed."

"That remains to be seen, and I should remind you that we are off the record."

"Do you see a notebook in my hand?"

"It doesn't mean you don't have a recorder in your pocket."

Marvin has made a career getting stories the old-fashioned way: get someone to talk and report on what they say. Not everything was strictly on the record. He has a reputation for playing hard and fast with that journalistic rule.

"What information could you possibly have that would interest me?"

"Marvin, you know my reputation. Do you really assume that I don't have my pulse on this presidential race?"

"I know you do."

"Then the question answers itself," Brian says, admiring the view up and down the Mall.

"What do you want in return?" Marvin asks.

"What makes you think there's a quid pro quo?"

"Because I know your reputation. You don't give out information for free."

Brian laughs. That's the first fact Marvin has been able to uncover. "Fair enough. I want you to tell the side of the story that others don't."

"That's journalism, Brian."

"That has never been journalism, and you know it. Tierra Campos tried to do it right and is getting crucified for it. Even Wilson Newman is in hot water over at *Capitol Beat*, and he's the patron saint of broadcasting."

"That's only a rumor."

"Not anymore. That you can run with."

"Okay. I'll do it, but don't you think for a second that you get to dictate what I write."

"Wouldn't dream of it. We'll talk soon, Marv."

Marvin scoffs as he stands and heads back up the sidewalk. So far, the day has been productive. Brian is about to leave when his phone rings. He checks the caller id and connects the call.

"Good morning, Brevin."

"Whatever. You get your wish: tonight, 6p.m. at the governor's retreat in the Appalachians."

"Thanks for all the advance notice."

"If you want this bad enough, you'll find a way to be there. And Brian? Don't be late. Colin doesn't like to be kept waiting."

Brevin hangs up, and Brian checks his watch. There aren't many flights to that part of the state, so he needs to get moving. He only gets one shot at this.

# CHAPTER THIRTY-ONE

## TIERRA CAMPOS

*Navy Yard Metro Station*
*Navy Yard, Washington, D.C.*

I hate feeling like this. Stress is one of the worst emotions to cope with. Grief is painful, but it gets used up. Anxiety is debilitating but can be managed. Stress takes a mental and physical toll, and for some people, it's always present.

The higher you travel up the ladder, the higher the expectations and demands. When I was at WWDC, my work was not stressful. I was an unknown human interest reporter. That changed following my reporting at Brockhampton and subsequent jump to *Capitol Beat*. I knew anchoring the number one news show would put me under a microscope, but I didn't expect the stress to be this bad.

I lug my rolling carry-on behind me as I step off the escalator and walk down the Navy Yard Metro Station platform. It's busy but not packed. The cavernous station and wide platforms provide an airy, open space that helps make rush hour volume tolerable.

Several college-age kids dressed in shorts and t-shirts stand behind me. I can hear them talking and feel their eyes on me, so I'm not surprised when I get a tap on the shoulder.

"Hi. Are you Tierra Campos?" one of them asks.

"Yes," I say with an upbeat tone to my voice.

For most of my life, I wished I was invisible. It started in Summerville when a gunman was trying to force his way into the closet I was hiding in. It happened numerous times at WWDC, including the day I was fired and discovered that my personal information was leaked on the Internet. Now, I like the idea of being recognized.

"You're a bitch!" the kid says, jabbing his finger in my face.

"Excuse me?" I say, reeling from the sudden verbal assault.

"You heard him," the girl behind him says. "You're a liar and a traitor. You should be ashamed of yourself."

"What are you talking about? I report the news."

"You spread propaganda," a third kid says as the rest nod their heads in agreement.

"You've been *listening* to propaganda if you believe that," I argue, beginning to lose my temper.

"We listen to the truth. You're the liar! That's all you do. You spread lies!" the girl says, her cheeks turning from pink to red.

"We should push you in front of that train," the guy next to her says. "We'd do the world a favor."

I've heard enough. I can deal with criticism, but that's not what this is. These are Oliver Jahn's disciples, and they take his words as gospel not meant to be questioned. I drag my small suitcase away from the edge of the platform. I can't know if that kid is posturing or serious.

"Where you goin'? You scared?" one of the other kids taunts.

"Don't run away."

"You need to pay, you ignorant bitch!"

My harassers are growing more aggressive. I look around to see if there are any uniformed police in the station, but I see none. I'm getting that familiar feeling of fearing for my life, and I'm shaken by it.

"You have no problem harassing other people, Queen of Pretenders. How does it feel when you're on the receiving end?"

The moniker confirms what I already thought. Oliver Jahn has his viewers amped up. These kids are only regurgitating the nonsense they hear on his show. Heads are turned in our direction. Up and down the platform, people watch the show these kids are putting on. I would have hoped that someone would come to my defense, but nobody does.

The train pulls into the station, bringing the verbal ambush to a halt. The doors open, and I enter a different car than they do. I take a deep breath as the train lurches forward. I was hoping that they wouldn't follow me into this car. My relief is short-lived when the kids open the door between cars and pile into mine.

"You ain't getting away that easy!"

"You know who this is? It's the liar Tierra Campos," another kid says to a passenger.

"I'm asking you to leave me alone," I say, trying to garner some sympathy from the people on the train with me.

"That's not gonna happen."

"Look, I don't want to argue with you. Everything you think you know about me is wrong."

"We know all about you."

"You've been exposed for the evil liar that you are. I hope you die!" the girl shrieks.

"That's what you deserve: a long, slow, painful death."

"While your family watches," the third kid adds.

Everyone else in the train car looks away. Not a single person reacts to the vile comment. That hurts as much as the words do.

The abuse continues as the train pulls into nearby Waterfront Station. I can't endure this all the way to L'Enfant Plaza, so I hurry out the door after the train stops.

"Look at her run!"

"What a coward!"

"You'll get yours someday."

The kids laugh until the doors close and the train pulls away. At least they didn't follow me.

My hands are shaking uncontrollably. I find a bench and sit on it, trying to regain my composure. As the adrenaline starts to subside, I feel my emotions rush to the surface. All I can do is sit on the bench and sob while the world goes on around me. Maybe I got my wish and am invisible again.

# CHAPTER THIRTY-TWO

## OLIVER JAHN

*Grammercy Citizens' Cafe*
*New York, New York*

It started with one person. Then another joined in. Then another. Before long, every patron in the small restaurant had started clapping. Now, some of the people are even giving him a standing ovation. All Oliver can do is smile and wave.

"Is this why you brought me here? To introduce me to your adoring fans?" Mi Sun leans over and asks Oliver.

"Hardly. I came because this place makes a mean Western omelet."

The applause dies down as the pair are shown to a seat at the back of the restaurant. It suits Mi Sun just fine. She has never pined to be the center of attention. Her comfort zone is behind the scenes with someone else baking under the white-hot spotlight. The applause was for Oliver, and she was uncomfortable enough standing next to him.

"You were chatty all the way here. Why so quiet now?" he asks after the waitress hands them menus and sets off to retrieve their cups of coffee.

"We've worked together for a long time," Mi Sun says with a shrug. "I don't recall a time when you've ever taken me to breakfast."

"I'm usually not up early enough."

"That's not the reason we're here today. Spill it."

"I wanted to talk something over with you."

"Okay, the last time you did this to me was in Times Square."

"I thought this would be more comfortable."

"For you, maybe. We're meeting in a public place, and that's ominous."

"You worry too much, Mi Sun," Oliver says, snatching up the coffee the waitress drops off. "This isn't bad news if that's what you're worried about. I want to talk about raising the stakes on our crusade against Tierra Campos."

The producer has time to think that over as the waitress takes their orders. He orders the Western omelet. Mi Sun is content with simple eggs and toast.

"Oliver, you got what you wanted. TNT is on the verge of becoming the number one show on cable news. The network will give you the deal that you want."

"That remains to be seen. I'm not talking about any of that."

"Then this is about Tierra Campos. Oliver, she was fired from *Capitol Beat*. The war is over. You won."

"No," he says, shaking his head. "The battle is won. The war rages on. Campos will land somewhere else. The only thing that will change is the channel she's on. That's not good enough. I want to destroy her."

"You know, you're starting to sound like Ahab searching for the white whale."

"I know."

"It didn't work out for him," Mi Sun warns.

"I'm going to rewrite the story. Everything I've said about Campos is factual, and they rewarded her by giving her a Peabody and a Pulitzer."

"Jealous much?"

"No, I don't care about those awards, just what they symbolize. We've spent years presenting the news in an entertaining and meaningful way. She stumbles on a story, and they hand her an armful of hardware for it. Her voice doesn't give her legitimacy. Her opinions don't compel people to listen to her. Those ridiculous accolades do."

Breakfast arrives, and their coffee cups are refilled. Mi Sun has lost her appetite. She doesn't like where this conversation is going. Oliver has always had a good compass for picking their direction. Right now, it's spinning in circles.

"You're getting carried away with this."

"No, I'm not. Times have changed since we were working out of my basement," Oliver says.

"Yes, they have. Now look me in the eyes and admit that you're also changing. This crusade against Tierra Campos isn't healthy. You're becoming the thing that you used to rail against on our show."

Oliver puts his fork down and leans back in his chair. "Are you saying that you won't support me?"

Mi Sun pouts, clearly unwilling to be guilted into agreeing with this tactic. Oliver knows that she owes him a lot and despises Tierra Campos almost as much as he does, but her allegiance and support doesn't come with obedient cheerleading.

"Don't be like that. I always support you, and I always will. You take risks, and I've trusted that they would pay off. And they have, but that doesn't mean I follow you blindly or withhold my opinions."

"What is your opinion?"

"That now you're gambling with our livelihoods. You are winning big, but you have to know when to get up from the table and leave the casino."

"I want to take the house."

"That's the problem. Don't be the cliche by becoming a victim of your own success. People like you because of your story—"

"People like me because I speak the truth."

"Nobody knows what that is, Oliver."

Now it's his turn to get angry. Mi Sun has never challenged him like this. Fear is compelling her to settle for what they've accomplished. She doesn't see the opportunities still in front of them.

"Our viewers know they get the truth from us," Oliver says, pointing his fingers between the two of them.

"That's only true until they have a reason to question the faith they place in us. Don't give them one."

"Mi Sun, I need to know if you're with me in this. It doesn't sound like you are."

"Just be careful."

Oliver nods. It wasn't the answer he wanted, but he'll take it. Mi Sun has always kept him grounded. The risks he takes are calculated ones because of her. If she is okay with this, then he is still on the right path. It's up to him to stay on it.

# CHAPTER THIRTY-THREE

## SSA VICTORIA LARSEN

*Former SOF Safehouse*
*South Hooksett, New Hampshire*

It's like returning to the scene of a nightmare. The tattered yellow police tape still marks off the property. Rigo parks in the cul-de-sac, and the team walks up the asphalt driveway. The ranch-style house looks different than it did that night. The broken windows and bullet holes have something to do with that. It still amazes Victoria that nobody was killed when the SOF opened fire on them as they approached.

"Now we've got the band back together," Seth Chambers announces as he meets them, Diego right behind him.

Victoria smiles at Seth and hugs Diego. Unlike the one with Takara, this feels natural. She owes a lot to these two men. The FBI often has strained relationships with local and state law enforcement, but she will always count these men as the best she's ever worked with.

"Careful, now. My wife is going to get jealous," Diego says after she holds the hug a couple of beats longer than expected.

"How are you?"

"I'm fine. My injuries get me out of doing housework. Latinas can be tough, but they melt when someone they love gets a boo-boo."

"Only in New Hampshire would you think getting shot three times is a boo-boo," Seth offers with a smile.

"Maybe you Massachusetts boys need to toughen up."

Victoria introduces the two men to the team. Dennis, Amanda, and Shawn have accompanied them up here, leaving Steve to man the fort back in Chelsea. Rigo's introduction to the men is chummy and brief. Victoria wonders how long he spoke to each of them when he was vetting her.

"Okay, we're all here. Now what?" Seth asks.

"Let's take a walk."

Victoria leads them up the remainder of the driveway, stopping just outside the front door. She takes a deep breath and walks in. The walls are gone, stripped down to the studs. All the furniture and fixtures were also removed.

"I wonder what this insurance claim looks like," Dennis muses.

"The forensics team was thorough. The NHSP and FBI tore this house apart and checked every inch of the property with ground-penetrating radar. The woods were extensively searched, and nothing was found."

"The only useful thing the SOF left behind was that hard drive and their bodies," Shawn says.

"Not that I'm sad to see you, Victoria, but you wasted a trip," Diego says.

"Not really. Everyone look around you."

The team complies, but there isn't much to see.

"It looks like a house," Rigo says.

"Or what's left of one," Amanda adds.

"Yeah, it's a house, and the secret it held was a dark one. It's also a testament that the Sword of Freedom didn't do this alone. They didn't write a rent check. It was paid in full, in advance, from a corporation that doesn't exist."

"We know," Amanda interjects. "We tried following the money trail."

"I know, but that's not my point. Why this place?"

"It's quiet and secluded, with limited access in and out," Dennis observes.

"It's close to Manchester," Diego adds.

"Exactly. What the SOF did took a lot of planning. These guys were mercenaries, not strategists. They reported all that reconnaissance and prep work to somebody."

"We scanned the hard drive, Victoria," Shawn argues. "There was no digital trail."

Victoria moves to the shattered window and stares out of it. This was the spot where Marx engaged with the M240B machine gun. Several of Diego's men were cut down by that fire. It sends a shiver down her spine.

"Maybe we're looking in the wrong place."

"We've been digging for months," Rigo says. "We haven't uncovered any SOF communication outside of Machiavelli's cell phone."

"And even that wasn't much," Dennis adds.

"Do you think that Machiavelli trusted them to do all this without oversight?"

"Unlikely," Diego mutters.

"The profile we created on him indicates that he's a control freak. He would have been more hands-on," Amanda says.

"That goes back to my original question. How did the SOF communicate?"

"Snail mail?" Diego asks.

"Too easy to get lost or intercepted," Seth argues. "They would have had to do it in person."

All eyes turn to Victoria. She must have already come to this conclusion to lead them down this road.

"We've assumed the big bad is a shady character smoking a cigarette in the corner of a dark room."

"I appreciate the *X-Files* reference, but what are you driving at, Vic?" Rigo asks.

"Whoever was working with the SOF was hiding in plain sight. Who spends a lot of time in New Hampshire and had the most to gain by what happened?"

"Burgess."

"Who else?"

"Standish," Shawn adds.

"Any politician." Everyone looks at Diego. "They spend months up here before the primary. New Hampshire takes that vetting seriously. There are people around here that won't vote for a candidate unless they've met and talked to them at least three times. Even Alicia Standish spent an eternity up here."

"The time that the SOF needed to do their research coincided with every presidential contender being in the state."

The group falls silent as they process that information. It makes sense but proving it will be something else entirely.

"It's a stab in the dark."

"Yeah, it is, but what else do we have left, Dennis? What other avenues are left to explore?"

"She's right," Rigo concludes. "There was a political angle to Ethan Harrington and the Brockhampton massacre. We know there was a political angle to rigging this primary."

"Do we?" Seth asks. "Since we're playing the game here, what if this wasn't just about the primary? What if it was something else?"

"Why would you think that?" Shawn asks.

"Burgess," Victoria interjects. "If he is Machiavelli, why would someone try to kill him?"

"To silence him," Dennis concludes.

"Over what? The primary is over. And if he had an accomplice, he would have outed him by now."

"Amanda is right," Rigo says. "And if he isn't Machiavelli, then everybody stops investigating when he dies."

"Leaving the real Machiavelli still free to plan who knows what?"

"To what end?" Diego asks.

"We don't know, and that's what scares me," Victoria says. "Diego, the state police covered political events in the state, right? Do you have video surveillance from any of them?"

Diego scratches his chin. "I don't know. I can check."

"National news didn't get up here until the primary," Rigo adds. "The local news will have video. I can ask them for the raw footage."

"With all due respect, this is the 'Live Free or Die' State. People up here are suspicious of the federal government. Let me make the request."

Rigo nods as Victoria cracks a slight smile. She's learning to like him more and more. This isn't an ego thing for him. He wants answers and isn't afraid to let others help get them.

"The FBI can run the footage. We can start with Marx and check the Burgess rallies first. That will be the fastest way to confirm that Burgess is Machiavelli," Dennis adds.

For the first time in months, there is excitement in the team's voices. Rigo moves closer to Victoria as the group begins talking among themselves and the state police's two detectives. They trade notes and listen to the rallies that the SOF would have been most likely to attend.

"Did we have to come up here for this, or were you looking for an excuse to see Diego?" Rigo asks.

"It's called multitasking. And besides, would the team have this much energy sitting in a conference room? The SOF is deadly. Machiavelli is a quaint name, but the man behind it is an accessory to murder. They needed to experience this place and see what happened here."

Rigo smiles. "You're going to be a great agent in charge someday."

"Unless somebody tries to kick me out of the FBI again."

Victoria moves over to the team and listens to the conversation. Diego is already off to the side, making a phone call. From the sounds of it, they have a long night of work ahead of them.

# CHAPTER THIRTY-FOUR

## BRIAN COOPER

*Reagan National Airport*
*Arlington, Virginia*

Brian thanks his lucky stars that he's a planner. He already had a suitcase packed and was ready to go while he waited for Brevin's call. It was just a matter of getting home, booking a flight, and hightailing it over to Reagan National.

With time before he needs to report to his gate for boarding, he wanted to stretch his legs by walking through the concourse. He didn't expect to bump into anyone he knew. That thought was quickly dispelled.

"Tierra!" Brian says, striding over to the young woman dragging a carry-on.

"Brian? What are you doing here?"

"For an astute journalist, you sure like asking dumb questions," he says, gesturing at the airport around them.

Tierra smiles. "I meant, where are you heading?"

"Charlotte and then on to Asheville via a puddle jumper."

"North Carolina? You're going to see Colin Bradford, aren't you?"

Brian puts a finger on his lips. "I know trusting that secret to a journalist is like trusting a toddler with the cookie jar, but that needs to stay between us."

"It won't be on *Capitol Beat*, that's for sure."

"I've heard you've been having a rough time of it over there. Oliver Jahn is way out of line."

Tierra's face changes. It's more wounded than angry.

"Yeah. My own network isn't backing me. My executive producer and the network head demanded that I apologize on air for asking Veach questions any real journalist would ask."

"That's because DeAnna Van Herten is a fool."

"You know her?" Brian cocks his head and grins as she realizes the stupidity of the question. "Yes, of course you do. I forgot who I was talking to."

"With the shit hitting the fan, I'm surprised to see you leaving town."

"I have some unfinished business with Isiah Burgess."

"I see," Brian says, caught off-guard by the admission.

"What? I remember that look."

"It's not my place to say."

"No, tell me," Tierra demands. "You are the most political animal I've ever met. You would have gotten out of this jam in ten seconds."

"No, I wouldn't have gotten into a jam in the first place."

Brian knows that Tierra is a gifted journalist with impeccable foresight. She missed all the signals on this one, though. *Capitol Beat* has been tacking toward more partisan stances for years now. He isn't the least bit surprised they are using Wilson Newman's retirement and Tierra's hiring as an excuse to accelerate that pivot.

"Unfortunately, I did. Since I'm going to get fired anyway, I thought I would do something useful."

"You should rethink that. The moment you leave town, DeAnna will use it against you."

"The outcome is predetermined."

"Is it? DeAnna likes strength. Wilson pushes back on her, and that's how he's lasted so long. Here's my advice: stick around and argue your case until your mouth goes dry."

"You weren't there, Brian. It won't do any good."

"I think it might. But if you aren't there or prepared for it, you'll never know."

"It should never have even come to this," Tierra says, looking down at the ground. She's unsure of herself. He's not used to seeing that from this young woman.

"I agree. Your interview with Veach was professional and on point. That's what Americans have come to expect from you and Wilson. Your reporting is something that every American on both sides of the ideological spectrum needs to hear."

Tierra offers a weak smile at the compliment. "Can you speak to DeAnna?"

"I would, but she doesn't like me much. This fight is yours, Tierra. You just have to be willing to take up arms and go to war for what you believe."

"I know you need to go. Thanks, Brian. Good luck with Bradford."

"Thanks. Good luck to you, as well. After all that we've been through, know that I'm in your corner."

Tierra squeezes his arm and moves off back down the concourse. He watches her go as he makes his way toward his gate and his own critical moment to navigate through.

# CHAPTER THIRTY-FIVE

## VASSYL STRACHENKO

*Fuller Residence*
*Somerville, Massachusetts*

Vassyl is sitting at the small breakfast table and reaches into the pocket of his black windbreaker when his phone vibrates. With a couple of taps, he opens the app and checks the text message he just received:

*Get to Chicago immediately. Await instructions.*

The assassin shakes his head and checks his watch. This will already be a long night, and he isn't looking forward to a thirteen-hour drive at the end of it. He replaces the phone in his pocket and fiddles with the suppressed pistol on the table.

"You had better be right about this, Jackrabbit. We have no margin for error."

"Oh, I'm right. He just pulled in."

Nothing needs to be said as the men get into position. They are professionals who have rehearsed this and know what to do.

Keys rattle in the door. Lance Fuller opens it and walks in, dropping them into a dish perched on the kitchen counter as he scans the mail. For an FBI agent, he has no situational awareness.

"Hi, honey," he calls out. "You haven't started din—"

Fuller looks up and stops cold when he sees Vassyl seated at the table with the SIG Sauer pointed at him. His mouth slacks open as the blood rushes out of his face.

"Dinner is going to be late tonight. Please don't reach for your weapon. I'm an excellent shot. You won't get a fraction of the way there before I make your kids orphans."

"Who are you?" he demands.

"Who I am isn't important. Who you are is."

"I'm an FBI agent."

"Oh, we are well aware of that," Ian says, rounding the corner from the living room. Fuller's mouth hangs open. Ian walks over and relieves him of his weapon. He tucks it into the small of his back and gives his old boss a pat-down, searching for a backup. There isn't one.

"You look surprised, Lancy Boy. You shouldn't be. You had to know it would come to this if I wasn't caught. Or you didn't, which makes you an idiot."

"Where's my family?"

"Damn, it took you long enough to ask. That's most people's first question. They're upstairs. To answer your next question, they're alive. For now. Whether they stay that way depends on you. Have a seat."

Lance doesn't move and gets a shove from Ian. He moves around the counter and sits in a chair. Ian pulls a glass out of the cupboard and fills it with water.

"You have a beautiful home, Agent Fuller. And a lovely family. Men like you often take those things for granted."

"What do you want? Revenge?"

"On you? For what?" Ian asks, joining the men at the table. "You're a nobody pretending that you're oh, so important."

He sets the water in front of Fuller and dumps a handful of pills on the table. Lance stares at them, fighting back the panic that Vassyl knows he's feeling.

"Why are you here?"

"That isn't important either."

"Focus," Vassyl says, tapping his weapon on the table to get Fuller's attention. "You have two simple options in front of you. You take the pills, and your wife and kids go free. If you don't, you will die anyway, and the coroner will haul four bodies out of here instead of one. Decide."

Fuller stares blankly at the table in front of him. Vassyl watches him, knowing what must be going through his head. He knows a fight is out of the question. There must be another way out of this situation.

"Dylan Spencer," he mumbles before looking at Ian. "This is how you killed him. You gave him an ultimatum in his car and had consequences for his family if he didn't comply."

"Nothing gets past you," Ian says, mocking him. "That was our early M.O., wasn't it? You have ten seconds to swallow those pills. You know the consequences if you don't."

One of the SOF's first missions was to remove a rich megadonor from the equation. Marx had Ian break into the man's house to kill his family if he didn't comply with the orders he was being given. It was all streamed from a darknet site right to the man's cell phone. The thought of losing his family was unbearable, so he drove up on the train tracks as requested. Less than a minute later, a train ran over his fancy sportscar.

"How do I know you'll let them live?"

"Because the Spencers did. I was five feet from their bedroom when Marx convinced Dylan to sacrifice himself. Enough talk. Ten seconds," Ian says, staring at his watch. Lance stares at them and then the pills without moving. "Five...four...three..."

Ian shakes his head. Dylan Spencer at least displayed courage and a shred of honor in what he did. The same can't be said for the agent in charge of the Boston FBI.

"All right. We do this the hard way."

Vassyl nods at Sven, who has quietly entered the kitchen from the basement stairs. Like a hunter stalking his prey, he stealthily comes up from behind Fuller with a wire garrote. He throws it across Fuller's throat with a flick of his wrist. The toggle lands effortlessly in the palm of Sven's other hand. He pushes his thigh into the back of the chair and pulls back. Vassyl is impressed. The man has done this before.

Fuller struggles to no avail as the piano wire cuts off all air and blood flow in his throat. The man is too big and strong to fight against, and the FBI agent goes limp. Ian checks the man's pulse. There is none.

Vassyl pulls out a twenty and hands it to Ian. "I hate losing."

"You didn't know Fuller like I did. Everything is about him. There was no way he was taking those pills."

"Oh well. Let's finish up here," Vassyl commands as Jackrabbit enters from the living room. "Get in touch with Dimitri and tell him that we're a go for tonight."

Ian pulls a can of spray paint out of his backpack. It's red this time, instead of the white they used outside the Burgess campaign offices they torched. He writes SOF on the table next to Fuller's head in thick letters.

"I've been waiting a long time to do that."

"Go ahead and take a few selfies if you want. I'll be back in a minute."

Vassyl walks upstairs and enters the master bedroom. Fuller's wife and two children are bound and tied on the bed. They have horror and fear in their eyes as he sparks a cigarette with his Zippo before sliding it back into his pocket.

"Don't be afraid. I'm here to free you."

He sees the woman relax a little before he raises his weapon and squeezes the trigger. It burps, pumping a round into her forehead. He shifts his aim and repeats the act with the two children. He takes another drag from his cigarette, watching the shocked, lifeless eyes stare back at him.

Satisfied that his work is done, he heads back downstairs to the three men waiting for him. As complicated as this mission is, so far, it has gone off without a hitch.

"One down. Two to go."

# CHAPTER THIRTY-SIX

## TIERRA CAMPOS

*Tierra's Apartment*
*Navy Yard, Washington, D.C.*

I couldn't say no to him, even though I wanted to. The television is off, and I didn't even uncork a bottle of wine following my trip back from the airport. I need to focus, and those distractions are unwelcome. So is this one.

"I got your text. Since I knew you wouldn't bother ordering dinner, I brought it to you," Josh says, holding the bag up at the door.

I let him in, not hiding how frustrated I am at the interruption. The gesture is sweet and thoughtful, but I don't have time for that right now. I have a lot to plow through, and the clock is ticking.

"You don't look happy to see me. I thought you—"

"I texted you so you wouldn't worry. It didn't mean to show up here."

Josh is taken aback by the comment but doesn't get the hint. "What happened to Chicago?"

"I didn't go."

"Obviously. Did you tell Victoria?"

"Yeah, I told her."

"What did she say?"

"What could she? I don't work for her," I say, growing more impatient by the second.

"I thought you wanted to talk with Isiah."

"I did. There was a change in plans."

"Just like that?"

"Jesus, Josh. What's with the inquisition? I don't need you grilling me right now."

Can't he see that I'm doing something important? Why does he feel the need to always give me the third degree about everything?

"I'm not *grilling* you. I'm curious. You were set on interviewing Isiah and then did a complete one-eighty."

"I ran into Brian Cooper on my way to my gate at Reagan National."

"He met you there?"

"No, he was getting on a flight."

"And he convinced you not to go see Isiah?"

"He gave me some guidance on how to handle DeAnna Van Herten. That's what I'm working on. I need to be bold to convince her that firing me would be a mistake."

"Tierra, you don't really think that's going to work, do you?"

Josh's condescending tone is about to set me off. I bite my tongue despite wanting nothing more than to lash out with it, get him to leave, and get back to work. Instead, I fork into my mouth some of the chicken parmesan he brought me, and answer after swallowing.

"I have to try."

"Why?"

"What do you mean, why?"

"DeAnna Van Herten wants you out. Just leave. You don't need that job."

I've had enough of the stupid questions. The last thing I want to listen to is another of Josh's lectures.

"That's easy for you to say, Mister 'I will work at Treasury doing tasks I could train a monkey to do until I die.'"

Josh recoils at the comment. I don't care. He started this, and I'm going to end it.

"Is that what you think—? I'm working—"

"You're working your way up. I know. You've used that excuse a hundred times. Tell me, Josh, how many promotions have you gotten since you've been there?" I know I hit the mark when he narrows his eyes. "Face it. You're content being a nobody because you don't fight to be something more."

"Wow. That's really what you think of me. Everyone is right – those awards did go to your head," he says, heading for the door.

"Excuse me?" I ask, shooting off the couch.

"You heard me. Have you ever stopped to think about why so many people are buying into Oliver Jahn's message? It's because they think you're arrogant and unlikeable. You're the big shot everyone wants to see fall now."

"There is nobody more arrogant on this planet than Oliver Jahn," I snap.

"That's probably true, but he's popular because he doesn't come across that way. You do, and that's why so many people want you to fail. I never thought they were right until right now."

"Get out. Go!"

"Yeah, I'll leave you to your futile work."

"You would know what that looks like."

Josh is about to reply to my snide remark but smothers the words before they escape his mouth. I've been best friends with him since high school. We saved each other's lives – mine during the Summerville shooting and his, as I only found out during the Brockhampton shooting investigation, when my phone call interrupted his suicide attempt.

I can see the mixture of hurt and anger on Josh's face. He wants to vent it but just offers a weak smile.

"Enjoy the rest of your dinner."

He leaves, and I close the door behind him. I return to the couch and open my laptop. I was in the zone, but now my focus is gone. Josh has some nerve. I slam the screen down and lean back into the sofa with what remains of my dinner. Damn him and his ridiculous interruption.

# CHAPTER THIRTY-SEVEN

## SSA VICTORIA LARSEN

*Boston FBI Field Office*
*Chelsea, Massachusetts*

Diego is a man of his word. It took him less than a day to send Victoria's team raw footage from dozens of rallies to sift through. It couldn't have been easy to obtain, and by bureaucratic standards, it happened at light speed. He also included some security camera footage from the venues where these events were held.

Rigo arranged for them to use some of the Boston office's equipment, and the team gets to work running facial recognition software on the videos. The first two rallies have been busts, but the third gets a hit. The group gathers around the monitor as Amanda works to confirm it. After trying a few angles, the software identifies the image with a ninety-seven percent match. Victoria didn't need a machine to tell her that it's Marx.

"What rally was this?" Rigo asks.

"One of Burgess's early ones. It was held at the same ballroom he gave his concession speech at."

"He stayed there during the primary," Victoria says. "Can we bring up the security footage and see if we can find Marx before or after the rally?"

"On it," Dennis says.

"If this pans out, I'm going to add Diego to my Christmas card list," Rigo says, leaning in to whisper in Victoria's ear.

"He knows how to get shit done," she adds.

The stress level inches up with every passing minute. After a half-hour without locating Marx, everyone is getting frustrated.

"I'm not finding anything," Dennis says, running his hands through his hair. "We know he was there, but not much more."

"Being there doesn't prove anything," Shawn says, also annoyed that such a promising lead is evaporating. "Marx was a socialist."

"Duh," Amanda says.

"SOF Marx, not Karl Marx," Shawn says. "I would expect anyone with his ideological bent to go to a Burgess rally. It's not enough to prove anything."

"Wait a second…hey, boss, I think we have something," Steve says, pointing at his monitor.

Victoria and Rigo move over to Dennis. The others get out of their chairs and gather around.

"What are we looking at?"

"It's camera footage from the hallway outside Governor Burgess's staging area."

"Staging area?" Rigo asks.

"Greenroom didn't seem right. It's a meeting room repurposed for him to wait in before the rally started and to retreat to after it was over. I watched the governor and his staff leave it before the speech started."

"When is this?" Victoria asks.

"About ten minutes after the speech ended. That's Marx, and he's standing with Isiah Burgess when the governor himself joins them."

"Interesting," Rigo mumbles.

The team watches as the governor shakes the man's hand, followed by Isiah. They both move into the staging room when another figure approaches with his back to the camera.

"Who is that?" Amanda asks.

"I don't know. They look chummy, though," Steve says as the team watches the animated conversation.

"He isn't turning to face the camera. C'mon," Dennis pleads.

Marx looks behind the man, and they abruptly end their conversation. He walks down the corridor toward the camera as the guy he was talking to enters the room.

"Whoa," Rigo says.

"Did he just walk right into the governor's staging room?" Shawn says, staring at the monitor.

"Back it up," Victoria commands. "Freeze it when he opens the door. I thought I saw a brief shot of the side of his face."

Dennis does as he's instructed. He advances it frame-by-frame until they get the perfect side view of the target.

"Should we get facial recognition?" Steve asks.

"No need," Victoria says, standing straight up and folding her arms. "That's Andrew Li."

"The consultant who's now working for Standish?" Rigo asks.

"Yup."

Victoria grabs at her neck and kicks a chair before pacing in the aisle between the workstations. The rest of the team stops what they're doing and watches her.

"What's wrong?"

"It was in front of us the whole time," Victoria says, dropping her arms and offering a distraught look.

"What do you mean?" Amanda asks.

"The cell phone number we got from Marx's device. It was the only lead we had. We used Tierra's interview to see if we could flesh out who Machiavelli was before voters went to the polls. We didn't know what would happen when that number got dialed."

"It rang Burgess's phone," Dennis says.

"Yeah, but he was surprised it rang because it wasn't his phone number. It was Andrew Li's. He's Machiavelli."

"Then why didn't Burgess deny it?" Shawn asks.

"The optics. Isiah was live on national television and might have been getting framed. The better tactic was to say nothing."

"Then why not cooperate with the authorities? If Burgess isn't Machiavelli, then he could have explained it to investigators and avoided an indictment," Steve offers.

"I don't know why, and he won't tell us. He must have a reason."

Victoria's mind starts racing. If he has a motive, she doesn't know what it could be. Most people assert their innocence before they're arrested and taken to a courthouse.

"I don't know. It's a reach, Vic," Rigo admits.

"I know it is, but on some level, it makes sense. We know what to look for now. Let's see if we can place Marx and Andrew Li together at any other events. If we find repeated meetings, we have cause to dig further."

"What are you going to do?" Rigo asks.

"Call the only other person that can help us and convince her to do something that she doesn't want to."

# CHAPTER THIRTY-EIGHT

## BRIAN COOPER

*Executive Mansion - Asheville*
*Asheville, North Carolina*

This is a beautiful spot. Brian admires the view as he steers his rental car up to the top of the mountain. This hideaway has served eleven governors and countless civic groups over the years. The split-level home on the eighteen-acre estate that is the Governor's Western Residence was almost impossible to find. Brevin didn't give him directions on purpose.

He is escorted past walls adorned with rustic artwork and rooms filled with mountain-themed furnishings to a living area on the main level. Left alone, he stares out the massive windows at the sun as it begins its descent toward the Appalachians that loom not far in the distance.

"You can see Mount Pisgah on a clear day," Colin Bradford says, entering the room wearing jeans and a casual shirt. Brevin Hawkins follows him in but remains quiet.

"It's a spectacular view. Thank you for agreeing to meet with me, Governor."

The two men shake hands, and Brian is gestured over to one of the floral-patterned sofas. He declines the offer of a drink, eager to get down to business. Brevin opts to remain along the wall, making it clear that he is not a part of this conversation.

"It was brazen to make a pitch to my campaign manager about working for me."

"I don't look at it that way, sir. We both want the same thing."

"Do we?" Governor Bradford asks, eyeing the consultant with suspicion. "I know that you despise Alicia Standish, but you have to admit that it's an odd request."

"I understand how you would view it that way. I also know that you need every advantage you can get. I have information that will provide you one."

The governor doesn't mask his annoyance. "You don't think I can beat her on my own?"

"No, sir, I don't."

Brevin scoffs. "We disagree."

"Does Monica Stengel?" Brian asks, taking a risk with the question. He doesn't know what she said to them or if they even spoke at all.

"Monica said that you aren't without your advantages. I agree with her, but your credentials aren't the problem."

"You don't know if you can trust me," Brian says, leaning forward. "I don't blame you. I wouldn't trust me either if our roles were reversed."

"Then you'll understand when I say no."

"Yes, but you don't want to do that."

The governor looks over at Brevin, who shakes his head slowly.

"Why?"

"Because you asked me to come here in person. A 'no' was easy enough to relay through Brevin. You want me to give you a reason to say yes."

"I don't think you can," Governor Bradford admits, offering a challenge.

"Pennsylvania is going to be the key state in this election."

"We know that," Brevin snaps from along the wall, suddenly wanting to participate.

"Do you want to know why Standish hasn't softened her stance on fracking? I know you must be wondering that yourselves. The oil industry is one of the state's largest employers."

"You think you know? I doubt that," Brevin says.

"The North Carolina Department of Environmental Quality authorized drilling exploratory wells for oil and gas in Cumberland, Hoke, and Scotland Counties in 2017. Those deposits would have been extracted through fracking the shale rock formations. You wrote an opinion piece for a local newspaper coming out against that."

"The samples didn't indicate the existence of oil or gas deposits," Bradford argues.

"Do you think that matters to her? To the media that support her? She won't care when Angela Mays uses this to show that you can't be trusted. Thirty-one states produce crude oil, and thirty-three produce natural gas. That's a lot of people that you'll need to explain your position to."

The governor leans back into the sofa and looks over at Brevin. His campaign manager has nothing to say now. He should have known about that article, considering the importance of the Keystone State.

"My supporters won't cast their ballot for Standish."

"She doesn't need rural voters to win. Pennsylvania is a numbers game. She only needs them not to vote."

"Why are you telling me this? Wouldn't it have made sense to hold that information as a trade for the job you want?"

Brian loves hearing buying signals. Colin Bradford is on the precipice of agreeing to this. All he needs is a nudge.

"It's only the tip of the iceberg for what I can do for you. I know Standish, and I know Angela Mays. Alicia has been plotting to win the White House for years, and I helped develop the game plan. I'm offering those insights to you in return for a consulting job. That's it. I don't want a permanent campaign position or a spot in your administration when you win. My services would be isolated and provisional. If you don't like the job I'm doing for you, fire me."

"Just like that?"

"I serve at the pleasure of the future president," Brian says, paraphrasing the line every appointee who works in the Executive Branch uses.

The governor rises from his seat. Brian does the same. All that's left to do is wait for the final verdict.

"Let me think about it. Thank you for coming down here."

The men shake hands, and Brian makes his way to the front door and his car in the driveway. It wasn't the answer he was looking for but wasn't the one he dreaded hearing either. Brevin will argue about this all night, but Colin Bradford is a smart man. He knows when he sees an offer that he can't refuse.

# CHAPTER THIRTY-NINE

## OLIVER JAHN

*Tomorrow's News Today Network Office*
*New York, New York*

Oliver is the last to enter the room. He takes his seat next to the trio of attorneys while the network brass watches from across the table. His lawyer leans over and whispers in his ear as the network lawyer fidgets. Oliver nods.

"Thank you for coming, Mr. Jahn. As your lawyer probably informed you, we are at a stalemate."

"He did. Then why am I here? My demands are non-negotiable."

"We understand your positions, Oliver," the executive says, "but you need to meet us halfway."

"Why?"

"Excuse me?"

Oliver leans forward. "Why do I have to meet you halfway?"

"Because we run a network, and there are more things to consider than just your show," one of the other executives says.

"I understand. How many shows on this network bring in the revenue that mine does?"

"That's not the issue," the man says.

"Then let's make it the issue," Oliver says, turning to the head honcho. "How many?"

"You bring in the most."

"And how many shows that air on this network cost more than ours does to produce?"

The head of the network turns to his executives. All except one refuse to look at him. He nods at the one woman who is brave enough to make eye contact.

"Eight," she says quietly.

"How many?"

"Eight."

"There are extenuating circumstances," the same obnoxious executive at the end of the table interjects.

"Like what?"

"There are more expensive costs associated with them."

"You mean salaries?" Oliver asks with a smile. "So, you are willing to pay others more even though they don't generate the revenue that TNT does?"

"The talent on those shows have bigger names," the executive continues to argue, much to the chagrin of the others.

"You saw the rankings that were published yesterday. Where did I come in?"

Oliver waits patiently but doesn't get a response. The executives all look down at the paperwork in front of them. He finally locks eyes with his sparring partner on the far end of the table.

"Go ahead, you can say it. Everyone here already knows."

"First," the man mumbles.

"That's right."

"That's only because *Capitol Beat* fell, not because you are growing your viewership," the woman says.

"We are growing it, and I will continue to do so."

"Oliver, we understand your position," the network head says, "but I'm afraid we can't meet your demands. That doesn't mean you aren't a valuable asset to our lineup for all the reasons you stated."

"Then prove it. I'm worth even more to this network than I asked for in my offer. That is my meeting you halfway. You will agree to the terms I spelled out, or I will take my number one show to a network willing to pay for this quality and ratings."

Oliver stands, although this time his three lawyers remain seated. They know there is more work to be done. His instructions to them were crystal clear.

"Let me know your decision because the clock is ticking, and my stock is on the rise. Don't miss a bargain by waiting for a steeper discount."

Oliver smiles as he walks out. He doesn't want to leave the network but isn't about to settle for less than he is due. It was risky not taking their first offer, and he is doubling down on it. He needs to make sure it pays off.

# CHAPTER FORTY

## VASSYL STRACHENKO

*The Big Dig Nightclub*
*Theater District, Boston, Massachusetts*

This nightclub looks a lot bigger when it's empty. He had almost forgotten what it was like to hang out in a place with pulsating LEDs, thumping dance music, and scantily clad women walking around with trays of shots. The trendy underground tunnel-themed hot spot in this converted basement was built to honor the Central Artery/Tunnel "Big Dig" megaproject. That undertaking turned the City of Boston into a construction site for a quarter of a century.

The Esme Hotel's owners must have been looking for ways to monetize a space best served for long-term storage of dusty boxes and old mattresses. It's cramped, claustrophobic, and loud enough to make Vassyl's ears bleed. It's also a haven for the drug dealers who can afford VIP bottle service. It escapes the assassin why anyone would spend seven hundred dollars for twenty dollars' worth of vodka.

Vassyl tracks Dimitri as he makes his way through the undulating bodies on the dance floor to a booth off to the side. A pair of henchmen stop him before Bertram Jackson waves him over. So far, so good.

Dimitri and the city's number one heroin dealer have an animated discussion. How either of them can hear over the synthesized noise coming out of the floor-to-ceiling speakers is beyond him. From the bar, Vassyl desperately tries not to pay too much attention to his associate. His eyes are on someone else taking a keen interest in the interaction.

Dimitri points at a man standing nearby. It's not much of a disguise but wasn't designed to be one. It only needed to be a credible deterrent to easy identification without making him unrecognizable. Bertram motions Ian over to the table. Vassyl needs him to be noticed for this plan to work.

The former FBI agent doesn't sit. The men shake hands before Ian gestures for the door. Dimitri and Bertram get up and follow him to the back of the club. Four men in Bertram's entourage follow closely, all probably armed despite the prohibition of weapons on the premises. It's showtime.

"Eagle is leaving the nest," Vassyl says into the microphone tucked into his sleeve. If Sven responds, he doesn't hear it in the device fitted into his ear.

After a couple of seconds, his target leaves his drink and follows them to the club's emergency exit. There was a good chance he wouldn't recognize Ian. It was fifty-fifty that he would follow the group out the door. Although Vassyl had a workable Plan B, the original is much more fulfilling.

"Prairie Dog on the move."

"*Waiting,*" Sven replies in his earpiece.

The club's back door leads to a corridor that bisects the basement. A set of stairs and a freight elevator at the far end lead to the loading dock. The passage serves as a convenient way to resupply the bar during the day. Vassyl slips into the hallway as his prey slowly moves forward. The target is keeping plenty of distance between himself and the men in front of him. It won't matter.

He passes a service entrance to the hotel's laundry. The door slowly opens, and Sven's hulking figure slips into the corridor behind him. The Swede twists his torso and swings a steel pipe hard into the back of the man's legs. There is a scream of agony as the man crashes to the ground. Sven slams the pipe into his ribs, probably breaking a few before checking with Vassyl.

The man flips onto his back and finds Vassyl's gun pointed right at his face. He freezes.

"Check him," the assassin commands.

Sven rifles through the man's pockets as Vassyl keeps his weapon trained on him. The search yielded the expected haul of identification, radio, and a concealed Glock.

"Loading dock."

Sven grabs the man and drags him up the stairs and through a set of double doors that open onto the raised concrete platform. Below, Dimitri and Ian stand with the drug dealers in a loose semi-circle where delivery trucks park. Sven tosses the man down, and he lands hard on the concrete in the middle of them.

"Who is he?" Bertram asks, looking at the man as if he were an insect as Vassyl takes the short flight of stairs down and joins them.

Vassyl holds up the badge and identification that has FBI in big blue letters for Bertram to see. "Special Agent Takara Nishimoto. He's been building a case against you for a couple of months now."

"How do ya know that?"

"It's not important."

"You'll never get away with this," Takara says, trying to climb up on all fours.

Vassyl nods at his guys, and they take turns pummeling the agent with blows to the head and kicks to the abdomen. He holds a hand up when Takara coughs up blood. The agent has plenty of fight left, but his body isn't in a condition to cooperate.

"We owe you for dis," Bertram says.

"Maybe someday. You aren't going to want to be around for what happens next. You should leave the club through the main entrance and make a show of it."

The drug dealer nods, and Bertram and his associates exit the way they came. Dimitri pulls out his phone and starts recording once the drug kingpin and his goons clear out of the loading dock. Vassyl circles Takara before pulling him up to his knees. All the planning for this mission has paid off. Now he gets to enjoy the moment.

"Your friends outside will begin wondering what happened to you, so time is short. You have a lot of questions. There is only one answer."

Ian circles into Takara's view and stands in front of him with his arms crossed. The man's unswollen eye narrows in recognition.

"It is you," he whispers.

"You remember me! I feel so special," Ian says, placing his hands over his heart. "Why now?"

"So many questions. It's what I always hated about the Bureau."

Vassyl smirks as he hands him the agent's gun. Ian does a press check to ensure a round is chambered. Satisfied, he holds it down at his side.

"Your question should answer itself, Special Agent Nishimoto. So long as one man lives to wield the Sword of Freedom, tyrants and despots shall never be safe. Long live the S-O-F."

Ian smiles as Takara stares at him. In one swift motion, the former agent raises the weapon and fires a single shot into his former mentor's head.

# CHAPTER FORTY-ONE

## TIERRA CAMPOS

*Capitol Beat Network Offices*
*Washington, D.C.*

This is not the kind of meeting to show up early for. The conference room is already filled with players from legal, human resources, and the production staff when I walk in. Wilson watches me as I take my seat next to him and fold my hands on the table in front of me.

"You ready for this?" Wilson asks.

"As ready as I'll ever be."

I took Brian Cooper's advice and stitched together my defense against DeAnna's accusation. Then I memorized all of it. The exercise smacked of final exam week in college. My argument with Josh was the only respite I got. The damage from that fallout will be one more thing I need to patch up when this is over.

DeAnna enters the room and takes a seat without acknowledging anyone. I expected to see some hint of emotion on her face but find none. I expected anything from sadness to joy, but the woman is impassive when she locks her eyes on me across the table.

"You can't seem to follow simple instructions."

"I have reasons for not following them," I say, mustering every ounce of confidence I have.

"I'm not interested in hearing them."

"You should be," I snap, causing her to cock her head. "We're talking about setting a dangerous precedent. Is apologizing every time we ask hard or uncomfortable questions the future of doing the news at this network? Is that what we want reporting in this country to be? I treated Senator Veach with a level of respect commensurate with his position. It was not a smear campaign, nor was it an attempt to do anything other than address legitimate questions and hold him accountable for his responses. I did nothing—"

"Save it, Tierra," DeAnna barks, holding up a hand. "There's no need to waste anyone's time with a discussion about what you did wrong, nor do you need to bore us with your sob story. I demanded that you apologize, and you refused. You're fired. Brock, have security escort her to the door."

Two men in security uniforms enter almost immediately. They must have been waiting outside the conference room. So much for mounting a staunch defense and showing strength to DeAnna. Josh was right. This result was a foregone conclusion.

Nothing I said here would have made any difference. It's the same thing that happened at WWDC when they fired me.

The men stand behind me as I rise from my chair and straighten my jacket. Wilson also stands in solidarity.

"Wilson, remain here," DeAnna commands, expecting his reaction. "We need to talk about the show's new direction."

"DeAnna I…" She narrows her eyes and stares intently at him. He looks over at me and frowns before turning back to DeAnna. "Okay."

That one four-letter word turns my world upside down. Since my first broadcast on the *Capitol Beat* set, I have always felt that Wilson was there for me. Now, when I need him most, he has turned his back. I can't help but feel betrayed, and the hollowness of it haunts me as I'm escorted from the building. The two guards return to their posts as I stand on another sidewalk outside another employer's office. The feeling of déjà vu is eerie.

People walk past me, oblivious to the pain I feel in my heart. I got my wish. I'm invisible again.

"You look like you're having a rough day," a familiar voice calls out from behind me. I turn to see Austin leaning up against the building's façade. I guess I'm not so invisible after all.

"You're the last person I want to talk to."

I turn and step off the curb. Screw the crosswalks. I need to get away from Austin and away from this place. I feel a hand grab my arm and yank me backward—the woosh of air and the sensation of something screaming past me register before the realization does. The bus only missed me by inches. I take a deep breath, knowing that my life very nearly ended.

"A bad day is no reason to commit suicide," Austin scolds.

"I…I never saw it," I say, staring down at my shaking hands. "Thank you."

"I'd say it was no big deal, but I just kinda saved your life. I'll let you pay off your life debt by buying me coffee. Come on. You need someone to talk to, even if it's me."

Part of me wants to argue, but Austin is right – on both accounts. We walk down the street in silence. It's not as awkward as it would have been had I not almost become a hood ornament. I appreciate the opportunity to regain control over my jitters. By the time we sit down with our drinks, my thoughts have shifted back from being roadkill to getting fired.

"How did you find me?" I ask before I take a sip.

"The news business is small, Tierra. You know that. Everyone knew what was happening in that conference room."

"Is this you gloating? Are you going to say that it would have always come to this and that I should never have left *Front Burner*?"

"Oh, God no. I gave you every reason in the world to leave."

"So…you want me to come back? Is that why you're here?"

Austin stares out the window. "Even if I did, there's nothing for you to come back to. *Front Burner* is dying a slow death. I'm here as the friend that I should've been all along. I can't tell you how sorry I am for that. The right words escape me."

I narrow my eyes. "And you came to this realization on your own?"

"As usual, I had help from a rather aggressive blond."

"You talked to Victoria," I say, smirking.

"Yeah, I asked her out on a date."

"It's about damn time. What did she say?"

"She didn't say no. Then she left for Boston. Victoria did take the time to point out that it's my fault that you ostracized your friends."

"I did no such thing," I argue.

"Are you sure about that?" Austin asks, taking a sip of his brew before replacing it on the table. "Logan still talks to Tyler. He told me about what happened at the wine bar. Victoria also told me about the terse conversation you had with her."

"That had nothing to do with any of this," I say, dismissing the comment. "Victoria's up there investigating the SOF. She thinks that Isiah may not be Machiavelli."

Austin leans back in his chair. He uses that particular body language when he is about to say something that I won't like. We may not have worked together for long, but he has more tells than a lousy poker player.

"Victoria is convinced of it now. What do you think?"

"That I'm unemployed and don't much care."

"Yeah, you do. You're one of the most dedicated journalists I've ever met. You want the truth to come out above all else."

"Tell that to Oliver Jahn," I moan.

"Screw him. Cancel culture came for both of us. We can sit here and whine about it or seize the opportunity it presents."

"What? To work together?"

My tone was more hostile than intended. Despite that, I'm not sure I would ever want to go down that path with Austin again. The way he treated me before I left last February was a personal betrayal that I'm not willing to ignore.

"Victoria thinks that Andrew Li is Machiavelli. She needs you to talk to Isiah and confirm that."

I shake my head. "That's why she returned your call about the date…and why you're here now."

"No. It was a reason to see you, not *the* reason. You have every excuse in the world to tell me to go pound sand. The way I acted…well, I can't say I wouldn't do the same if our roles were reversed. I knew you would need to talk to someone, and I desperately wanted to give you the apology I should have a long time ago."

"Then why didn't you?"

"I don't know. I was afraid you would leave *Front Burner*. Then I pushed you out the door and convinced myself that I did the right thing. It took time to realize just how wrong I was. I don't want you to fall into the same trap. Please don't take it out on Victoria, Tyler, or Olivia. Friends that you can count on aren't a dime a dozen — they're more valuable than gold."

I turn the coffee cup on the table several times. He's right. I may not have deserved the treatment I got from Austin, but they didn't deserve the cold shoulder they got from me after leaving *Front Burner.* That's for another time. What Victoria needs is more pressing.

"I'm not sure I have the money to get out to Chicago now. I already live in an apartment that I'm not sure I can afford."

"Victoria said the FBI would fly you out on one of their planes if needed. She will make the arrangements if you agree to meet with Isiah."

"What do you get out of this?"

"The first step in atoning for a mistake that cost me a colleague and a friend."

"That's it?"

"It's more than enough."

I finish my coffee and grab my purse. As if I didn't already have enough on my mind, Austin has given me a lot to think about. I stop and look back at him.

"Have Victoria make the arrangements. Maybe we can talk some more when I get back."

Austin smiles. "I'd like that."

# CHAPTER FORTY-TWO

## BRIAN COOPER

*Jefferson Memorial*
*Washington, D.C.*

Brian is not used to idle time. Washington politics is a rat race through a never-ending maze. The most successful people in this town are workaholics. Despite taking countless meetings to lay the groundwork to get off the bench and back into the game, it takes only a fraction of the time he's used to spending with his extensive network of contacts.

The downtime has given him plenty of opportunities to walk and think. Today's sojourn took him down the National Mall, past the MLK and FDR memorials, and across the Ohio Drive Bridge to the Jefferson Memorial. This is one of his favorite monuments in Washington. Families and tourists still mill about, but not in numbers seen at the Lincoln Memorial. The walk to the south side of the tidal basin is far enough to deter many pedestrians from making the trek. That doesn't stop tour buses from discharging large groups of camera-wielding tourists, but the grounds never seem busy to him.

Brian admires the third president of the United States and author of the Declaration of Independence, but has little in common with him. Jefferson was a powerful advocate of liberty, once writing in a private letter, "I have sworn upon the altar of God eternal hostility against every form of tyranny over the mind of man." Brian thinks that such notions smack of naiveté. By its very nature, government exercises tyranny over people's minds. So do politicians. It's how they get elected.

The two men do have one thing in common: like Brian, Jefferson was eloquent in his correspondence but a lousy public speaker. His pen, not his voice, was his weapon. Brian thinks of himself in the same light, which is why he's content operating behind the scenes. That's if he can get back into the show at all.

The wait is eating at him. The rest of his life may be riding on a decision he can no longer influence. He made a compelling case to Colin Bradford, but he knows that Brevin Hawkins is dead-set against hiring him. Colin trusts his campaign manager implicitly. Not having his support is a formidable obstacle to maneuver around.

There is a myriad of debilitating psychological states that hold people back. Self-doubt is among the worst of them. Brian has spent his career casting aside misgivings about what is possible to reach ever-higher goals. To him, doubt is a cancer that will metastasize and destroy everything it touches. For the first time in years, he feels it creeping in.

Brian's phone rings and he checks the caller id. The wait is over…he's about to find out whether there were reasons to doubt himself.

"Hello, Brevin. I was beginning to wonder if I would hear from you before Election Day."

"If it were my choice, you wouldn't have. I'd let you twist in the wind while I told anyone who would listen the multitude of reasons you should never work on a campaign again."

"Thank you. I appreciate your willingness to stab me in the chest instead of the back," Brian says.

"Unfortunately, I can't do either. I underestimated you, Cooper. I never thought you could convince Colin of your worth."

"The governor agreed?"

"Yes, against my counsel," Brevin admits. "We have a rally tomorrow in Scranton. It's only about a four-hour drive, so I expect you to be there. I will have someone text you the details."

Brian can't resist smiling. The self-doubt has disappeared. He is the former chief of staff and campaign chairman of the Democratic candidate for president. Now he's working for her opponent at the highest level. It may not be a first, but it's unheard of in modern politics.

"You could try sounding a little happier about this, Brevin. I want to work with you, not against you."

Brevin scoffs. "That remains to be seen. I don't trust you, Cooper. The governor shouldn't either, but he's willing to give you a chance."

"One that I will not squander."

"We'll see. Understand that you're on a short leash. If you so much as cough in a manner that I don't like, you're out. Am I clear?"

"Perfectly."

Brian does understand. Campaign managers are trusted to make decisions about personnel unless they are overridden by the candidate. That's what happened in Brian's case. Brevin can't fire him without Colin Bradford's blessing. He just can't give the governor a reason to.

"Good. See you tomorrow."

The call disconnects. Brian pockets his phone and climbs the stairs up to the monument. He stops in front of the bronze statue of a man whose accomplishments he could never match. Not that he's worried about trying. Brian has never longed to be immortalized in bronze. His mission is to make damn sure that Alicia Standish isn't either.

# CHAPTER FORTY-THREE

## SSA VICTORIA LARSEN

*The Esme Hotel Loading Dock*
*Theater District, Boston, Massachusetts*

Rigo pulls the SUV up behind a line of Boston Police vehicles, all of which have their strobes on. Victoria jumps out and heads to the yellow police tape cordon even before he jams it in park. She flashes her badge and walks under the partially opened rolling door of the dock.

Several uniforms and Boston PD detectives are watching a forensics team go about its work. One man is up on a ladder inspecting a camera affixed to the corner of the loading dock. Victoria trains her eyes on the white sheet covering a body in the middle of the lower concrete pad. She begins shaking as she approaches the body.

"You don't want to see that, Victoria," Seth says, rushing over to stop her.

"Let me go, Seth!"

"Victoria, trust me—"

She fights against the muscular detective, and he puts her in a bear hug as she breaks down in tears. Seth presses her head against his chest as she sobs. The men in the room don't offer disparaging looks or mock her in any way. Victoria knows every man in this room, and they know all about her legendary toughness. It's a rare moment of vulnerability in a woman that any one of them would trust with their life.

"What happened?" Victoria asks, regaining her composure and wiping the tears from her eyes.

"He was on his knees and shot in the forehead."

"Takara was executed?"

"It looks that way."

Victoria looks around the loading dock. His death in a raging gunfight would have been easier for her to handle. Takara deserved better than to die on his knees in this horrible place.

"What was he doing here?"

"Surveillance on a drug kingpin named Bertram Johnson," one of the FBI agents says as he joins them. "I was on his support team outside when it happened. Bertram is the number one heroin dealer in the city. We were cataloging his activities, accomplices, and associates."

"So, he's the prime suspect," Victoria concludes.

"Actually, he's not. We already know where to start looking."

Victoria doesn't need to ask the next question. Seth grimaces and removes a second tarp adjacent to Takara's body. The letters "SOF" are scrawled with bright red spray paint in block letters. Rigo comes up alongside Victoria and stares at the message as if E.T. wrote it in alien hieroglyphs.

"Son of a bitch," he mumbles.

"There's more," Seth says with a sigh, looking down. "I don't know how to say this."

"Just spit it out."

"Lance Fuller was found dead in his house an hour ago."

Victoria rocks back on her heels. That's not what she expected him to say. She closes her eyes and lets the information burn into her soul.

"We're keeping it quiet for the moment. Fuller didn't pick up his phone when the office called to inform him about Takara. After attempts to reach him failed, someone in Chelsea dispatched an agent to his house. They found him slumped over his kitchen table, killed with a garrote."

"Why didn't his wife report it?"

The agent joins Seth in looking at his shoes, and the reality of what happened hits Victoria with the force of a freight train.

"His wife and two children were found shot in the upstairs master bedroom."

Victoria puts her hands on her head and walks away. She's losing the second battle with her tears and doesn't want the men here to see her cry again. She never liked Lance Fuller. He was a pompous administrator who never appreciated how hard fieldwork was. Despite her difference with him, he didn't deserve that. Neither did his family.

"There was a calling card left there," Seth says when she makes her way back to the small gathering. "SOF was spray-painted on the table next to his head. It was probably from the same spray paint can."

"Someone has declared war on the FBI," the agent says.

"It was Ian Drucker."

"Or other members of the SOF that we missed," Seth adds.

"No, it was Ian. This was personal."

"He killed two FBI agents back-to-back in separate locations? No way," the agent argues.

"Unless he had help," Seth surmises as Victoria stares at the camera in the corner.

"What's the word on that?" she asks, pointing.

"Disabled," Seth says. "The cord is cut. Hotel security says it went down yesterday. They have a work order in to replace it."

"What are you thinking, Vic?" Rigo asks.

"This wasn't a random location. They chose this spot, which means planning and surveillance. They probably also knew Fuller's routine."

"Seth, see if you can get all the security footage from this hotel for the last week. One of them must have seen something. You, go back to the office and pull Fuller's itinerary. Check the video from the parking lots. If someone was tailing him, maybe they caught something," Rigo instructs the agent.

"Already in the works," he says.

Victoria is lost in thought when Rigo touches her arm, startling her. "We need to get you out of Boston."

"No chance. I'm not leaving."

"Vic, if Ian can get Fuller and Nishimoto, we have to assume you're a target."

"I don't care. I'm not going to run from that prick. We have a job to do, and that means finding Ian Drucker and putting him down once and for all."

Victoria spins and ducks back under the loading dock door on her way out. Seth and Rigo share a look. Lined up in Victoria's sights is the last place either of them would want to be. She's on a mission now and will see this out to the bitter end. There is nothing anyone can do or say that will deter her.

# CHAPTER FORTY-FOUR

## VASSYL STRACHENKO

*Interstate 90 Westbound*
*South of Erie, Pennsylvania*

Vassyl stares out the window and lets his mind wander. There isn't much else to do. He doesn't need the vehicle's navigation when getting to Chicago from Boston is this easy. He steered the car onto Interstate 90, knowing that in fifteen hours, depending on rest breaks, he'll be standing in front of the Willis Tower.

The journey will be beautiful but excruciatingly dull. The trip has already taken them across Massachusetts and north of the finger lakes to Buffalo. Now in Pennsylvania, he will continue down the Lake Erie shoreline through Cleveland, passing south of Toledo and then cutting across very northern Indiana. The interstate then curls up around the southern tip of Lake Michigan, and they'll be there. It would have been much easier if they could have flown.

Vassyl pulls out his smokes and sparks one with his Zippo before opening the window. He glances over at Ian, who is crashed out in the passenger seat. Lucky bastard. Yesterday was a long day, but he still won't chance Ian driving a leg of the journey. The consequence of that decision is a constant fight against the drowsiness determined to overtake him. The adrenaline dump into his bloodstream last night has brought on a heightened feeling of fatigue. The faster he gets this trip over with, the better.

He flicks the cigarette out the window after sucking it down to the filter, returning his thoughts to what lies ahead. The instructions were vague, as they often are. He would prefer to get to Chicago quickly and rest while he awaits clarification than take his time and have to hurry when it finally comes.

"Oh, shit," Vassyl says, noticing the pulsating red and blue strobes atop a slate-gray Pennsylvania State Police SUV in his mirror.

The reason for the stop is apparent when he sees his speed. Losing focus in his line of work can get you killed or land you in prison. He may have just done the latter.

"Look alive, Ian," Vassyl barks as he turns on his emergency flashers and guides their car to the shoulder.

"What?"

"We have a problem."

"What did you do?"

"It doesn't matter."

The trooper pulls up behind them and sits in his vehicle as Vassyl kills the engine. He must be running the rental car's plate. It will come back clean, so that's the least of his concerns. Next to him is a man atop the FBI's Ten Most Wanted list.

"What do you want to do?" Ian asks.

"Follow my lead. If there are two troopers, you're responsible for the partner. Don't let them see your weapon until I make a move."

"How will I know?"

Vassyl turns and looks at him. "When I shoot this one in the head."

The trooper knocks on the window, standing to the side of the window so an assailant can't get off a clear shot. Vassyl notices that he has his hand on his gun. And people wonder why everyone feels threatened by the police.

"Good afternoon, sir."

"License, registration, and proof of insurance."

Vassyl complies without protest. The fake identification he is carrying is the best money can buy, but his identity won't hold up to much scrutiny.

"A rental?" the trooper asks, checking the paperwork the assassin handed him.

"Yeah, I didn't want to add the miles to my BMW."

The man eyes the base model sedan. "This is hardly the ultimate driving machine."

"Tell me about it," Vassyl moans.

"Then why are you driving it that way? The posted speed limit is sixty-five. I clocked you going eighty-one."

"Yeah, that sounds about right," Vassyl says to the surprise of the trooper. "I got punchy driving through upstate New York. I wasn't paying attention to my speedometer like I should have been."

"Where are you going, sir?"

"Chicago. We left Boston early this morning."

"Long drive. You could have flown."

"I would have, but my friend here is aviophobic. You'd have to knock him out like B.A. on the A-Team to get him on a plane. He also can't drive for shit. Thus, here we are," Vassyl says, gesturing around him.

The trooper smiles and stares down at the paperwork in his hands. Vassyl glances at Ian sliding his hand down to his side, and warns him off with his eyes. There is no reason to panic yet.

"All right, Mr. Beane, I'm going to let you off with a warning. Just slow it down. I want you to get to the Windy City in one piece. The troopers in Ohio won't be as forgiving if you speed through their state."

"I will, thank you, sir," Vassyl says as the trooper hands his paperwork back. He rolls up the window and feels himself breathe for the first time since the interaction started. One good look at Ian, and this would have gone much differently.

"You know that I flew all the time in the military, right?" Ian asks.

"He didn't know that," Vassyl says, starting the engine and checking his mirror to merge back into traffic.

"If the assassin gig gets old, you have a bright future as a con man."

Vassyl pulls out and accelerates, sure to mind his speed. A simple mistake almost cost him. Even if they have escaped the officer, they would have had to deal with a manhunt, and would never make it to Chicago when Robespierre wants them there.

He peers out his window with a newfound determination. With two successes under his belt, this is no time to get sloppy. They are too close to their goal.

# CHAPTER FORTY-FIVE

## OLIVER JAHN

*Bryant Park*
*New York, New York*

Oliver stares at his watch as he dabs his brow. He dressed down today, but it's still hot and humid in New York. There is no heat like city heat. Places like Phoenix may push the mercury up the thermometer more than the Northeast does, but the urban heat island makes high temperatures feel more oppressive.

While he hates it when people are late, Oliver at least picked a nice place to wait. Situated behind the New York Public Library to the west, Bryant Park is a lovely green space that serves as a retreat for city denizens and tourists alike. The park distinguishes itself by hosting a relentless free entertainment schedule during the summer, including outdoor movies on Monday night that draw large crowds. In the winter, an ice skating rink surrounded by pop-up shops draws big crowds during the holidays.

"I expected to meet in some parking garage," his photographer says, parking himself in a green iron chair across the small table from Oliver.

"I'm a television personality, not a covert agent."

"Then why not do this on the phone? Why force me to take the Acela up here and then face a three-and-a-half-hour trip back to Washington?"

"I missed your face," Oliver says, holding his hands out and shrugging.

"Oliver, I know you're a clown on television, but I don't see any cameras around, so cut the crap."

"You're no fun."

"You wouldn't be either."

Oliver disagrees but doesn't say anything. He's made the trip to Washington, D.C. dozens of times on the Amtrak's Acela and Northeast Corridor trains, and doesn't remember ever whining about it. It's not like he's up in the engine running the damn thing.

"You're here because I want to discuss expanding our business relationship face-to-face."

"Expanding it?" the photog asks, his facing contorting at hearing something unexpected. "As in growing it?"

"That is one of the traditionally accepted definitions of the word, yes."

"Oliver, I'm a one-man shop. You hired me to take pictures of a subject."

"And paid you handsomely for it," Oliver interjects, sensing he is about to get a long-winded excuse as to why he won't consider this request.

"Yes, and I have done my level best to do what you asked. But that's where this ends. I cannot expand my business."

"Cannot, or will not?"

"Is there a difference?"

"Absolutely. One implies impossibility, while the other is the consequence of a choice. I cannot fly like Superman. I will not jump out of a perfectly good airplane."

"You're growing more arrogant and pretentious by the day," the photographer mumbles.

"Thank you. The Campos pictures are great, but I need more."

"There are only so many shots I can get unless you want me to barge into her apartment and take pictures of her in the shower."

Oliver smiles. "You were a card-carrying member of the paparazzi before you opened your studio, right?"

"Forget it."

"Good, because that's not at all what I'm asking. I have different targets I want the same coverage of."

"Just pictures?" he asks warily.

"You're no more of a secret agent than I am. Just pictures and postings to the site. That's the deal."

"What are you doing with these?"

"That's not your concern," Oliver answers immediately, expecting the question.

"It is when I'm taking them."

"Are you doing anything illegal? Are any of them on private property, or are they all in public spaces with no expectation of privacy?"

"You know the answer to that," the photographer snaps. "I can ask you the same question."

"Candid shots in public places aren't something you blackmail people with, if that's what you're asking. Can you do it? You must have friends that don't mind making some extra cash."

The mention of money gets his attention. Oliver knew it would. Paparazzi don't stalk celebrities because they are fanboys. They want money shots, and the more salacious, the better. It's not the line of work you go into unless you're a money-grubbing whore.

"How much?"

Oliver reaches into his pants pocket and hands him a folded bank check. "That's the down payment. I will arrange for more when I see results."

The photographer can't hide his surprise when he unfolds it and sees an amount more than double his initial payment. "What are the targets?"

"Get me the people first. We'll talk then."

Oliver stands and walks away from his table, enjoying Bryant Park before he leaves it to return to the concrete jungle of 42nd Street. He has no doubt that his photographer will play ball. The key to poker isn't playing your cards but those of your opponents.

When they aren't holding much, they can be forced from the game. The hard part is knowing when to raise and by how much. Oliver just did.

# CHAPTER FORTY-SIX

## BRIAN COOPER

*The Keystone State Hotel & Suites*
*Scranton, Pennsylvania*

Brian stares at the news report on the television. It's more than a distraction from the awkward silence coming from the staff assembled in the governor's suite. He expected that they wouldn't have much to say to him. No, this report hits closer to home and has his undivided attention.

"The murdered agents are identified as Special Agent in Charge Lance Fuller, head of the Federal Bureau of Investigation's Boston Division, and Supervisory Special Agent Takara Nishimoto. Fuller, his wife, and his two children were found murdered in their Somerville home. Nishimoto was working a case at the Big Dig Nightclub and was found dead on the Esme Hotel's loading dock above the local hotspot.

"Authorities have no leads in the case and have yet to confirm whether they are related. The murders come as the division is still reeling from its handling of the Brockhampton school massacre investigation. Its reputation has also been tarnished by the manhunt for one of its agents accused of being a co-conspirator in the Burgess campaign firebombings last winter. Reporting from the Esme Hotel in Boston, I'm Jasmine Adams, WBOS News."

"We thank our local affiliate for that report," the morning news anchor says. "There is another high-profile divorce rocking Hollywood this morning as—"

"You know those guys?" Colin Bradford asks, toweling off from his workout downstairs in the hotel's small fitness center.

"I'm sorry, Governor. I didn't hear you come in," Brian says, caught off-guard. "No, I didn't know them. I know someone who's friends with someone who did."

"You are nothing if not well-connected. I'm going to say a few words about it at the rally. Do you think that's a good idea?"

Brian takes a quick look around the room and sees every set of eyes staring at him. The test is starting early this morning.

"It's appropriate. What else are you planning on talking about?"

"Brevin put together a hit list of Standish's support for bills that weaken law enforcement. She has a weak record on crime during her time in the Senate. We figured that was a good place to start in Pennsylvania."

Brian is only half-listening. He is still thinking about the report on television. It's precisely what he thought it would be: bland. The media reported the story, and now they want it to quickly die.

"Snap out of it, Cooper! We hired you for your input, not your mopey silence."

Colin shakes his head at his chief of staff. Brevin scowls and checks the messages on his phone.

"Did you hear the tenor of that report, Governor?"

"Yeah, it was better than they usually are."

"Only because they didn't have an agenda to push. Fuller was white. Nishimoto was Asian, and neither ranks high on the intersectional scale. If either had been black, this would dominate the news for a week."

"That's a cynical view," Bradford says, uncapping a bottle of water and taking a sip.

"It's also the truth. This race isn't against Alicia Standish. It's against the media. Your tactics not only need to counter her moves but account for how news organizations portray them."

"We need them on our side," Brevin argues.

"They will never be on our side. If that's your goal, you'll get crushed."

"What do you suggest, Brian?" Colin asks as Brevin shakes his head.

"I'm working on it."

"Bunch of nonsense," the campaign manager mutters.

"Is it, Brevin? This was a Boston news report, and the reporter tried to color this as business as usual. It's not. The murder of two FBI agents in cold blood within hours of each other *is* the story. It sounds like a coordinated effort, yet there was nothing more than a passing mention of it. Instead, she focused on the Bureau's involvement in Brockhampton and the New Hampshire Primary. Social media trolls will interpret that as a signal that these FBI agents deserved to die because they did something wrong."

"That sounds like a PR problem for the FBI. What does this have to do with us?" the governor asks.

"Sir, everything you say and do will be reported the same way. Every statement you make against Alicia Standish and the Democrats will be characterized by her allies in the media as decisive and inflammatory. Even if every word you utter is backed with facts and one hundred percent accurate, reporters and pundits will dismiss it as catering to your base while trying to divide the country."

"Do you expect me not to go after her?"

"No, you need to. But it has to be done using the right issue at the right time, or it will boomerang back on you. If you choose to charge up this hill now, you'll die on it. Standish will deflect your attacks, and the media will circle the wagons. Then she'll seize control of another news cycle by using something in your background against you. That will become the story."

"There isn't anything she can use against me," Colin says reflexively.

"You've been governor for seven years. There is. More than one thing, actually."

The governor stares at Brian, wondering what he knows and growing more comfortable with the decision to hire him. Every politician has skeletons in the closet. The most prominent ones have entire graveyards. Colin is somewhere in between.

"What do you want me to do?"

Brevin throws his hands in the air. "Governor, the speech is locked in. I—"

"Brian? What do you advise that I do?"

"Talk about crime in America like you planned. Don't mention Standish at all."

"What?" Brevin practically shouts.

"Make it about criminals and why people are forced to turn to a life of crime. Outline your policies that will make America a safer place, bolster law enforcement, reduce the prison recidivism rate, and create opportunities for crime-ridden communities. Be positive and upbeat by the end. Don't mention Standish at all."

Brevin is beside himself. He storms up to Brian and sticks a finger in his chest. There was no doubt that the suggestion would be controversial. Brian knew that the campaign manager would push back hard. This is something else. The real reason for Brevin's outburst is that he feels his influence over the candidate beginning to slip away.

"You want to get zero coverage out of this?"

"For now, yes. Any coverage you get will likely be negative. If you do it my way, Standish will get frustrated and make a tactical error. Then you can go after her."

"How do you know?" the governor asks, weighing his options.

"Patience was never her virtue. She is expecting you to be aggressive. I have no doubt that Angela Mays's whole strategy is centered around counterpunches."

"What if you're wrong, Brian?"

"We had this conversation, sir. Play it my way for a couple of weeks. If what I say doesn't pan out, I know where the door is."

"We don't have two weeks to spend in Fantasyland," Brevin argues.

The governor walks over to the window. With rare exceptions, most people who win their party's nomination get only one chance to make it to the White House. There are no mulligans at this level. The decision may be the most important one he's made in his life.

# CHAPTER FORTY-SEVEN

## TIERRA CAMPOS

*Anacostia Riverwalk Trail*
*Navy Yard, Washington, D.C.*

I do my stretching at the entrance to the Yards off Water Street. This is a section of the Anacostia Riverfront Trail, a paved walkway that stretches nineteen miles between the Tidal Basin and Bladensburg Marina Park in Maryland. It's an excellent place for a jog, and countless people use the trail to bike-ride, walk their dogs, or take a casual stroll.

Exercise provides two things that I need right now: time to reflect on everything that has gone wrong and physical exertion to forget it for a spell. Cooper's advice, while good-intentioned, was way off base. And then there's Wilson. Not only did he fail to back me up in that conference room, but he also hasn't even bothered to call me since. We were friends. At least I thought we were.

That's what hurts the most. The cancel culture has taken my job, but I never thought it would cost me a friendship. It has done just that, and all over a few interview questions that I not only had the right but the responsibility to ask. It's what any good journalist would have done. Maybe that's the problem – nobody knows what good journalism is anymore.

I start my warm-up walk through the trees and wavy benches in the Yards. I pop in my wireless earbuds and crank up some music. As I reach the water, I turn them off and look around. Something feels wrong. There are people exercising and families with their children, but nothing out of the ordinary. I'm getting paranoid. I start my jog at the Yard-Park Bridge and head west down the trail. When I reach the long boardwalk that runs along the river, I glance behind me.

Seven kids are there, all jogging. That wouldn't usually be out of the ordinary except that they aren't in workout clothes, and every one of them is staring intently at me. I feel a tingling sensation in my shoulders, and it isn't from the exercise. It's the creepy feeling I get watching horror movies when something terrible is about to happen.

My thoughts return to what happened on the metro platform. I don't want a repeat of that incident, and I scan my surroundings. There are people around, so I don't feel like I'm in any real physical danger. That really isn't the point. I came here to think and escape life for a while. This is not the time or place for a confrontation with some jackasses getting programmed by a media determined to bury me.

I glance back again and see that the kids are gaining on me. That won't do, and I pick up the pace. My feet hit the planks and immediately pop back. I'm flying now, not at a dead sprint, but something close. My lungs begin to burn as they crave more and more oxygen.

The hoard behind me picks up their speed as well. They may have youth on their side, but I'm determined not to let them catch me. That and they don't look like the fittest bunch I have ever seen. Not that I'm in the best of it myself.

I stride past HQO, the ultramodern O Street headquarters of DC Water. I see the end of the trail past the boat rentals ahead and push myself into a dead sprint. My breathing is even more labored, but the adrenaline that comes from being chased propels me forward as much as my legs do.

At the four-way intersection to the left are a dock and a dead end. Straight ahead is an apartment building with shops on the bottom floor. If their thoughts are to harass me, that won't be much of a deterrent. I break to the right and join red-and-white-clad throngs of people moving in every direction. Thank God for Nationals home games.

I do my best to lose myself in the crowd. The pink workout shirt I'm wearing stands out, so I duck behind a vendor selling Nats gear.

"How much for a woman's small tee and a hat?"

"Forty-five."

I pull out a fifty that I keep for emergencies from the clip behind my phone.

"Keep the change," I say, quickly donning the shirt and letting my hair out of its ponytail before sticking the hat on my head.

I head off past the front of the stadium while forcing myself not to stand out by looking around. I act like any other fan going to a game. The bump causes me to jump at the shock of it.

"I'm sorry," a man says, holding his hands up to show he meant no offense.

"I told you to get your nose out of that phone and watch where you were going!" his girlfriend says, chastising him.

"Yeah, babe, I know."

I keep walking, hoping my heart settles back into my chest. Some college-age fans are in front of me, and I tuck in behind them to make the group look one person bigger than it is. To my relief, they continue walking around the far side of the stadium. No longer being able to resist the urge, I turn my head to see if I can spot my pursuers. They are nowhere in sight. I want to keep it that way.

I walk up S Capitol Street toward M and get on my phone to order a rideshare. It will be a short ride home, but it's the safest option for me right now. There is no doubt that the punks know where I live, so I'm not about to risk heading home on foot. I'm beginning to wonder if this is going to become a common thing. Cancel culture has driven me from my job. Now they want to make me a prisoner in my own home. I need to get out of this town for a while.

# CHAPTER FORTY-EIGHT

## SSA VICTORIA LARSEN

*Lexington Common National Historic Site*
*Lexington, Massachusetts*

Victoria stands in Lexington Common, trying to imagine what it looked like on April 19, 1775. She can't picture it without a reference, and settles for knowing that it was far different from what she sees around her today. Despite the progress, this is still hallowed ground.

She is no history scholar but remembers learning that the first shots were fired here in the cause of American independence. Seventy-seven militiamen faced off against nearly ten times that number of British Regulars, ending in eight Lexington men's deaths. The Redcoats moved on to Concord and the Old North Bridge to find staunch resistance from several thousand farmer-soldiers who would drive the Redcoats back to Boston and place the city under siege. Victoria smiles. That's what happens when you piss off Americans.

Lexington is only a thirty-three-minute drive from the Chelsea office, taking the scenic route. It was an odd place for her to come, but anything beats the stifling atmosphere of that conference room. That, and she wasn't given much choice.

"You should go through Minuteman National Park up to Concord and see the Old North Bridge," Seth says as he comes up beside her wearing jeans and a polo shirt. "It's a great place to visit on a beautiful day like today. You might want to dress down a bit for it."

Victoria subconsciously checks her own pantsuit, which is a bit too much for this hot, sunny day.

"I'm not in the mood for sightseeing, let alone dressed for it."

"Then what are you doing here? I'm a little shocked that they let you stay in Boston under the circumstances."

"I didn't give Rigo a choice. I'm not running from Ian Drucker."

"Except to Lexington."

Victoria sighs. "I was sent away for a while to clear my head."

The explanation causes Seth to belly laugh. "Okay, let me guess the real story: you were ripping people's heads off in the office, so Rigoberto sent you out before he had a mutiny on his hands."

"Yeah." Victoria needs to remember that she will never get much past Seth. He's as sharp a detective as you will ever find.

"We've all been there. I would have expected you to walk around on the Charles River waterfront or something. You don't strike me as the nerdy history buff type."

"I'm not. I did a paper on Lexington and Concord in college. It stuck. I found something romantic in the notion that a militia made up of farmers and everyday colonists would be brave enough to stand toe-to-toe with the most feared professional army in the world."

"It didn't work out so well for them here."

"No, but it was the British who had to run for their lives back to Boston when the day was over. Four years later, Lord General Cornwallis surrendered at Yorktown to a man the British didn't think was worthy of a commission two decades prior."

"George Washington."

Victoria nods. "Tierra agreed to travel to Chicago to meet with Isiah. The half of Rigo's team still in Washington is setting it up."

"What changed her mind?" Seth asks, not missing a beat following the quick change of subject.

"She didn't get specific, but something has her spooked down there."

"I figured it has to do with her being canceled. The stuff I've seen online is brutal."

"Probably," Victoria says, nodding. "Things haven't been right for us since I came back into the Bureau."

"You know, it's still weird to think that a federal agent is BFFs with a journalist."

"It just kinda happened."

The pair begins to stroll on the sidewalk that outlines the common's small patch of triangular grass. "Do you think Isiah has anything useful to say to her?"

"I don't know. I hope so. It would be nice to catch a break. If Isiah is jerking my chain, I'll make sure he gets thrown into the deepest hole in our prison system."

"No news on Lance or Takara?"

"No," Victoria says, looking down as she walks.

"How are you holding up?"

"I'm managing."

"Are you? You're Ian's next logical target, and your colleagues kicked you out of the building."

"That's not quite how it happened," Victoria says, trying to correct the record.

"Okay, but still."

"Are you saying that I shouldn't be upset?"

"No, not at all. I'm saying that you're the best I've ever seen, and you're off your game when you're needed most."

Victoria's head jerks around. She takes the comment personally.

"Did that detective badge come with a psych degree?"

"Hey, *you* called *me*, remember?" Seth holds his hands up in mock surrender. "I just call it like I see it."

"Sorry."

"You don't need to apologize. Like I said, we've all been there. You know that you're not in this fight alone, Vic. You have a good team working with you. I have no doubt that you'll get to the bottom of this."

"You're not the first to tell me that, but how do you know? Why don't you, or anyone else, have an ounce of doubt when I'm not convinced of it myself?"

"You see? That's your problem, right there. Ian Drucker is living rent-free inside your head, and it's taking a toll. If you want to end this, you have to stop playing defense and get back on offense. You were successful with Ethan Harrington and Machiavelli because you don't play by the rules. You fix bayonets and charge when you should retreat and regroup. It's what makes you special."

"Some would say reckless."

"Those are the people who don't have the balls to take a risk," Seth says, looking around. "I have to get back to the barracks. Before I leave, do you want to grab a quick bite? I'm starving."

"Are you asking me on a date, detective?"

The big detective laughs. "My wife might take umbrage with that. She already doesn't like you."

"Why not?" Victoria asks, slightly offended.

"You're a beautiful woman, for starters. But mostly because you've almost gotten me killed a couple of times."

"Okay, yeah, there is that," Victoria says, offering a genuine smile for the first time today as the two of them head for a café.

# CHAPTER FORTY-NINE

## OLIVER JAHN

*The On Now with Guldan Cormack Studio*
*New York, New York*

Guldan sits behind his desk as they return from commercial break. He has always hated that his show's format follows the template of every other late-night show on television. Unfortunately, it's a winning formula, his ratings are good, and there is no way either his producers or the network wants to change anything. It's too bad.

"Our first guest tonight started off doing live streams and videos in his basement. His show *Tomorrow's News Today* was picked up by a cable network, and he can now claim that he hosts the number one news program on cable television. Don't think for a moment that I'm not jealous of that! Please welcome Oliver Jahn."

Oliver walks onto the stage to a standing ovation from the studio audience. He waves enthusiastically before shaking hands with the host. He sits on the couch beside the desk and settles in for what will undoubtedly be a fun interview.

"How are you, Oliver?"

"I'm doing well, Guldan. You have nothing to be jealous over. Our shows are nothing alike."

"Because you don't interview guests on yours?"

"No, it's because I'm actually funny," Oliver says to the amusement of the audience.

"Ouch. Okay, okay, it's going to be like that. I've been tuning in to your show for a long time. It is very funny."

"We go to great lengths to present news and commentary in an interesting and entertaining way."

"And it must be working," Gulden says. "Number one in the country."

The audience applauds and Oliver nods his head in appreciation. "Thank you, thank you. Yes, we're very excited about that."

"Your latest shows have been a bit more serious, haven't they? You have a competitor in your sights. Where did this crusade against Tierra Campos come from?"

"Simple. Journalism is a cesspool."

"Wait, wait, wait," Gulden says, waving his hands before pointing a finger at his guest. "You're a journalist."

"I am. Thank you for noticing. I'm one of the dookies floating on the top of the putrid water," Oliver says to laughs. "No, I am. I don't deny it. But there is far worse in the tank."

"Alligators?" Gulden says with a serious look on his face.

"Yes, along with snakes. Maybe even Swamp Thing."

"That must be Tierra," the host says with a smile to the applause of his audience. "You have dedicated your show to going after her."

"Not her, specifically. I'm so tired of people pretending they are something they're not in this country."

"Like what...can you give me an example?"

"Yes. Honest politicians."

The line causes laughs and applause that only grows louder before studio staff intervenes to get the crowd to simmer down. What seems like a natural crowd reaction when it's watched on television is very scripted and orchestrated in the studio.

"I'll, no, wait, I'll go a step further...a politician who honestly gives a shit about everyday people," Oliver continues.

"We'll have to bleep that out," Guldan says playfully as he looks off to the side of the set.

"I forgot that this isn't cable."

"It's okay. That's what our censors get paid for."

"Well, shit, I'll keep doing it then," Oliver says, as the audience gives their roaring approval.

Guldan holds his face in his hands. "I'm going to get hate mail from them after this. So, Tierra Campos is one example. You call her the Great Pretender."

"She is one. Does anybody really think she cares about the truth? She cares about her fancy awards and getting the next story to stay relevant."

"You sound jealous."

"I am. I want a Peabody award. I have this door in my apartment that keeps swinging open."

"It's a very prestigious award. You're going to use it as a doorstop?" Gulden asks.

"Why not? What other good is it? Do you think the American people care?"

"No, probably not," he admits. "Now, you're a partisan."

"And a proud one. Every journalist is. It all comes down to those who admit it and those who don't."

"Don't you think that people are entitled to unbiased news? I mean, that's what people claim they want, right?"

"It doesn't exist."

"It doesn't?"

"Never has, never will. Not only are reporters naturally biased, but so are editors, producers, and the owners of the networks. They are the ones who decide what you see. Reporters only control the presentation. That's the world we live in. It is what it is. Let's just collectively stop pretending it's something else."

"Where do you go from here? You're already hosting the number one show on cable news."

"A fact that I am very proud of."

"And you should be," Guldan says, nodding his head and clapping to elicit applause from the audience. "So, when you're done cleaning up journalism, what's next?"

"Middle East peace," Oliver declares. "It may be easier."

"That would be a miracle."

"So will cleaning up journalism. If I can add getting peace in the Middle East, I'll only need one more miracle to be eligible for sainthood."

"Screw the Peabody. Keep it. I'm a saint!" Guldan exclaims.

"Saint Oliver does have a nice ring to it," Oliver says, playing along.

"I think so. We're going to have more with the saintly Oliver Jahn from *Tomorrow's News Today* and play a clip from his show when we return from the break."

The music plays them into the commercial as the two hosts talk amiably with each other while the audience applauds. Oliver may have to lobby the execs to add a studio audience to his show instead of playing to a laugh track. He likes the energy they bring and the applause even more.

# CHAPTER FIFTY

## TIERRA CAMPOS

*Isiah Burgess's Safehouse*
*Winnetka, Illinois*

Isiah picked a lovely town to lie low in. Winnetka is only sixteen miles north of downtown Chicago and has one of the nation's highest household income averages, perennially ranking in the top ten on the Richest Places Annual Index. Houses built on quarter-acre lots here run just under a million dollars but are worth every dime with all the golf courses and tennis courts I've passed.

The FBI agent who picked me up at the tarmac when the plane landed steers the Suburban into the driveway of a traditional English-style brick home. He puts it in park and turns to me.

"This is the address. Are you sure that you don't want me to come in with you?"

"The instructions were clear. I'll be okay," I say, not sure if I mean it.

I exit the SUV and make my way up the sidewalk to the front door, which opens without the need for me to ring the bell. Isiah waits behind it, keeping himself out of sight from the outside world. He's dressed in jeans and a polo shirt. This is not a formal meeting.

"Mr. Burgess."

"Miss Campos. Please, come in."

I enter the majestic entry hall, and he closes the door behind me, locking it. "This is swanky. Are you staying here?"

"No," Isiah says, motioning me to the well-appointed and expensively furnished living room. "I'm only borrowing it from a friend for this meeting. You don't need to know where I am staying."

"I wasn't going to ask."

"Can I get you anything?"

I want to say bourbon because I feel like I will need one to get through this. "Coffee would be great."

"Cream and sugar?"

"Black is fine."

Isiah nods and moves over to the pot that smells like it is freshly brewed. He returns with a cup for each of us, and we take our seats on the couch. Neither of us says anything for what feels like an eternity. He wanted this meeting, so I'm determined to let him make the first move.

"I half expected you to pull out a notepad or tape recorder."

I offer Isiah a half-smile. "There was nothing that led me to believe that any of this discussion would be on the record."

"Because it isn't. I want to be very clear about that. I'm trusting that you will not let a word we say in this room end up in print or broadcast."

"It won't."

"Okay. Then let's start. I'll go first. It was a bold move to present a case against someone on live television without knowing all the facts. Some would call it irresponsible."

I frown. There was no shortage of journalists and partisan pundits who did. The *Capitol Beat* interviews I conducted at Granite State University in New Hampshire included the two front runners and campaign managers for each party. It was also an excuse to hammer the Burgess campaign about what we learned about the arsons and campaign manipulation.

Victoria secured a cell phone number from one of the conspirators. It was a shot in the dark, but it was all we had to stop Machiavelli from successfully keeping his thumb on the election scale. The interview was covered heavily by the media, and the attempt to steal the election was thwarted. I take pride in my part in maintaining election integrity, at least for this cycle.

"How many scandals have dragged on for years based on assumptions and rumors? I had one shot at getting answers and got them in fifteen minutes."

"Yes, you did," Isiah says, sipping his coffee. "And I wanted to hate you after that interview. I did hate you."

I should be more offended by the comment than I am. There was no intent behind it in Isiah's eyes. It was more of a statement of fact than an admission he's been pining to get off his chest.

"Is that why I'm here? So you can tell me that you detest me and what I did to find the truth?"

"No," Isiah says, staring down at his hands. "I've watched that interview a hundred times. When I got past my anger, I realized that you weren't after me. You didn't know who Machiavelli was."

"I thought it was your father."

"Why?" Isiah asks, cocking his head.

"I'm not going to divulge any more than that," I say, not wanting to give him more details than he needs to know.

"Did Victoria Larsen give you the number you dialed?"

I shrug. "Does it matter? I was staring at your father when I made the call. I wanted to see his reaction. Then your phone rang."

Isiah chuckles. "Nobody was more surprised than I was. I did use several untraceable prepaid phones, but that wasn't one of my numbers."

"If that's true, why didn't you ever refute it?"

"How would I do that? Look offended and scream my denials at the top of my lungs?"

"For starters, yes."

Isiah sets his coffee down and rubs his hands together. "The moment that phone in my pocket rang, I was the man holding the smoking gun over the body. It doesn't matter if someone else put it in my hand. Part of being in politics is knowing how people react to information. I knew what the country was thinking at that moment. Nothing I did or said would have changed that."

I purse my lips and think about that for a moment. Isiah is right. I wouldn't have believed his denials, and neither would anyone else have. I'm still not sure I do, despite the FBI's reservations.

"You don't believe me."

"I don't know what to believe," I admit.

"For what it's worth, I don't blame you. I acted guilty. You had every reason to think that you found me out. In reality, all I wanted to do was get off that set so I could start finding out who was framing me. Now I know."

"You believe that Andrew Li is Machiavelli."

Isiah cocks his head. "From the sound of your voice, part of you thinks so, too. I know he is and can prove it."

"There's where I have my first problem with all this. You say that you're innocent, but you don't take any steps to clear your name. You were uncooperative during your FBI interviews. You let yourself get indicted. If you have proof, why stay silent?"

"'No proceeding is better than that which you have concealed from the enemy until the time you have executed it. To know how to recognize an opportunity in war, and take it, benefits you more than anything else. Nature creates few men brave, industry and training makes many. Discipline in war counts more than fury.'"

I shake my head. "Please tell me that you didn't just quote Machiavelli."

Isiah smiles. "Andrew was right about one thing in that interview: I quote him all the time. I'm impressed that you recognized it."

I don't bother telling him that the first thing I did after that interview was read and reread *The Prince*. "You didn't answer my question."

"No, I didn't. I haven't said anything because Andrew Li might fancy himself as cunning as Machiavelli, but he isn't working alone."

"What do you mean?"

"I spent almost every waking moment with him for more than eight months. He's a brilliant strategist and master manipulator. Honestly, those are the best traits for any political consultant to have. What he doesn't have much of is networking skills. There is no way he could have recruited the members of the SOF to work for him."

"That's flimsy reasoning."

"I know, which is why I needed time to prove it."

"How?"

"Unlike him, I do know how to network. When your father is the governor of the sixth most populous state in the union, you get to do favors for people. I cashed a lot of them in to get the information I needed. At least two more people are working with him that I identified: Robespierre and Nietzsche."

"Who are they?"

Isiah shakes his head. He's not about to give that information up, or he doesn't know.

"What are they trying to do?"

"I don't know for sure. Machiavelli was interfering with a primary. My working theory is that they are planning something for the general election."

"That's one hell of an accusation without any proof."

"I know. That's why I asked you to come out here. I don't expect you to believe a word coming out of my mouth, but I needed you to hear it."

"Why?"

"Because you're Tierra Campos. You aren't beholden to any party or candidate, and you still give a shit about finding the truth. You won't bury it because it doesn't advance an agenda or conflict with your chosen ideology."

"Tell me who they are."

"I can't. Not yet. Robespierre is someone high up in the federal government. Nietzsche is some sort of business tycoon, probably in Silicon Valley. Both are more powerful than you can imagine, but that's why I'm not telling you. I have reason to believe neither is the mastermind behind this. Until I can determine who that is, the information stays with me."

"I don't understand," I say, shaking my head.

"The moment I tell you, or anyone else, everything I know, I'm dead," Isiah says without a hint of humor in his voice. He's serious.

"If that's true, they could kill you before you can tell anyone."

"I understand what makes you a great journalist, Miss Campos. You like poking holes in every conclusion. You're right, but then they won't know what I've learned."

"They'll still be able to stop the information from ever getting out," I argue.

"No, they won't."

Isiah slides his hand into his pocket and pulls out a slip of paper. He leans over the table and hands it to me. I unfold it, expecting to see some tantalizing piece of information. As I read the prose, that's not what this is.

*The city never sleeps, full of villains and creeps / That's where I learned to do my hustle, had to scuffle with freaks / I'm a addict for sneakers, 20's of Buddha and bitches with beepers / In the streets I can greet ya, about cons I teach ya / Inhale deep like the words of my breath / I never sleep, 'cause sleep is the cousin of death / I lay puzzled as I backtrack to earlier times / Nothing's equivalent to the New York state of mind*

"What's this?"

"The lyrics to 'New York State of Mind,'" Isiah says, using a tone that makes me feel like an ignorant idiot for somehow not knowing that. "One word was changed."

"This doesn't look like a Billy Joel song."

Isiah closes his eyes and lets out a breath in disappointment. "Different song, same title. You've never heard of Nas?"

"Should I have?"

"Nasir bin Olu Dara Jones is one of the most mercurial lyrically gifted hip-hop artists to ever hold a microphone."

"I'll take your word for it. When I asked you what this was, I meant, why are you handing me a piece of paper with lyrics scrawled on it."

"It's the key to a lock. If something happens to me, you will get the location of what it opens. All you'll need to figure out is how."

"Seriously?"

"From everything I've read about you, you like puzzles. You proved that in Brockhampton. I have no doubt that you'll figure it out should you ever need to."

That's the downside of what happened with me during the Brockhampton investigation. I don't like puzzles. I got lucky when I realized that the key to finding Lizzie Schwarzer's journals about Ethan was hidden in some of the last words she told me. By applying that to the letter she released to the media, the result pointed me right to the most incriminating evidence ever found against a public figure until someone finds the missing thirteen minutes of Nixon's Watergate tapes.

"You think something is going to happen to you, don't you?"

Isiah gets up and pours himself another cup of coffee. He stares out the kitchen window for a long time.

"They've already tried to silence me once. It was only luck that I didn't leave that hotel in a body bag. There's no reason to think that they won't try again."

I stare down at my hands. Victoria briefed me about what happened in his Chicago hotel room. He's right. There isn't a reason to think that they wouldn't take another shot at him.

"Then go deep underground and wait this out," I say, raising my eyes to meet his.

"There's no hiding from these people," Isiah says, shaking his head. "Even if I bury myself in the hole that Saddam Hussein was hiding in, they'll just find a pressure point and squeeze. I have an obvious one."

"Your father."

"I have already destroyed my relationship with him. I won't let them destroy his career."

There is a real sadness in Isiah's voice that I didn't expect. Politics is such a dirty business that it's easy to forget the real emotions and relationships involved. Public service often means sacrifice. Most don't realize what the cost could be when the last shots are fired. I find myself admiring Isiah far more than I ever thought I would.

"Tierra, I need you to understand something. I may have made you a target by inviting you here. Whatever you do, tell no one that you have that. Don't mention it to your friends, colleagues, and definitely not the FBI. That includes your friend Victoria."

"Why not?"

"I have my reasons."

I take the small slip of paper and place it behind the mirror in my compact. I give it a quick inspection. The plastic tabs that hold it in place aren't broken or damaged. It might not be the last place anyone looks, but it won't be the first.

"Where can I reach you if I need you?"

"Contact Victoria. She doesn't know where I'm staying but knows how to contact me."

I shake Isiah's hand. "For what it's worth, if I end up being wrong about you at the interview, I apologize."

"You can make it up to me by bringing these conspirators to justice. We owe that to Frederick Lamm, Dylan Spencer, and to America."

I nod, fighting off the shiver that runs down my spine. Lamm and Spencer were both murdered by the SOF. Marx may have been responsible, but the belief is that he was acting on orders that came from Machiavelli.

If Isiah is him, then I shook the hand of a man who has blood on them. I'm beginning to see why Victoria asked me to speak with him. The pieces that once looked like they fit no longer do.

# CHAPTER FIFTY-ONE

## VASSYL STRACHENKO

*Near Isiah Burgess's Safehouse*
*Winnetka, Illinois*

A long dirt driveway that meanders between soccer and lacrosse fields lies across the road from the street leading to the house where Tierra was dropped off. It's the perfect spot for Vassyl and Ian to watch the crossroads without looking suspicious. The residential streets in this part of Winnetka are long and straight, providing an easy line of sight down them. After circling the block when the FBI Suburban ducked into the driveway, they positioned themselves to watch it leave the area.

"We should have parked along the curb," Ian mutters from the passenger seat.

"Sure, while we were at it, we could have just pulled in behind them."

"We can't see anything from here."

"This is one of the richest towns in America. Do you think there is a house on that street that doesn't have a top-of-the-line surveillance system?"

Ian knows that Vassyl is right. He may think the assassin is more paranoid than he should be, but it comes in handy. Instead of complaining further, the former FBI agent goes back to staring out his window at the crossroads.

"Why didn't the agent stay with Campos after he dropped her off?"

"I don't know. He should have. You know, we can do this right now and take out both targets. We could be done in fifteen seconds and still make it look like a murder-suicide."

"Those weren't our instructions," Vassyl says, checking the mirrors.

"Who cares?"

"I do."

The assassin types up a secure text and sends it to Robespierre's number. He doesn't usually have it powered on, but he knows what's happening today.

> *Target located*
> *Good. You know what to do*
> *We have a development that you should know about*

Vassyl waits for a response but gets none. He glances over at Ian, who is showing no interest in the conversation.

> *Campos and Burgess are alone in the house. We have an*
> *opportunity to eliminate both*
> *Negative. Stick to the plan*
> *Are you sure?*
> *Campos is Rasputin's responsibility. Our mission is to*
> *handle Burgess and Larsen. Clear?*
> *Yes*

Vassyl powers down his device and places it in the center console. With nothing to say, he stares out the window. As much as he hates to admit it, Ian has a point. They can literally kill two high-profile targets in a single instant, and they are letting the moment pass. It's a shame, but orders are orders.

"Stupid," Ian mutters, assuming that the request was denied. "These guys are so wrapped up in their plans that they miss the importance of getting results."

"Do I need to quote Tennyson back to you now?" Vassyl asks.

"No. It doesn't mean that I don't have an opinion on the matter. Now what?"

"We wait for Campos to leave."

Another half an hour goes by before the FBI vehicle makes a right turn onto the tree-lined street. Two minutes later, they spot Campos in the passenger seat as the Suburban makes a left and heads back toward the interstate. Vassyl waits a couple of minutes before leaving the dusty gravel access road, crossing the street, and making his way down to the house.

"Showtime," he says, pulling into the driveway.

The two men exit the rental car and walk quickly up the sidewalk to the front door. Vassyl nods, and Ian rings the bell.

"Can I help you?" a voice asks from the other side.

Ian flashes his badge. "FBI, Mr. Burgess. We need to have a quick word with you."

Nothing happens immediately. Vassyl and Ian dressed the part in planning for this eventuality. Both could pass for federal agents. That doesn't mean that this is going to work.

The door opens, and Isiah hides behind it. "We had an understanding. There is to be no…wait, I recognize you from somewhere."

Ian nods. "Yes, sir, we met in New Hampshire during your father's campaign. My name is Special Agent Ian Drucker."

Isiah attempts to force the door closed, but Vassyl expects the move and blocks it with his foot. He pulls out his weapon and puts the barrel against Burgess's forehead.

"I'm betting you also remember me now."

"Yeah, I kicked your ass in my hotel room."

"There won't be a repeat of that," Vassyl says, forcing the man back into the foyer.

Ian scans the houses up and down the street to see if any neighbors are around. He doesn't see any. Content, he closes the front door and stares at a defiant but scared Isiah Burgess as he locks it.

# CHAPTER FIFTY-TWO

## BRIAN COOPER

*Executive Mansion - Asheville*
*Asheville, North Carolina*

The governor wrapped up campaigning early, and Brian joined him and Brevin for the flight back to Asheville. The finale of the Democratic National Convention will dominate the news cycle when Alicia Standish accepts the nomination. It gives their campaign a brief respite before their own convention in a couple of weeks.

"Thank you! Thank you for that amazing welcome," Senator Standish says, taking the stage in front of a raucous crowd of delegates.

"This ought to be interesting," Brevin mumbles as Alicia thanks her family and friends for their support.

Brian doesn't think any of it will be interesting. He already knows what she's going to say. He's been prepping the governor all day for what he thinks is about to happen. Brevin couldn't be bothered to listen.

"And… and I want to thank Luther Burgess," the senator says over the applause of the crowd. "Governor, you inspired millions of Americans, particularly the young people who poured their hearts and souls into your campaign. You've put economic and social justice issues front and center, where they belong. Your input will always be welcome in my administration because our country needs your ideas, energy, and passion."

"And socialism, apparently," Brevin grumbles before sipping his drink.

"She's smart to reach out to his supporters," Bradford says, glancing over at Brian, who nods.

"My friends, we've come to Phoenix this week to celebrate America's proudest and most cherished tradition: the choice the citizens of this great nation make every four years to determine who will represent them and who will lead them. It is the foundation of our Republic and something we must safeguard for this and all future elections."

"Easy for her to say. She benefitted from the debacle in New Hampshire."

"Brevin, are you going to provide a running commentary through this whole speech? Because if you are, there are about a dozen other televisions in this house that you can watch."

Brevin holds his hands up in surrender before the governor turns to Brian. "Does she think that she can bury what happened in Manchester during the primary?"

"No. It's embarrassing to Democrats, so the liberal media won't cover it. When conservative outlets do, Alicia will spin what happened into a hero's journey and proclaim that she will ensure election security for generations to come."

"And then do nothing," Brevin adds.

"No, she'll team with sympathetic members of Congress to offer a bill just distasteful enough to poison the effort. Then she can claim obstructionism without really putting any effort into it."

"Sometimes I hate politics," the governor grouses.

"Powerful forces are threatening to pull us apart," Senator Standish says from the stage. "The bonds of trust and respect that hold us together as a nation are fraying. Our own primary showed that. We have to decide whether we all will work together so we all can rise together.

"Our country's motto is 'E Pluribus Unum': out of many, one. Colin Bradford doesn't subscribe to that. He wants to divide America from the rest of the world and from one another. He's betting that the perils we face in today's world will blind us to its unlimited promise. He wants us to fear the future and fear each other. I refuse to let that happen.

"We are clear about the obstacles our country faces and unafraid to confront the challenges we must rise to meet. We will not make choices based on deep-seated bias, nor govern by penalizing one race over another. There are other elected officials who adhere to that racial dogma."

Brian looks at Colin to measure his reaction. To his surprise, the governor doesn't have much of one. He either doesn't realize that Senator Standish is laying the groundwork for future attacks on him, or is oblivious to some of the things he did in office.

"We are a diverse and dynamic nation stuck in a system with rampant inequality, a dearth of social mobility, and far too much paralysis among our elected representatives in Washington to do anything about it. We are languishing as our most enduring values have remained out of reach for people of color: freedom and equality, justice and opportunity.

"We need to build a country where the economy works for everyone, not just those at the top or with one skin color. Good jobs and good schools must be made available to all Americans no matter what zip code they live in. The effects of systemic racism must end, and the proponents of it relegated to the dust bin of history—not forgotten, but preserved as a warning to never return."

Brian rubs his chin. He has to hand it to Angela and Andrew – they put together a great speech. It has the right tone and drops breadcrumbs for the media vultures to feed off for weeks. He knew they wouldn't make this race easy for him, but now he knows that it's going to be a steep climb to November.

"The Republican nominee for president has done nothing but offer empty promises. What are we offering? A bold agenda that will improve the lives of people across America. Safety, good jobs, better opportunities, and a system that works for you, not against you. We stand in stark contrast with each other. If that is what you value, the choice in November is clear."

Brian gets up and moves to the back of the room to pour himself a drink as the senator goes on to talk about her family's background. He stares at the bookcase along the back wall and takes a long sip as the governor joins him.

"Heard enough?"

"I know this part," Brian says. "What's your excuse, sir?"

"I'm nauseated and need to let my stomach settle. Listening to Alicia Standish talk about freedom and values is like listening to an abortion doctor wax poetic about the sanctity of human life. That woman doesn't give a damn about people's rights. She's spent her Senate career taking them away."

"I know. I spent years helping her. How badly do you want to win, Governor?"

"What do you mean?"

"There's going to come a point when you have to make a choice about which path to take. You can go left, or you can go right, but you will have to choose. Before you decide, you'll have to ask yourself how badly you want to win the presidency. How badly do you want to stop her?"

Brian points at the television, and the governor's eyes track to it.

"And, with your help, I will carry all of your voices with me to the White House. America is not a government or a president. It's all of us working toward a better tomorrow. It is with humility and boundless confidence that I am the person to lead us through our challenges and accept your nomination for President of the United States!"

# CHAPTER FIFTY-THREE

## TIERRA CAMPOS

*O'Hare International Airport Hotel*
*Chicago, Illinois*

A loud rap on the door rouses me from a deep sleep. I'm staring at the ceiling when another knock confirms that I'm not dreaming. The glowing red LEDs on the cheap alarm clock read almost two in the morning. What the hell could this be about?

Without turning on a light, I slide into a complimentary hotel robe and peer out the peephole into the corridor. Two men in suits are standing in the hallway, and one of them is holding up a badge.

"Who is it?"

"FBI, ma'am."

"What do you want?"

"Open the door, please, Miss Campos."

Against my better judgment, I unlatch the guard. I take a deep breath and open the door, needing to squint when the bright corridor lighting pours into my room.

"What's this about?"

"I'm Special Agent Smeele, and this is Special Agent Mebrahtu. We need you to come with us, ma'am."

"What's the problem? Did something happen to Victoria?" I ask, tugging at my robe to make sure it's closed as a panicked sensation grips me.

"Not to our knowledge. Please get dressed. We need to leave now."

I do as instructed and am taken down to a waiting car for the longest trip of my life. It's not the forty-five minutes it takes to get here; it's the complete silence. The two agents in front haven't even spoken to each other. Most unnerving for me is not knowing what is going on or why I'm being hauled into the Winnetka Police Station.

I'm immediately shown to an interview room with a table and multiple chairs. It's more spacious than the ones I've seen on episodes of *Dateline* or *20/20*, and the extra space is needed. FBI agents and law enforcement in both uniforms and plainclothes file into the room and shut the door as the lone other woman sits across from me.

"Good evening, Miss Campos. I'm Supervisory Special Agent Deka Kimathi. You've already met Agents Mebrahtu and Smeele. The guy in the corner is Detective Tony Gambello with the Illinois State Police. Next to him is Daniel McMahon with the Marshals Service.

"I'd say it's nice to meet all of you, but it's after three in the morning, and I'm supposed to be getting on a flight in a few hours. Can you tell me what the hell this is about?"

"You met with Isiah Burgess today," Agent Kimathi says, not pulling her eyes off me.

"I did."

"Did you tell anyone what you spoke about?"

Alarm klaxons start sounding in my head. Whatever has happened, there is no reason they would need to know that information. I remember what Isiah told me and prepare to do something I never thought I would do when confronted by law enforcement. I formulate a lie.

"I gave a detailed account of the meeting to Victoria Larsen."

"Is there anything you left out?" one of the agents who picked me up asks.

"I had a long conversation with Isiah, so probably. I didn't omit anything intentionally if that's what you're implying."

"How did you leave the conversation?"

"He was going to get back to me."

"He knows how to reach you?" Detective Gambello asks.

"Not directly. Our communications are through Agent Larsen."

"Did he threaten you?"

The question catches me off-guard. "Threaten?"

"Yes. With violence."

"No."

"Did you threaten him?"

"No."

"Do you own any weapons, Miss Campos?" Agent Smeele asks from his spot along the wall.

Now I know what the Inquisition must have felt like. The four men and one woman in this room are doing everything they can to intimidate me. I might feel that way if I had any idea what these questions are about, and even more so had I done anything to warrant this early-morning grilling.

"I have a set of kitchen knives," I say, meaning to be as sarcastic as possible. They don't flinch.

"Do you have any firearms?" Agent Smeele continues.

"No."

"Do you know how to use firearms?" Agent Mebrahtu asks.

"Yes."

"So, you've fired one?" the police detective asks.

"And had one fired at me. Countless times, as history recorded. I'm going to ask again. What is this about?"

"Recently?"

"Fired one or been shot at?" I ask.

"Don't play games with us, Miss Campos," the woman warns me. "Do you have any firearms in your possession now?"

"No."

"You didn't bring one on the flight to Chicago?"

"I don't own a weapon," I say, my tone beginning to betray my rising anger at their questions.

"Did you bring any firearm, owned or otherwise, on your flight to Chicago?" Agent Kimathi leans forward and asks.

I match her body language. "No. I certainly wouldn't bring one on a plane."

"You took an FBI plane here, correct?" Agent Mebrahtu asks.

"You know that already. I wouldn't bring one on *that* plane, either."

"You have been threatened lately," Agent Smeele interjects. "You didn't buy one for protection?"

"Good luck with that in Washington, D.C. I've been very patient, but—"

"Did you have any contact with Isiah Burgess after you left his apartment?"

I have to restrain myself from lashing out at the interruption. I know the agents are trying to rattle me. It has the desired effect, but I'm not about to let it show.

"No."

"Did he give you anything?"

"Only a lot of B.S."

The three FBI agents look at each other. The police detective and US marshal in the room have no reaction at all. They aren't after the same information that the Bureau is. That's interesting.

"I'm waiting. What happened to Isiah?"

"What makes you think anything did?" Agent Kimathi asks.

"Seriously? You dragged me out of bed to ask me questions about a meeting that I've already discussed with an FBI agent. Is Isiah okay?"

"No, he's dead," the marshal says, tiring of the game.

He puts a folder on the table and pulls out several pictures of Isiah lying dead on the floor with a single gunshot wound in his head. I cover my mouth as tears begin to pool in the corners of my eyes. This isn't a random stranger or some pictures that got leaked on the Internet. This carnage is of a man I talked to only hours ago. Now their collecting me for questioning makes perfect sense.

"When?" I ask in a whisper.

"We don't have a time of death yet. It's likely right around the time you left your meeting. Given your history with the deceased, you can understand our suspicion."

"Isiah Burgess was alive and well when I left that house."

"For your sake, I hope that's true. We will need the clothes you wore to the meeting and want to swab your hands for GSR. It's—"

"I know what gunshot residue is. Feel free. The clothes are packed in my suitcase in the hotel."

Kimathi nods at Agent Smeele, who gets on the phone. They must have an agent waiting for the call back at the hotel outside O'Hare. That's not surprising. It wouldn't be the first time that law enforcement has rifled through my underwear. Hopefully, the FBI will be more professional about it than the Massachusetts State Police were during the Brockhampton investigation.

"Am I under arrest?" I ask, wondering what their next move is.

"No, not at this time."

"Then, once you have what you need, I'm leaving."

"I'm afraid we have more questions for you, Miss Campos," Agent Mebrahtu says. "We need to know what you said to Isiah Burgess."

I lean back in my chair. That's an interesting question to ask for a second time when the man was just murdered.

"That's privileged information."

"Not anymore, it isn't. Things will go much faster for you if you cooperate," Agent Kimathi warns.

"I am cooperating. The conversation itself is not germane to the questions that you need answered."

"We feel otherwise. Keep in mind, Miss Campos, that murder becomes a federal crime when a suspect crosses from one state to another. Even if you satisfy state officials, a federal prosecutor can still push forward."

"I understand what concurrent jurisdiction is, Special Agent Kimathi," I say, ratcheting up my hostility.

"Good. Then you should get comfortable, Miss Campos. You're going to be here until we get the answers that we're looking for."

# CHAPTER FIFTY-FOUR

## OLIVER JAHN

*Tomorrow's News Today Studio*
*Hudson Yards, New York, New York*

"I am going to kick off tonight's show by commending you, my loyal audience, on a job well done," Oliver says once the opening credits finish and the camera clicks on. "I know, I know, it sounds a little arrogant and contrite, but I assure you, it does come from the softest spot of my otherwise cold, hard heart.

"You, ladies and gentlemen, have done it. With your help, you have made this country a better place. How? By bringing world peace? Of course not. We still have plenty of work to do on that. No, you have taken a major step in holding frauds that fancy themselves as unbiased journalists accountable. You did it by knocking over their hive.

"Earlier today, the digital echo chamber that calls itself *Front Burner* announced that it's closing its doors next month. It's shutting down! I'm astonished. I literally danced a jig when I heard the news. *Front Burner* is closing up shop, and Tierra Campos is gone from *Capitol Beat*. I say good riddance to both of them!"

Music plays, and Oliver breaks into a bit of dance at the anchor desk. He knows it looks ridiculous and can imagine Mi Sun rolling her eyes, despite this being her idea. There is one thing he knows for sure: he will never get a spot on *Dancing with the Stars*.

"You are helping to reclaim journalism from the charlatans that masquerade as objective journalists. Go ahead and pat yourself on the back. You saw through their lies like clairvoyants. To that, I say 'bravo!' It was your pressure that forced them to close. It was your comments on social media that pushed Tierra Campos out the door at *Capitol Beat*. It is because of you, the greatest audience in the history of television.

"Unfortunately, the victory lap needs to be a short one. There is still much more work to be done. Silencing their voices is nothing more than stopping the screeching nails on the chalkboard. Others will rise to take the place of the Great Pretender. Another company could form to be the next *Front Burner*. Worse, either or both could resurface like a bad case of herpes."

Oliver glances at the monitor and sees the image Mi Sun selected to put over his shoulder. He recoils. She couldn't have picked a more graphic one.

"Okay, that's disgusting. I'm sorry for that. It's gross. This show has lost all standards," Oliver says with a laugh. "You cannot allow that to happen."

He points his finger. "Campos is the enemy of the American people as much as raging herpes is. They are enemies that need to be defeated. But more than that, you need to make them pay. Tierra Campos should never work in this town again. Never work in journalism anywhere. Neither should anybody that aspires to be like her. I don't care how many Peabodys or Pulitzers she's won. I want her working as a gas station attendant ringing up bad sushi, lottery tickets, and stale Twinkies when this is over.

"She shouldn't be free from criticism for how she has misled you. It's more than just calling her out online. You need to get in her face. You need to make her feel pain. Confrontation is the only way to stop these people and dissuade others from following in her footsteps. They need to know in no uncertain terms that they cannot spread their poison free of consequences. You are the antidote to this ridiculousness. We're back after this."

Oliver smiles when the camera clicks off. He loves this job, and his loyal audience means everything to him. He knows that they'll continue to come through.

# CHAPTER FIFTY-FIVE

## SSA VICTORIA LARSEN

*Boston FBI Field Office*
*Chelsea, Massachusetts*

Victoria inhales deeply, exhales slowly, and pauses her breathing as she squeezes the trigger in quick succession, letting all nine rounds fly at the target. She pulls her weapon back and thumbs the magazine catch to eject it before removing her hearing protection and flipping the toggle to retrieve the target from the far side of the range.

The Boston Division's headquarters in Chelsea is relatively new and comes with some features not found in most FBI buildings. A shooting range in the basement is one of them. For her, it's a Godsend. Shooting is therapy for her. It sharpens her mind by focusing on something other than whatever problem she is facing. Today isn't about that; it's about channeling her rage.

"Damn. Not on my best day," Shawn says from behind her. She turns back to check the target. The tight shot group in the center is not her best work.

"Did Rigo send you down here to spy on me?"

"Not very trusting, are you?"

"Nope. I don't really know him yet. Or you."

Shawn lets out a chuckle. "Shit, I've worked with the guy for a year and a half, and I barely know him. As for me, I'm an open book. Ask me anything."

"I just did."

"Okay, you have me there. No, the boss asked for someone to check up on you, and I volunteered."

"Why didn't he do it himself?" Victoria asks as she reloads her magazines.

"He doesn't like to hover. Or he's scared of you. We have a pool started about which one it is."

"I'm fine."

"Yeah, you sound it," Shawn says, handing her a fresh target. She isn't in the mood for jokes and playful banter today.

Victoria clips the new target onto the bracket and sends it to the back of the range. She's the only one firing, and every sound echoes in the concrete and steel box she's standing in.

"Is Tierra Campos still being questioned?"

"Yeah," Shawn says, looking down at his shoes. "The GSR test came back negative on her hands and clothing, though."

"Then why is she still there?"

"We don't know."

She puts on her ear protection, and Shawn hurries to do the same before she fires nine more shots. She ejects the magazine and places the weapon on the tray in front of her.

"You wanna go?"

"No, I'm embarrassed enough just watching you. Where did you learn to shoot like that?"

"Girl Scouts."

Shawn raises his eyebrows, uncertain whether she is joking. "Remind me to buy more of their cookies when they ask. Look, Victoria, I understand why the Campos interrogation's eating at you. I know you two are close."

"She's my best friend," Victoria says, fighting the feeling that Shawn has an agenda for bringing that up. "It took some getting used to for both of us."

"You met during the Brockhampton investigation, right?"

"Yeah. I took a leap of faith when we traded notes on Ethan Harrington. I wasn't sure I could trust her. Now I trust her more than almost anyone else. Certainly more than anyone here."

Victoria turns to check Shawn's reaction. One of her gifts is the ability to read people through their reactions. Her trainers at Quantico said she was the best they ever saw at recognizing and interpreting microexpressions. Even the best liars on the planet cannot hide them completely. It's a skill that comes in handy in her line of work. In this case, there is no hint of deception, so she allows herself to relax.

"I know you were close to Takara Nishimoto. Did you know Lance Fuller well?"

Victoria shakes her head as the memories come rushing back. "I spent a fair amount of time in his office if that counts. You know all that, Shawn. Rigo told you all about me before I was even hired. Why are you really here?"

"We're worried about you, Victoria."

"Why?"

"Because I've been where you are. Did Rigo ever tell you how I ended up on his team?"

"No."

"I was working in Atlanta when there was a double murder in the Old Fourth Ward. It was run-of-the-mill stuff so far as jurisdiction goes; a local case that didn't warrant any FBI involvement. They were two kids, ages thirteen and eleven. Local police weren't doing much, and I remember seeing the grieving mother on television. It was one of the only stories I saw about it on the news.

"So, I made the mistake of going to see her. I looked into her eyes and felt her pain. I went into her kids' rooms, and everything was left just as it was when they went to school that day. They were beautiful children who had no reason to die.

"I started working the case in my spare time and against orders. That must sound familiar. Then I got a lead, and another, and another. Before you knew it, I was neglecting my own casework to pursue them. I was obsessed with catching the bastard. I was never going to stop until I brought him to justice."

"Did you catch the guy who did it?"

"No. I was placed on probation and taken out of the field. I handed over everything I had to the Atlanta PD detectives working the case. They were going to process me out of the FBI before Rigo intervened."

"What does that have to do with me?"

"Honestly? Nothing. I just don't want this to consume you like it did me. I almost lost my badge over my obsession. Once you start down that path, it's hard to get off it."

"You think that's what's happening to me?"

"Only you can answer that."

Victoria doesn't like psychologists or being analyzed, especially by a colleague. She isn't sure what Shawn's background is, but he's either gone to school for it or spent a lot of time on a therapist's couch. Either way, she is old school and doesn't want to talk to anyone about her feelings, even if it might do her some good. Tierra talked about her therapy following the Summerville shooting and how it saved her life. It's just not Victoria's style. Losing a colleague is tough, but it comes with the job. So does making someone pay for it.

"Anything else?"

Shawn turns to go and then stops himself. "Yeah, one more thing. Somebody here told me that you are like a cat with nine lives at the Bureau who's used eight of them. Don't let your search for Ian Drucker be the ninth."

"Shawn? Did the detectives ever find out who killed the two kids?"

"Yeah, he was a junkie who just thought it would be fun to kill someone. He was killed in a shootout six months later."

Victoria nods and sends a new target back downrange as Shawn leaves the firing line. She plows eight rounds into the center of the target and then pauses before lowering her weapon. Shawn missed the point of his own story. Had he not done what he did, Victoria doubts the detectives assigned the case would have cracked it. Sometimes it takes a maverick to cut through the bullshit and get stuff done. She takes a deep breath, raises her weapon, and fires in one fluid motion, plugging the final shot right into the silhouette's forehead.

# CHAPTER FIFTY-SIX

## VASSYL STRACHENKO

*Abandoned Mill*
*Loughborough, Massachusetts*

Vassyl and Ian grab their clipboards and hop out of their rented white pickup truck. They're only for show, much like their hard hats and the vinyl sticker for the fake consulting company slapped onto the sides of the vehicle. It is a deception meant to assuage a slightly curious onlooker, but won't hold up under close examination.

Not that they expect trouble. Loughborough is a dump. The unemployment rate nearly matches the sky-high crime rate. This may have been a thriving industrial center in its golden years, but it's a city on life support now. It is in the early phases of an urban renewal that gives some plausibility to the sight of a pair of consultants initiating a redevelopment project on a riverfront property.

"Where do we start?" Ian asks.

"The beginning. You said this is the likeliest avenue of approach. Let's find a way to cover it in a crossfire."

The men scout the building. The roof has partially caved in on the east side of the mill. That will make it easy to hide the boat Jackrabbit is procuring. After getting familiar with the structure, they move to the boiler house, with its partially collapsed second floor.

"This will do nicely," Ian says after climbing the stairs and surveying the parking area out the window.

"We can use the materials from the collapsed floor to fortify the walls for more cover," Vassyl notes. "We'll just have to do it quietly."

"I didn't think assassins spent much time worrying about cover. Only concealment."

"We worry about every contingency. I'm going to check to see how hard it will be to get what we need up here. Figure out the sectors of fire while I'm gone."

"You got it, boss," Ian mumbles as he stares at the residential area to the south.

The twin buildings that make up the old mill are easily two football fields long and only a fraction of that wide. He has no idea what they made here since all the machinery was removed ages ago. What he knows is that the brick walls are sturdy, the avenues of approach are limited, and there is a sublevel that will allow the team to stay out of sight until they are ready. Vassyl picked a good location, even if it has its drawbacks.

A white truck pulls up next to theirs in the construction parking lot. A man in khakis and a polo shirt gets out and inspects the signs on the sides of theirs. This can't be good. He looks around before heading for the entry to the mill. Ian is about to call out to Vassyl but thinks twice about it. He may be too far into the bowels of the dilapidated structure to hear him.

Ian tries to look busy. He was silhouetted against the window, so he assumes that the portly man already spotted him on the second floor. His conclusion is confirmed when the visitor enters and climbs the stairs.

"Hey. What are you doing here?"

"Working," Ian says, trying to sound innocent.

"Not here you're not. You're trespassing. You need to leave," the man orders. "Now."

"I'm afraid you're mistaken. The city sent us here to do a demolition evaluation of these structures."

The man shakes his head emphatically. "I work for the city."

"I don't know what to tell you."

"Who are you?"

"Sorry. The name's Arnie Blanchette. I'm a civil engineer with TRC Consulting," Ian says, extending his hand.

"The man folds his arms across his chest. "Arnie? You're a little young for that name."

"I was named after my grandfather, but I'll take the compliment. Who are you?"

"Doug Armstrong. I'm the head engineer for the City of Loughborough."

Ian tries not to react. Of all the dumb luck. There must be a hundred bureaucrats working for the city, and he runs into the one who can blow their cover in two heartbeats. Ian is anything but an engineer. One probing question, and the game is over.

"Good to meet you, Doug."

"You need to leave."

"I can't do that. The boss gave me a task to do and warned me it'd be my ass if it wasn't completed. We were given strict deadlines for this project."

"Which would have come from my office, and I didn't issue any. In fact, I've been living in Massachusetts all my life and have never heard of TRC Consulting. I'm not going to ask again. You need to leave these premises, now, or I will call the authorities."

"Look, I'm sure there's a way we can clear this up without escalating a bureaucratic SNAFU up to the police," Ian says, trying to sound exasperated as anyone would in that situation. "I'm sure they have better things to do."

"No, I think I'll let them handle this."

Doug digs through his pocket for his cell phone. Stalling isn't working, so Ian decides to change his approach.

"You really don't want to do that."

"Yeah, I really do," the city engineer says, sneering as he finally jerks it from his pocket.

"Doug, I'm trying to be reasonable with you. You aren't making it easy."

"Reasonable? You're the one misrepresenting yourself and why you're here, Arnie, or whatever your name is."

The wood floor creaks behind him, and he starts to turn.

"In a few moments, you're going to wish you were more cooperative," Ian says, keeping the man's attention with the ominous tone in his voice and a threatening step closer.

"You wait right there," he says, pointing his finger at Ian and missing the telltale sound of another creak.

"Doug, are you a hunter?"

"What?"

"Hunting. Have you ever gutted a deer before? It makes an awful mess. As you're about to experience."

Doug gives him a puzzled look when an arm clamps around his throat and a blade slices through his side. He tries to scream, but with both lungs punctured, only a whisper escapes his lips. Several more stabs to the lower back perforate his diaphragm before he's released. He collapses to his knees as blood gushes out of his wounds. He stares at Ian in confusion and terror.

"I tried to warn you to be reasonable, Doug."

The man falls face-first to the floor. It's all done now except the dying. Vassyl cleans off his knife with the man's shirt as he takes his last shallow breaths. The shock and panic on his face will be the final look he'll ever have, frozen in death for eternity. Or at least until he gets to a funeral home for burial.

"What took you so long?" Ian asks.

"Every board in this place creaks. I had to move slow."

"You would have made a ninja proud. I thought I was on my own. I didn't hear a damn thing until you were right behind him."

"It was an unexpected challenge," Vassyl admits.

"What do we do with this guy? Someone is going to come looking for him."

"Let's find out who," Vassyl says, pulling the man's wallet from his pocket and opening it.

He pulls out his own cell phone and presses the speed dial for Jackrabbit, who answers on the first ring.

"Yeah?"

"Get on your computer and find out everything you can about Douglas Armstrong. He's the city engineer in Loughborough."

"Why?"

Vassyl takes a deep breath. He hates being questioned. "We had an unexpected run-in with him at the mill. It did end well. I need to know his family or marital relationships, enemies, old grudges…anything we can use to pin his death on someone."

"That won't hold up long," Jackrabbit warns him.

"It doesn't need to. Get on it," Vassyl says, ending the call. "Let's finish what we're doing here while Jackrabbit works his magic."

"And if he doesn't?"

Vassyl glances at the man's body then moves closer to the broken window to stare at the brightly lit space between the buildings.

"The crime rate here makes South Chicago look like Disneyland. We'll make it look like a mugging or carjacking that went wrong. Either way, we need to accelerate our plans."

"I thought you said patience was the key to this."

"I did, but that was before Mr. Armstrong crashed the party. We have no choice now. I'll run it past Robespierre. Sooner or later, someone will piece together his movements and come here to take a look. We have to be done before they do."

"All right. This is taking too damn long anyway. How do you plan on moving this along?"

"Simple," Vassyl says, turning to Ian. "Once we get the green light, you're going to make a phone call."

# CHAPTER FIFTY-SEVEN

## TIERRA CAMPOS

*Red & White Wine Bar*
*Navy Yard, Washington, D.C.*

I admire the view from the window, fully realizing that I won't have much longer to enjoy it. With no salary or future job prospects, my savings will go fast, and I will need to find a new domicile to spend my self-imposed exile in.

Until then, this beautiful apartment has become a prison, and I am its only inmate. There are no visitor's hours, not by design, but because I don't get visitors anymore. My recreation yard is a trip to the building's small gym since I won't risk venturing outside. I won't even go to the rooftop bar reserved for the building's residents. Who knows whether neighbors would refrain from harassment?

I glance over at the closed laptop. I made the mistake of checking social media a few hours ago and shouldn't have. #CancelCampos is still trending on the top social media sites. Whether the comments are from actual people, bots, or tech giants manipulating the algorithm to keep the hashtag trending is irrelevant. The hate mob feels real enough. Many of the commenters have blue checkmarks, so I know that they aren't fake accounts. Videos have popped up that mock me and my reporting. Most sign off with the Great Pretender moniker that Oliver Jahn bestowed on me.

I've been accused and found guilty of a crime that I didn't commit. The facts about Senator Veach have finally hit the mainstream media over the past day, despite their flagrant attempts to bury it. I doubt he's on anyone's shortlist for re-election now, much less vice-president. My facts were accurate. The questions I asked were legitimate. Why are they still coming after me?

The reasons are obvious – once you are in their crosshairs, there's nothing you can do or say to exonerate yourself with the cancel culture. I thought having my identity stolen sucked. Getting canceled has been far worse. I'm not immune to criticism and have received plenty of threats. Lord knows that I got my fair share of them from Ethan Harrington's disciples before the truth about his actions that led to the Brockhampton school massacre came to light. I even shared some of them when I met the team at *Front Burner*. More threats even came in after he was indicted.

How does a young man, through his failure to report an imminent shooting and then lying about being a victim, still garner that level of support? Are people so wedded to their beliefs that they're willing to pardon an accomplice to mass murder in their heads? It's unconscionable to me. It also doesn't matter anymore.

I feel like my whole world is imploding. It could just be my being overtired from getting grilled by federal agents, state, and local police for hours over a crime I didn't commit. I knew that I would be released eventually, but getting cleared didn't make me feel any better about the experience.

Now the news that *Front Burner* is raising the white flag and calling it quits is hitting me. Everything I have ever worked for during my professional career is dead or dying. *Capitol Beat* has slammed the door in my face. *Front Burner* is as good as gone.

I lean forward and pour the final drops out of my last bottle of wine and sip it, not able to resist feeling sorry for myself. Why not? Nobody else will. On the mantel over the gas insert fireplace rest my Peabody and Pulitzer awards, along with some shots of family and colleagues at *Front Burner* and *Capitol Beat*. They were happier times and the realizations of dreams I once had. Now I feel like I'm living a nightmare.

I have alienated everyone that I have ever cared for, and for what? Fame? Notoriety? To be the "best journalist in the country?" None of those things were worth the price of admission. I would trade every award I have earned or ever will to undo all the damage I've done.

This will eventually pass. No leg of any journey lasts forever. The only question that remains is what will become of me when I arrive on the other side. I am an accomplished journalist who may never work in the industry again. That's assuming I even want to. Can I spend my life running the gantlet every time I do or say something a small percentage of people find disagreeable? Is it worth it?

I sink deeper into the sofa and stare at my muted television. Those are all questions for another time. I don't have the physical stamina or the mental energy to work them out now. All I can do while locked in this magnificent apartment is exist. It's what my life has been reduced to. I got my teenage wish to be invisible and have come to an uncomfortable conclusion: it isn't what it's cracked up to be.

# CHAPTER FIFTY-EIGHT

## BRIAN COOPER

*Emergency Campaign Strategy Session*
*Jacksonville, Florida*

The battle has been raging for over half an hour. The campaign booked the hotel conference room so all the key staff members could have input into the conversation. The problem with hearing all the voices is the analysis paralysis that results. Everyone wants to make a good impression on the man who could become the next president of the United States.

Alicia's comments at the convention had the desired effect on the mainstream media propaganda machine, as Brevin characterizes them. None of that was a surprise to Brian, considering his time spent in the opposing dugout. Her words were a dog whistle to them to start digging.

What remains to be answered is how the governor wants to address it. His record is public. Anything he did wrong will be dissected by an army of pundits rotating on and off the air in a continuous loop. The things he did well will enter the laundry and run through the spin cycle to make them seem nefarious and wrong. It's the ugly nature of modern politics.

"We've already spent enough time discussing Brian's ridiculous idea, Governor," Brevin says.

"You've heard everyone's comments and positions, Brian. Have you been swayed at all?"

"No, Governor, I haven't."

"My campaign manager and a majority of the people in this room disagree with you. Why are you so insistent on adding fuel to the fire ahead of our convention?"

"Because if you don't, Standish continues to get to set the narrative. Her convention speech was a means to an end. She knows that you are struggling with black voters already. If you don't begin correcting that, you might as well save the millions you'll spend on this campaign for the next election cycle."

"Why would I admit guilt when I did nothing wrong?"

"Nobody is perfect, Governor. There are always improvements to be made. If you admit that with honesty, the American people will respond favorably to you."

"Brian, did you move to La-La Land after Standish fired you?" Brevin says with a sneer.

"Standish is going to make the cornerstone of this election about race. She will dole out memes of you doing your Civil War reenactments to drive home the point."

"I'm proud of my heritage!"

"And you should be, Governor, but that's not what people will see when the photo of you on a horse surrounded by Confederate battle flags hits the media. It will dominate the news cycle for weeks, and reporters will gobble up every morsel the Standish campaign gives them about your policies toward minorities, and then lick the plate when they're done."

"Being a Southerner shouldn't preclude anybody from becoming president, Brian. It's not 1860."

No, it was a Northerner who got elected in 1860, then South Carolina seceded and opened fire on the Union garrison at Fort Sumpter. Brian doesn't say that, though. Bradford would likely fire him on the spot.

"They don't care that you're a Southerner. It's that you're a Republican. This is a tool to defeat you and the media will harp on it for weeks. By the time the story dries up, it's late October, and there will be no time for recovery. Early voting will start, and she'll get handed an easy win on Election Day. If you combat the narrative now, it takes her queen off the board."

"This is ridiculous," Brevin says, not finding any stronger argument to articulate.

"What do you have in mind?" the governor asks.

"Admission of anything you said or did during your time in public office that can be portrayed in the wrong light."

"The governor didn't do anything—"

"Then show me a single video clip of the governor talking about the horrors of slavery," Brian snaps at the campaign manager. "Is there one, Brevin? I know I couldn't find it."

"Brian—"

"Show me a video or soundbite where you denounce white supremacy, sir. While your campaign is searching for either of those, figure out how you're going to respond when a reporter asks why you cut the budget for free school lunches for disadvantaged children. What your answer will be as to why funding for the state's urban youth opportunity initiative was slashed or why black unemployment went up in your state while every other group saw theirs decline."

"I'm not a racist!" the governor shouts, pointing his finger at the consultant.

"I know that, and you know that. Everybody in this room knows. The American people only know what the media tells them, and the press works for the Democrats. They will say you are one, and you'll spend the rest of this campaign trying to convince them otherwise."

It's hard for Brian to hold back. He has one more ace up his sleeve courtesy of Anika, but now's not the time to play it. Still, he wants to so badly. Brevin Hawkins would look far better with his foot not only in his mouth but shoved all the way down his throat.

"Sir, you should—"

"Shut up, Brevin. I want to hear this," he says, causing his campaign manager to recoil at the intensity of the rebuke. "What do you think I should do?"

"Come clean about your entire record in front of the American people and then acknowledge that diversity is one of this nation's greatest strengths."

"Yeah, like that's going to work," Brevin interjects as he seethes on the opposite side of the table.

"Then make a series of policy proposals about what you are going to do for minorities in your presidency. You will get hit for pandering and grilled about reparations, which you will say are empty promises meant to assuage white guilt, not uplift blacks who need good jobs, better opportunities, safer neighborhoods, and good schools. You will say your policies are the first small steps in what needs to be done to make black Americans the part of the American fabric that they always should have been. Do all that, and you control the narrative while putting Standish on the defensive."

The governor looks at Brevin. The campaign manager shakes his head.

"It's a mistake before the convention. End of story."

Colin rises from his seat at the table, and everybody in the room stands.

"I'm going for a walk. I'll think all this over. Thank you, ladies and gentlemen."

# CHAPTER FIFTY-NINE

## SSA VICTORIA LARSEN

*Boston FBI Field Office*
*Chelsea, Massachusetts*

Victoria's eyes are tired and dry, like only her staring endlessly at a computer screen can make them. She leans back in her chair and rubs them hard. Office work isn't her cup of tea. The FBI appealed to her because, despite the paperwork, active fieldwork kept her out of an office. She doesn't know how people who toil behind desks or in office cubicles eight hours a day do it.

A cup of coffee materializes in front of her, and she turns to see Rigo standing beside her. She nods and pulls the stopper out of the lid before taking a long sip of the hot black liquid. If heaven had a taste, Victoria imagines that it must be dark roast coffee.

"You look like you needed that. When was the last time you slept?"

"I don't know. What day is it?" Victoria asks, not meaning it to be the joke that Rigo took it for.

"Tierra has been officially cleared from being a suspect in Isiah's murder by the Chicago Division."

"I would hope so."

"You don't look happy. What's bothering you?"

"I read the transcript of Tierra's first interrogation," Victoria says, leaning back in her office chair. "The three FBI agents in that room were more interested in what she and Isiah spoke about than determining who was at fault for his murder."

"You don't think that's a coincidence?"

"I have a long history of not believing in them."

Takara could have explained that better than anyone. Coincidences exist, but in the law enforcement world, they are unicorns. It's more likely that one is a piece to a puzzle that has yet to be completed.

"You don't think that the agents were involved in his death, do you?"

"That would be hard to believe. It's more likely that the Chicago FBI was under orders to find out what Tierra knew. I've been poking around to see if I can find anything."

"Have you?"

"No."

Victoria sips her coffee. Rigo looks like he wants to say something but waits patiently for her to speak first. If Victoria were in a better mood, she would toy with him by making the silence last forever. Today isn't the day for that.

"Do they have any new suspects?" she asks, letting him off the hook.

"None of the neighbors saw anything, but a lot of them have home security systems, and we have multiple angles of the street. The cameras are all pointed at each other's houses. It's kind of a digital neighborhood watch."

"Or a scheme to have leverage on the guy across the street when you return the lawnmower you borrowed from him broken."

"You have a twisted side. You know that, right? Come see this."

They walk over to his laptop, and he logs in. Victoria looks over his shoulder as he surfs through a file structure to find the archived video footage he's looking for. When he clicks play, nothing happens until a car pulls into a driveway. Two men exit the vehicle and take the sidewalk up to the front door. He pauses it when both look across the street.

"These aren't detailed enough for facial recognition."

"That's Ian Drucker," Victoria says, pointing at the guy on the left.

"How do you know?"

"I know."

"If that's true, how the hell did he get all the way to a town north of Chicago?"

"Driving would be their only option."

"Then they would have dumped the car and found another when the deed was done. Maybe we'll luck out."

"Unless it was rented under an alias. In that case, good luck."

Rigo crosses his arms and grins. "You're full of optimism today. We don't know who the guy with him is. Another member of the SOF?"

Victoria stares hard at the monitor and shrugs. "I don't recognize him. Maybe. It's not my first concern. These guys killed two FBI agents and then drove halfway across the country to kill Isiah Burgess. Why?"

"Wrapping up loose ends?"

"It makes sense, but it was a hell of a risk to take. When I spoke to Tierra, she said that he was close to figuring out who is behind all this. He said it was powerful people."

"That makes Isiah sound like a paranoid conspiracy theorist."

"It's not paranoia when they're really after you. It cost Burgess his life," Victoria says, heading out of the conference room.

"Where are you going?"

"For a walk."

She doesn't mean a random stroll around the building. Victoria needs to talk to someone outside of her team, and there is only one person left in this building that she trusts enough to confide in. That leads her to the part of the building that houses the New England Regional Computer Forensics Laboratory and its star examiner, Miranda.

"Well, hello, Your Majesty!" Miranda bellows. "What brings the great Queen Victoria to our humble cube farm? Do you have something you need me to do?"

"Not this time. Just dropping in to say hi."

Miranda was instrumental in the last investigation she did for the Boston Division. Her ability to crack into Marx's cell phone allowed Tierra to stop the rigging of a primary election during her interview with the Burgess campaign. Or so she thought. Now, the truth is proving more elusive than she thought it was.

"Oh, this is bad. You look like Atlas with the weight of the world on your shoulders."

"Yeah. I'm stuck here playing the worst of games."

"Charades?"

"Catchup."

"This is about Drucker, isn't it?" Miranda says, almost forgetting that the murder of Agent Nishimoto must be hitting Victoria hard and that she has no reason to laugh right now.

"He's three steps ahead of us, and I can't manage to close the gap."

"I'm no therapist. You know that. I will say that self-doubt isn't a part of your psychological makeup."

"Most of the time, you're right. I can also usually figure out a motive. There isn't one here," Victoria admits.

"Or you're overthinking it. Sometimes it's just about settling scores. Drucker is seeking revenge on the people who did him wrong, end of story."

Victoria sighs. "That's what Rigo thinks. He wants me out of town in case he comes after me next."

"Not for nothin', that's not a bad idea."

Miranda gets the side-eye. "Drucker and another man just drove from here to Chicago to kill Isiah Burgess. I'm betting that he would go to the moon for a shot at me. No place is safe, so I might as well stay."

Miranda nods. She can't argue with that logic, although the thought of taking on Victoria is anything but appealing to her. Only a man with an oversized ego would relish the idea.

"Can I help?"

"You scoured Marx's device for everything, right?"

The rarely offended computer forensic analyst doesn't appreciate the question as her face contorts into a look of annoyance. "Of course."

"Machiavelli was the only person he talked to?"

"It was the only number I recovered. Why?"

"Because I think that someone else is behind this, and I don't know who or why," Victoria says, picking a stress ball up off of Miranda's desk and compressing it to a fraction of its usual size.

"You'll figure it out. If anyone can, it's you. One thread to pull is all it takes. When you find it, the whole plot will unravel."

"What makes you think that there is one?"

Miranda smiles. "Because you do, and your instincts are the best in the Bureau."

Victoria nods and tosses the stress ball back to her. Like Seth, Miranda has more confidence in her than is deserved. Everyone surrounding her thinks she'll crack this. The end result is self-doubt and an increasing amount of pressure on her.

"Thanks, Miranda."

The analyst watches her head out of the room. "Good talk!"

Victoria heads for the elevator. That met her expectation of not being particularly useful. She needs to catch a break before Ian strikes again. Without one, the body count could go higher before she can put him down for good.

# CHAPTER SIXTY

## OLIVER JAHN

*Tomorrow's News Today Studio*
*Hudson Yards, New York, New York*

Oliver walks into Mi Sun's office without knocking. The two have always had an informal relationship and a long-standing open-door policy that doesn't include knocking before entering. The practice dates back to the small Ikea desk he put in the corner of his basement for her back when TNT was nothing more than a fledgling podcast.

Mi Sun is surfing the net and not trying to hide her lack of focus on today's show. It's a rarity for a woman with boundless energy who seems to work far more than she sleeps.

"I see you're hard at work," Oliver says, a slight frown following the comment.

"My heart's not in it right now."

"Since when? What's the problem?"

"Do you really want to know?" she asks.

"Oh, boy. That sounds ominous."

"What are we doing, Oliver? I mean, I know why you wanted to go after Tierra Campos. At least initially. Now, she's gone from *Capitol Beat*, they're hemorrhaging viewers at a rate even Wilson Newman can't slow down, and our show is number one."

"Those are all good things."

"Yeah, so why are we still harping on this? Every show we do is centered on Tierra Campos."

"It's a story," Oliver argues.

"No, it isn't. We're in the middle of a presidential election, and you've spent all of about ten minutes on it this week."

"The world does not revolve around the race for the presidency."

"It doesn't revolve around Tierra Campos and *Front Burner* either," Mi Sun fires back.

"Do you really think journalism will survive with people like that in its ranks?"

"Do you really think you deserve to be the arbiter of who gets to report the news and who doesn't?"

Mi Sun has always been hard to argue with. She likes making her point by forcing people to defend theirs. Oliver finds it infuriating. The lack of sex may be the only difference between her being a work wife and a real one. Although he thinks that some married men may argue with that.

"Yes, I do deserve it. I paid my dues."

"Oh, please. You had an entertaining video blog that got noticed, by me included. Don't you remember the MSM's reaction when you signed a cable news contract?"

"The mainstream media—"

"Hated you. You didn't go to a fancy journalism school or come up through the reporting ranks. You had a streaming show on the Internet, and they barked about how that didn't qualify you to do the news. I remember. I was there."

"What's your point?"

"How is what you're doing different?"

"I tell the truth," Oliver says, his tone sharp and voice rising.

"Really? Let's not sit here and pretend that you aren't selective about what truths you tell and how you tell them. By your own admission, you're partisan."

"I have an agenda, yes. I make that very clear every night. I don't profess to be objective, but that doesn't make what I say untrue. That's the point."

"And my point is that this show is no fun anymore."

The words hack at his heart with all the subtlety of a chainsaw. He has always taken pride in creating an atmosphere around his personality and show that makes delivering the news fun. It's what draws in his viewers and earned him the respect of his staff. To hear Mi Sun say that is devastating.

"You agreed to go on this crusade with me. You said you would always support what I was doing."

"I am supporting you. That doesn't mean that I do it blindly or don't have an opinion. Unless my voice doesn't matter either."

"You know that it does."

"Do I? You never asked mine. You dictated the direction like a parent would to a five-year-old."

"You are invaluable to me. I never would have gotten here without you," Oliver says, lowering his voice to throttle down the tension.

Mi Sun stands and collects a few things from her desk. "Then listen to what I'm saying and take it to heart. TNT is a brilliant show because you are willing to tackle any subject head-on. The audience listens to you because of that. They still are in big numbers, but for how long? This crusade against Campos is popular now, sure, but what about a month from now? A week? A day? If you don't start blazing a new trail on something people actually care about, you might find that you have no audience left when you do."

"Where are you going?"

"The control room. I have a show to prep."

She leaves him sitting in her office. Oliver just stares out the window. Mi Sun doesn't really get what this is about or what it could do for them. It doesn't matter how many times he tries to explain it. She is a stubborn woman and has to come around on her own. He only needs to keep her placated long enough for it to dawn on her.

# CHAPTER SIXTY-ONE

## VASSYL STRACHENKO

*Back Bay Safehouse*
*Boston, Massachusetts*

The supplies have been procured, and the necessary equipment is in place. All that's left is the waiting. Any soldier in war will tell you that it's the worst part. Just ask the paratroopers waiting to load their planes on the evening of June 5 before D-Day or the hundreds of thousands of allied soldiers anticipating the order to breach the Iraqi defenses on the Kuwaiti border in 1991. It's agonizing.

This is no different. Vassyl's team may not be preparing an invasion, but they are declaring war on the FBI. For the rest of their lives, they will be hunted. Fortunately, the money these men are making will make this the last mission they ever need to undertake. Vassyl isn't sure that retirement will come so easy for him. It's the action that drives him, not the financial benefits of what he does.

He glances at his watch and looks around the room. He'll miss the conveniences of this Boston apartment, indoor plumbing included. Where they are going is far less hospitable. Vassyl has stayed in worse places. They all have, including the prima donna Ian.

The assassin disappears into his bedroom and closes the door. Taking a seat at the small desk along the wall, he logs on to his computer, opens an online game system, and rechecks his watch. He should be on it now.

Vassyl selects *Knights of the Crusade* from the menu and launches it. It's an old-school game, and the graphics in it are terrible. He's not here to level up his knight or slaughter the enemies of Christianity. It has a feature that makes perfect sense for men in his line of work. Some conversations shouldn't be had over a cell phone, regardless of the encryption level. This offers the opportunity to have deeper discussions in relative anonymity.

The map of players online comes up, and he double-clicks on the appropriate character. The map zooms in and shows his avatar galloping over to a dismounted knight who's admiring his sword. That's fitting.

The chat on the side of the screen opens, and the character name Robespierre pops up in calligraphy style script:

Robespierre>>> Where are you?
KnifeKnight>>> Back in Boston.
Robespierre>>> Excellent. Good work in Chi-town.

KnifeKnight>>> It was fun. Any heat on us?
Robespierre>>> Some. The neighbors had cameras. Your colleague was identified. You'll be next.
KnifeKnight>>> That's unfortunate, but it was unavoidable.
Robespierre>>> It won't matter.

Vassyl grimaces. That's easy for Robespierre to say. He's not the one who will be hunted to the ends of the Earth when this is over.

KnifeKnight>>> There is a development here. We need to accelerate the execution.
Robespierre>>> No.
KnifeKnight>>> We have no choice. Our quest will be compromised without immediate action.
Robespierre>>> Handle it.
KnifeKnight>>> Unable. We bought time, but not much. The longer we wait to take the Holy Grail, the worse our chances for success. Permission to proceed?

There is a long pause in the conversation. The character on the screen goes through a series of fighting moves, swinging and lunging his sword. Vassyl hopes that he isn't trying to kill his character. He doesn't even know how to play this stupid game. The knight finally bows his head.

Robespierre>>> Don't screw it up.

With that pearl of wisdom, Robespierre's character disappears from the screen as he logs off the game. Vassyl does the same and closes his laptop. He got what he needed and heads back into the living room.

Dimitri and Jackrabbit are trying to make dinner. The aprons they are wearing make them look more ridiculous than domesticated. Sven is on the couch watching television with Ian. All four men look at him when he emerges from the bedroom.

"What's the word, boss? Sven asks.

"Pack your shit for tomorrow. We have the green light to proceed."

"About damn time," Ian says as Dimitri claps. The men all perk up, knowing the wait is coming to an end.

Ian gets off the couch and approaches Vassyl. "When do I get to do my thing?"

"Soon. Very soon."

# CHAPTER SIXTY-TWO

## TIERRA CAMPOS

*Tierra's Apartment*
*Navy Yard, Washington, D.C.*

I'm staring out my apartment window at the muggy Washington night when my phone vibrates in my hand. Nobody has texted me in days, not even Wilson. I glance down at the number and see 867-5309. I know it isn't Jenny reaching out to me for a good time, so I smile and open the message. There's only one person I know who speaks binary.

01000110 01110010 01100101 01100101 00100000 01100110 01101111 01110010 00100000 01100011 01100001 01101100 01101100 00111111 ?

I open an app that translates binary code into plain text and paste the message into the window. I tap "convert," and the result displays in the lower window: free for call?

I return to the text and type "yes." A few seconds later, the phone rings.

"It's been a while, DP," I say.

"It has," the voice on the other side of the line replies without the usual digital disguise of his voice. That ship has sailed.

DialPirate was one of the hackers involved with Ethan Harrington. I learned their real names through Brian Cooper and called upon them to help me with the New Hampshire investigation. They did, begrudgingly, except Dial Pirate, who was more helpful than he should have been. I haven't had any reason to reach out to the others, but DP still checks in on occasion.

"I'd ask you how you're doing, but I already know," the hacker says.

"I wish I could say the same about you, but I suppose you would think that it's a good thing that I can't. To what do I owe the honor?"

"I have something for you. Call it a thank-you."

"For what?"

"Not turning me in to the feds," he admits. "You easily could have. I know that Agent Larsen has some friends in FBI Cyber that would love to know my real name."

"We had a deal. I had no interest in breaking it."

"Integrity isn't common in today's society. That's why I like computers. There's predictability and truth in ones and zeros."

"Only when you're comfortable using one. I have a beef with those infernal machines right now."

"No, your problem is with the people using them. That's why I reached out. I've been watching what's happening."

I shake my head. "You mean the grassroots mob of cancel culture disciples trying to destroy me?"

"Yeah, only it's not grassroots at all. Everything happening to you on social media is organized."

That gets my attention. I sit up on the couch and focus my eyes on a spot on the coffee table.

"What do you mean?"

"It's not organic. The smear campaign is centrally coordinated."

"Oliver Jahn?"

"Good guess, but no. He doesn't have the power, resources, or technical expertise to do this."

"Then who is doing it?" I ask, feeling a rush of adrenaline that comes with new information and the fear of not knowing what it means.

"I don't know, but it's someone with a lot of clout and an army of social media experts and computer-savvy people. Anti-you hashtags have been trending for weeks. That doesn't happen unless someone is working on the inside, and would still only be possible because there are people good enough at gaming the algorithm."

I clench my teeth until my jaw begins to hurt. I don't understand the technology behind social media, so how that's possible will have to remain a mystery to me, and I'll take DP's word for it. He's forgotten more about computers than I will learn in three lifetimes.

"Great. I have an army of nerds mobilized against me."

"This is serious, Tierra. A powerful enemy is driving this, and they know what they're doing. It's a sophisticated operation, and that's not all. Have you been getting harassed at all in the RW?"

I do the translation in my head. "Yeah, some real-world things have happened. Mostly verbal abuse. Oliver Jahn's viewers, no doubt."

"Let me guess: a metro station, someplace near the water, a bar, and an airport."

"A couple of those places, yeah," I say, stunned over how he could know that.

"I did some digging after I saw the picture of you and Alicia Standish on TNT."

"Please tell me you don't watch that show," I say, almost tasting the vomit in my mouth.

"Sometimes. Anyway, I found the photographer who took it."

"It's old news, DP, and certainly not what Oliver Jahn portrayed it to be."

"I believe you, but it's not exactly old news at all. The guy's name is Mulder Scully. He has a photography studio in D.C."

"You can't be serious."

"I am. Scully changed his name when he joined the paparazzi and spent almost a decade in L.A. selling salacious pics of celebs he dubbed the 'X-files' to the highest bidder. He gave up the chase to move to the East Coast to sell portraits and scenic shots of the capital. Despite his new business model, he's still a scumbag."

Most people seek fame and fortune without really understanding the consequences that come with the territory. It's something that I now have firsthand experience in. Celebrities have it far worse. There is no such thing as the expectation of privacy when you're in the public eye. As bad as it is for me, I never thought I would have to worry about people hanging out of trees or shooting me with a telephoto lens from a quarter-mile away.

"He took a picture of me with a politician. So what?"

"That's not all he's doing. He's been following you and posting shots of you in public places."

My phone chirps, and I go back to my text messages. I open an image of me on my phone as I'm walking into the Metro. Another text comes in with a timestamp. It was the day I ran into those kids on the platform.

DP sends a few more from Reagan National Airport and in the Navy Yard along the water. The latter was the day of the footrace down the trail with those kids.

"Jesus."

"Those are just a select few. Scully is posting these to an Internet group with a location and timestamp. Anyone in the group knows where you are within minutes of them being taken."

I can feel myself shaking. Of all the creepy things that have happened to me in the past year, this takes the cake. This isn't voyeurism or sending a few mean tweets. This is stalking a target for an end I don't even want to contemplate.

"How many belong to the group?"

Dial Pirate exhales. "Almost 30,000, with a sizable chunk in the D.C. area."

"Why is he doing this?"

"I don't know, but you can bet he isn't doing it for free. I'm trying to get into his financial records to see what I can unearth. Until then, watch your back. Some of the people on this site are downright crazy."

"Thanks, DP."

"You betcha."

I end the call and settle back into the couch. As bad as I thought my life was ten minutes ago, it just got worse. I'm making enemies through the simple act of reporting the news. The question is, why?

# CHAPTER SIXTY-THREE

## BRIAN COOPER



*Bradford for America Campaign Rally*
*Cincinnati, Ohio*

Brian has been to hundreds of campaign rallies during his career. He's seen young, energetic politicians light a fire under their base and enlist the help of thousands of volunteers per event. He's also seen polite applause in arenas that feel like morgues. This more closely resembles the latter, but the lack of enthusiasm isn't what has him concerned.

The governor's stage time is trickling down, and he still hasn't addressed his record or done anything to appeal to voting blocs destined to make or break this election. No matter how compelling Brian thought he was, his argument down in Florida fell on deaf ears. He shouldn't be surprised. Brevin pulls his strings like a marionette. It was surprising that Governor Bradford eschewed his campaign manager's advice and hired him in the first place.

The crowd applauds as the governor begins railing about how Alicia Standish has been bought and paid for by Wall Street fat cats. He doesn't need to characterize her as a career politician. She is one. So is he. What will he say when she tells the media that he took millions in donations from pharmaceutical, tobacco, and health care insurance companies?

Brian shakes his head as he watches the show from the crowd's fringes off to the right of the stage. He will never understand why politicians willingly walk into minefields. It is so easy not to do. At a minimum, each knows what they did or didn't do to get into office and how they conducted themselves once they assumed it. That's why the word "hypocrite" is increasingly used in the modern age to describe leaders and representatives.

Digital media and the Internet make it possible to quickly search for every sentence a politician utters and then match those words to what they do. Too often, the language and actions don't match, and the term is applied. That's all before the media and critics latch on to broken promises.

Examples are aplenty. If a candidate took big-dollar political action committee donations from unpopular and morally bankrupt special interest groups, he or she shouldn't be railing against dark money in politics. That's the trap that Bradford is falling into. Unless he didn't know who funded his campaign war chest, which Brian would find remarkable.

He feels the phone in his pocket vibrate and pulls it out as the audience offers another weak, unenthusiastic round of applause. The text is from an anonymous source, but he knows who it is.

> *I'm assuming that this speech wasn't your idea. If it was,*
> *you're making this too easy for me*

Brian shakes his head and types a response.

> *We haven't reached Election Day yet*

> *Keep this up and it won't matter. Start bringing your A-*
> *game or this will be over in a week*

Brian doesn't bother acknowledging the last taunt and deletes the texts. He's not worried about the exchange ever being seen, even though he knows that he should be. If it was ever discovered who he was talking with, the consequences would be severe for both of them.

"You look bored," Brevin says, walking up behind him. "Who was that?"

"A member of my fan club," Brian grumbles, pocketing the phone.

"From the look on your face, I take it that you don't like our next president's speech?"

"It's fine."

"I figured that you would be screaming at me," Brevin admits, trying to provoke a reaction.

"You're the boss. I'm sure you've spent millions in campaign funds on focus groups and research to form a strategy you hope will lead you to two hundred and seventy electoral votes and a scheduled move-in day at the White House."

Brevin is taken aback a little. "Is there a 'but' coming?"

"Not at all. I'm a consultant hired to help you divine how Alicia Standish is going to campaign against you. I get paid for my opinion and to outline a possible course of action. I did that. You get paid to guide the candidate to a decision. You did that. We're all doing our part."

"Just remember that moving forward. I don't want a repeat of what happened in Jacksonville."

Brian would love to argue that point but doesn't. He fights the urge to pucker his mouth like he ate something spoiled. The words tasted that bad coming out. Instead, he just forces a nod.

Satisfied that his annoying consultant is finally playing for the team, Brevin walks away. There is nothing to be gained by a confrontation here. The campaign will just have to learn the hard way that their strategy is playing right into Alicia's hands. Andrew Li and Angela Mays must be salivating over this right now.

Unfortunately, Bradford's failure to heed common sense advice will make Brian's job that much more demanding over the next three months. In politics, the two most important commodities are time and money. When you dig a deep enough hole as a candidate, there is never enough of either before the clock runs out and America goes to vote.

# CHAPTER SIXTY-FOUR

## SSA VICTORIA LARSEN

*Boston FBI Field Office*
*Chelsea, Massachusetts*

The frustration is getting to everyone. Tempers are flaring amongst the team working fourteen-hour days away from their homes in a cramped conference room. Despite all the grunt work, there isn't a single lead on the whereabouts of Ian Drucker.

There isn't much progress on the Isiah Burgess case either. Rigo has some contacts in the Chicago Division that provide him regular updates, unlike the agents leading the case. They may have been interested in Tierra's conversation with Isiah, but that hasn't translated into them working on his murder.

Most of the details about Isiah's death haven't been publicly released. Victoria knows that Ian was involved. She knows there was a man with him. That's about it. There are no insights into where they went or are now. Rigo bursts into the room with new energy, and Victoria hopes that the information drought is over.

"We have a hit on our unsub," Rigo says, holding some printouts in his hand. "His name is Vassyl Strachenko, age unknown. He's a Kosovar Serb who spent some time with the Solkovi Battalion of the 72nd Special Forces Brigade."

"Spec Ops?" Shawn asks.

"It fits with the SOF motif," Steve adds.

"Only Marx and his guys in the Sword of Freedom weren't special forces. They were only stationed together in Europe."

"Well, Strachenko was," Rigo continues. "The Solkovi Battalion's focus is counter-terrorism. Once he left the military, his history disappears into a black hole until a couple of years ago, when he was implicated in a pair of low-level assassinations on Eastern European political targets. Interpol started a file on him, but nothing ever stuck. This is the first time he has surfaced in the U.S."

"How did he get here?" Amanda asks, listening in on the conversation from the far end of the conference table.

"We don't know. CBP has no record of him entering the country."

"He came through Canada," Victoria mumbles, shaking her head. "Check with their immigration."

"How do you know?"

"It's how I would have done it. Come into Canada and then slip across the border. There are plenty of places to do it where you don't need to go through a checkpoint."

Her phone rings, and she snaps it up without bothering to look at the caller id.

"Victoria Larsen."

"Hello, Victoria," a familiar voice says on the other end as the blood drains out of her face and her body stiffens. It feels like she was just hit with seventy-five amps.

"Ian," she says, getting the undivided attention of everyone in the room.

"I'm betting that I'm the last person you expected to hear from today."

"Yeah, you could say that," Victoria says, too stunned and angry to come up with anything witty. "What do you want?"

"I just thought I would check in to see how the search for me is going."

"It's going great. You can help speed up the process of your inevitable demise by telling me where you are right now."

Ian chuckles, amused at the thought. "Nah, I'm not going to make this that easy for you. Everyone knows that you're the best and brightest agent in the FBI. You can figure it out without my help. Then again, they said the same thing about Takara. Look where that got him."

He has a set of balls to even mention Takara's name to her. "How many of you did it take to kill him that night? I know it wasn't only you. You're too much of a coward to work alone."

"Sticks and stones, Agent Larsen. Don't be like that. All's fair in love and war. Ask Lance Fuller. At least I had some respect for Takara. Fuller was a pussy who got what he deserved."

"Neither of them deserved that."

"Sure they did," Ian sings out. "I'm willing to bet you fantasized about choking that man to death once or twice while he was trying to run you out of the Bureau. Speaking of which, you should come over to the dark side. We have way more fun."

Rigo puts a hand on Victoria's shoulder, trying to calm her down. It isn't working.

"Ian, when this is over, you are going to pay for everything you've done. Manchester. Takara. Fuller. All of it. I am going to make sure they throw you in the deepest, darkest hole I can find."

"Empty threats are so not you. You're better than that, Victoria."

"They aren't empty. You'll see."

"You have to catch me first. That's assuming I don't get to you before you can."

"You won't."

"Don't be so sure," Ian says, a knowing tone in his voice. "I'm closer than you can imagine. Don't think that your instincts or looking over your shoulder every couple of seconds is going to save you. You'll never see me coming."

Victoria looks around subconsciously. She doesn't let people get under her skin. When she took down the Devil Rancher before the Brockhampton shooting investigation consumed her life, he made some wild threats, too. Nothing ever materialized. Some people are all talk. Ian Drucker is one of them.

"Ian, on your best day, you were never that good."

"Time will tell, Victoria. This has been a good talk. We should do it again. That's if we don't see each other very soon."

Ian ends the call, and Victoria drops her phone on the table. She plants both hands on it, locks her elbows, and hangs her head. It's pounding with the unhealthy mix of rage and stress.

"What did he want?" Shawn asks.

"To gloat."

"Or get you spun up," Rigo counters.

"If that's what his goal was, it worked."

Rigo sits on the edge of the conference table alongside her. "I know you're going to argue with me, but I think it's time for you to go back to Washington."

"No."

"Victoria—"

"The answer is no, Rigo," she says, getting inches from his face. "I'm not running away."

"Ian is making this personal for a reason. Don't fall into the trap."

"He isn't *making* it personal. It already is. He's going down, and I have every intention of being there when it happens."

Victoria storms out of the conference room. There's nothing more left to be said. She's not about to allow herself to be benched over this. Rigo needs to understand that, or every word he said to get her to join his team was a marketing pitch and nothing more.

# CHAPTER SIXTY-FIVE

## VASSYL STRACHENKO

*Abandoned Mill*
*Loughborough, Massachusetts*

Sven pulls their white king cab pickup truck rental into the small construction site lot next to the two abandoned mill structures, and the five men climb out. Dressed in jeans and work boots, he hopes their attire serves both a practical and illusionary purpose for any prying eyes in the apartments around them.

"We want to leave this here?" Dimitri asks as the others except Ian look around.

"For now, yes," Vassyl says.

"Do we have to wear these dumb things?"

Sven takes the hard hat off and fiddles with the adjustment knob on the plastic strap. Even opened up to its maximum size, it's too small for his head.

"Illusion is everything. You can take it off once we're inside. Grab the generator and lighting. We'll get the rest later. Let's go."

Sven and Dimitri grab the bulky gas-powered generator while Jackrabbit hefts a coil of construction lighting. The men move inside the structure, careful to avoid tripping on the debris littering the floor.

"Ain't this a garden spot," Dimitri moans.

Vassyl ignores the comment, switches his LED flashlight on, and leads them to a set of concrete stairs that take them down to the basement level, where the turbines' machinery was kept. It's a much smaller space, but serves their purposes. It has no windows for light to escape, making it the perfect place for the team to lie low until the rest of the pieces are in place.

Sven gets to work getting the generator fired up, finding a way to vent the exhaust outdoors through a crack in the foundation so that they don't die of carbon monoxide poisoning. Dimitri and Jackrabbit string the lights up using U-bolts to secure them to the roof. The industrial lighting is more than enough to illuminate the space once it glows to life.

"Can't we just stay in Boston until we're ready?" Dimitri whines.

"We are ready," Vassyl says, laying out a schematic of the area.

The men gather around, and he walks them through the plan. The firing positions are annotated, as are the likely, secondary, and tertiary avenues of approach and how they will respond to each. He also explains what will happen if key personnel go down and what the escape route and rendezvous will be once their mission is complete.

"There will be an overwhelming response once we open up," Ian says. "We have to be fast."

"How fast?" Jackrabbit asks.

"Fifteen minutes. We need to be on the boat in ten."

"That isn't much of a margin for error," Dimitri says.

"If all goes well, it won't even take that long. Most will be down in the first ten seconds."

"We expect only a few lightly armed agents," Vassyl interjects. "They shouldn't be hard to handle."

"What if they bring more?" Sven asks.

Vassyl moves to the corner and uncovers a pair of M240B machine guns that they brought in earlier. Ian walks over and touches one of them before smiling.

"We must have the same arms supplier. Did our bosses get a bulk rate?"

Ian didn't spend any time at the South Hooksett safehouse during the Manchester operation, but he knows that Marx and the others were armed to the teeth. In addition to the explosives buried along the property's perimeter, they all had AR-15s modified for automatic fire and an M240B machine gun.

"How will we get the feds here?" Jackrabbit asks. "Without them thinking that they're walking into an ambush."

"Ian will take care of that. Any other questions?" Vassyl asks.

There are none.

"Remember, you guys are demolition consultants. Whenever you leave this room, remember to have your hard hats on. Go scout your positions. Look like you are doing an inspection of the place. Stay away from the windows."

The men move out. Vassyl snags the smallest of them by the arm as he starts to follow them.

"Jackrabbit?"

"Yeah?"

"When it gets dark, grab Sven and move the dinghy to the far east end of the building. Make sure it's well-hidden."

"The feds will scope this area before moving in," Ian advises them. "If they see that boat, our escape route will be blown, and we'll be spending the rest of our lives in a federal penitentiary."

"Roger that."

Jackrabbit leaves, leaving Vassyl and Ian to look over the map.

"What are you going to want me to do during this?" Ian asks.

"You're with me."

"Seriously? Hiding down here?"

Vassyl doesn't like the tone of the question. It makes him sound like a coward, which he's not. Sven, Dimitri, and Jackrabbit are all getting paid handsomely to do the heavy lifting in this mission. They are the soldiers in this war. He's the stealthy assassin.

"You want to kill Victoria Larsen?"

"More than anything," Ian says.

"Then when the dust settles, you get the kill shot. The only caveat is that you have to be alive to take it. I didn't bring you into this so you could get yourself planted before you could make that happen."

Vassyl pats Ian on the shoulder and heads up the stairs, leaving the former agent alone in the dingy basement to study the plan. He hopes that Victoria Larsen is so focused on vanquishing her nemesis that she rushes into this. If the FBI has air support assets available and rappel a tactical team in at the far end of the mill, they'll be in trouble. His alternate strategy is workable but not desirable. Worse, Vassyl knows that if he has a Plan B, Ian probably does, too.

# CHAPTER SIXTY-SIX

## TIERRA CAMPOS

*Neighborhood Supermarket*
*Navy Yard, Washington, D.C.*

Not showing my face in public without fear of humiliating verbal assaults has meant quarantining myself in my apartment. Food delivery services are convenient, but the total cost adds up. I have some money tucked away, but with rent and utility payments coming up and no discernible means of income on the horizon, I have to watch my spending.

That means cooking, a skill which I don't possess. Even if I could put together a casserole, I don't have any ingredients. Worse yet, the mac and cheese that I rely on as my go-to comfort food ran out two days ago. Faced with no other prospects to fill my stomach, I decide to brave the short walk from my apartment to the market to pick up some groceries.

It's not something I want to do. I can't help but be hypervigilant after my conversation with Dial Pirate and my Anacostia Riverwalk experience. I check everything around me and note every detail. Soldiers call it keeping your head on a swivel. That's fine in a combat zone with roadside bombs and armed insurgents trying to kill you. This is America. I shouldn't have to feel like I'm about to walk into an ambush every time I step out of my building.

Nobody is waiting for me. None of the pedestrians pays me any attention as I walk up the street. For so long, I wanted to be invisible. Some days I lamented that I was. Today, it's the only wish I have, and it might have been granted. I could also just be getting paranoid. How couldn't I be? I have to take what Dial Pirate said at face value. I don't know him well, but it serves him no purpose to lie about my being followed.

The supermarket is quiet this time of day. I pass people in the aisles who go about their shopping without giving me a second look. I pick up some instant meals from the freezer section and get some chips, knowing that I'll need to get back in the gym, but it won't be this week. Next week doesn't look promising either.

I pay for the groceries and exit the store. Seated at one of the half dozen tables that run alongside the market is a group of hipsters talking among themselves. A couple of them have their phones out and are looking around. I get a sinking feeling as I try to nonchalantly pass by them.

"Hey! Tierra Campos?"

I don't react. I don't look back or acknowledge the group in any way.

"It is her," one of them says as the entire group leaves their table. "Hey! I'm talking to you, bitch!"

They follow me down the sidewalk, talking more amongst themselves than addressing me. My apartment building is up ahead. I'm thinking about making a run for it but won't be very fast carrying two grocery bags. I'm better off walking as quickly as I can and trying to ignore them.

"She is the Great Pretender," one of the girls says, evoking the term that Oliver Jahn uses for me. "She's pretending we're not here!"

The group laughs as they speed up and surround me. I'm scared, and it probably shows despite my attempt not to let it. I feel like I'm at school getting picked on by bullies. We've all either been that kid, been one of the bullies, or seen a movie that depicts it.

"Please move," I say. The guy stands fast. "Okay, I asked nicely. Now move!"

"Or else what?" one of them taunts.

"You think that you're a tough guy by harassing a woman on the street like this?" I ask, hoping to appeal to the girls in the group.

"You think you're a big shot because you can tell lies and get away with it?" one of the girls asks in return. That didn't work.

I try to step around the kid in front of me, who pushes me back in the middle. He goes to grab at me, and I turn my shoulder violently, knocking his hand away from me.

"Keep your hands off me!"

"You're in no position to make demands."

One of the kids snatches a bag of groceries and begins rifling through it. I'm angry, scared, and anxious at the same time. All I want is to be left alone. Is that so hard?

"You eat worse than I do," his friend says after peeking in the bag.

"That's it. I'm calling the police," I say, retrieving the phone from my pocket and turning away from the two most aggressive kids in the group.

The phone gets swatted out of my hand by a third kid who glares at me but says nothing. I know the look in his eyes. I've seen it before. It's hatred, and it's the same look that the kid who entered my school library all those years ago had before he pulled out his rifle and opened fire.

"No, you aren't now," another says, causing the others to laugh.

This is escalating quickly, and my fight or flight instinct kicks in. I choose the latter and drop my remaining groceries to make a run for it, but I feel one of them grab my arm. He spins me around, temporarily throwing me off-balance. I start to protest when a fist crashes down on my temple. My vision explodes into stars, and I stagger. I'm hit in the head again from another direction, and my legs give out. I crash down on the sidewalk and try to clear my vision.

"Get her! Get her!" one of the kids shouts.

I am kicked in the stomach, and then again. I curl into the fetal position and try to shield my face as a flurry of kicks lands on my abdomen and back. I feel a heavy foot come down on my side, forcing the air from my lungs.

"Let me in there."

One of them forces me onto my back and straddles me. I try to throw a punch, but it's weak and lands on his shoulder with no effect other than to annoy him. He hits me in the face several times with closed-fist punches. My cheek...my nose...my eye again...my chin. I feel my lip split open and can taste blood as more punches land in rapid succession. He then grabs my hair, lifts my head, and bangs it hard against the concrete. I sense him move his face inches from my ear.

"Too bad that we aren't by ourselves where we could have some real fun," he says, rubbing his hands over my chest. "Not that you're looking all that good right now."

"Ew!" shrieks one of the girls. "Don't be gross! She's dirty."

He gets off me and spits in my face. "You've needed your ass kicked for a long time, Campos. Hope you enjoyed it."

"Come on," another kid says with urgency to his voice. "We've got to go. Someone is gonna call the cops."

"Yeah, yeah," the leader of the mob says as he brings his foot back. I see it coming forward at me but can't react fast enough to do anything about it. It hits me in the face, knocking my head in the other direction. I feel myself starting to black out. Seconds feel like minutes without anything happening.

"What the hell are you doing?" another voice screams. "Are you stupid or something? Stop taking video and use the phone to call 9-1-1."

"Hey, I wasn't gonna get involved, man," the man says in his own defense.

"Yeah, well, I just involved your useless ass. Call the police. Now!"

I feel someone kneel and hover above me. I can't make out the face. Scared that it could be another assailant, I try to shield myself.

"It's okay. You're going to be okay. Nobody is going to hurt you. Help is coming," the voice reassures me.

Both my eyes are swelling shut. Blood pours out of my nose, and I can taste it in my mouth. It is making me nauseated. The feeling is made worse when the world starts spinning around me.

"Stay with me, ma'am."

"Yeah, I'd like to report an assault. A woman was just beaten...we're on 4th Street Southeast in the Navy Yard near the supermarket. Yeah, she's in bad shape...I don't know, some kids...no, they took off. Okay, we'll wait for it...yes, I'll stay on the line."

Everything hurts. My chest starts to heave as my eyes try to force tears out of my swollen eye sockets. All I can think of is the pain. And sadness. A deep sadness as the sound of a distant siren rises above my ringing ears.

# CHAPTER SIXTY-SEVEN

## OLIVER JAHN

*Tomorrow's News Today Studio*
*Hudson Yards, New York, New York*

Oliver forces himself to get through the opening two segments under the crushing weight of Mi Sun's disapproval. She hasn't said anything specific, but the edge in her voice is noticeable even through an earpiece. And then there is the atmosphere on the set. You would need a jackhammer to break through the tension.

He ends the segment, and the show goes to commercial break. Makeup shows up to powder his face as he reviews his notes. Mi Sun is still silent, and he knows that she's about to blow.

*"Well?"*

"And there it is," he whispers. "Well, what?"

There is no response, and he looks at the digital clock that marks their return from the commercials. He thinks he might be off the hook when the door that leads to the set from the control room bangs open, and Mi Sun storms up to the anchor desk.

"You're a third of the way through the show, and you haven't mentioned Tierra Campos once. Tell me that's an accident."

"I thought my not mentioning her is what you wanted?"

"Don't play dumb with me! The woman was attacked in broad daylight walking home with groceries, and people are starting to point fingers at you. If you don't address it, they will accuse you of burying it."

"We didn't review it in show prep," Oliver says, looking back down at his notes.

"Since when has that ever stopped you? It's not like you use a script or rundown. You fly by the seat of your pants when there is breaking news in Uganda, but somehow you can't make a single mention of what happened to Campos?"

She's right. It was a weak defense to a question that Oliver knows he should have been prepared to answer. The fact is, he doesn't want to mention it for a lot of reasons.

"Okay. Good," Mi Sun says after Oliver doesn't respond.

"Do it in this segment. We're back in sixty," his EP says, storming back toward the control room.

A minute is an eternity in broadcasting unless you aren't sure what you want to say. In that case, it flies by. Oliver has to not come across as callous. Mi Sun is right. He could get scapegoated for this. Maybe that's the angle.

*"Ten seconds,"* she says in his ear. *"Get it done."*

"We're back on *Tomorrow's News Today*. Before we continue to our next subject, I wanted to send my best wishes for a speedy recovery out to Tierra Campos, who was hospitalized after being brutally attacked in Washington.

"No, that wasn't a joke, and what happened to her isn't one. I have my differences with Miss Campos and have created some colorful nicknames about her and how she practices journalism. None of that matters. She is still a person, and while I don't like her, I will also say that no person deserves to be brutally beaten like that.

"Critics are going to say that I'm the cause of the assault. Nothing could be further from the truth. I live in New York. I use words, not fists, and would never advise or call upon any viewer to use violence as a solution to a problem. Tierra Campos will be defeated in the arena of ideas about what good journalism is, not by vigilante justice that lands her in a hospital bed."

Oliver checks the monitor in his peripheral vision. There is no graphic over his shoulder like he's so used to seeing. The camera is centered on him. It's his words that have to leave the impression.

"I also know that there are some out there who cheered when this happened to Miss Campos. I understand the feeling that she brought this upon herself. A part of me agrees with that. But violence should never be condoned, nor should it be forgiven. I sincerely hope that the thugs who did this are brought to justice, and that it never happens to Tierra Campos or any other journalist ever again. Those are my thoughts on the matter, and they're for the record."

Oliver continues with the show. The tension in the studio hasn't subsided, and if anything, it's gotten worse. What more does Mi Sun want? It's a question bound to be answered after he shaves some time off the next topic and they go to commercial break.

"How was that?"

There is a long pause of dead air before Oliver finally looks at the camera.

*"Wrong, on so many levels. A part of you believes that Tierra brought it on herself to get brutally beaten on a street in the nation's capital? Are you serious?"*

"It's true."

*"No, it isn't. She did nothing to deserve that, and you came off as unrepentant and cold in your delivery."*

"I said what I needed to," Oliver argues.

*"And for a man who delivers the news with passion, it was obviously flat. You might as well have been reading from a script."*

"It will be fine."

*"Sure. That must be why you got one more jab in by using the Capitol Beat sign-off for the final thought segment."*

"Did I?"

Oliver looks up again. He honestly didn't realize he had done that. He used to mock Wilson Newman and now Tierra Campos all the time about their tacky show ending, but that wasn't the time to do it. The great part about unscripted news broadcasting is the flexibility it provides. The downside is that it makes him prone to mistakes.

"*Yeah, you did,*" Mi Sun says, her anger and disbelief evident in her tone. Oliver can imagine the look on her face. He's seen it before.

"*Don't worry. You'll be hearing about it all day tomorrow.*"

# CHAPTER SIXTY-EIGHT

## BRIAN COOPER

*Turtle Creek Hotel*
*Lebanon, Ohio*

Every day is long during campaign season. This one feels longer because it's painful to travel down a road and find yourself even farther from your destination. The whole campaign effort is flat, uninspired, and floundering. Everyone senses it except the two men who matter most.

Brian props himself up on his hotel room bed and opens his computer to find the video of Standish's rally in Pennsylvania. He keeps a notepad and pen close and jots down a couple of items as she responds to Bradford's attacks. One thing is evident – Angela Mays and Andrew Li work well together.

It also helps that their candidate has an ounce of common sense and listens to them. For all her faults, Alicia Standish knows that she needs help to become president. All candidates need it to get elected to office, but many still eschew advice or the path to victory professionals devise for them. Sometimes it works out better. Often, it doesn't.

Alicia Standish wants to be president more than anything in the world. If her winning demanded a human sacrifice, she would offer up her own children first. She has put a lot of thought into adopting her strategy, and it shows.

"Yes, I have taken money from Wall Street tycoons," Standish admits at the rally. "I know that many people aren't happy about that. As much as I would love to only accept small-dollar donations like Colin Bradford does. Wait, he does that, right? Someone should probably check on that."

Brian shakes his head. That's brutal. She just threw her attack dogs in the media a big, juicy steak.

"I would also love to know how many of my opponent's donors are people of color. Every candidate will tell you that they welcome all Americans, regardless of their race. Very few of them walk the walk. We do. I have spent decades in politics supporting minority communities and have the record to prove it. Put mine up side-by-side against Governor Bradford's on education, social services, and community support. You'll see."

This is painful to watch. Right now, media companies around the country are doing just that. She played another race card, and the media will run with it. The news articles will all be a comparison while the reporters go after him about donors. He's caught in a pincer movement, to use a military term. She is hitting him on two flanks at once. As predicted, Bradford will spend the week before the Republican National Convention on the defensive. Well played.

Brian checks his watch. It's the time when the office will be empty, and the phone will be picked up, even if it's him calling. The man is a workaholic and will be at his desk poring over numbers. He lives for this, and with that thought, Brian finds the contact in his phone and hits send. The call is picked up on the second ring.

"What do you want, asshole?"

"Seriously, Cubic? That's how you're going to be?"

"I don't like being blackmailed into giving my work away, Brian."

"It's not blackmailing. It's a mutually beneficial arrangement. We are enjoying the benefits of a non-zero-sum game. You are giving me information in return for me not sharing mine with others. We're both getting what we want."

"Yeah, right," the pollster mumbles. "What do you want?"

"You know the answer to that. What are your latest polls saying?"

He laughs. "That your candidate is an idiot."

"I'm aware. Can you be more specific?"

Cubic sighs. "He's losing support nationwide, almost equally. That level of consistency is almost impressive. He's down in all demographics and is hemorrhaging what little support he had in the black community. College-educated males are abandoning him, and support with women is softening, even in the red states."

Brian rubs his chin as he listens. He knew it would be bad but didn't think it would be this bad.

"Is there any good news?"

"Yeah. Alicia Standish won't win all fifty states and the district. Although, if he keeps this up, she might be close. She has a message that resonates with voters without saying anything meaningful. The media doesn't press her on issues because they don't need to. Bradford attacks, she counters, and they chase after him. If this election comes down to a candidate's personality with voters, Standish wins in a walk."

"Have you revised your prediction model for the race?"

"Not yet. I'm going to wait and see what happens at the RNC. If the convention goes well, Bradford's still in the fight. If it fails to motivate his base or start attracting support from outside the party, he's toast."

"So, it needs to make a splash?"

Cubic laughs. "Why is it that all you political types are so narrow-focused?"

"It comes with the job description."

"It must. Look, none of the long-term trends benefit Bradford right now. The convention will give him a bump in the polls, but he needs more than a splash. He needs to do something in Detroit to change the narrative of the whole election."

Brian continues to watch Standish's speech on television. Their applause lines are far more enthusiastic than anything he sees at Bradford's rallies. Her attacks on him are more subtle, and they are working. Standish is laying the foundation for the media to make this election about race, and she'll win if that's one of the top three voter issues in November.

"What about Standish's likability?" Brian asks.

"It's not sky-high but not in the cellar either. Like I said, she resonates even though voters characterize her as cold and calculating. The more the electorate sees her, the more they are starting to get used to her. She's not the kind of candidate that will make their spines tingle, but I suppose that's better than being irrelevant."

"You know that our internal polling is telling a different story."

"Your internal polls are garbage," Cubic counters. "I've seen them. They are overweighting all the wrong groups in this election cycle and ask leading questions. They don't paint an accurate picture because your pollsters don't want one. Someone over there has an agenda and is skewing the results to support it."

That explains a lot. Brevin must be feeling more threatened than he thought. He will only remain as campaign manager if he gets results, so he's fabricating them. Typical. He is more interested in hanging on to a job for the next three months than focusing on winning and earning a bigger one for four years.

"Okay, thanks, Cubic."

"Screw off, Cooper. Don't bother me again until after the convention."

The pollster hangs up. Cubic is a valuable source of information who may never speak to him again after this. Brian knows that he can spin it any way he likes, but it is blackmail. It's also a concern for another time. Election politics is about momentum. Right now, he needs to figure out how to keep his candidate in the game because Alicia Standish is running up the score.

# CHAPTER SIXTY-NINE

## SSA VICTORIA LARSEN

*St. Elmo's Fryer*
*Revere, Massachusetts*

Victoria has always had a weakness for fried food. When she left the Boston Division never to return, it was assumed that she would never again visit her local haunt a mere ten-minute drive from the Chelsea office. Victoria was a regular at the St. Elmo's Fryer for years and still managed to stay impeccably fit.

She watches Rigo enter the diner, remove his sunglasses, and look around before spotting her in the corner. He walks over and slides into the opposite bench in her booth table without invitation. He's the boss, so technically, he doesn't need one. It's not like she would tell him to leave.

"This is the place, isn't it?"

"What place?"

"I asked your old friend Audric LeClair about you, and he said he betrayed you in a diner. I'm guessing this is the one."

"It's close to the office."

The waitress comes up, and Rigo orders a bacon cheeseburger and fries with a Coke without even looking at the menu. It's a stark difference from what happened the last time she sat in here. She offers him a slight smile.

"What?"

"Audie whined about the food here."

"Yeah, well, you won't hear me do that," Rigo says, leaning back.

"How did you find me?"

"I put a GPS on your car," Rigo says, forcing a smile after earning a displeased look from Victoria. "I asked some of your former colleagues where you might disappear to during the day. Apparently, your love for this place isn't a secret. What is a mystery is why you haven't touched your food."

Victoria looks down at her uneaten cheeseburger. "It turns out that I'm not very hungry. Are you here to try to talk me into leaving town again?"

"Nah. You won't listen."

"You're my boss, Rigo. You could order me back to Washington."

Rigo smiles. "Let's not pretend that you'd listen then either."

Victoria nods. He's right. Even if he sent her back to D.C., she would find a way around the order. "Tell me something. If our roles were reversed, would you leave?"

"Hell no. We're similar in that respect. It's part of the reason I hired you. How's Tierra doing?"

She has cracked ribs, bruised eye sockets, a fractured nose, a couple of lacerations, contusions everywhere, and a concussion. She's in rough shape but will live. She's lucky…they could have killed her."

"Tierra told you all that?"

"No. She can't really speak until the swelling in her face goes down. She gave the doctor permission to share the information with me."

"I'm sorry, Victoria. What did the Metro PD have to say? I know you contacted them."

"Their working theory is that it was a mugging gone bad."

"But you don't believe that."

"Not for a second."

"Do you think it was Drucker? Maybe his way of getting back at you?"

"No. Ian would have killed her."

It was a definitive statement. The former FBI agent also wouldn't have risked doing it outside a supermarket in broad daylight. All it takes is a veteran or off-duty Marine to see what's happening and intervene. The story would have been different had the one who rushed to Tierra's side after the attack been half a block closer when it happened.

"Maybe it was random violence."

"Not likely. Tierra was fired from *Capitol Beat* over a perfectly acceptable interview. A competitor has mobilized a social media mob to cancel her, and she was beaten on a street in broad daylight. Two of my colleagues were murdered, and Ian Drucker called my personal cell phone to taunt me about it." Victoria leans forward and looks directly into Rigo's eyes. "Why?"

"You think they're linked," he says, taking the question and turning it into a statement.

"Tierra and I have a history. It's no secret that we are friends and that we're both looking into the SOF."

"Coincidence?" Rigo asks before grimacing. "That's right. You don't believe in them."

"There is something bigger going on. I just don't know what."

"If any other agent said that, I'd say they were imagining things."

"But?"

"Every single person I spoke to said that you have incredible instincts. If you're saying that there's something more to this, I believe you. Where do we start?"

"I don't know. I thought we would find something with Isiah or the SOF. Nothing has panned out."

"It doesn't mean it won't."

"No, it doesn't, but it feels like we're looking in the wrong place."

"Where should we be looking?"

Victoria shakes her head and stares out the window at the side parking lot. There's nothing of interest out there. She just doesn't want to have to admit that she has no idea what to do next.

"Do you think that Ian is close?" Rigo asks, changing the subject after the waitress arrives with his food.

"I think he's trying to spook me. He's in the area but not lurking behind some corner ready to ambush me."

"Do you think he'll call again?"

"I don't plan on giving him the opportunity," Victoria states, a steely determination in the tone of her voice. "He's going to mess up. When he does, we need to be ready to pounce."

"What are you thinking?"

"We need a tactical team on standby."

Rigo rubs his chin. "That's overkill, isn't it?"

"Maybe, but after what happened in South Hooksett, I don't want to take any chances. A small army of New Hampshire State Police officers walked into machine gun fire like we were in Afghanistan. I'm not making that mistake again."

"Okay. I'll make it happen. Anything else?"

"Yeah, enjoy your burger, and let's talk about anything but work for the next twenty minutes."

"Okay," Rigo says, reaching for the ketchup. "So, babe, come here often?"

He offers a wink and a cheesy first-date smile, managing to get Victoria to laugh for the first time in days.

# CHAPTER SEVENTY

## TIERRA CAMPOS

*Washington Memorial Hospital*
*Washington, D.C.*

I lie on my back and count the tiny holes in the ceiling tile above my head. I don't get very far before losing track and having to start all over. There is nothing else to do. The television is unbearable to watch. I don't have anything to read. There is nobody to call to even bring me my Kindle or buy me a paperback.

This is the loneliest I have ever felt. Despite regaining the ability to speak and actually be understood, there is nobody outside of doctors and nurses for me to talk to. Victoria at least checked up on me when she heard what happened. There are a couple of bouquets and cards around the room, but none from the people I care about most. The worst part of it is, I know I'm the one to blame for it.

I roll my head to the right when I hear a knock on the open door. I would smile even more broadly at the sight of Josh carrying an enormous bouquet if it didn't hurt so much.

"How are you feeling?" he asks as I raise the head portion of my adjustable bed and adjust my hospital gown.

"Like I got hit by a train. What are you doing here?"

"Did you seriously think I wouldn't come to visit?"

"After the way I treated you the other day, no."

"You should know me better than that. I would have been here earlier, but I wasn't sure if you wanted to see me," Josh says, pulling up a chair to my bedside.

"You only thought that because I'm a jerk."

"You're not a jerk."

"Yes, I am. I came to the conclusion that I'm a terrible person even before this happened."

"That's not true."

"It is," I argue. "I've had a chance to do a lot of thinking."

"Getting hospitalized will do that."

"Yes, but no...before that. Be serious for a second, please. I've made so many mistakes. I need to apologize to you."

"What drugs do they have you on?" he asks.

"I asked you to be serious," I say, trying to keep a grip on my emotions.

"You don't need to apologize."

"Yes, I do. I lashed out at you in my apartment, but not because you were interrupting me. It's because everything you said was right, and it touched a nerve. I've pushed everyone I care about away from me, and for what?"

"Tierra, everyone goes through this at some point in their life. It's a part of each of our journeys."

"No, mine is worse. After the Summerville shooting, I was lost. I was stuck at a dead-end job that I hated with no prospects for a bright future. You snapped me out of that."

Josh shakes his head. "The interview with Ethan Harrington did."

"And it was you who convinced me to follow my instincts and go after him. I was so angry after losing my job and so unsure that I did the right thing. It ended up with me getting the best opportunity I could ever hope for. I should have been happy with that, but I wasn't. I wanted more."

"*Capitol Beat*."

I nod. "I knew in my heart that was why Austin was acting the way he was. I should have talked it out with him. Instead, I let it fester to the point where leaving was my only option."

"Tierra—"

"No, let me finish. Please. When I left, I turned my back on everyone. Who does that? What kind of person abandons their friends like that?"

"The lead character of almost every Lifetime movie ever made."

I start to laugh, but it hurts. "And now me. Josh, I'm so sorry for everything. You're the best friend I have ever had. You saved my life both literally and metaphorically. I need to start listening to you more. Like I should have all along."

"Now I know you have a concussion. I need you to repeat that once I hit record," Josh says, reverting to the joking as he pulls out his phone.

I begin to cry. There is no fighting it any longer.

"I can't afford to lose my friends over this. I can't afford to lose you."

Josh takes my hand in his. "You're not going to lose me. I know you think you owe me an apology, but you don't. I forgave you seconds after I walked out of your apartment. That's why I'm joking around with you, even though I know it annoys you."

"Jerk," I say, forcing a smile while I wipe the tears off my cheeks.

"Your other friends will understand if you give them the same heartfelt apology you gave me. I'm going to bet that they won't hold it against you either."

"If they do?"

"Then they were never your friends to begin with."

"How do I find out?"

Josh gives me a knowing smile and retrieves my phone from the tray table next to the bed. He holds it up and wiggles it in his hand.

"It starts with a phone call. Then we're going to break you out of here."

I offer him a smile. "Sounds good to me."

# CHAPTER SEVENTY-ONE

## VASSYL STRACHENKO

*Abandoned Mill*
*Loughborough, Massachusetts*

Vassyl watches from the doorway to the boiler house as Ian gets dropped off in the asphalt residential parking lot and walks down to the site. He adjusts his ridiculous hard hat and moves back into the bowels of the building, or what's left of it. Despite misgivings about the former FBI agent's role in this plan, he actually views him as competent and reliable. It's a shame what will happen to him when this is over.

"How did it go?" the assassin asks when Ian enters the structure.

"Done deal. The truck was returned to the rental place, as requested."

"Were you recognized?"

"I don't think so. I did make sure a camera or three got a good look at my face, though."

"Do you think that it's enough for the FBI to catch on?"

Ian shakes his head. "They're closed-circuit systems. The FBI will only get access with good reason, and they have to be looking in this area first."

"Then let's make sure they are."

Vassyl pulls out his cell and calls a number that he never thought he'd use. Contact of any manner with law enforcement is usually avoided by people in his line of work. For that reason, he's been looking forward to this and switches the phone to use the speaker so Ian can listen.

"FBI tip line," the overworked operator informs him.

"Hi. I live in Loughborough, Massachusetts. This may be nothing, but there's been some strange activity at the abandoned mill behind my apartment."

"What kind of activity, sir?"

"A couple of men have been walking around. They show up in a white pickup."

"Do they work for the city?" the woman asks.

"They might. I don't know. Here's the thing: the truck was there all night. No reason for that. That building is abandoned and doesn't even have a working bathroom."

Ian nods emphatically. He's the second-most to complain about the lack of facilities, with Dimitri getting the "Whiner-in-Chief" award at their spartan conditions.

"Can I get your name, sir?"

"I'd rather not if that's okay. I don't want to get involved. They could be cooking meth in there or somethin'. I don't want to endanger my family."

Ian covers his mouth to prevent himself from laughing. The way Vassyl made that sound was priceless. He knows how to play the role of the scared informant. He's probably run into a few during his career who are no longer living.

"Do you have reason to believe they are manufacturing methamphetamine?"

"Uh, no. It could be the guys who killed your agents, for all I know."

"Where is this mill?" the woman asks.

"It's next to the river off Bridge Street. You can't miss it."

"Okay, thank you for the information. If you see anything else suspicious or feel like you are in immediate danger, please don't be afraid to call the local authorities."

"Okay, I will. Thank you."

Vassyl ends the call.

"Brilliant."

"Unless my assumptions are wrong and the tip line just sends the information to the local police department."

"Yeah, that'll be the day," Ian says, rolling his eyes. "The FBI doesn't share. They deal with federal crimes and like to hog all the glory. It will be logged in the system by the woman who answered the phone but won't make its way down the food chain."

"Let's hope they manage to put two and two together before we die of boredom down here."

Vassyl waves Ian over to the stairs, and they return to the basement. The three mercenaries are starting to go a little stir crazy. It won't be long before the Russian roulette starts, and he's cleaning brains off the walls.

"Larsen will if she gets the information. They would have flagged anything mentioning me for analysis," Ian explains as they reach the musty basement level. "It could be compelling enough to dig into."

"Showtime?" Sven asks with the eagerness of an eight-year-old on his first trip to Disney World.

"Soon. Let's make the final preparations and take your last pisses. In an hour, we won't be going outside until we know whether or not they took the bait."

The three men look at each other in confusion. "How will we know?"

"I know a guy," Vassyl says. "Jackrabbit, go check the boat one last time. Make sure the engine fires up quickly. We'll have to get out of here fast when this is over."

"Roger that."

"Move all the ammo up to your positions. There is no reason to leave any down here. I should have the composition of the force once they decide to move in. For now, we assume the worst."

"What happens if they don't figure out that we're here?" Dimitri asks.

"Then we stay hidden and tip them off again. We'll repeat the cycle as long as it takes."

"Where will we piss until then?"

Vassyl walks over to the supplies along the wall and throws Sven a milk jug.

"Aw, come on, man? You serious?"

"They are expecting two lightly armed men," Ian interjects. "If the FBI learns that you guys are here, or they see our firepower, tactical teams will arrive in force from all directions, and we will die."

"Don't let this place be the last you ever see because you got sloppy. We are in ambush mode. Stay away from windows and no unnecessary movement. Understood?"

The men nod grudgingly. Vassyl knows they will do as instructed, although not without complaints. It's the nature of all foot soldiers, whether they belong to professional armies or are freelancers for hire.

"This operation will be over soon. If things go as planned, seventy-two hours from now, you'll all be sipping drinks on a Caribbean beach."

# CHAPTER SEVENTY-TWO

## SSA VICTORIA LARSEN

*Boston FBI Field Office*
*Chelsea, Massachusetts*

Victoria sits in an empty meeting room doubled over and staring at the ground as she listens to Tierra explain what happened. The shock has worn off. The guilt is just setting in. They haven't said much to each other since she returned to the FBI and took this assignment. It breaks her heart that they are drifting apart and hurts worse that she can't be back in Washington with her friend.

"This wasn't a random assault, Vic."

"What do you mean? I thought you said they were young thugs?"

"I did, and they were. That's only half the story," Tierra says, her words muffled as she speaks through a swollen mouth, making her hard to understand over the phone. "It was coordinated."

"Coordinated? You mean some teenagers got together and decided to silence you?" Victoria asks, skeptical of the dubious claim.

"No. This is different. I got a phone call from Dial Pirate."

Victoria perks up. She won't tell Miranda that one of the most hunted hackers in the country is on a first-name basis with her best friend. They have a history that dates back to Ethan Harrington and the Brockhampton investigation, but only Tierra knows who he is. The FBI's Cyber Division pressed her more than once to see if she could find out. Victoria rebuffed them, but she isn't looking forward to revisiting those awkward conversations again.

"What did he want?"

"The short version is that he said pictures of me in public spaces were being posted online to geo-tag my location. They were timestamped so people could hunt me down to harass me."

"How many times did that happen?" Victoria says, suddenly taking this very seriously.

"On two occasions at least. This was the first time they got violent. Now, who do we know called for that?"

"Oliver Jahn," Victoria mumbles.

"The kids called me the Queen of Pretenders. They were his disciples. I think he's behind it all, Vic."

"Can you prove it?"

"Not yet. DP has a lead that he's following. If he manages to uncover something, I'm going to cut the bastard off at the knees."

"There you are! I've been looking all over for you," Shawn says, bursting into the room. "We have some leads on Drucker. Come on."

"I'm sorry, I have to go, Tierra."

"I know. Go get the bastard. We'll talk later. Good luck."

Victoria hangs up and rushes to catch up with Shawn, who is striding back to the main conference room they have been huddled in for weeks. This had better be good. Victoria already feels guilty that she hasn't been there for Tierra. Now she just abruptly ended their conversation.

"What is it?" she demands as the two of them charge into the room. It already has an air of excitement that has been absent since Fuller and Takara were murdered.

"What are *they*," Rigo says, correcting her. "As in two of them. The first was an anonymous tip from a residential complex in Loughborough about strange activity at an abandoned mill."

Steve brings up images on his screen, and Victoria peers in.

"It's a construction site. So what?"

"The company awarded the contract by the city went bankrupt, and all work stopped months ago," Amanda explains.

"So why would anybody be there?" Shawn asks.

"I can think of a dozen reasons," Victoria says, hoping that they have more than an anonymous tip and a boatload of speculation.

"Let's find out. Amanda, call the city," Rigo orders. "Find out what the deal is. We need to know if anyone is authorized to be on site."

"You got it."

"That place is long past its prime," Steve says.

"And a great hiding spot," Shawn adds.

"You said there are two leads?"

"Yeah, a man matching Ian's description returned a white pickup truck at a rental location a few hours ago. The anonymous caller reported that a similar vehicle would stay overnight at that site for no apparent reason."

It's still a stretch, but more that they've had to go on than anything they've uncovered so far, and they might as well chase it down. It's not like leads are pouring in.

"All right. Shawn, can you check the cameras in the Loughborough area? Start with the rental company. I want to see if that bastard was dumb enough to show his face."

"Hey boss? The city has me on hold while they put me through to their engineering department."

"Figures."

"Yeah, but get this – the city's chief engineer went missing a couple of days ago. They found his truck outside town, but he wasn't with it. His last known location was an abandoned mill."

Rigo looks at Victoria. "I don't believe in coincidences either. Let's check rideshare companies for any activity in that area," Rigo says. "I want to see if anyone was picked up at that site today. If so, I want to know where they went."

They walk over to his end of the long table to start making phone calls. While Victoria salivates at the thought that Drucker finally made a mistake, it's almost too much to hope for.

"Rigo, we need to get eyes on that site. If this pans out, we need to know if they move. We might not find them again if they do."

"I will coordinate to get a tactical team there. They can do surveillance from the adjacent apartment building.

Victoria nods. The last thing she wants to do is tip Ian and Vassyl off that they are onto them. She let Ian slip through her fingers once before and isn't about to let that happen again.

# CHAPTER SEVENTY-THREE

## BRIAN COOPER

*Republican National Convention*
*Detroit, Michigan*

Everything is bigger when the political conventions start: the media coverage, the personalities of those involved, the attention span of the public, and the price of failure. While a poor performance doesn't necessarily spell disaster for a candidate, it puts them on the path for a rough November.

Right now, Bradford is the Union Army at Little Round Top. He needs to hold the hill to have a shot at winning the battle and the war. Right now, his defenses are about to collapse. Nothing short of a bayonet charge will save them, and he doesn't have it in him to order one. Brevin certainly doesn't.

"Hey, Aimee," Brian says, walking into a makeshift office buried deep in the heart of the arena that temporarily houses the campaign's speechwriting staff.

"Hi, Brian. What can I do for you?"

"I'm looking for the draft copy of the governor's acceptance speech. I haven't seen it come through my inbox yet."

The other writers immediately return to what they were doing, each going out of his or her way to avoid eye contact with Brian. It's a bad omen. Maybe not getting a copy of the speech wasn't the oversight he thought it was.

"I'm sorry. I'm not authorized to share it with anyone," Aimee says.

"With anyone? Or just with me?"

Aimee gets up and gestures him out to the hallway. The arena is bustling with activity, so it isn't any more private here than it is in the room they were just in. Whatever is on her mind, she doesn't want to say it in front of her peers.

"Look, we were all instructed not to provide you with anything."

"Who ordered that?"

She gives him a look. "Brevin. He was unambiguous about the consequences of violating it. Brevin also said that he would fire all of us if he can't specifically determine who leaked documents to you. Nobody in there is willing to lose their jobs."

"No, no, I get it. You don't look like you agree with it, though."

"I've listened to the guidance you've given the governor. I think you're an arrogant pain in the ass, but you're right more than you're wrong. I think it's a mistake that the candidate and his chief of staff aren't listening to you."

"Then help me. Brevin will never know."

"I can't. I want to, but I need this job and won't risk theirs," Aimee says, pointing back to the room. "We'll be out on the street and unemployed until the midterms. Money aside, my peers also don't want to give up a shot at working at the White House."

"On our current trajectory, none of you will be," Brian complains.

"I know, but it's not my decision to make. I write what I'm told and do the best I can at it."

"I know you do. Since you can't give me the speech, will you at least tell me what's in it?"

She shakes her head before glancing back into the writers' room. "Nothing you're going to like. That's all I'm going to say, so please, don't ask me for more."

Brian nods. He doesn't want to put Aimee or any of the other speechwriters in a bad spot. He nods and takes a deep breath.

"Fine!" Brian shouts, catching her off-guard. "Your lack of cooperation will be noted! If you won't tell me about the speech, then I'll find out myself. Get out of my face!"

Aimee cowers at the sudden violent outburst until he gives her a wink. She relaxes and mouths "thank you" to him. Brian just gave her the cover she needed. There's no doubt that every other person in that room would have grilled her about this conversation, and probably wouldn't have believed her denials.

He storms down the hallway until he rounds the corner and adopts a normal gait. He needs to talk to Bradford. After a few minutes of searching, Brian finds one of the governor's campaign staffers.

"Where's the candidate?"

"He's conducting a strategy session with Brevin," the guy says, trying not to pay the consultant any attention.

Now he's getting pissed off. "Why wasn't I told?"

"I was specifically asked to keep that from you. I'm sorry, but the orders came from—"

"I know who they came from. It's all right."

This is not good. As much as Brian doesn't want to follow Tweedledee and Tweedledum into the jaws of defeat, there really is no other option. He could go to the press with his concerns, but that would get him fired even faster.

With nothing more to do in the arena, Brian heads to the staff entrance and spends a few minutes chatting with the guards on his way out. The one thing near sports arenas and stadiums in any city are a selection of good bars. He could use a drink.

He sits and orders a beer before noticing Standish on television again. She is taking questions, and the media is gushing over her. She doesn't even need to do fundraisers with all the free air time and softball questions she gets. It's good to see that the propaganda arm of the Democratic party is still hard at work. The only thing that breaks him from his trance is the phone vibrating in his pocket. He hopes it's Brevin calling, but no such luck.

"Miss Campos. I've been meaning to call you but wasn't sure you were up to it."

"Hi, Brian. Thanks."

"How are you?" he asks, with genuine concern in his voice.

"I'm looking rough and am sore as hell, but I'll be okay."

"What happened to you is nauseating. That kind of thing should never happen in this country."

"I couldn't agree more. It's almost funny that the mob is coming after me, and I'm not even reporting the news right now. Oliver Jahn saw to that."

"He's a poser. I didn't even like that jackass when I worked for Standish, and he agreed with everything we said and did."

"I'm happy to hear you say that."

"Uh, oh. This is about the time that I should be ordering another drink."

"I'm taking the fight to Jahn and all his disciples."

Tierra has a lot to learn about how Washington works, but he admires the woman's guts. She isn't one to shy away from tough battles when most people would. It's an admirable quality.

"That's a bold plan. Is there anything I can do?"

"It's funny that you should ask. I'm calling you because there is something."

Brian listens to Tierra as she makes her sales pitch. He can't stop his jaw from hanging open. He may admire her, but she's crazy and is asking for the impossible.

"You want to do *what?*"

# CHAPTER SEVENTY-FOUR

## OLIVER JAHN

*Republican National Convention*
*Detroit, Michigan*

Oliver's network-rented town car pulls up to the arena access point designated for the media. The main entrance where the who's who of the Republican establishment draws all the cheerleaders decked out in American flag paraphernalia. The men and women congregated here are a decidedly different flavor.

If you are an obnoxious demonstrator who believes that the media is to blame for all the ills of modern society, this is the place to be. There are barricades and uniformed police to keep them back, but media personalities and reporters still have to run the gantlet to get inside the building. There is no doubt in Oliver's mind that it was done on purpose.

The jeering and boos start the moment he and Mi Sun exit the vehicle. He's not a popular figure amongst the Bradford faithful, not that he has given them any reason to embrace them. Still, the insults are jarring, vulgar, and often deeply personal. More than one reference is made about him having improper relations with his mother.

"I don't think they like me," Oliver says, leaning over toward Mi Sun as they walk the short distance to the arena under the hateful eyes and louder mouths of the hecklers.

"Whatever gave you that idea?" she replies, looking around anxiously.

"I don't know. Maybe it's the effigies of me and all the incorrectly spelled signs."

"You probably shouldn't enjoy antagonizing them so much."

"What fun is there in that?"

Mi Sun stops a few paces from the door, making the security guards anxious.

"They're Americans, Oliver. Just like you and me."

The pundit paints a smile on his face to hide his own nervousness. "How much are you willing to bet that they don't think that when they look at you? Come on."

He grabs her arm gently before she yanks it away, but he's relieved that his executive producer at least enters the arena. He is in no mood for a confrontation.

"You don't know that," she barks as they reach the magnetometers.

"No, I don't. Look at that crowd behind us," Oliver says, pointing back toward the doors as she empties her pockets into a plastic dish. "See its diversity? There isn't any. Most of them are white, with a few other token colors mixed in."

"What's your point?"

"I think I just made it."

The doors open after another journalist passes through the crucible. The insults are even worse, although he can't imagine why.

"God, I love Republicans," he says as he passes through his metal detector, and they get the okay to proceed from security when their credentials are checked.

"Since when do you care about the conservative point of view?"

Mi Sun grimaces. "Just because I don't agree with them doesn't mean that I discount their opinions."

"Oh, the racist, xenophobic, misogynistic ones, or something else?"

"How many stereotypes can you fit into one sentence?"

"It's true," Oliver argues.

"It's not, and you know it."

Oliver and Mi Sun wind their way down the passage in silence. He's unnerved knowing that he hasn't been on the same page as his EP for a while. Now the stress fractures are getting broader and deeper.

"You never used to complain about this before. How long have you felt this way?"

Mi Sun doesn't look at him. "Long enough."

"You say that you respect their opinions. Well, I don't."

"Clearly," she mumbles.

"There is nothing they think or say that is worthy of my respect."

"You know, Oliver, for a man who is intent on growing his audience, you're very willing to disregard half the population."

Oliver waves a hand. "I don't need or want them to be a part of my audience."

"Yeah, groupthink has always worked out so well. Perhaps you can push for having thought police or the Ministry of Truth. It's almost too bad that the cancel culture wasn't around when Orwell wrote *1984*."

"It's a tool."

"It's the Salem Witch Trials."

"No, it isn't. What cancel culture does is necessary."

"Yeah, sure," Mi Sun says, picking up her gait as they get closer to the elevator bank. "If you think you can achieve some sort of ideological purity by shaming offenders and forcing the rest into silence out of fear, you're mistaken."

Oliver smiles. "All evidence to the contrary."

"Then what you aren't noticing is the seething contempt that is building. Someday, it will erupt, and it could destroy America. In the meantime, it's sure to destroy our show."

"Our show is about building a better America," Oliver says, pressing the up button.

"And you think that Tierra Campos almost getting beaten to death is a step in that direction?"

"That's not fair."

"It was the next logical step. If an ounce of accountability existed today, you would be getting questions about what you've said about Campos on the show, and challenged as to whether you're partially to blame."

"I had nothing to do with what happened to her!" Oliver shouts, now losing the fight to control his temper. Why doesn't she see?

"I never said you did. But it's undeniable that the kids who did this probably watch TNT."

"We don't know that."

Mi Sun rolls her eyes. "Oliver, you've made a living injecting speculation and opinion into your broadcasts. Don't stop now just because it's inconvenient."

She climbs aboard the elevator once the doors open. She waits patiently for her boss, whose feet are welded to the floor with the heat of his anger.

"Come on, we're running late."

Oliver finally joins her, content to let the conversation die. Mi Sun has always been in his corner, but something has changed. He needs to have a reset with her. Unfortunately, it will have to wait until after the RNC concludes. This is not the time or the place for showing anything other than a unified front.

# CHAPTER SEVENTY-FIVE

## TIERRA CAMPOS

*Front Burner Washington Office*
*Washington, D.C.*

It's beyond eerie in here. An office building that used to be a hive of activity is entirely desolate. There is no receptionist, no security, and worst of all, no reporters. The sensors trigger the lights to come on as I navigate the corridors to my old stomping ground. The place is that empty.

My old office is no different. All the desks except one are cleared off. Most of the computer equipment has been removed and probably sold for operating cash. It's depressing.

"Depressing, isn't it?" Austin says from his doorway.

"That was my exact thought, yes."

"How are you doing?"

"I'm sore and still on some potent painkillers, but I'll be okay," I explain. "It looks worse than it is."

"I'm so sorry," Austin says. The look on his face tells me that he means it.

He waves me into his office. On the wall opposite the window is his gigantic whiteboard that I half expected to be empty. Instead, it's filled with sticky notes, pictures, arrows in different colors, and boxes with either names or question marks.

"What's all this?"

"Oh, just something I've been working on. I'll explain another time."

"Hello, Tierra," Logan says after he materializes in the doorway.

The tone is cold but not overtly hostile. The room still gets tense until I turn, and he gets a good look at my face.

"Oh, my God!"

He walks over and gives me a hug. The three of us chat about what happened until we hear Olivia and Tyler arrive. Their reaction to my appearance mimicks Logan's. After some more explanation, we get down to the reason I asked everyone to meet here.

"What's this all about, Tierra? I don't think anybody is comfortable being here right now," Olivia offers.

"We're not here to revisit the whole Hatfields and McCoys thing."

"It's kind of hard not to, don't ya think?" Tyler asks.

"No, I don't think that at all. But I'm also not here to patch up friendships or help us get past all the bad blood."

"Then why are we here?" Logan asks.

"I want to put the band back together."

"That's all well and good," Austin says, "but *Front Burner* isn't going to be here."

"What if it was?"

"How?" Olivia asks.

"Follow me."

We head to the elevator and go up to another desolate floor. I open the double doors to see the desk and equipment just as it was before I left. The *Front Burner* podcast studio has never gotten much use.

"Now it's a party," Naomi Merritt says from a chair in the corner. I don't think we've ever had this many people in here.

"You're still here, Naomi?" Tyler asks.

"Yeah, not doing what I was hired for, obviously."

Naomi was hired only about six months before I started at *Front Burner*. She had success launching podcasts and was brought on to do the same thing here. It didn't work out, so management found other roles for her in the office because they didn't want to lose her.

"What are you doing?"

"Everything I can until they turn the lights off for good."

"I think I know where you are going with this, Tierra," Logan says. "You want to monetize podcasts to do what? Save *Front Burner*?"

"That's crazy. We couldn't get this off the ground when we had the money," Tyler adds. Even Austin offers a nod after a quick glance at Naomi.

"That's because we didn't have the right frontman."

"You?" Olivia asks.

"No. I said front*man*."

The three men look at each other and shake their heads.

"I ain't doing it," Logan says.

"You're not pretty enough anyway," Tyler argues in a tone reminiscent of the days when they would always clown around with each other.

"None of you guys would," I say. "I already have a plan in motion. It's a crazy idea and a long shot at best, but we used to make a living off of those. Since there's nothing to lose, why not give it one more try?"

"You want us all to work together again?" Olivia asks, not sold on the idea of coming back.

"It's not possible," Austin decrees. "Even if we all agreed to try it, we have no money."

"So, let's make some. We start small and add sponsors and advertisers as we go. It's how *Front Burner* was built in the first place."

"Podcasting is cheap. It's why they're so ubiquitous," Naomi says. "All the equipment is here. We just need someone to host it and compelling source material to present."

"Leadership won't go for this," Austin interjects.

"The honchos are all interviewing for new jobs. What do they care? It's basically down to you and me now," Naomi says, her eyes pleading with him. "We have a plan, Austin. This fits in with it. Tierra is right. What do we have to lose?"

Austin rocks on his heels a few times. I think a big part of him wants to do this. Something is holding him back, and it isn't about the cost or what the soon-to-be-former directors have to say about it. It must be something more personal.

"What plan?" Olivia and Tyler ask at the same time. They both look at me as if I have any idea what Austin and Naomi are talking about.

"It's a story for another time."

"Way to leave us hanging. Just like old times," Tyler grumbles, earning a sharp look from Austin.

"Enough, guys. I know there are still many bad feelings, but three of us are unemployed, and the rest will be soon. We can look past our differences and work on fixing our relationships later, or we can all go down in flames while our enemies clap."

"Do you really think we can do this?" Logan asks, warming to the idea.

"There is nothing in the world more dangerous than a group of determined people with nothing to lose."

Austin looks over at Naomi, who smiles. The line struck a chord with both of them. Whatever they are cooking up must have been on the stove for a while.

"Okay. Why the hell not? What's your plan?" Austin asks, at least willing to hear her out.

"I think someone needs to run to a liquor store. You're all going to want to be sitting down with a stiff drink for this."

# CHAPTER SEVENTY-SIX

## BRIAN COOPER

*Republican National Convention*
*Detroit, Michigan*

Brian is shown into a conference room that he supposes the executives of Detroit sports teams use. All the power players are here, including Governor Bradford and Brevin Hawkins from the campaign, Monica Stengel and GOP strategists, party brass, and convention organizers.

His request on behalf of Tierra must have made waves. Brian assumed that it would be quickly dismissed. From the looks on the people's faces, there was a contentious debate on the subject. It's good to know that common sense still exists in some form.

"Have a seat, Brian," the governor says. "We discussed your request at length. We're not comfortable allowing Tierra Campos to take the stage for the journalism roundtable tomorrow."

Brian frowns. Common sense may exist, but it rarely wins.

"What?" he asks.

"Her request has been denied," Brevin says, almost thumping his chest as he delivers the rebuke.

"Why? She's the one non-partisan journalist left in the country."

"Do we need to spell it out for you, Brian? We need people on that stage who share our ideology, not someone who will turn it into a spectacle."

"Oh, I see. You want to act like the Democrats."

"That's not—"

"You're holding a roundtable about fairness in journalism. Except you're omitting the woman with the most compelling story to tell about it."

"It's not one we're interested in hearing."

"Are you serious? If you're afraid of causing a stir, you might want to think about how you're going to defend not having her on that stage in light of what happened."

"Your objection is noted and dismissed," Brevin concludes.

"You're okay with this, Governor?"

Bradford leans back in his chair. He rubs the edge of the table with his hands as he avoids eye contact. Then he stops and regards Brian.

"I'm not the nominee yet. I have no say."

"You're the leader of the party, if not formally, then definitely in spirit. This convention and what you say at it tomorrow will go a long way in determining whether you're filling out a change of address form for 1600 Pennsylvania Avenue or giving a concession speech and wondering what could have been."

"It's not my call."

"This isn't Monica's first go-round either. She knows the stakes. If you insist, she'll make it happen."

Monica performs a perfect impression of a Renaissance sculpture from her seat at the table: stone-faced and impossibly motionless. She also doesn't argue against Brian's point. If he didn't know better, he would think that she almost seems inclined to go along with it.

"I'm not comfortable having Miss Campos here on the night of my acceptance. She's a wild card, and the media would love to have a reason to bury my speech. Even you would agree with that, Brian."

That's the whole point, but Brian can't say that. He rubs his hands together and grimaces. Cubic's words ring in his head. There needs to be a spectacle, but he's out of moves. Almost.

"It's a mistake, sir."

"The decision stands," the governor says, rising in a signal that the discussion is over. The rest of the room follows suit.

"Then I will let her know."

"I already took the liberty."

Brian glares at the campaign manager. This was a lost cause from the outset. The verdict was rendered before he was even summoned here. Typical.

"What's the matter, Brevin? You don't trust me?"

The campaign manager smirks before leaving with the candidate. Most of the other staff and GOP bigwigs follow suit. Monica stays behind, and Brian sees an opportunity.

"Do you agree with this call? You look like you're on the fence."

She shifts her weight between her feet. "I know what happened to Tierra Campos. It could be an opportunity to set the narrative. Unfortunately, Bradford is right – it could also be a complete disaster. I'm not blind. I know his campaign is floundering. We can't risk anything detracting from the governor's acceptance tomorrow."

"You should have backed me."

"That's not my job. I understand both sides of the argument. I made sure all the points were heard. The governor made the call, and I respect that. You should too."

Monica leaves the room, leaving him alone. There is one card left to play. It's a long shot, and the consequences could be dire, but he has nothing left to lose. The odds aren't in his favor, but he didn't make it this far without being bold and taking chances.

"Hey, it's me. I have a proposition for you. How fast can you get to Detroit?"

# CHAPTER SEVENTY-SEVEN

## VASSYL STRACHENKO

*Abandoned Mill*
*Loughborough, Massachusetts*

Vassyl receives an encrypted text and puts the wheels in motion. Ian did his job. The feds have zeroed in on Loughborough and have an approximate location based on Vassyl's phony call to the tip line. He closes the app, causing the message to self-destruct and become unrecoverable. It isn't that he plans on losing his phone, but he didn't stay alive this long by being careless.

The men quietly assume their positions, taking care to remain out of sight and well-hidden from agents with binoculars who will be scoping the place before moving in. So long as none of them does anything stupid, nothing should tip off the authorities.

Now it's all over except the wait. Vassyl checks the monitors showing the feeds from the half dozen cameras he emplaced. About a dozen motion sensors are also protecting the mill's flanks and rear, just in case. Just because they think they know the FBI's attack plan doesn't mean they do.

It all comes down to this. Months of planning and several pre-execution missions all laid the groundwork for this moment. Ian is right – it's a lot of effort to kill one person who could have been dispatched while she slept. He knows that this is only a part of Robespierre's agenda but still thinks it's risky and foolish.

Vassyl's phone chirps. He reads the second text that comes in:

*RAID IMMINENT*

The assassin takes a deep breath. "Look alive, Ian. They're coming."

"About damn time," he says, jumping off the crate he was seated on.

Vassyl stares at his screens. He's the only one in a position to spot their movements. Once the FBI team begins their assault, the rest of the team can come out of hiding and man their guns. There will be no escape from the kill zone even if they're noticed in the windows.

He pockets his phone. Part of him wishes he had explosives like the SOF had. None of his men have that expertise, and he figured it wouldn't be needed for this assignment. A few charges and some shrapnel would be a great way to ensure that nobody escapes, especially Agent Larsen.

"Almost showtime, gentlemen," Vassyl says into his mic.

"Roger."

"Standing by."

"Affirmative."

Minutes go by after the three men check in. Vassyl takes another deep breath. Where are they?

"Got 'em! Movement, seven o'clock. Hold position until my signal. One FBI tactical team with windbreakers in support coming right down Broadway."

They are commencing their assault on the building just as he hoped. Vassyl checks the motion sensors on the east flank. Nothing. The camera pointed at the sky shows no helicopters overhead. The river is also clear of any boats. Thank God.

"The windbreakers are being careful. They don't have much intel on this place and are acting accordingly. That's why they're moving slowly along the wall," Ian says, pointing at the screen.

"Where is Larsen?"

"Right there. She's hanging back."

"Coward. Larsen identified. Twenty meters to the rear and left of the main formation. Man your positions slowly and quietly."

The FBI team stacks along the wall at the corner of the residential building to their south. They squat and make a few hand signals to each other. At once, they begin a sprint across the flat empty construction lot. They won't clear the danger area fast enough, as they are about to learn.

"Wait...wait..."

One of the tactical team members gives the freeze signal when he spots someone in the window. The recognition comes far too late.

"Now!"

The FBI team is about halfway between the apartments and the abandoned mill when the two machine guns open up in a deafening roar that bounces off the surrounding buildings.

# CHAPTER SEVENTY-EIGHT

## TIERRA CAMPOS

*Republican National Convention*
*Detroit, Michigan*

Road trips can be fun. They can also be monotonous hours of driving on an interstate and seeing nothing of interest. This was neither. The drive from Washington to Detroit was therapeutic for the three of us.

We had a lot of issues to work through. Doctors didn't want me to risk flying due to my injuries, so Tyler offered to drive me across the country. Olivia agreed to help, and they split the driving duties. After checking into the hotel, we park the car and wait a couple of blocks from the arena hosting the Republican National Convention.

The delegates have already cast their votes, and tonight Governor Colin Bradford of North Carolina will formally accept his party's nomination for the presidency. Brian didn't brief me on the specifics of his plan. All I know is that we are to meet here and that I'm not officially allowed in the building. I feel like I'm in a spy movie.

"This could go horribly wrong. You know that, right?" Olivia asks from the passenger seat.

"Luckily, I'm not concerned about my reputation at this point. By the way, thanks for doing this, guys."

"No need to thank me," Tyler says. "I would have volunteered for this out of morbid curiosity even if we weren't back on speaking terms."

"There he is," Olivia says, pointing.

Tyler flashes his headlights a couple of times from our spot along the curb, and Brian hustles over. Olivia lowers her window, and Brian sticks his head partially in. The look on his face is the same one I've gotten from almost everyone since leaving the hospital.

"My God!"

"Just what every woman wants to hear," I say, forcing a smile that probably doesn't look like much of one.

"I'm sorry. I didn't know how bad it was. I'm so sorry that this happened to you."

"Me too. It's not your fault. Let's stick it to those who actually are to blame," I say, climbing out of the car.

I say goodbye to Tyler and Olivia, who will watch the fireworks from our hotel room. That's assuming that Brian can get me through the door to the arena on one of the biggest nights in American politics.

"I don't mean to be rude, but you look terrible. Are you sure you're up for this?"

"The bruising gets worse before it gets better. I didn't drive halfway across the country to wimp out now. That's assuming you're willing to risk your career and Colin Bradford's wrath to get me in the door."

"Trust me. You're helping me as much as I'm helping you."

I don't understand what he means, but there is no time to talk about it. We arrive at the staff entrance and are greeted by a pair of security guards.

"Back so soon, Brian?" one of the guards asks.

"You know me, Tony. Always on the move. Angela can't be happy that you're still here. I thought you were coming off shift."

"My replacement didn't come in. My wife might hate the time away from her and the baby, but she'll like the money when she gets to spend it. Who's this?"

Brian gives him a quizzical look. "You don't recognize her?"

"Tierra Campos, right?" he asks after studying my face. "I'm sorry, I..."

"I know. It's okay. I'm a mess."

The guard checks his clipboard. You would think in the modern age that political parties would have gone digital with tablets that could update lists, changes, and check-ins in real-time. Not so much.

"She's not on my list, Brian."

"She wouldn't be. Monica Stengel wants to make her a surprise speaker, and it's being kept very hush-hush. That's why I'm taking her through this entrance. There are only a handful of people who know she's here, and we need to keep it that way."

Tony nods. "I gotcha. Knock 'em dead tonight."

"I will. Thank you," I say as Brian and I walk through the double doors into a long service corridor. "Is he going to get in trouble?"

"No more than I will be in."

"I'll bet Tony and his high-maintenance wife won't find that reassuring."

"No, probably not."

"What do we do if we run into someone on the way to wherever we're going?"

"Hope that they don't notice you," Brian deadpans.

"Are you kidding? I look like Sloth from *The Goonies*. Do you really think nobody will notice that?"

Brian smirks. "How old were you when that movie came out?"

"I wasn't born yet."

"Pssh. Thanks for making me feel old. This way."

He steers us down another corridor. This place is a maze. How he knows where he's going is beyond me. The convention would be over before I managed to learn the layout of the arena.

Without a word, he steers us into a utility room just as I hear voices around the corner. Brian closes the door and waits for them to pass. He opens it, peeks out, and then beckons me to follow. Yep, this definitely starting to feel like a spy movie.

# CHAPTER SEVENTY-NINE

## OLIVER JAHN

*Republican National Convention*
*Detroit, Michigan*

"We're back on *Tomorrow's News Today* live from the Republican National Convention in Detroit, Michigan. I know, I know. It wasn't my idea. Believe me.

"Here is breaking news...nothing at all has happened. Which pretty much describes this entire convention. I have to hand it to the GOP, the Grand Old – and I stress "old" – Party. They have earned high marks this week for consistency. They are killing us, not with drone strikes or cages at the border, but with boredom.

"Calling this dull would be a generous exaggeration. We've heard this all before. Policy points aside – and there aren't many good ones – the speakers remind me of something you would hear during a seminar on the mechanics and processes of paint drying."

Mi Sun is right on time with the image of a paint can and brush. It then changes to a freshly painted wall with absolutely nothing of interest in the shot. She's a genius.

"And now, we will watch intently as the coat of latex paint you meticulously slathered on this wall becomes permanent through a process of evaporation, or however the hell it dries. Who cares?

"This whole thing is mind-numbingly dull. Can you imagine if Governor Bradford wins? Doctors would prescribe his State of the Union address as a sleep aid. I know it's all the other Republicans who have spoken so far, but you've seen him. He's no better. Take an Ambien and watch any Bradford speech.

"The only people who are really into what the speakers are saying are this lady..." Oliver says as Mi Sun posts the video of a person yawning full-screen. "And this guy."

The video jump-cuts to show another man dressed in full political regalia rubbing his eyes and slapping himself to stay awake. A picture says a thousand words. Videos are their own narrative worthy of a novel.

"Maybe they had a late night out last night, I don't know. Those Republicans are party animals."

Oliver scrunches up his face and shakes his head. He wasn't sure he just said that. It was an obvious joke but still tasted funny coming out of his mouth.

"Conventions are supposed to be a showcase that inspires people to vote for a candidate. They're usually electric and brimming with enthusiastic partisans hoping for the promise of a better tomorrow. That's what the Democrats had at theirs. By comparison, this has all the kinetic energy of Michelangelo's David statue. It's frozen, immobile, static – yes, I'm on a synonym tear here. Cut me some slack. It's all I could do not to slit my wrists this week. Although I think Tierra Campos would like that.

"Here's a bit of irony for you, speaking of the Great Pretender. No, she isn't here. She's still fired, as she should be. Too bad, because I wish she were. I could destroy her on live television. Maybe we can teleport her here or something.

"Anyway, *Capitol Beat* is right next door to me. Ah, the wonders. I kid you not. What poor intern did the Republicans have assigning the media areas before this started? Does he even watch the news and see what I've said for the past few weeks? No, probably not.

"'Sure, I just got off a three-day bender. So, I'll just assign media outlets places and put absolutely zero thought into it. What could go wrong?' It's the same question people ask with gas station sushi or hang gliding."

Mi Sun is quick tonight. The video she posts is a hang glider piling his flimsy craft into the ground. That's fitting for this debacle.

"Tonight is the big night for Republicans. Fortunately, they have set the bar so impossibly low that it ought to be a raging success. Rest assured, I'll be watching so that you don't have to. Should you want to watch the train wreck in real-time, we will be doing live commentary during the speeches. How else can I keep up with pointing out all the lies they're telling? Someone needs to inject some humor and entertainment into lectures with all the flavor of a wet saltine cracker.

"I'm here for you all," Oliver says, alternating putting his hand over his heart and gesturing with it to the camera. "We will endure this together. But not for another three minutes because that's when we'll return from our break."

# CHAPTER EIGHTY

## BRIAN COOPER

*Republican National Convention*
*Detroit, Michigan*

Tierra must think that he's either crazy or lost. Brian wouldn't blame her considering the route that they're taking. Navigating the guts of this arena would make anyone feel like a rat running through a maze. She hasn't said anything, nor has he mentioned that he reconned this route in advance to find the least-traveled spaces.

Sneaking around the arena completely unnoticed is impossible. Thousands upon thousands of delegates, party members, media, and arena employees fill the space. Most are centered around the floor, and Brian avoids any corridor leading to it. There are a lot of rooms, but few places to hide. It's why he selected a special one on the skybox level.

"Are you sure coming up here is a good idea?" Tierra asks. "This is where all the media outlets covering this convention are."

"I know. It's the second to last place we should go."

"So why are we?"

"There aren't any better options. At least this is the one place where privacy is respected."

"Assuming you can get me there without bumping into…well, anybody."

"Yeah. Assuming that."

"Are you sure you thought this through?"

Brian smiles before peeking his head around a corner. It's clear, and he waves her forward. All it takes is for one reporter to leave a suite at an inopportune time. They're a curious group by nature and make careers out of asking questions. Even if Tierra tries to hide her face, it will do no good.

The pace quickens, and Brian finds the suite he's looking for. He pushes the door open and ushers Tierra in. She expects to see it empty but instead finds herself standing face-to-face with Wilson.

He checks her appearance with a wounded look on his face. For a moment, it looks like tears are forming in the corners of his eyes. Wilson hugs her, letting it linger for a couple of beats longer than usually acceptable. When they release, he tries to say something but the words won't come out. She doesn't want to dwell on it.

"Is it safe for me to be here? If Brock Puttman comes in—"

"He won't. He's too busy sucking up to people."

Brian nods and walks to the other side of the suite to make a call.

"I'm surprised you agreed to all this," Tierra says, getting a quizzical look from her mentor.

"Why?"

"We didn't talk after I was fired."

He sighs. "I wanted to, believe me. It was better for both of us that I didn't. They were watching me."

"So?" Tierra asks, anger in her voice. "I'm a friend."

"Yes, you are, only more than that. You're like a daughter to me. Your getting fired was heartbreaking, but not talking to you since killed me inside."

"Then why not call me?"

"Shame, for starters. I felt guilty not standing up to DeAnna in that conference room."

"Then why didn't you?"

"Because I needed to stay on the inside to fight this war. If we were both out on the street, it was over. I thought if I could stay in the fold, there was a chance at getting them out and you back."

"Is there?"

"No. It's why I was more than happy to agree to this."

"I still don't understand," Tierra says, turning away from him.

"Puttman made it very clear to me that if I talked to you, I was out."

Tierra jerks her head back around to him. "Is that even legal?"

"Probably not," Wilson says with a shrug, "but I played along. I made them think I was afraid to lose my deal."

"Are you?"

"Would I have agreed to this otherwise?" Wilson asks with a devious smirk.

Tierra reaches into her pocket and holds up a thumb drive. "Then you're going to need this."

"What is it?"

"The information that Dial Pirate gave me proving who was behind my harassment and assault. It's all the proof we will ever need. Do you have a technician that you still trust?"

"I have one or two that are still loyal."

Wilson takes it like she just handed him irrefutable proof of the Roswell UFO crash. He stares at it for a long moment.

"This is going to be fun," he says, smiling.

"Are you ready for tonight?" Brian asks, rejoining them after making a call.

"I'm not sure what I want to say. The words never come out right in my head."

"May I give you a piece of advice?" Wilson asks.

"Always."

"Speak from the heart. People know genuine truth when they hear it. It's why so many of them hate politicians, even the ones they agree with. Be yourself. You have facts on your side. The rest will take care of itself."

"I agree one hundred percent," Brian adds. "You'll do great."

"I wish I had your confidence."

"You'll find it. Wait and see," Wilson says, getting a nod from Brian.

"I'm going to leave you here for a while. The gantlet we just ran was the easy part. I have some more arrangements to make. I'll be back to get you when we're almost ready. Whatever you do, don't go anywhere."

Tierra agrees, and Brian leaves the room. It's just her and Wilson, and she could use one of his patented pep talks right now. All she can do now is try to settle her nerves and figure out how to convey the message that she needs others to understand.

# CHAPTER EIGHTY-ONE

## SSA VICTORIA LARSEN

*Abandoned Mill*
*Loughborough, Massachusetts*

The world erupts in deafening blasts of machine gun fire, forcing Victoria to dive on the ground. She recognizes the sound immediately, having heard it before. The M240B has a distinct guttural sound when it's fired. The same one announced it was cutting down the New Hampshire State Police officers during the SOF raid in South Hooksett. Now, it brings back a nightmare that she has tried desperately to forget.

They should have listened to her. She told the team's commander that there wasn't enough intelligence on the building and its surroundings. His assurance that this was a low-risk operation just got them all killed.

Victoria presses her head down as she sees the men caught in the exposed construction parking area. Some of them manage to return fire, but one by one they fall like bowling pins. Their body armor doesn't stand a chance against the high-caliber bullets fired by weapons with their muzzle velocity. Their lives were over the moment the assault started.

Her team isn't in any better shape. They are pinned against the future residential building. They haven't drawn the machine gunners' attention so far, but it's only a matter of time. One of the belt-fed behemoths stops firing to reload, and the other slows its fire.

"We can flank them. Let's go!" Steve shouts.

He stands and manages only one step before a rifle burps from the far side of the old structure. A pink mist erupts from his neck, and he collapses back to the ground.

"Steve!" Amanda shouts as she tries to reach him. She takes several rounds to the chest, the final two defeating the plate in her body armor.

"He's going to pick us all off if we don't get out of here," Rigo shouts.

"We're dead if we try!" Victoria shouts back.

One of the tactical team members moves across the ground. Victoria can't believe any of them are alive after that volume of fire. His desperate escape attempt is short-lived. The machine gun fires a couple of bursts, the second one hitting the smoke grenades secured to the man's tactical vest. They belch out plumes of white smoke, some of which drifts back towards the building. The firing stops as they struggle to make out targets with their reduced visibility. This is their only chance.

"Make for the building!" Rigo shouts.

All three of them jump up and break for the spot where the larger mill, the smaller building that houses the boilers, and the renovated building's north wall converge. The rifle opens up in what seems to be a desperate panic fire. It's still effective.

Shawn gets hit in the leg and falls. Stopping for him is suicide. Bullets stitch the wall and kick up off the ground all around her. He has a bead on them. Victoria and Rigo almost make it to cover when two rounds hit him in the shoulder and side.

"Damn it to hell!" he shouts, covering his wounds with his hands as he lies prone on the ground.

Victoria stops, grabs him by the body armor, and drags him closer to the building. It was a desperate, even stupid move. Had it not been for the light breeze that shifted more smoke between her and the gunman, she would have joined Rigo on the ground, bleeding.

They reach a spot along the wall and take some cover behind a concrete step that leads into the dilapidated building. She pulls out a couple of hemostatic bandages impregnated with kaolin to force Rigo's blood to clot faster. Both machine guns are silent now. The only noise is the ringing in her ears.

"Ah, this sucks," Rigo says grimacing as his head falls backward.

He's losing a lot of blood, and Victoria presses harder against the wound. The jolt of pain snaps him back into the present. His eyes grow wide as he sees something behind her.

"Look out!"

Bullets skip off the concrete slab, missing her by only a foot or two. She draws her weapon and pivots, seeing a man hanging partly out the window while trying to fire his machine gun from the hip. That explains the inaccurate fire.

Victoria fires off three quick shots, hitting the man at least twice. The machine gun falls to the ground as he's thrown backward. The gunman slumps forward on the windowsill before his momentum teams up with gravity to pull him from the window. He crashes to the ground with a thud.

"You have to go," Rigo orders.

"I'm not leaving you here."

"You have to."

"No. We can wait for Seth. He's on the way."

"Victoria, look around you. This place is designed to be a kill zone. Even if they got here now, it would be an hour before they move in, and we'll be long dead. You have to go. I'll be fine."

Victoria surveys the ground and knows he's right. She should have seen it before. The Sword of Freedom chose their remote safehouse because of the escape routes it offered. Ian and his pal Vassyl chose this place because of the lack of them. There is only one way in and out unless you want to swim. It was the perfect place for an ambush.

"What about Shawn?"

Rigo glances over to the spot where their colleague fell and shakes his head. "He's only alive because they want to draw us out into the open. Go. Go now."

"Okay, but I'm not leaving you exposed like this."

Victoria drags him inside and through an opening that leads into the dilapidated mill. There are enough beams and boards on the floor to provide him with some cover and concealment.

"Stay hidden," Victoria orders her boss before handing him his weapon. "Don't let anyone get past you if they come this way."

Victoria raises her weapons and moves into the boiler house. It's long and narrow with almost no cover outside of an old cylindrical steam boiler that must weigh a hundred tons. Past that is the partially collapsed second floor that the team was ambushed from. That's where her targets are.

She hears a noise and scampers behind the boiler. It provides ballistic protection, but there is no escape. It's a bad place to be. She gets low as two men emerge from the basement level armed with rifles.

They were underground, and that's why they were never spotted. Victoria shakes her head and then recognizes Ian. She resists the surge of adrenaline that pushes her to jump out and surprise him and his buddy. Common sense wins out. Victoria would have the element of surprise but a terrible shooting angle. If she misses her shot, they will pin her down, and it will only be a matter of time before they get her. She needs to wait for her opportunity.

The two men raise their AR-15s and exit the building, sweeping in front of them as they pause just outside the door. She has never felt so helpless...and alone. Rigo is out of the fight. It's one against at least four, not counting the one she got in the window. She's outgunned and on unfamiliar ground. There is a good chance that this isn't going to end well. With that thought, Victoria closes her eyes and says a quick prayer.

# CHAPTER EIGHTY-TWO

## VASSYL STRACHENKO

*Abandoned Mill*
*Loughborough, Massachusetts*

Ian and Vassyl both raise their weapons when they step out the door. They don't need to. The machine guns did their work. None of the bodies on the ground are moving. It doesn't mean that they aren't playing possum. It also doesn't mean that they got all of the agents, although he doesn't see how any of them could have escaped the carnage.

"Sven, any movement?" Vassyl calls up to the man in the window to their right.

"Negative. Dimitri? Dimitri?"

"Vassyl, we have a man down," Ian says, taking a knee and pointing his weapon down the narrow convergence of the three buildings.

"Damn it," the assassin says, seeing the body outside on the ground. "Check him."

Ian complies, carefully moving over to where Dimitri lies. Vassyl already knows the man's fate. He's gone—poor bastard.

"Cover us, Sven."

Ian rejoins Vassyl, and they move over to the tactical team. They were more of a threat than the other agents along the renovated building were. Most of the men on this team were shot multiple times. All of them are gone. Ian nods at him, agreeing that the job is done.

"Let's find Larsen."

"Gladly."

Vassyl didn't task one of the machine guns to take out the windbreakers because they wanted Victoria Larsen alive. He had made a promise to Ian that he wanted to keep. Jackrabbit had more control with his rifle and could choose his targets more easily. With the bodies littering the ground, he may have been a little too overzealous. It's a shame, but he won't cry about it. Ian won't either, at least not for much longer.

Ian checks the bodies of the FBI agents, starting with the blond woman. He picks her head up by her hair.

"It's not her."

"Shit. Where is that bitch?"

One of the agents shot near the convergence makes his move and scrambles for a gun on the ground. He's badly injured and doesn't move as quickly as he should. Vassyl stomps on his arm, causing the wounded agent to withdraw it. He kicks the weapon away.

"It looks like we have a live one. What's your name, friend?"

"Screw you."

"Okay, Screw You. That's an odd name, but whatever," Vassyl says to Ian's amusement. "Where are the rest of your friends?"

"Go to hell," the man says with pure contempt and hatred in his eyes.

"You first, buddy." Ian trains his gun on the man's forehead and moves his finger to the trigger.

"Hold on. This scumbag still has some use in the waning moments of his life."

"Seriously?" Ian says as the sirens in the distance grow slightly louder. "The clock's ticking."

"Agent Larsen!" Vassyl bellows, looking around. "I'm sure you can hear me. There is no escape from here without going through us. You must know that by now. So, we're going to make this easy. I'm going to count to five. If you don't present yourself, Ian is going to put a bullet in your colleague's head."

"What are you doing?"

"Baiting a trap."

"You know that Victoria Larsen is a crack shot, right?"

"So I've heard. She won't be able to hit us from anywhere we don't see her first," Vassyl says, keying the mic on his walkie-talkie. "Sven, keep a lookout to the south. Jackrabbit, watch the area between the buildings. Keep a listen to your surroundings. She may have made it inside the mill."

"Roger," the two men say simultaneously.

"This isn't a good idea," Ian warns. "Don't play with her."

"You're the one who demanded the opportunity to kill her. Now's your chance," Vassyl says before taking a deep breath. "Five!"

Ian raises his weapon and points it at the door to the boiler house. She must be in there. Surrender is her only option. There is no way she is willing to let a fellow agent die. It's her weakness.

"Four!"

"Do the right thing, Victoria," Ian calls out. "We're not bluffing."

"Three! Are you really not willing to trade his life for yours? Two!"

"You come out, and he lives.

"One!"

Vassyl shakes his head and points his gun at "Screw You," who is staring up at him from the ground.

# CHAPTER EIGHTY-THREE

## TIERRA CAMPOS

*Republican National Convention*
*Detroit, Michigan*

I have never obsessed over clothes like many women do. I always tried to present myself well, especially when I was reporting for WWDC. Unfortunately, human interest stories aren't always glamorous, and I learned to dress for the occasion lest I ruin outfits that I could barely afford in the first place.

It wasn't until I got to *Capitol Beat* when I had an entire wardrobe designed and purchased for me that I realized how important it was. Some colors don't work on television. Green is a horrible color for anyone who could find themselves in front of a lime-hued screen for the digital graphics overlay. Black and white can both be problematic.

I change into the navy blue suit with a low-cut sleeveless blouse that shows the bruising. My face, battered and still somewhat swollen, tells the rest of the story. My abdomen looks far worse, but any attire that shows off my midriff would likely be too racy for this crowd.

"It's time," Brian says after a quick knock on the door. "You look fantastic. Act natural, like you're supposed to be here. If you look nervous, it will stand out."

"I'll be doing my best acting job. I'm completely winging this."

"It wouldn't be the first time," Brian mutters. He's right. Winging it is how I ended up on this long journey.

"You're not helping. Whose spot am I taking?"

"Does it matter?" Brian asks with an impish smile.

"No, but they can't be happy about me taking their air time."

"The governor of North Dakota. Apparently, she's a fan of yours. Don't worry — there will be an upside for her. It'll be okay. Let's do this."

Brian walks me the short distance from the room and guides me to a quiet corner. He pulls out his phone and has a short conversation, nodding when it ends.

"Wait here."

Brian goes and hands one of the producers a slip of paper. They engage in an animated conversation that I can't hear. The man objects but isn't in a position to argue. Brian must have laid the groundwork for this all day.

Butterflies the size of pterodactyls are jockeying for space in my stomach. I wasn't anywhere near this nervous for the Ethan interview, and that was my first one ever.

The last speaker just finished to thunderous applause, and the show must go on. A woman's voice fills the auditorium.

"We have a special guest speaker tonight. She was a teenaged school shooting victim who rose to national prominence following her bombshell interview with gun control activist Ethan Harrington. That resulted in exposing him as complicit in the mass murder in Brockhampton, Massachusetts, and earned her a Peabody Award for Online Journalism and a Pulitzer for Investigative Reporting. Please welcome the former *Front Burner* reporter and *Capitol Beat* anchor, Tierra Campos."

There is applause mixed in with murmurs from the audience as I walk out on stage. The assembled delegates and party faithful are confused, and rightfully so. Most of them were expecting a hugely popular governor. Instead, they are treated to seeing my beaten face on giant screens on each side of the stage.

There is a gasp that sucks the oxygen out of the room. The applause quickly fades into a stone-cold silence. I see so many people up front covering their mouths. I didn't try to hide my appearance under layers of foundation and cover-up. They need to see this. All of America does.

The shock at the sight of my face is likely the same in every household tuning into this. It's a harrowing thought, causing my anxiety to reach stratospheric levels. My mouth goes dry, and everything I wanted to say rushes out of my head—one line. I need to focus on getting one line out and then take it from there.

"My fellow Americans," I say, uttering the first line that comes to mind and gesturing at my face. "I stand before you tonight as a victim of cancel culture. This is the end result."

# CHAPTER EIGHTY-FOUR

## SSA VICTORIA LARSEN

*Abandoned Mill*
*Loughborough, Massachusetts*

Victoria emerges from her hiding spot as the count dwindles to one. Part of her can't resist the urge to plow out the door and start firing at the two men. She thinks twice about it. The success of that move would rely entirely on hope, and hope is not a tactic.

She begins climbing the rickety staircase that leads to the second floor. It's time to even the odds a little. That's when a single shot rings out from outside. Victoria closes her eyes.

Guilt is already racking her body and mind, even though in her heart, she knows that there was nothing she could do. She takes a deep breath, determined to deal with the emotional ramifications of that decision if she survives this. There's work to do.

Victoria comes to the top of the stairs and finds herself face-to-face with a big man. He is the first to overcome the surprise and swipes the gun from her hand with a paw attached to a forearm as thick as a four-by-four. He reaches for the tactical holster on his hip, but Victoria kicks the weapon away before he can aim it at her.

"Time to pay, bitch."

There is an arrogance to underestimating an enemy because she's a woman or is smaller than you. It's on full display as he cracks his knuckles. Both sexes are capable of being aggressive, and while it's true that men are generally stronger, that doesn't mean a woman can't kick his ass. It's about who has the better physical and mental conditioning resulting from continuous training. Victoria takes up a fighting stance, determined to find out.

The man takes a couple of aggressive swings but hits nothing but air. Victoria deftly moves around him, sliding around his hooks and straight punches unpredictably. He favors his right and rarely uses his left. Victoria keeps that in mind.

The bulging muscles from hours of chest presses and bicep curls might make him look good on a beach, but make him slower and more cumbersome in a fight like this. That doesn't mean he cannot knock her unconscious with one blow. She needs to avoid getting hit and not get caught in a grappling match where his strength plays to his advantage.

The giant grunts and swings wildly three or four more times. Victoria keeps her guard up but moves around the punches instead of trying to block them. There's no point in trying to absorb blows with a block unless she has to. He's already starting to get winded and reaches out and grabs her body armor as he reaches back to throw another right hook. Victoria makes a move.

In Krav Maga, you aim for the sensitive and vulnerable parts of the body. It's all about finding an opening to successfully strike by bypassing an opponent's defenses. Victoria doesn't need an extraordinary amount of power, but just proper technique, agility, and speed.

She brings her elbow down on his grabbing arm and raises her left forearm to block the punch. Her non-blocking arm snakes under his armpit and pulls him forward, changing his center of gravity. As he bends at the waist, she pumps two knees with her left leg into his head. Victoria still has positive control of him but doesn't use the leverage to try and dislocate his shoulder like she would a smaller man. Instead, she pushes him away and resumes her fighting stance as he shakes off the blow. This guy can take a hit, and now he's angry.

Four more haymakers get launched at her in a fit of rage, forcing Victoria to slide to the right. Her foot catches a piece of debris, causing her to almost lose her balance. She recovers from the stumble in time to be ready for the fifth. Fatigue has set in, making his attacks even slower. She blocks a straight punch using an inside defense with her forearm and guides his fist across her body. The move prevents him from landing a left as Victoria turns her hips and executes a perfectly placed palm-heel strike to his solar plexus. It has the desired effect.

The solar plexus is a center for nerves that control the cardiorespiratory system, and the painful blow takes the breath from her already tiring opponent. The giant staggers, dropping his guard. Victoria recognizes the weakness and goes on the offensive.

She bunches the fingers on her left hand to make them rigid and plunges them at his right eye in a quick strike. He howls and immediately brings his arms to his face in reflex, leaving him exposed to the knife hand strike that lands on his throat. He goes down on one knee, allowing her to pound a double hammer punch into his collarbone.

The man pushes off his knee and throws a wild uppercut that must be painful to attempt. Victoria once again turns her body, nudging his fist away as she pivots and swings her elbow at his face, hitting him below his nose. With her back to him and risking a bear hug that could crush her ribs, she slams her foot on his instep and lands a knife-hand to his groin.

Her massive opponent doubles over again. Victoria plants another knee to his face, followed by an elbow to the back of the neck. Out of desperation, he thrusts a fist out that catches her abdomen and follows it with a kick that crashes into her thigh with the force of a sledgehammer. She doesn't fight the momentum and does a side break fall, popping back to her feet, much to his surprise.

He knows he is losing. Intent on changing his fortunes in this fight, the big man telegraphs his next move and rushes at her. With his torso open and exposed, Victoria lands a heel kick directly into his chest as he bears down on her. The strike knocks her off-balance and forces her to do a backward break fall. It was a planned move. She comes out of the roll right next to her gun. She picks it up, causing the behemoth of a man to stop dead in his tracks and frown.

"Shit."

This is not the time for a witty, movie-style retort. Victoria squeezes the trigger and puts three shots center-mass. The man is so wide that it isn't much of a feat. He drops to his knees before collapsing face-first into the ground, his eyes welded open.

One more down. A salvo of bullets rips past her head. The popping sounds next to her ears alert her that death is only inches away, forcing her to dive and shoulder roll behind a support column. It's narrow but is about the only cover in this part of the floor.

The gunman's bolt locks to the rear. He's empty. Victoria rolls out from behind the column and fires at the man as she walks forward. Initiative is a game-changer in a firefight. The stress levels are sky-high, and aggressive maneuvers create panic. Panic leads to mistakes, and mistakes lead to death.

The man fumbles to change magazines. He gets one locked into place and looks up in time to see Victoria line her sights on him and fire from thirty feet away. Two of the three shots hit him, causing him to drop the rifle. That's what she needed.

Victoria surges forward in a race to close the distance before the man can retrieve his weapon. She's going to lose as he snags the sling and drags the rifle over to him. She pulls up and fires a shot. And another. One hits its mark. The other goes just wide. Shot three times, the younger man stares at her. With no emotion, Victoria squeezes the trigger and puts a round through his forehead.

She holsters her weapon and grabs his rifle. Pressing the catch above the magazine well, she checks to see that it's fully loaded. She digs through the man's ammo pouch and grabs three more mags, tucking them into the pocket of the windbreaker zipped over her body armor.

Victoria rushes back east to the edge of where the floor collapsed. She arrives in time to see the assassin burst into the building. They heard the firefight and came running to catch her in a pincer from behind. A few seconds longer, and she would have been caught in a crossfire with cover from one direction but not the other. Now they are the ones exposed.

She opens fire, forcing the two men to scramble behind the massive boiler near where she hid. She shifts her position moments before both men unleash a hail of bullets with their AR-15s, forcing her to retreat. She returns fire from a new position, compelling the pair to get intimate with the steel boiler. They're pinned down, and now it's two on one with a small army of reinforcements getting closer with every passing second. She's starting to like the odds of surviving this after all.

# CHAPTER EIGHTY-FIVE

## OLIVER JAHN

*Republican National Convention*
*Detroit, Michigan*

Oliver can only watch in horror as Tierra stands on the stage and presents her battered face for the entire world to see. The audience in the arena is aghast, as he's sure his own viewers must be. She looks far worse than he thought and he is beginning to regret playing this off like he did.

"I am not the victim of a random mugging. It was planned, coordinated, and the kids who did this to me were acting on instructions. I know that sounds like yet another unverifiable accusation that floats around today. It could easily be another conspiracy theory meant to defame an enemy. It's neither of those things. Everything I am about to tell you I can prove definitively."

Oliver's mouth hangs open. Adrenaline dumps into his bloodstream, causing an instant fight or flight reaction to kick in. He feels helpless to stop what is about to happen.

*"Say something, Oliver,"* Mi Sun chirps in his ear. *"This is a big moment for commentary, and you're a statue right now."*

"Uh, it looks like we have a guest speaker tonight," he says, still focused on what his nemesis is about to say on the stage below.

*"Yeah, how about something not quite so obvious?"*

"I know who is responsible for the attack on me – not the kids who perpetrated it, but the individual behind it. There will be a reckoning. Not because I want revenge or to destroy another human being, but because it's what America should demand."

"Cut my mic," Oliver demands, knowing it's still hot.

*"You're live, Oliver,"* Mi Sun cautions.

"Cut my microphone, now!"

*"Okay, okay, it's off."*

"Keep the video on Tierra. Don't put me on the air."

*"What's this about?"*

"We need to go to commercial," Oliver says, ignoring the question.

*"Why?"*

"Because I don't want this garbage aired on my program!"

Mi Sun doesn't say anything for a long moment. This kind of behavior isn't something that she's ever seen him display in the years they've been working together.

Oliver isn't the type of man who shies away from a story, especially one as rich as the Republicans subverting their own list of speakers on the night of the nomination.

*"This is news, Oliver."*

"It's not."

*"Are you kidding? Tierra Campos is on stage."*

"So what? It's nothing more than propaganda from the Great Pretender. Cut to commercial."

*"We can't do that,"* Mi Sun protests.

"You can, and you will."

*"Fine,"* she says, recognizing the threatening tone in his voice for what it is. *"We're on break, but we're back in two and a half minutes. Now, tell me what you're doing."*

"Just what I said. I refuse to let that bitch slander me while I'm airing it on my own broadcast."

*"Slander you?"*

Oliver is in a panic. He clenches his fists tighter and tries to focus through the nervous energy coursing through him. Tierra may be bluffing, but she may not be. If she was able to trace Mulder Scully back to him somehow, it could end his career. This would be the perfect stage to do it on for all his viewers to see. He can't let that happen.

"Mute the stage mics when we return," Oliver blurts out. "I'll go on air and talk instead of her."

*"Are you serious? I don't have a graphics package ready,"* Mi Sun argues.

"We don't need one. I will explain to our audience why we aren't airing it."

*"You're going to have a lot to answer for. I've been listening in on her speech. She's creating tomorrow's narrative in real-time while we sit on the sidelines."*

"I don't care, and neither will any other media outlet," Oliver says, hoping it's true. "They won't waste air time covering criticism of journalism and how it's done today. It's self-defeating. Has anyone else cut away?"

There is another long pause. Mi Sun must be checking the other networks, or at least he hopes she is.

*"No,"* she finally answers.

"I can't believe they didn't after we did," Oliver mumbles. He's losing his touch.

*"Why would they? The networks understand that it's more damaging to do what we just did."*

"They don't care! She isn't talking about them...she's talking about me!"

*"She hasn't mentioned you or TNT even once. What is going on, Oliver? Level with me."*

"Nothing that you need to know. Give me a minute to prepare for when we come back."

*"Whatever."*

Oliver knows that Mi Sun is pissed, and he will be spending a lot of time explaining himself and the hole he just dug. That's a problem for later. Right now, he needs to focus. Tierra's appearance on the stage of the RNC has thrown him for a loop. Her proclamation about knowing what happened to her and why has Oliver on the defensive. That's not where he wants to be. He has about thirty seconds to figure out how to recover from this nightmare he just walked into.

# CHAPTER EIGHTY-SIX

## BRIAN COOPER

*Republican National Convention*
*Detroit, Michigan*

Brian pumps his fist as Tierra gets going. For a moment there, he thought she was going to choke, but he should have known better. If there is any lesson that Brian has learned over the past year, it's never to underestimate her. There are few people he's willing to say that about.

The area backstage explodes with activity. Everyone is trying to figure out what just happened. Brian is almost surprised they haven't rushed the stage to tackle Tierra. There is no telling what she will say to a primetime audience, but what's done is done. If they overreact, it will become a hall of fame moment for live television. Instead, they're likely going to channel their anger at him.

"What the hell is this?" Monica asks right on cue as she storms up to him.

"What does it look like?"

"Who gave you permission to put her on stage? Where is the governor who was slated to speak?"

"She yielded her slot for this."

Monica's face turns bright red, and she looks as if she is about to burst a blood vessel. "That's not how this works, Brian!"

"Maybe not, but it's how it did work."

Brevin stomps up to them with his fists clenched. "What the…are you stupid?"

"I could ask you the same thing, Brevin."

"Come with me. Governor Bradford is demanding to see you. I hope he fires you right here and now."

The trio heads down one of the corridors behind the stage. Two more aides rush over to ensure that Brian is heading for one of the back rooms. Brevin goes to a door, knocks, and opens it. The corner of Brian's mouth curls. This is right next to the room that Tierra changed in. Talk about him pulling this off right under their noses.

"You wanted to see me, sir?" Brian asks, cutting Brevin off before he can launch into a tirade.

"I think you have some explaining to do. Was there anything about my order that was unclear?"

"You said that she couldn't attend the roundtable. She didn't."

"Damn it, Brian! Don't play games with me!"

Brian is playing with fire. Although technically correct, he knows why he didn't want Tierra Campos here. That extends to what's happening on the stage right now.

"No, sir. You were clear."

"So, you took it upon yourself to disobey it?"

"Yes, that's exactly what I did," Brian admits.

"Nobody helped you?"

"No."

"And you didn't clear this through Brevin, Monica, or anyone else?"

Brian would love to throw the campaign manager under the bus right now but would be lying. The information would be easy enough to confirm. Once it was, Brian would find himself holding a pink slip faster than Alicia Standish accepts a check from special interest groups.

"Brevin wouldn't have the balls."

"Watch yourself, Cooper!"

"Monica would, but she won't go against the candidate on this matter."

"I see," the governor says, pacing the room with the napkins still tucked in his collar to protect it from the makeup and powder applied to his face and neck. Everything in national politics is about appearances.

"Do you understand what you did tonight?" Brevin asks. "Changing speakers will make us look like clowns."

"Or it will be spun as a shrewd political move. Whatever Tierra is saying out there, you can bet it has everyone flocking to their televisions less than an hour before the governor gives his acceptance speech."

"The Democrats won't look at it that way," Monica argues.

"They aren't voting for the governor anyway. This convention is about swaying independents and firing up your base."

"I don't hear any cheering," Brevin says, seething contempt dripping from his voice.

"You don't hear jeering, either. People are listening, and that's what you want right now."

"Governor, you need to fire him right now. I will issue a press release—"

"That's a little hasty, don't you think?"

"No, it's necessary!"

"Governor, the media knows that there was a last-minute change in speakers, and they'll learn that I'm responsible. When they do, I can still be employed and under the control of your campaign or fired and free to say anything I want."

"We clearly don't control you now, Brian," the governor says.

"I'm acting in the best interests of you and the party. Your campaign manager just hasn't figured that out yet."

"I swear to God, Brian. You need—"

"Enough!" the governor shouts, losing his temper for the first time in this conversation. "I'm about to give the speech of my political life. We will deal with this later. You are still employed by us, Brian, but all your responsibilities are curtailed until further notice. Leave here, and we will talk in Washington after the convention concludes. Talk to nobody until then. If I see one quote attributed to you before we speak, you won't be able to get a dog catcher elected in Podunk, Alabama. Understood?"

"Yes, sir."

"We can have security escort him out."

"No, Brevin. I don't want to make a spectacle of this. Brian understands the consequences if he does."

The consultant nods and leaves the room. Tierra knows what to do next. The moment she leaves that stage, they will try to remove her from the building. There is only one way around that, and she will have to be convincing to pull it off. Either way, it's up to her now.

He will have to watch what Tierra says later. There is no doubt that clips and full video from her speech will be everywhere on the Internet. This is a Hail Mary. Brian managed to get the ball off before getting buried under a pile of political linebackers. Now it just has to find a receiver in the end zone.

# CHAPTER EIGHTY-SEVEN

## SSA VICTORIA LARSEN

*Abandoned Mill*
*Loughborough, Massachusetts*

Vassyl clenches his teeth together. This is hopeless. All they are doing is burning through their ammo with no chance for resupply. Every time they dare open fire, their target isn't where they thought she would be. They can't risk spraying the entire second floor and being exposed to her fire if they miss. Instead, they are pinned down and trade shots three at a time.

"Holy shit!" Ian shouts as accurate fire ricochets just over his head.

The assassin peeks over the boiler, waiting for Sven or Jackrabbit to intervene. Neither does. That means they are down. Either of them would have responded a long time ago.

"This is bad," Vassyl says, resting his back against the steel cylinder as he catches his breath.

"Yeah, no shit. Now what?"

"I'm an assassin, not a soldier. Gunfights aren't my forte."

"You should have thought of that before you tried drawing a seasoned agent like Victoria Larsen into a trap, and just killed her on the street like I told you to."

There is no arguing about that point right now. Vassyl wishes he had told Robespierre to shove his ridiculous plan and done just that. It's not his ass that's on the line against a pissed-off FBI agent hell-bent on killing them for murdering her colleagues.

And determined is exactly what she is. No ultimatums are being issued, nor is she hurling insults or smack talk. Victoria isn't gloating that she has them hemmed in. She is patiently waiting until one of two things happens: the cavalry arrives, or they get desperate enough to make a break for it.

Ian goes to pop his head up and fires his rifle before almost having it shot off.

"Damn," he says, ducking back down.

"We can't stay here," Vassyl says.

"Yeah, well, the moment we move away from this boiler, we're as good as dead. We need a distraction.

"Or a tank."

They don't even have flashbangs or smoke grenades, which would come in handy right now. It's just the two of them with two rifles and whatever ammunition they happen to have left.

"I have an idea that might get us out of this," Ian says. "We'll have to be fast. We're going to let loose on three. One...two...three!"

The two men pop up and fire, forcing Victoria to retreat. Vassyl's rifle goes dry, and they duck to avoid a return volley. Ian sets his rifle down. Vassyl wonders what he's doing as he pulls out the magazine and reaches for one of the last remaining spares in his ammo pouch. He only carried a small combat load, expecting them all to be on the dinghy and motoring away from this place by now.

"What's the plan?"

"This."

Ian pulls the handgun from his thigh holster and fires it into Vassyl's side. The assassin looks up at him, his eyes wide with horror and disbelief as his legs fold underneath him.

"Don't give me that look, Vassyl. You were going to do the same thing to me when this was over. That boat that Jackrabbit secured only has room for four."

"What? We would have fit you in there!"

Ian shakes his head. "No, you wouldn't have."

"You said you had a distraction to get us both out of here," Vassyl says, trying to change the subject.

"I did," Ian says with a smirk. "I lied, just like you did. That was your plan, right? Use me to bait Larsen and then kill me to slow the feds down from hunting you down? Go ahead and tell me I'm wrong."

Vassyl lowers his eyes. He doesn't know how or when Ian figured out his plan. He never even told any of the other men. Not that it matters now.

"I thought so. Well, I'm not about to let you kill me, and since the only way to get out of this mess is for one of us to sacrifice himself, I just volunteered you."

"I should have killed you in South Carolina."

"Probably, but you didn't. I'll give Robespierre your regards."

Vassyl is about to protest when Ian raises his rifle and gives him a buttstroke to the head. It wasn't enough to knock the assassin unconscious, but his vision explodes into bursts of light, and he gets instantly woozy. Ian slaps a fresh magazine into his rifle. He has thirty rounds and keeps count as he wildly fires off about two-thirds of them. He then tosses the weapon into the kill zone at the boiler's far side between them and Victoria.

"Fetch, Vassyl!"

Ian climbs over the boiler. Vassyl has no choice but to go for the rifle. Unarmed, he's as good as dead. His legs are rubbery as he reaches the end of the big steel cylinder. This is taking too long. He stumbles forward and begins to reach down for the rifle, glancing up to see Victoria emerge on the second floor and point her own AR-15 directly at him.

# CHAPTER EIGHTY-EIGHT

## TIERRA CAMPOS

*Republican National Convention*
*Detroit, Michigan*

I stare at the faces of the people closest to the stage. I wasn't sure what their reaction would be to my appearance. I knew that my bruised and swollen face would catch their attention, but these are conservative die-hards. I am not left or right and have both liberal and conservative viewpoints, although neither side will ever characterize me that way. All I know is that, in the end, these people here know that I am not one of them.

"I am not here to talk about what happened to me. You can see the information for yourself and allow your own opinion to form," I say, then pause. "That's something that most people don't do these days. Instead, they quickly rush to conclusions, adopting the views of a few vocal members of the online community rather than deciding for themselves.

"That's what the cancel culture feeds on: uninformed people who make snap judgments. One journalist, in particular, has professed in a passionate defense of the mob that such tactics are necessary to hold people accountable. Others have argued that cancel culture is no more than a political slogan conjured up by those they disagree with. It's neither of those things.

"The medieval village mob has now gone virtual in America, and they suffer from the same hysteria. It's a modern shunning with punitive consequences. Transgressions are admonished no matter how much time passes since they occurred, like when social media activists called for a governor to resign for wearing blackface in a college skit...over fifty years ago."

There is a smattering of boos that come from the crowd.

"It is also unforgiving, like when an aircraft manufacturing executive was dismissed because he wrote an article opposing women as fighter pilots back in 1987. Or when a college trustee was forced out for wearing a fake Nazi uniform to a *Hogan's Heroes*-themed college costume party way back in 1980. It doesn't matter that both men sincerely apologized for failing to meet the modern standard of political correctness, nor that they exhibited no misogynistic or anti-Semitic behavior since.

"You see, the cancel culture believes that everyone is intrinsically bad and incapable of learning from mistakes. There is no room for error or misjudgment in the eyes of a mob that illogically believes imperfect people must always be perfect. You are no better than your worst moment and are measured accordingly. It doesn't matter how young you were or what the situation was, or even if it was an isolated incident.

"What results is a breeding ground for societal dishonesty and cover-ups by people who can never achieve the level of purity the cancel culture demands. The sad irony is that many of those doing the accusing refuse to hold themselves to the same standard. That is especially true when we consider what is happening today."

I hazard a glance off to the side of the stage. I half expect to see a team of burly security guards poised to remove me. They aren't. I have been granted the stage without interruption, knowing that consequences will come later. I can live with that.

"People are no longer just canceled for their actions; having a disagreeable viewpoint is enough. No longer do we believe in the maxim, 'I don't agree with what you're saying, but will defend to the death your right to say it.' On social media, now it's, 'I hate what you are saying and will cancel you because of it.'

"The practice of calling for repercussions against someone simply because of their viewpoint is a proverbial slippery slope. The blacklisting of people in the 1950s reinforced our national belief in the protection of political speech and affiliation. We have collectively forgotten the lesson.

"Our freedom of speech is one of our most cherished rights. Do we want to live in a world where someone is fired for reposting a Princeton study concluding that peaceful protest is more effective than violent ones? Should our academic elites be given the power to punish faculty for "racist" research, as some have requested?"

There is grumbling in the crowd, and heads are moving left and right. I expected them to agree. The right has been railing about this for years, but that isn't who I am trying to reach. I am relying on the media covering this event to do the right thing. We'll see if that's the case when this is over.

"I am sad to say that the media has helped elevate outrage politics over genuine engagement and dialogue. Cancel culture marched through our academic institutions and is now pervasive in our newsrooms. Journalism, and our democratic principles, are worse off because of it.

"You see, cancel culture tactics start with social media attacks that escalate into accusatory videos. Sooner or later, the news media gets involved. At that point, these attacks are viewed as legitimate by reporters and editors willing to inflict their own denunciations in the name of ad revenue and Internet clicks. They're quick to label these cancel culture crusades as news to cater to the cultural elite's identity-politics dogmas.

"There is no objectivity or verification of facts. Nor is there room for anyone to debate the mob's accusations. The media's role is to participate in the trial, report on the verdict, and help deliver the punishment. The end result is that someone loses a job or, in some cases, winds up in a hospital. It's no wonder why so many Americans have lost faith in the media."

There is rousing applause from the assembled attendees waiting to hear their candidate formally accept his party's nomination to run for president. They didn't expect this but are receptive to what I am saying. I had prepared myself to hear nothing but silence.

"Respect for a free press is the cornerstone of any democratic society. After all the dishonesty, fake news, fabricated sources, and slanted reporting, it's hard to fathom how public confidence in our news media will ever be restored in our lifetimes. Can journalism, the once-esteemed fourth estate of our nation and watchdog of our rights, ever manage to shrug off lazy and dishonest reporting? Will they ever have the people's interests in mind, or is everything now about revenue and promoting an agenda?

"The great men and women of journalism once proudly reported stories that inspired and informed. They did not speak individual truths but universal ones. They were feared, trusted, and revered for their objectivity.

"Identity politics, cancel culture, and political correctness run amok have made that objectivity an evil to be exorcised. Modern reporting instead feeds noise into the echo chamber. Reporters quote other journalists instead of attempting to locate their own first-person sources. The speed at which an article is posted online is of higher importance in its value than its factual content.

"That reality has left real reporters defenseless and voiceless. Most journalists are nothing more than marionettes with hidden editors and news directors pulling their strings. Journalists possessing any integrity and or respect of standards find themselves bullied and forced out of their organizations. I am a testament to that."

The applause has grown louder. I'm not a Republican any more than I'm a Democrat. I am certainly not a cheerleader for either. The response that I'm getting is more than I hoped for: they are listening and responding.

"Ladies and gentlemen, please take a long look at me. I am the face of what the future of cancel culture looks like. I am a woman of color who was beaten in the streets for the crime of asking difficult questions. It is a warning to those with the audacity to disagree with the mob. If the cancel culture can come after me, trust me, they can and will go after you.

"The time has come for Americans to reject their line of thinking and demand more of those we rely on for information," I continue when the applause dies down. "I will not let time-honored journalism standards erode into extinction. I will not cave to the mob bent on canceling me for doing my job. My voice will not fall silent simply because I was forced off of a popular news broadcast. That is my word. All I ask in return is for every man and woman in this country to use theirs. That is what freedom expects and what liberty demands.

"I want to thank the Republican Party for letting an outsider come and speak on this important night for you," I say, offering them a chance to save face about my taking the stage. "And I thank all of you for listening to my story."

I step back from the microphone and listen as the applause builds. It continues to grow louder for the next few moments until every man and woman in this massive audience is clapping and screaming their approval at the top of their lungs.

# CHAPTER EIGHTY-NINE

## VASSYL STRACHENKO

*Abandoned Mill*
*Loughborough, Massachusetts*

Vassyl knows that he's dead in her sights. There is nothing he can do. Unarmed and exposed, he can only hope that death comes quickly. Then he catches a break.

Victoria notices Ian making a break for it at the other end of the boiler and raises her rifle to engage him first. The distraction of pushing Vassyl into the open has given him enough time to climb over the boiler and jump to the other side without drawing her fire.

Ian darts for the door as Victoria's rifle goes empty. She transitions to her 9mm. They may kill equally effectively but sound much different in doing so. Her nemesis escapes unscathed out the far door. Vassyl won't make it that far. He won't even make it to the nearer of the two exits, so he takes the only course of action he has and breaks across the boiler house floor and crashes out the window.

He lands hard on the ground, cutting himself on shards of broken glass. Vassyl wills himself to his feet and moves as quickly toward the convergence as his abdominal wound will allow. If he can make it to cover between the buildings, it at least buys him some time. A bonus would be stopping Ian before he can launch the boat. He looks back at the door as he gets within ten feet of the narrow opening. She's not there. He might make this after all.

The pain in his shoulder precedes the report of the weapon by a few milliseconds. It spins him before knocking him to the ground. Vassyl catches a glimpse of Victoria in the second-floor window as he crawls into the shadowy convergence and takes a couple of deep breaths.

He can't stay here. It's a chokepoint, but the fatal funnel will only live up to its name if he finds cover to engage targets coming through it. Vassyl rises and stumbles forward until the pain becomes too much to bear. He makes it to the five-story brick chimney and collapses at its base.

"This will have to do," he mumbles to himself as he slides up against it.

There's no other place for him to go, even with more mobility. The river is behind him, and the whine of the dinghy's small outboard engine announces that Ian's escape is a foregone conclusion. He will make his last stand here, between an old brick chimney and the propane and gasoline tanks fenced in next to him that the construction crews used.

With his right arm unusable, Vassyl positions himself to rest the rifle on its magazine. He opens fire when he catches movement. The bolt locks to the rear, and he labors to eject the magazine and force his last one into the well. He has to be disciplined. Thirty rounds is all that separates him from certain death.

A flash of a figure causes him to fire off two more rounds. Three bullets come back at him, slamming into the gasoline tank to his left. He lets loose with five more when Victoria darts through the opening at the convergence.

The more he fires, the sharper the pain in his shoulder from the buffered recoil. He has no angle on her and slides farther out from behind the chimney to fire in her direction. Another shot hits him in his left arm this time.

Unable to dress the wounds and losing blood at an alarming rate, Vassyl finds himself getting woozy. He spots her creeping toward him along the mill wall and swings the weapon around, firing off the remaining rounds out of sheer desperation. She hits the ground, waiting as his shots scream over her head. Then the bolt locks to the rear for the final time. He stares at it for a long moment before tossing the gun away. It's over.

Vassyl leans his head back against the brick chimney. He finds himself waiting once again. This time, it's different. The hours before a mission is set to start are nerve-racking and stressful. Counting the seconds until you die is far worse.

All the planning was for nothing. Victoria Larsen is still breathing, and he's taking his last breaths. He struggles to reach into his pocket for his smokes and Zippo before the pain becomes too much to bear. Vassyl stops when he feels her approaching him. Waiting. It's always the worst part.

# CHAPTER NINETY

## SSA VICTORIA LARSEN

*Abandoned Mill*
*Loughborough, Massachusetts*

Victoria's eyes sweep left and right, searching for movement as she approaches the man leaning against the wall. She has already walked into one ambush today and isn't about to walk into another. Drucker is still here somewhere. If she's going to die in this hell hole, it's not going to be because of that son of a bitch.

One of the man's hands is in his lap, and the other is clutching an abdominal wound. She spots the weapon that was tossed out in front of him. He isn't an immediate threat, but that doesn't mean he doesn't have a trick up his sleeve. Whoever this guy is, he's formidable. She tightens her hands around the grip of her weapon and closes to within ten feet of him.

"You're an amazing woman, Agent Larsen," he moans, fighting the pain.

Victoria stops and bends at the knees to pick up the cell phone that the man dropped. He shakes his head as she tucks it in her pocket.

"There's nothing of any use on it," he informs her.

"We'll see. Where's Drucker?"

"Gone."

"Where?"

"We had a boat stored by the river. He's on it."

Victoria is a little surprised that he is willing to give up that information. There is no sign of deception in his voice or face. She stares at the end of the dilapidated mill but doesn't see any movement.

"He didn't stick around?"

"No. The bastard shot me instead."

"What did you expect?" she asks with an amused laugh.

"A little loyalty would have been nice. I had a gun to Ian's head and could have killed him a while back."

"You would have done the world a favor if you had," Victoria says, her head still swiveling as she scans for threats.

"That may be the only thing we will ever agree on, Agent Larsen."

"You're a long way from Serbia, Vassyl. Did you come to the U.S. for this or something more?"

The corner of his mouth curls up. "I was wondering if you were able to identify me. As for your question, it's none of your damn business."

"Oh, you just made it my business when you killed my colleagues and shot at me. This is how this is going to work, Vassyl. You tell me what I want to know, and I'll call an ambulance for you. If you don't, I'll watch you bleed out right here. The choice is yours. Let's start with an easy one. What's the code for this?"

Victoria pulls out the phone and wags it. Vassyl shakes his head.

"You have nothing to lose now."

"That's probably true," Vassyl says with a moan. "Tomorrow is a different story. If I cooperate with you, I'm as good as dead anyway."

She pockets the phone. "We can protect you."

"Not from Robespierre, you can't. He's more powerful than you can imagine."

"Give me his name."

Vassyl laughs. "Save your breath. You're a good enough agent to know that I'm not going to talk. I will say that your marksmanship is top-notch. That was an incredible distance to hit a moving target from with a handgun. Hanging out a window added to the degree of difficulty."

"I'm glad my routine earned high marks from the Serbian judge," she says as he continues to clutch his side to stem the blood loss. It isn't working.

"It takes a lot."

"You're running out of time."

"Meh," Vassyl says, waving a dismissive hand. "I heard that you took out Marx in a similar way. In the woods, I believe."

Victoria hears the sirens pulling into the residential parking lot. Seth and the Massachusetts State Police will be here in minutes. Despite Rigo's misgivings about her calling for state backup, she's happy she decided to do it anyway.

"Marx got what was coming to him. Just like you."

Vassyl nods his head slowly. "There is one difference."

He signals that he is going to light a cigarette so that the movement doesn't spook Victoria. Vassyl grunts as he sticks one in his mouth and sparks his Zippo. He takes a long drag on it, holding the smoke in before yielding a satisfying exhale.

"What's the difference?" Victoria asks as she notices that his blood loss is taking its toll on him.

"I always pledged that if I was caught, I would take people with me."

A sadistic smile crosses his lips like Napoleon's army marching across Europe. Vassyl holds the flaming Zippo up before tossing it in the direction of the gasoline leaking out of the ruptured tank positioned next to the five-hundred-gallon propane cylinder. Victoria notices the wet ground, and bullet punctures. Her eyes grow wide as she turns back to the assassin.

"See you in hell, Agent Larsen."

He lets out a maniacal laugh as the gasoline catches fire, and Victoria turns and makes a run for the adjacent building. She sees an entrance to a cellar carved into the ground and sprints toward it, desperate to reach it in time. She has only seconds left.

The flames race along the river of gasoline to the tank, and it erupts into a fireball. The force of the blast lifts her off the ground and sends her hurtling through the air. Her ears are ringing from the overpressure, and time seems to move in slow motion. She slams hard into the building and falls to the stairs leading to the basement entrance that she was sprinting for.

The heat and pressure rupture the propane tank, sending another shockwave out across the ground. Unable to move, Victoria can only watch as the white-hot sheet of flame smacks the side of the building above her. A massive rumbling precedes the gigantic smokestack violently crashing to the earth. Victoria struggles to shield her face as chunks of brick rain down on her. The blackness from her peripheral vision creeps to the center. Seconds later, darkness envelops her, and her head collapses on the concrete stairs.

# CHAPTER NINETY-ONE

## TIERRA CAMPOS

*Republican National Convention*
*Detroit, Michigan*

Tierra leaves the stage to thunderous applause. A winning three-pointer at the buzzer in the last game of the NBA Finals wouldn't shake the building this hard. She feels exhilarated and needs to remember to breathe once she reaches the backstage area. It's a short-lived high.

"Wait here, please, ma'am," a severe-looking guard says, holding up a hand.

"Am I in trouble or something?"

"I know nothing about that. I was just asked to keep you here."

"On whose orders?"

"Mine," Monica Stengel says, walking over to them.

"Is there a problem?" I ask, scanning the backstage area. Where is Cooper?"

"You just crashed a major political party convention. What do you think? Oh, and if you're looking for Brian, he has left the building. We need you to do the same. I'm sure you appreciate the reasons."

I'm about to agree before I think twice. "No, I actually don't understand the reason. Please explain it to me, for the record."

I rarely pull that card out. Journalists who engage in a version of blackmail with people because of their ability to reach the masses is a distasteful exercise. It is a valuable tool with the political class, though. It reminds them to be on their best behavior.

"Whose record would that be, Miss Campos?"

Okay, that works better when you're employed.

"I'll escort her out, ma'am," another guard says. I turn and see Tony, the guard who let us into the arena. He stares back at me impassively. I wonder if he knows how much trouble he's going to be in. Probably.

"Very well. Good night, Miss Campos," Monica says.

Tony gestures me forward, and we begin walking through the same series of corridors that Brian used to get me back here. I'm trying to remember how to reach the media area and find the best time to make a break for it. The whole second phase of this plan is worthless if I don't make it up there.

"If you're thinking about running, don't," Tony warns. "You won't get far, and I don't feel like chasing you."

"Tony, if you're pissed about—"

"I'm not. Brian made everything right."

That gets my attention. "How did he do that?"

"It's not important. Just know that if you run, you'll never make it up to Wilson. If you stick with me, you will."

I didn't see that coming. Brian must have known that he wouldn't be around at the end of the speech and made alternate arrangements. That man is a master planner.

"Aren't you going to get fired for this?" I ask.

Tony just keeps walking to the elevator. "Like I said, Brian has made it right. All I have to do is my part, so that's what I'm doing."

True to his word, Tony escorts me straight up to the media area. It's buzzing with activity, for obvious reasons. When I'm spotted, the corridor becomes jammed with reporters. My new friend clears the way to the *Capitol Beat* suite, where one of the technicians opens the door.

Wilson is on the air when I step in. That's what I get for being a couple of minutes late. Fortunately, nobody ad-libs better while waiting for an interview subject than Wilson Newman.

"And our next guest has arrived, right on time. Well, almost. Welcome back to the show, Tierra," Wilson says as I sit in the chair at the end of the small anchor desk.

"Hi, Wilson."

The sound is picked up by studio mics, but it's no doubt quiet and muffled. A technician affixes my mic right on the air. Wilson watches for a moment before turning to the camera.

"This is what happens on set when all you good people are watching commercials," he says with a smile. "How are you, Tierra?"

"I'm good, Wilson. It's nice to see you again."

"Likewise. Now that we have your sound levels, we can get started. That was quite a speech you delivered down there."

"Thank you."

"You didn't read it off a teleprompter, did you?"

"Did I make that many mistakes?" I ask, knowing I didn't. Puttman must be barking in his ear, and he's buying time.

"Not at all. It was fantastic. It's just a rare occurrence on a night like this."

"I was a last-minute addition to the list of speakers. I didn't need to read a script explaining what happened to me and how I feel about the state of journalism today."

"Many will agree with what you said on that stage."

"And many won't. That was one of my points. The beauty of America is our freedom, and one of its strengths is the ability to agree or disagree with what others are saying."

"Speaking of disagreeing, if you will pardon me for one moment, Tierra. Ladies and gentlemen, my executive producer Brock Puttman is threatening to pull the plug on this interview. If we suddenly cut to a commercial, it's because he feels that this isn't important and that you're not entitled to the information. I believe you should make that determination for yourselves. I just thought you should know what's happening. Brock, if you want to pull the plug, I'll give you five seconds to do it now. Don't be a coward and do it later when I'm in mid-sentence."

Wilson leans back and waits. I do the same. I honestly don't know which direction this is going to go. The red light over the camera continues to glow. Even the cameraman is watching it to see if they are still live on the air.

"Good, then I won't need this," Wilson says, pulling out his earpiece and tossing it. "My apologies, Tierra. I know you spoke philosophically about cancel culture and journalistic integrity on the stage, but I want to ask how it relates directly to you. You said that you know who was responsible for your assault. Can you walk us through that?"

"Of course. It all started with Oliver Jahn on a *Tomorrow's News Today* broadcast. He started coming after me in a very personal way."

"Why would he do that?"

"I don't know. To my knowledge, he's never explained it other than to say that I embody everything wrong with journalism."

"You probably aren't aware, but he's right on the other side of that wall. He claimed before you took the stage that he wished you were here. Now's his chance to say what's on his mind."

Wilson waits, and I enjoy the moment. "I guess not."

"It was worth a shot," he says with a chuckle.

"It turns out that Oliver was doing much more than dragging me through the mud on his program. If it had been just that, I could live with it. I'm in the public eye and not immune to criticism, nor should I be. Only he took it further."

"Are you saying that he was involved in the attack on you?"

"Not directly, but yes. I have learned that Oliver contracted a photographer named Mulder Scully to follow me around and take pictures of me in public places."

"Mulder Scully?"

"I know. I laughed, too. Apparently, Mulder was a paparazzo before opening a studio in Washington. Now, there is nothing wrong with taking my picture, but this is where it gets creepy. Oliver Jahn had a tech company set up a forum where the geotagged pictures would be posted."

"A forum dedicated to what?"

"Making my life miserable through harassment. Once a picture was posted, an alert was sent out to its subscribers. If they happened to be in the area, they would come looking for me. I was verbally assaulted on one occasion, right after this picture was posted."

The technician displays the photo of me entering the Washington Metro station. It's not a day that I remember with fondness. From the angle, Mulder Scully couldn't have been more than fifty feet away. The thought of being stalked like that still sends shivers down my spine.

"Wait…are you alleging he set this up with the explicit purpose of having people harass you?"

"Yes, and I have proof in the contract he signed with the company to set the forum up. I was chased by some teenagers following this one."

The production team posts the picture of me stretching at the entrance to the Navy Yard.

"Before we continue, assuming Oliver Jahn set up the forum, how do you know that he controlled the content? Mulder Scully could have been acting on behalf of the Smoking Man, or someone else for that matter."

Wilson is having as much fun with the *X-Files* references as I did. "Because it was his checks that Mr. Scully deposited. Here is his studio's redacted bank statement. A second check from Mr. Jahn was just deposited for double the amount. I'm curious what that was for."

"I think we all are. Then what happened?"

"This photo changed my life," I say, as the shot of me entering the supermarket pops up on the screen. "It was the first time I had left my apartment in a while. It led to this."

I lean back in my chair as the cell phone video of my getting beaten plays. It's hard to watch as I see it for the first time in its entirety. Wilson exhales deeply when it cuts off after the man rushes to my aid and belittles the guy shooting the video.

"Wow. That's powerful stuff. Why hasn't this been aired on the news?"

"I will leave it to people to ask that themselves."

"Fair enough. Do you believe that Oliver Jahn wanted these kids to become violent with you?"

I sigh. "I can't prove that. I sincerely hope not, but it's undeniable that his actions were contributing factors. Words have power. Oliver used his to characterize me as evil and to say that I needed to be punished. Listen to what my attackers said. They are parroting him. He may never have explicitly called for violence, but his words and actions led to it. His lack of apology in the aftermath speaks volumes about his true feelings."

"What will you do with this information, Tierra?"

"Turn it over to the authorities to determine if any laws were broken."

Wilson nods in approval. "What about the kids who perpetrated the attack?"

"I just got some news about that a few hours ago. They were arrested this morning, and I'm told that they are cooperating with authorities."

"Let's talk about your plans. Are you going to become a spokeswoman against the cancel culture?"

I spot Puttman entering the suite and watch as he makes a slashing gesture across his throat. Wilson spots him, too. Short of jumping over the anchor desk and tackling a septuagenarian, there isn't much Brock can do to stop the broadcast at this point without embarrassing himself.

"Unfortunately, we may have to wait to get the answer to that question. My executive producer Brock Puttman is standing behind the cameras and demanding I end this interview. Before I do, why were you fired from *Capitol Beat*, Tierra?"

"End this broadcast!" Puttman demands, throwing his hands in the air.

"I was given an ultimatum to either apologize for embarrassing Senator Veach on air or be dismissed from my job," I say, ignoring my old boss.

"But you did nothing wrong during that interview," Wilson decrees.

"I agree, which is why I chose not to apologize for it. The head of the network followed through on her threat."

"Our audience was told that you were pursuing other opportunities. I know because I was the one who was told to relay that. It was false?"

"One hundred percent fake news."

"That's enough!" Puttman bellows from behind the cameras.

The studio microphones definitely picked that up. Wilson and I turn our heads in his direction. This was fun while it lasted. I never really thought he would let us go this long. Now for a finale to remember.

"Yes, Brock, that is enough," Wilson says. "There have been a lot of secrets revealed tonight and more to come in the future. I'd like to once again thank Tierra for that. Now I'm going to reveal one of my own. I was ordered by this network not to contact Miss Campos after she was fired. That included after she was hospitalized following the brutal assault on her. If I had called her, as any friend or colleague would have, I was told that my contract would be voided."

Puttman has gone pale. The handful of technicians in the room all stare at him. They may have known the truth about Tierra's firing, but none of them were in the loop on that tidbit. It makes the network look petty and uncaring, and I'm sure they feel the same way.

"It has been a privilege and an honor to have all of you invite me into your living rooms each night. Hosting *Capitol Beat* has been the highlight of my career. Unfortunately, I cannot continue here under this network's current leadership. So go ahead and void my contract. I don't care. There are a great many things more important in this world than money. That is my final thought, and it's for the record."

I can't resist a smile. Wilson has closed his final segment with those words since I was a teenager. We pull off our microphones and walk past a stunned Brock Puttman. He looks like a deer caught in headlights.

"You can't leave! Go…go to commercial break. No, just…no, do it!"

He is so busy giving orders to stop them from beaming an empty desk into people's living rooms, he can't also stop us from leaving the suite. I almost can't wait to see how he deals with this mess.

I glance back just in time to see the anchor desk go dark. The red light over the camera is still on, so everyone saw the lights go down in tribute to Wilson. He did have some loyal technicians working here, after all. When the red light clicks off, I close the door. It's the end of an era and a new beginning for both of us.

# CHAPTER NINETY-TWO

## OLIVER JAHN

*Wolfwood Estate*
*Vienna, Virginia*

The driver follows the circular drive around the fountain until he reaches the front entrance. Oliver waits patiently to open the door and exits, taking a moment to stare at the mansion's massive façade. The home of DeAnna Van Herten is nothing if not impressive.

Oliver is escorted into a grand foyer and then down a long, ornate corridor to a sitting room to wait for his host. If that's what you want to call the room. It would easily fit his whole Manhattan apartment.

Minutes pass, and Oliver pulls out his smartphone and continues playing the newest *Front Burner* podcast. It's only been four days since the closing of the Republican National Convention, and Wilson Newman has already found a new gig two days after his epic on-camera walk-off. He never thought he would see the day that the venerable anchor would trade his fancy *Capitol Beat* studio to take up the dark art of podcasting. He certainly wouldn't have thought it would be good. It is, and his podcast debut reminds Oliver of the early days of *Tomorrow's News Today*. It may even be better.

The most disturbing thing about the video is its numbers. The views and likes are off the charts. Even his best show back then never came close to this many viewers and likes. Then again, he has never had Wilson Newman's name recognition. That alone will guarantee that the *Front Burner* podcasts get picked up by News Source and dozens of other aggregators. Too bad that Wilson is spewing the same nonsense that he did on *Capitol Beat*.

"Catching up on current events?" DeAnna asks as she waltzes into the room.

"I'm sorry, I…I was checking out Wilson's new podcast."

"You have to hand it to him. The man knows how to land on his feet. Unfortunately for me, he took a huge chunk of his audience with him. We've never been formally introduced. I'm DeAnna Van Herten. Please, have a seat, Oliver."

"Wilson must have had this lined up before Tierra Campos's stunt at the RNC."

DeAnna smirks. "No doubt about it. Miss Campos was given an ultimatum. Once she decided not to comply, she decided to burn my network down. It won't work, but I admire the balls it takes to attempt it."

Oliver relaxes in his chair and feels the edge of the circular mahogany table. This is a strange conversation to be having. He never expected anything this informal or honest with a woman as powerful as DeAnna.

"I never realized that you were so involved with the operations of the network."

"I usually don't need to be, but it's an election year, and a lot is happening in the world. I decided to dispel my reputation as a brainless debutante who's out of touch with the people. Sometimes misinformation is a strength."

"Sometimes. The view changes when you are constantly in the public eye. Reputation is everything in the news business. More than a few big names were even taken down over the years. What Tierra did to me…it cost me a lot."

"You went too far, Oliver. You had it coming."

"I was misinterpreted. I never meant to advocate violence against Tierra Campos."

"I'm sure, but that was the perception, and the perception is reality. She used your words and actions against you, and you got the blame. You do that on your show almost nightly. This time, you got a dose of your own medicine."

Oliver starts to feel uneasy. DeAnna sounds like she's gloating, even though neither of her stars is working for her anymore.

"Why did you request this meeting?"

"Simple. You are out in the cold. If a journalist had done that ten years ago, the network would have backed them, even considering your childish cut to commercial. Now it is all about optics. That's why your network backed away from the negotiating table for your contract, correct?"

"It's not dead yet," Oliver answers quickly.

"I know all of those people. They're spineless. They'll give this some time to blow over as a courtesy, but keeping you off the air won't help you recover, and they know that. Tierra Campos got the best of you at the RNC. Wilson Newman got the best of me. We each lost battles, but the war rages on."

"You didn't answer my question. Why am I here?"

DeAnna offers a smirk as her eyes twinkle. "I want *Tomorrow's News Today* to replace *Capitol Beat* in our eight p.m. timeslot."

Oliver's mouth hangs open. He hoped that she was interested in the show, but he never expected that. He tries to recover before he makes a complete fool of himself.

"Replace?"

"I'm not keeping the show. It was Wilson Newman's and will always be associated with him. It would have taken Tierra Campos years to make it hers, and that's with his support. With both of them gone, it's not a viable brand."

"What about Wilson's contract?"

"I have an army of lawyers who will deal with that. He's the past. My job is to look toward the future. I'm rebranding the entire network, Oliver. The wheels are already in motion, and the change will be announced next week, with it taking effect the following. I need a show to anchor it, and I want it to be yours."

Oliver exhales deeply. "That's asking an awful lot. I don't know—"

"If you can do it? Is that coming from a man who took a podcast in his basement to the number two show on cable news? That was impressive but not good enough for you. You could have taken the money your network was offering and lived a comfortable life, but you wanted to be number one. So you took your chance."

"And it failed."

"Did it?" DeAnna asks, raising an eyebrow.

"If I do this, I need full creative control. I determine the direction of the broadcast."

"And as the network's owner, I want some input. I'm not going to tell you how to do your job, but I determine the network's direction. I think you'll find that we are in alignment for most things."

"That's fair. I also maintain the rights to TNT."

DeAnna stares at him and presses her lips together before shaking her head. "No, not this time."

"TNT is mine. I have no intention of letting it go for any amount of money."

She pulls out a folded piece of paper and taps it slowly on the table. When she knows Oliver's curiosity has reached the appropriate level, DeAnna slides it across the table.

"Any?"

He opens it, and his eyes almost pop out of his head when he reads the number written on it. It's more than three times what his current network is offering to keep him.

"You know how to command someone's attention, Ms. Van Hertgen. I'll give you that much."

"You will be worth every penny in the long run."

"What about Ahn Mi Sun?" Oliver asks.

"What about her? From what I understand, she helped make you who you are. I would expect her to join you."

"At her current salary."

"No, I'm afraid that's not possible."

Oliver looks down at the paper and studies the numbers long and hard. He'll never see an offer like this again, but he did wrong by her for the first time ever with the Tierra Campos fiasco. The relationship is already proving difficult enough to repair. He isn't about to double down on the mistake. Oliver slides the offer back across the table.

"I'm sorry. That just won't do."

DeAnna raises an eyebrow at him before grinning. "Good. I was hoping you would say that. I admire loyalty, Oliver, and your loyalty to your EP is admirable. Therefore, I expect her to come with you at triple the salary."

"What?"

"She's as valuable to you as I expect you will be to me. Mi Sun has been underpaid for years, from what I understand. Triple her salary. Add it to that total if you must."

"I don't know what to say."

"I imagine that doesn't happen often, so let me help you. Say yes, Oliver."

"I need time to think this over."

"You won't get it," DeAnna says, rising from her chair and prompting the TNT personality to follow suit. "You have two more meetings with other networks. If you are thinking about taking this to one of them in hopes they'll match it, they won't."

"How did you know?"

"The news business is about information. My business is to know what to do with that information. The offer in your hand expires the moment you walk out the door. I want you to work for me, and that figure shows my commitment to you. Now I need you to show one to me."

Oliver extends his hand, and she shakes it.

"When do we start?"

# CHAPTER NINETY-THREE

## SSA VICTORIA LARSEN

*Stone Garden Cemetery*
*Valhalla, New York*

Victoria gingerly climbs out of Seth's car. Every bone in her body still hurts, and the concussion is still messing with her balance. She looks and feels like hell, and it's only by the grace of God that she's still alive. Against the advice of her doctor, she extricated herself from medical confinement. She'll take a long, tortuous car ride over another day in a hospital.

Seth takes her arm as she admires the grounds. At least this is a peaceful resting place. The six-hundred-acre Stone Garden Cemetery claims to be the largest in the world. The thousands of stone markers and monuments surround winding roads and paths, ponds, shade trees, and benches that all give the grounds a park-like appearance.

"Ready?"

"Yeah."

Victoria walks slowly through the grass. When she was released from the hospital, there were two places she was committed to visiting. This is the first, and given her questionable physical condition, Seth was nice enough to offer to drive her down here on his day off. As if digging her out of the debris from the chimney after the explosion wasn't enough.

She and Seth stand quietly in front of the freshly covered grave. They have both experienced the pain of loss before. It doesn't ease the anguish — it only makes it more familiar.

"They killed him to get to me," Victoria whispers, her words carried by the light breeze that blows through the hallowed ground.

"I don't know what to say to that."

"I wasn't looking for a response. It's the truth."

Seth bites his lower lip and chooses his words. "Maybe it is, but beating yourself up over it won't solve anything."

"If Ian hadn't escaped from New Hampshire, this never would have happened. I let him get away."

"You did no such thing. Even if that were remotely true, nobody has the means to know what would have been. Had you caught or killed Ian back then, it wouldn't have stopped Vassyl Strachenko."

Victoria knows he's right despite not wanting to hear it. A single tear rolls down her cheek. She's not the emotional type. Now she is a cauldron of them. Fear, anxiety, sadness, anger, guilt…they are all fighting to bubble up to the surface. Seth senses that, too.

"I'm going to wait over by the car. Take as much time as you need," he says, touching her gently on the arm.

Victoria nods and squats next to the gravestone, using it to stabilize herself. Slowly she reaches out and runs her fingers across the etching of Takara Nishimoto's name.

"I must look like hell. I know you would have some snarky comment about that. You always did. We were on quite the journey, weren't we? How many cases did we work on together? I may have gotten the credit for the Devil Rancher indictment but could never have done it without you. Then there was the Brockhampton shooting and New Hampshire."

Victoria shakes that memory from her head. "I was so frustrated when I left Boston. The hardest part was leaving the people I worked with. I knew I would miss that camaraderie. I think that's part of the reason I decided to come back. I don't really know how to be anything else. I tried…well, sort of. I even wore a sundress a couple of times, if you can believe it.

"You met Rigo. When he came to see me while I was on vacation, he said you would have been a great agent with a different mentor. I didn't argue at the time, but he was wrong. I always thought you were a great agent. You deserved better than this.

"We tracked down the men responsible," she says, wiping away stubborn tears from her eyes. "We lost others in the process. Most of the team in Boston was killed. I barely survived. Maybe you already know all this.

"Here's something you might not know. We had our differences, but I always respected you. You pledged to have my back. I feel like I didn't have yours when you needed me most. I let you down, Takara. That's not going to be easy to live with."

Victoria places the bouquet of flowers she's holding next to the marble stone. She straightens the arrangement next to it and hangs her head.

"I need you to know something else. The men who killed you were acting under orders. If it's the last thing I do, I'm going to find out whose orders they were. I'm going to find Machiavelli and Robespierre and take them down. They will pay for what they've done. That's my promise to you."

Victoria kisses her hand and touches Takara's gravestone. She stands slowly and walks back toward the car, more determined than she has ever been.

# CHAPTER NINETY-FOUR

## TIERRA CAMPOS

*Illinois Statehouse*
*Springfield, Illinois*

I've never been to Springfield, much less to its capitol building. A city statute does not allow buildings taller than it. Not that it needs help dominating its surroundings. The Illinois Capitol is taller than its federal counterpart in Washington and is the tallest non-skyscraper capitol building in the country, thanks to its zinc-covered massive central dome.

After leaving Tyler and Olivia at the car, I walk through the entrance of the cross-shaped structure that houses both legislative chambers of the Illinois General Assembly, committee rooms, staff offices, and the governor of Illinois. After being greeted by a member of his staff, I'm shown directly into his office.

"Good morning, Governor."

"Tierra Campos. You know, I thought long and hard about what I would say to you if we met again. To be honest, the last thing I expected was for you to ask for a meeting with me," Luther Burgess says, rising from his chair and buttoning his suit jacket.

"I appreciate you accepting."

"Please, have a seat," he says, offering a sofa as he moves around his desk and sits in the adjacent one. "Are you here on behalf of *Front Burner?*"

"No, sir. I'm here for me. This isn't work-related. This conversation is strictly off the record."

The governor laughs. "I've been in politics a long time. Nobody is ever strictly off the record with a journalist, Miss Campos."

I nod. "Unfortunately, there is more truth to that than there should be. In this case, it is, though. Our conversation is private. And personal."

"I see. What do you want?"

"To express my condolences for the loss of your son and to apologize to you."

Luther stares down at his giant hands as he presses them together and wrings them. I know that this meeting is as awkward for him as it is for me.

"I understand you spoke with Isiah the day he was…murdered."

"Yes, sir, I did," I say in a near-whisper.

"Was he polite or hostile?"

"Both…and neither. Isiah was firm and determined."

"That sounds about right. Isiah was unstoppable as a child. When he put his mind to something, he often made it happen. We ended up in the emergency room several times as a result. Tell me…was he Machiavelli?"

It's my turn to break eye contact. "I don't know. If Isiah was, he could have been working with somebody else who didn't want him to talk. Or, he could have been a patsy that the real Machiavelli wanted to silence."

"What does your gut tell you?"

I take a deep breath. My gut told me that the governor himself was Machiavelli. It also tried to convince me that he wouldn't take this meeting or would berate me if he did. It's been wrong so often that I'm not sure I trust it anymore. I can't tell him any of that, though.

"That it wasn't him, and I made a mistake at the end of the interview in New Hampshire."

"Was that your apology?"

"No. It would be a piss poor one if it was. I am very sorry for assuming your son was guilty without concrete proof. I'm sorry for how your campaign ended and my role in it. I am truly sorry about what happened to him."

Luther scoffs. "Miss Campos, I would like nothing more than to yell and scream at you so loud that the state police come running."

"Then you should."

He shakes his head. "I can't. I want someone to blame and would love for it to be you. Unfortunately, none of this was your fault, as much as I want it to be. The moment his cell phone rang when you called the number, I thought it was him, too. So did the rest of America. It was logical."

A long silence grows between us. The governor is right – everyone jumped to that conclusion. The difference is, I should have known better. I convinced myself of his guilt. It's the same thing I criticize other journalists for. It was bias and opinion that blinded me to a simple truth: despite appearances, a ringing cell phone is not an admission of guilt.

"Did he say anything about me?" the governor asks.

"His murderer ended his life, but what killed him was knowing that you didn't believe him. He wanted to clear his name to make things right with you."

"And I pushed him away. That's the other reason I can't blame you, Miss Campos. It's just as much my fault."

"That's not fair, sir."

"Maybe, but that's also the truth. You don't have children, do you?"

"No, sir."

"Any parent who loses a child will tell you that it's a fate worse than death. The day a child is born, you stop living your life so they can live theirs. Only I didn't do that. That's why Isiah joined my campaign, even though he hates politics. I never learned the lesson from that. The moment I was told that Isiah was gone, I realized I was a lousy father. My political career is coming to an end, and it has already cost me everything I should have valued."

"You're being too hard on yourself."

"I didn't talk to my own son for the last seven months of his life. Now I never will again. How can I not be?"

Words escape me. The governor felt betrayed by his son that night in New Hampshire. Most people would have reacted the same way in his position. Not that any of them would ever admit that. It's easier to criticize someone using the prism of hindsight than to look in the mirror and admit you would have done the same.

"Some things can't be undone in this world. One thing can. I need you to do something for me, Miss Campos."

"What is it?"

"Find the truth," the governor says, grave and serious. "I need to know if my son was Machiavelli or if this was an elaborate ploy for his defense to play up in court. Can you find out?"

I don't like to make promises. They are too hard to keep in this world. In this case, I'm compelled to make an exception.

"I promise that I won't stop until I find that answer."

Burgess nods. "Then let's end this conversation until you do. Goodbye, Miss Campos."

The governor rises and moves back to his desk without looking at me. I didn't know how this meeting would go. I thought an apology to his father might ease the burden I feel over Isiah's death. It didn't. We are still both seeking absolution for our sins. For him, it's about his parenting. For me, it's about my reporting. Maybe the truth will help bring us peace over what has happened. Or perhaps it won't.

"Good day, sir," I say, leaving the governor's office.

My stomach is in knots. Like Governor Burgess, I got caught up in my career, and it has cost me.  Friendships I once valued are strained after months of neglect. It will take time and dedication to repair them if I can at all.

I want to believe that I'm leaving Springfield with a purpose. Motivation comes in many forms. Isiah's nonsensical note still tucked behind the mirror of my makeup compact is one example. Luther Burgess just provided another, more emotional one. I should be hell-bent on finding answers but that's not how I'm looking at it.

Old demons are resurfacing. I can feel the doubt and uncertainty tugging at my soul. After Brockhampton, I felt like I could take on the world. Now, I find myself dreading the thought of another failure and breaking a promise I may not ever have been able to keep.

# CHAPTER NINETY-FIVE

## BRIAN COOPER

*The Hay-Adams Hotel*
*Washington, D.C.*

Located just off Lafayette Square, the Hay-Adams is as close a person can get to the epicenter of political power short of staying at the White House itself. Brian hopes it isn't the closest Colin Bradford gets to it. The hotel is cozy and elegant, with the Old World charm of oil paintings, wood paneling, crystal chandeliers, and working fireplaces. Brian peels his eyes off the unobstructed view of the White House from Bradford's suite. Like most candidates, he's running late.

Brian's phone vibrates in his pocket, and he checks to see who it is. With a smirk, he accepts it. This call is long overdue.

"This is a pleasant surprise," he says, seizing the opportunity to goad one of the most powerful women in America.

"Cut the crap, Cooper," DeAnna Van Herten says.

"Crap? Wow, DeAnna, that's the worst word I've ever heard you use. You had better check your blood pressure."

"Did you think that I was going to let that stunt at the RNC go unanswered?"

Brian returns to looking out the window at the White House. He might as well admire it while he can.

"I'm sure I don't know what you're talking about, DeAnna."

"Yeah, and you're standing in Bradford's suite at the Hay-Adams because you're waiting for a promotion."

"How did…?"

Brian doesn't finish the question. He looks around and then shakes his head. No, she doesn't have a camera in here. One of her reporters must be posing as an employee. That or she has an informant working here.

"You're not the only expert in this town at getting information."

"I guess not. What do you care about what happened at the RNC? You got what you wanted – rumor has it you landed the hottest cable news show on television."

Now it's DeAnna's turn to be surprised. "I'm not sure how you know that."

"Like you said, I'm an expert at getting information."

"Right. Oliver Jahn is damaged goods thanks to Tierra Campos."

"He would have inked a new deal with his network without her putting him on blast. If anyone can rehabilitate his reputation, it's you. That's why you paid such an exorbitant amount."

"Stop with the flattery. It's tiring. I don't know what game you're playing, Cooper, but tread carefully."

"We've known each other for a while, DeAnna. Our interests have always been aligned."

"We'll see if it stays that way. Tell Colin I said hi."

"He's not here yet."

The words no sooner cross Brian's lips than Colin Bradford comes barging into the suite. He closes the door behind him as Brian looks at his phone and sees that DeAnna hung up. She always has to get the last word. He pockets his phone and turns to face the Republican candidate for president.

"Who was that?"

"DeAnna Van Herten. She's displeased with me."

"She isn't the only one. Drink?"

"I think I need one."

The governor moves to the wet bar and pours two healthy glasses of scotch. Brian is surprised that Brevin isn't here for this. The consultant meets him in the middle of the room and accepts the drink. The two men eye each other as they take sips.

"I'm a Southerner, Brian. There are two things I value: my heritage and loyalty. I don't ask for more. The people who work on this campaign put in long hours because they want to, not because it's expected. But what I do demand is that those around me respect my decisions, and you countermanded mine. You know what that means."

"I do," Brian says, straightening. "You like people who kiss your ass."

"Excuse me?"

"Governor, was it your decision not to let Campos speak, or was it Brevin's?"

"What does it matter? He's my campaign manager. His loyalty is unquestioned. I know that he's looking out for my best interests."

"I know you believe that. I think that Brevin does, too. Neither of you sees what's really going on."

"What's that?" Colin asks, swirling the scotch in his glass.

"It doesn't matter. Brevin warned you that I can't be trusted. Then I defied you, and he probably said, 'I told you he was toxic. Cooper is a maverick who used to work for Democrats. He doesn't belong here. You need to can him.' How am I doing so far?"

"Spot on."

"If that's what you believe, then fire me. I'll leave without a fuss, but not before I say one last thing. I'm not here to blow sunshine up your ass, Governor. I'm here because I want you to win. Not because of your politics or policies. I don't give a damn about them. I want you in the White House because I know Alicia Standish, and she can't be allowed to move in."

"You use that line a lot."

"I do. It's also true. I snuck Tierra Campos on that stage because the convention had all the life and energy of a rotting corpse. Since you weren't willing to shake things up, I did."

"It was fine—"

"Fine is not going to beat your opponent. You needed a bump because you're boring. You may be a good governor, but that isn't enough in modern politics. You need to be entertaining and exciting, and you're neither. Count your lucky stars that Standish won the nomination. She isn't much better by comparison. Burgess would have crushed you head-to-head."

"You defied me to make a spectacle?" the governor asks. "The media aren't even talking about the convention. It's all about Campos and what she did to Oliver Jahn."

"And that's better than them telling the American people how lifeless the Republicans are. Tierra Campos is a rare, non-partisan believer in good journalism. She gave a brilliant, full-throated defense of it in front of a captive audience. She believes in fairness – something that the GOP has been screaming about for decades. Her appearance gave the convention the shot in the arm it needed. The views of her speech on social media are higher than every speaker at the Democratic convention combined."

"So what?"

"She gave your base the red meat that they didn't get from you and your milquetoast acceptance speech."

"You have some nerve!"

"I do. And that's what you need – someone with a backbone."

The governor swallows a big gulp of his drink and moves toward the window. "That's not a good enough reason to keep you around."

"No, it isn't. I told you that I understand Standish, so let me tell you what is about to happen. She laid the groundwork that you are an uncaring racist in her convention speech, and the media ran with it. Now they're going to use the Southern pride rhetoric you spewed out on that stage against you.

"Angela Mays will hit the Sunday morning news circuit tomorrow and offer a teaser to the audience. Something like, 'that explains a lot about him and what happened.' Nobody will know what she's talking about, and the media will go nuts speculating over it for a couple of news cycles. And then the campaign is going to drop a name: Tyrell Grant."

Bradford turns pale white. "How do you know—? Those records are sealed!"

"Presidential politics is a grudge match with no rules, Governor. Everything is fair game, including sealed court documents. Since I know, you can bet your ass that someone as resourceful as Alicia Standish does."

Brian finishes his drink. Now he really owes Adika. It might be better if he doesn't tell her about this.

"You can fire me now or wait twenty-four hours," Brian says, offering Bradford an alternative. "If my prediction pans out, we can have a conversation about how

Standish is going to link Tyrell Grant to your Southern heritage and checkered track record with blacks to dismantle you. Then I'll tell you how to beat back her attacks and put her on the defensive. Without good counter-punches, rural and suburban whites will get discouraged at your tanking poll numbers, and Latinos will turn their back on you. You'll be lucky to get 150 electoral votes, let alone win the race to 270."

"And if she doesn't?"

"Then I'm not much of a political consultant. Do you remember what I said in North Carolina during her speech? I asked you how badly you wanted to win, and warned you that a day would come when you would need to choose which path to follow. You're at that fork in the road now. Left or right? Brevin or me? The decision is yours to make now, Governor."

Brian sets his glass down on the coffee table. The governor stands there, stunned by a name uttered that he never thought he would hear again. It must have been a shock, but he should have known it would happen.

"Have a good night, sir. I'm sure we'll talk tomorrow one way or the other."

That went better than Brian expected, and he smirks as he leaves the hotel suite. Russian roulette is a deadly game to play. It's reckless to even try unless you know precisely which chamber the bullet is in.

FIVE DAYS LATER

# EPILOGUE

## SSA VICTORIA LARSEN

*Charles River Esplanade*
*Back Bay, Boston, Massachusetts*

"The Esplanade," as it is known to the locals, is a state-owned park in the Back Bay section of Boston. It's best known for hosting the city's July 4th celebrations with the Boston Pops. The seventeen-mile stretch of parkland alongside the Charles River is also a popular path for exercise enthusiasts and family strolls. It's also a great place to meet somebody, assuming you have a specific location and don't have to go looking for them.

"It's about time you got here, Queen V," Miranda says once Victoria gets into earshot.

"Sorry, I left my transporter at home. What's so important that we had to meet outside the office?"

Miranda stares at Seth before shifting her eyes to Victoria and shaking her head.

"You can trust him."

"Not with this."

"Miranda, I trust him with my life. He's saved it more than once."

"It's not personal, Detective. This is just…sensitive."

"I understand."

Miranda cracks open her laptop. She checks to see if anyone is around them and logs on using the embedded facial recognition software and a couple of keystrokes. It's paranoid, even for a computer analyst.

"This is from the device you gave me."

"I thought you said you didn't get anything off Vassyl Strachenko's phone."

"Officially, I didn't, and I would testify under oath to that if I had to. Unofficially, there was something. Vassyl Strachenko was sent a file."

"That doesn't look readable. What was in it?" Seth asks, staring at the screen.

"It's hard to tell. Most of the file wasn't recoverable, even using our best tools. The pieces that we were able to assemble resemble an operations plan. See?"

Miranda scrolls through the recreated document and points out the chunks. It's not hard to decipher. They are in English, and the rest of the text is in nonsensical ASCII characters.

"An ops plan for what?"

"The murder of Lance Fuller."

Victoria and Seth look at each other as that settles in. "Who sent it?"

"It's complicated, and I'll get to that in a second. I was able to recover this section as well. It's an outline of a plan to ambush an FBI team with one primary target: you."

A shiver runs down Victoria's spine. She thought Takara's and Lance's murders were Ian's version of payback against his supervisors in the Bureau. She was wrong. They were bait.

"They were after me the whole time," Victoria whispers.

"Vic, don't go down that road."

"Why not, Seth? How many funerals did we just attend for good people killed or wounded because of me?"

"None of this is your fault," he says. "How sure are you of this, Miranda?"

"One hundred percent."

"Okay, here's a dumb question. Why would an assassin carry those plans on his phone?

"Now is where we get to the good part. It was transferred to Strachenko from another device."

"He didn't make the plan," Victoria says, catching up.

"No, like Marx and his merry band of socialists in the SOF, he was following orders."

"Did this come from Machiavelli?"

"No. The sender was aliased as another code name: Robespierre."

"There is another player. Got it. That doesn't explain why we're here or all the cloak and dagger stuff. What has you spooked, Miranda?"

"I know when the file was transferred and where. It was 8:11 in the morning back on July 22nd at Theodore Roosevelt National Park in D.C."

"Five days after the first attempt on Burgess," Victoria mumbles.

"I took the liberty of contacting cellular carriers to see who was pinging off the towers in that area. It took some doing, but I managed to isolate eleven phones in the park that morning."

"Do you have the list?"

"Yes, but ten of them aren't interesting. It's the eleventh you need to pay attention to. It's an unlisted cellular number assigned to the government. Fortunately, we have access to that database as well. I checked it against what I found on the phone. There is an app on it that sends encrypted texts that self-destruct when it closes. Vassyl left his open before the ambush. The last message he received was from that number."

"Your knack for the dramatic is admirable, Miranda, but you're killing me here."

She pulls up a file and spins the laptop around. Victoria's eyes grow wide.

"No, it can't be."

"You said yourself that someone must have tipped Strachenko off about the raid. How many people knew about it? I'll guarantee that he did," Miranda says, pointing at the screen.

"This is why you didn't want to meet in the office."

"After we're done, I'm giving this to you and Captain America here and am forgetting that I ever saw it," she says, pulling out the thumb drive and holding it up between her fingers. "This isn't a rogue detective obstructing an investigation in Brockhampton or a political operative playing games with a primary election. This is treason at the highest levels."

"Miranda—"

"No, not this time, Queen V. You're better than Black Widow on her best day, and they still went after you. You barely survived that ambush. The cancel culture all but destroyed Tierra Campos, and I'm willing to bet that was orchestrated, too. You were both vital targets, and someone nearly succeeded in taking you both out. This is too big for me to be involved in. I have a family to think about."

"Okay."

She hands Victoria the memory stick and stands. "Good luck. Know that I'm rooting for you and the rest of the Avengers," Miranda says.

She pats Victoria on the shoulder before heading down the path along the river. Seth takes her seat on the bench. They both stare at the shimmering river as the minutes pass. Neither knows what to say until Seth finally breaks the silence.

"Now what?"

"I wish I knew. If Miranda is wrong about this, losing my badge will be the least of my concerns. If she's right about it, I may get myself killed trying to prove it."

"We can't let him get away with this. We sure as shit can't sit on our asses and do nothing."

"We won't," Victoria says, staring at the thumb drive in her hand.

Miranda has every reason to be frightened. She helped uncover a conspiracy involving a man appointed by the president and confirmed by the Senate to serve at the Justice Department. Victoria wanted a target, and now she has one. She never imagined that Robespierre would be Conrad Williams, the deputy attorney general of the United States.

# ACKNOWLEDGMENTS

Many of us were thrilled to turn the chapter to 2021. For many reasons, both personal and professional, nobody was more thrilled than I was. After finishing a rewrite of *The Eyes of Others*, I finally finished the latest installment in Victoria and Tierra's adventures. *Vital Targets* has given you another piece of the puzzle, and I promise you that there is much more to come.

I recently read that there are an estimated 2.2 million titles published worldwide each year. There is a massive selection of great novels from fantastic authors to choose from, and I thank you for deciding to pick mine up. I hope you will continue to find my stories thought-provoking and entertaining enough to read in the future.

As an author, the stories I write may come from my head, but it is only with plenty of support that they come to life. Much of the credit belongs to my wife, Michele, who is gracious about the amount of time I spend behind this keyboard. My mother, Nancy, sister, Kristina, brother-in-law, Ken, and nephew Gibson are always there to cheer me on. Maybe not my nephew. He's too busy shooting at me with a Nerf gun.

Thank you to Michael Waitz at Sticks and Stones Editing for the incredible job of correcting my horrible grammar and pointing out the inconsistencies that creep in after constantly rewriting certain parts. He has done a fantastic job polishing the first novels of this series and keeping me on the right path in this one.

While I won't pretend that Victoria's life in the FBI is typical of what agents deal with daily, it is grounded in some fact. Thank you to Meg for the guidance she has given me throughout this series and for not laughing too hard at some of the more unrealistic scenes.

For once, I actually had an idea of what I wanted the cover of Vital Targets to look like. Usually, I only offer thoughts and leave the rest to the designers. Kudos to JD&J for taking that vision and creating something vivid. I couldn't be more pleased with the way it turned out.

# ABOUT THE AUTHOR

Mikael Carlson is the award-winning author of *The iCandidate* and the Michael Bennit Series of political dramas. *Vital Targets* is his twelfth novel and the third book in the Tierra Campos series, following the award-winning lead book *Justifiable Deceit* and *sequel Devious Measures*. He is also the author of the Watchtower political thrillers, among other works.

A retired veteran of the Rhode Island Army National Guard and United States Army paratrooper, he deployed twice in support of military operations during the Global War on Terror. Mikael has served in the field artillery, infantry, and in support of special operations units during his career on active duty at Fort Bragg and in the Army National Guard.

He conducted over fifty airborne operations following the completion of jump school at Fort Benning in 1998. Since then, he has trained with the militaries of countless foreign nations.

Academically, Mikael has earned a Master of Arts in American History and graduated with a B.S. in International Business from Marist College in 1996.

He was raised in New Milford, Connecticut and currently lives in nearby Danbury.